Death of a Unicorn
An Unconventional Romance
Cheryl Terra

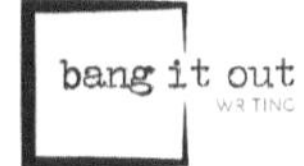

Bang It Out WRiting

Content Warnings

Please note this book is written in Canadian English, which has aspects of spelling from both American and UK English.
This is book 3 of a 3 book series. For the best reading experience, begin with The Unicorn Confessions.
I have tried to address potential triggers here without spoiling the story, however if you have concerns about any of the items listed and wish to know more, please reach out to me via email at info@cherylterra.com

This book is intended for mature adults. There are multiple explicit scenes and profanity. This book is categorized as "why choose" and discusses non-traditional relationship structures, including discussions of "unicorn hunting," polyamory, ethical non-monogamy, unethical non-monogamy, and casual sex.

Themes + Plot Points: cheating (not by the main characters and not presented in a positive light), toxic relationships, job loss, discussions of genetic diseases, serious illness of a family member, death of a family member, funeral preparations. Brief subplots including newborn baby difficulties and adoption discussions, toxic parenting, and child abandonment. Body image and fat positivity are main themes of this book. There are brief mentions of fatphobic situations or comments, but that is not a primary focus of the series and is not internalized by the main character.

SA + Consent: Blackmail occurs with implied threats about leaking explicit photos and videos that were taken without consent.

Coming Out: There are scenes that discuss the trauma around this and inclusion of negative reactions from family or friends.

Spice Variety: Characters in this book enjoy casual hook-ups, "breeding," using the endearment Daddy, and public hook-ups. Pairings include MFF, MF, FF, and MMF. These scenes are explicit.

Other: There are moderate mentions of alcohol use, anxiety, pressure to have children, homophobia, biphobia, transphobia, and misogyny.

Prologue

CHUCK WAS RUINING THE Monday morning meeting.

On any other day, I would have been enjoying the chaos of Loni stomping around the boardroom, the sound of her stilettos like knives clacking against the floor as splotches of red tinted her porcelain white cheeks. I would have nodded along to her ranting while coming up with the next thing I could say to annoy Dinah. And Chuck and I would have made faces at each other and exchanged exasperated glances.

But not that day.

"It's sabotage, plain and simple," Loni spat, picking up the brochure she'd brought in and slamming it on the table for the fifth or sixth time. "It's sabotage and classless and... and... plagiarism. I want a lawyer on retainer immediately. Paige Martelle is plagiarizing us and I simply will not stand for it."

Dinah fiddled with a crispy-looking strand of her white-blonde hair. "It's... it's not, though. I mean, it's bad form to copy us, but we can't copyright or trademark a gala concept. And we didn't invent the concept of a date auction."

Loni turned to her, eyes flashing. "Is it you?"

Dinah frowned. "Is it me what?"

"You're the saboteur," Loni said. "The traitor. The Roman horse."

"I'm not!" Dinah said, horrified. "I would *never*. And I think you mean the Trojan horse."

Loni gave her a disgusted look. "Educate yourself, Dinah. I'm speaking of *mythology*. Not condoms."

"No, I mean—" Dinah cut herself off, taking a deep breath and letting it out. "I'm just saying we can't sue Paige Martelle for plagiarism. It... it just wouldn't apply here."

"So you're saying I have to just bend over and take it, Dinah?" Loni folded her arms across her chest. "Sounds like something a saboteur would say."

"I'm not a saboteur!"

"You are advising me to let Paige Martelle culturally appropriate our date-auction idea—"

"That's *not* what cultural appropriation is!"

"—in an attempt to make ArtCycle look better than CARE and expect me to believe you're *not* the saboteur?"

And on and on it went.

Had it been a normal Monday, I would have loved it. I would have enjoyed the absolute bedlam of Loni's accusations, especially when Dinah was making them drag on like that. And the petty, vengeful part of me would've loved watching Dinah's face turn redder and redder as she tried to convince Loni she was not, in fact, doublecrossing us by working for ArtCycle, like that was something people would do for recycling-oriented charities.

But Chuck was staring at me so hard I couldn't even enjoy it.

And when I said staring, I mean staring. I wasn't sure he blinked even once during that entire meeting; every time I glanced over, he had that intense gaze focused on me and I'd glance back and look determinedly at Loni in an effort to avoid the wrath barely concealed in his dark brown eyes.

It wasn't my fault. Well, it was, but it was my fault in a funny way, so that should've made it better. But my intent had been to tell Chuck everything as soon as I saw him.

He just had immediately walked into the boardroom that morning, dropped his things on the table, and started yammering.

"You'll never guess—" I started.

"Uh-uh," he said. "No way."

"What?"

"Every Monday, you come in here with an insane story from the weekend and I'm so flabbergasted by the disarray that is your life that I forget to tell you about the insanity that was *my* weekend. So shh. I have to tell you the *most* insane thing."

"Uh... okay."

He sat in his chair and crossed one leg over the other, pausing for dramatic effect as he gave me a significant look. "Charles wants me to meet his family."

I waited, but that seemed to be it. "Oh."

Chuck looked offended. "Don't look so shocked."

"Sorry," I said. "I just... when you said it was the most insane thing, I thought you were going to be like, 'We were in the middle of sex and Charles put it in the wrong hole' or something."

"Why would that be insane?" he asked, bewildered.

"No one likes surprise anal." I sipped my coffee. "And I'd also be very confused about there being a wrong hole when I know for a fact you only have one."

He rolled his eyes. "No, Tessa Eileen Lane, my boyfriend did not put it in the wrong hole. He didn't put it in any hole last night, actually, because I was so shocked at the suggestion of going to his parents' for a barbecue in a couple of weeks."

"Because you suddenly went vegan or...?"

"Oh my God," he huffed. "You're the worst."

"Generally, yes," I said. "But in this case, I think you're being a bit—"

"Don't you dare say I'm being overdramatic," he said dramatically.

Shrugging, I grabbed my phone and tapped on the screen. "Okay. You're being a bit histrionic. Theatrical. Sensationalized, if you will."

"Did you just Google synonyms for overdramatic?"

"I didn't not do that."

"You are such an asshole."

"Again, generally, yes," I said. "But you're being over... the top."

"I am not." He leaned back in the chair and worry creased his forehead. "I've only done this a few times before and it's always gone horribly."

"What do you mean?"

He held up a hand, counting on his fingers. "Kayla. My first girlfriend. We were in high school and she brought me to her family's Easter dinner. Her uncles sat me on one side of the table and all sat in a row on the other side like I was being interrogated."

"You're joking."

He shook his head. "One of them had a flashlight. And none of them seemed to realize how fucked up all that was when I was the only non-white person in the room."

I grimaced. "Well, yeah. That's... bad."

"Mm-hmm. And then I didn't let anyone introduce me to their family again until I was dating Alexis, and we both know how that turned out."

"I mean, I know how the relationship turned out, but—"

"Not the point." He glared at me. "And the only other one that came even close was when I slept with that redhead who ended up being that rock star Theo Barker's personal assistant and introduced us because they were 'practically brothers.'"

"That doesn't count."

"Exactly. I'm not ready for this."

"I mean, that's fair. But it has to happen sometime."

"Of course." He sipped his coffee and I felt a little bad because he did look miserable. "That doesn't mean I'm not going to put on a brave face for Charles and kick and scream to you the entire time."

"So you're going to be... overdramatic."

Chuck's mouth twitched into a smile. "Maybe a smidge. But I'm just nervous about what might happen."

"I wish I could tell you," I said.

"Well, why don't you get your crystal ball out, you witch?"

"I checked it this morning," I said. "The spirits said you're a dick."

He laughed, shaking his head before sipping his coffee, which I took to mean he was done.

"Alright," I said. "So you're not going to believe—"

"Ah, ah, ah," he said, holding up a hand. "Nope."

"What?"

"I want my baby update."

I tilted my head back, rolling my eyes. "You don't even know this child."

"I will," he said. "On Saturday when we throw her baby shower. I'm looking forward to finally meeting Kira, too." He held out his hand. "Update and baby photos now, please."

Resigned, I passed him my phone, which he snatched out of my hand and brought up the album of baby photos I had saved just for him. "They're doing okay as far as I know. I didn't talk to Kira much this weekend. I was in Burnsley for the bridal shower. But I think she's a little overwhelmed."

Chuck looked up from the phone, genuine sympathy on his face. "Is she okay?"

I nodded. "It's just been a roller coaster. She went from planning to be a mom to being told she wasn't going to be a mom to being called up out of nowhere and asking if she still wanted to proceed with the adoption because the birthmother changed her mind. It's a lot. But she and Jackson both adore Velma. She's already the most spoiled little thing in the world."

"I still can't believe they went with *Velma*," Chuck said.

"It makes her happy and I'm not saying a fucking word about it otherwise," I said. "She's loved the name since we were kids."

"It's very Scooby-Doo."

"That's where she got it from. Velma was her hero."

"Hmmph," Chuck said, then finally passed my phone back to me. "Alright, Tessa Rose Lane. *Now* you can tell me how your weekend was."

And yes. I absolutely could have said I'd tell him after the meeting. That so much had happened, there wouldn't be anywhere near enough time to get into it before Loni got here.

But where was the fun in that?

"Well, I fucked Finn last night," I said.

And while Chuck could be one of the most overdramatic people I knew, the way he nearly spit out his coffee and turned to me so fast that he almost fell out of his chair was completely genuine.

"You *what*?!" he asked.

And then, with timing so perfect that I couldn't have planned it, Dinah walked into the room, followed by a ranting Loni.

So that was why Chuck was sitting at the boardroom table, staring at me like a creepy, rage-filled doll. And that was also why when Loni finally finished her tirade about there being a snitch in CARE's ranks that was telling Paige Martelle all our public trade secrets, he didn't stay to calm Dinah down like he usually did. Instead, he grabbed my arm and physically pulled me down the hallway, even as I protested that I was right behind.

"Finn?!" he shouted when we got back to our office and he'd slammed the door behind us. "Finn the *ghost*?!"

"Well, sort of," I said.

"You *fucked* him?!"

"That's not even the most interesting part of the story, actually," I said.

"You better start telling me the fucking story, Tessa Bernadette Lane. I can't believe you kept this from me!"

I shrugged as I settled into my desk chair. "You were telling me about Charles and being all scared about his parents and stuff."

"This is text-me-immediately worthy stuff. Why did you not *text* me?!"

"Because I was busy fucking him," I said. "Remember that thing I just said?"

"You texted me when you fucked Zain. Which was also yesterday."

"Yeah, after I left."

"Yes, but—wait." Chuck blinked at me. "Are you saying that you didn't leave?"

For some reason, I couldn't look at him. "Not exactly. But like, it was also late after we fucked, so..."

"What about Julie?" he asked.

I bit my lip, staring hard at my hands, then shook my head.

His voice got lower. "Does she know you and Finn...?"

"Well, no, but—"

"Tessa," he said, so much disappointment in his voice I almost cringed.

"It wasn't like that," I said. "You know I'd never do something like that. Well, not without a good reason. But this whole thing is... it's kinda fucked up."

He folded his arms. "Tell me what happened right now."

And God, wasn't that the fucking question.

Part One

Confession: Things aren't always the way they seem.

One

It took me a while to recognize the man on his knees as Finn.

His longish blonde hair was messy, stuck to his head in some places and sticking out in others. Shock-widened blue eyes were staring at me, wet with tears that were barely holding on behind his lashes. On his chin was a layer of hair I'd never seen him with before.

But it was Finn. It was definitely Finn fucking Goodman.

Unfortunately for me, Finn grimed down as good as he cleaned up. The chiselled line of his jaw was even more defined with that almost-a-beard on his chin. There was a mark of dirt on his shirt, though that might have been from Alfie's paws, since the small dog was still clutched tightly in his arms. Either way, Finn looked like the kind of guy who worked in a dive bar kitchen as a greasy line cook that dealt weed out of the back entrance, but would give you the dirtiest, nastiest, most shamefully unforgettable sex of your life.

And that man was kneeling in front of me.

For a moment, at least.

"Oh my God! Tessa!" he exclaimed, and then he was on his feet, a huge grin on his face as he threw his arms around me. I stood there, stunned as the dogs jumped at his legs because they were as excited by his excitement as he was, but eventually hugged him back with the arm that wasn't clutching the leash.

"Um... hi," I said.

"Hi!" he said as he parted from me, genuine happiness in his eyes that a second ago had been sad, deep pools of blue. "It's so good to see you! It's been *ages*. How are—"

And then he stopped.

The wide smile on his face faded and the happiness in his eyes dimmed into worry.

"Oh," he said. "I'm sorry."

"What?" I asked, because what else was I supposed to say?

"You probably don't want to see me."

Which was true, as much as I hated to admit it to someone who just greeted me like my very existence thrilled him. But that hug, warm and welcoming as it was, had opened a world of pain I hadn't known was still there.

Because there wasn't supposed to be anything there.

It had never been serious. I hadn't mattered to him and Julie. They had cut *me* out and that was fine. They could feel that way and I could feel my way and it should have been clear, even to Finn, that I had no desire to see either of them ever again.

But I couldn't bring myself to say that to the unkempt man standing in front of me with dogs sniffing at the cuff of his grey sweatpants.

"It's fine," I said. "I guess I'm surprised that you... do. Want to see me."

He smiled, though it wasn't his usual bright, heart-melting smile. "I get it. Totally. I just wish I could've said, like, thank you? I guess?" He shrugged, glancing down, which was also weird because Finn was very much an eye-contact guy. "I was lucky you were into it as long as you were and it's still one of the most fun things I've ever done. But like, also, I can't say I don't... you know. Miss you."

He looked up again, holding up his hands as though I'd been about to snap at him.

"But I totally respect that you didn't want to talk to us anymore. I just got excited to see you and forgot and—"

"Wait," I said, frowning. "What?"

"What?"

"I didn't stop talking to you," I said. "You and Julie stopped talking to me."

He stared at me, blinking once, then twice, then a slow realization dawned on his face. I watched it travel through his body, shoulders sagging and his head tilting back.

"Damnit, Julie," he breathed. "She told you we didn't want to see you anymore?"

I laughed. I had to. What the fuck else was I supposed to do? "I wish."

He frowned. "What?"

"You can't be serious, Finn," I said. "You guys ditched me at my work gala and then blocked me without saying anything. *You* ghosted *me*."

"No," he said. "No, that's not... I had no idea. I'm sorry, Tess."

There was a lump of anger in my throat. I wasn't entirely sure what I was angry at, whether it was from what they did to me or the fact that Julie apparently lied to Finn about it, but I swallowed it back all the same.

"Well, that's what happened," I said. "You and her can talk about it if you want. I hope it doesn't cause any problems for you."

"Oh, it won't," he said.

Somehow, the confidence in his voice stung. I forced another smile. "Good. I'm glad you have the kind of relationship that can overcome something like that."

"What relationship?" he asked.

I thought he was being facetious because of course I did. Because that was... like, what? What the fuck? But there was genuine confusion in Finn's eyes.

"You and Julie," I said slowly. "Your girlfriend?"

"Ohhh," he said, drawing the word out. "Yeah, no. She broke up with me a couple of weeks ago."

And fuck.

That hurt to hear.

I mean, it wasn't my business if any of the couples I had fucked didn't last. It wasn't my problem. They knew what they were getting into and it was on them if they couldn't handle it.

But the thing was, I would never know otherwise.

Because I was supposed to see couples one time and one time only.

"I'm sorry," I said.

Finn smiled. "It's okay. Actually, seeing you has been super helpful 'cause it all kind of makes sense now, you know?"

"What does?"

"Well, she said she was starting to get that zombie thing," he said. "Like that rule you made about having to tell everyone if you got feelings so no one turned into a zombie? And she said when she told you, you said you couldn't see us anymore."

That fucking...

"She didn't tell me that," I said. "I asked, but she said she didn't have feelings. That's why you broke up?"

"Oh, no," he said. "That was because she realized she's a lesbian."

Well, I hadn't seen that one coming. "Oh."

"Yeah. Which is fair because women are super hot, right?" he said, grinning. "But yeah, she just had something, like, click for her. And I didn't want her to stay with me if she wasn't into it. That wouldn't be fair and I want everyone to be happy."

"You, um, seem to be having a bit of a tough time, though," I said as diplomatically as I could.

"No, no. Not at all. Jules didn't choose for that to happen, you know? It's just who she is. We parted on good terms and we're still friends, sorta. It's good. It's all good."

I didn't say anything. That statement wasn't done. He'd said it like it was done, but something told me it wasn't. Sure enough, a few seconds later, his jaw twitched and he laughed, though it was more forced than usual.

"I just, uh, kinda wish... well. It's not important."

"Yes, it is," I said. "Tell me."

The smile faded and he looked away from me again, his throat flexing as he swallowed. "Well, I just kinda wish we could've stayed in our apartment a little longer, you know? Instead of breaking the lease? But like, it made sense. It was a one-bedroom and it was awkward with two of us there and she had a friend who was willing to let her move in. So it just... made sense." He forced another smile. "It's not her fault I'm stupid."

"You're not stupid, Finn."

"Well, I used to be," he said. "More than I am now. But like, when I first moved out, no one told me rent was the amount you paid every *month*, you know?"

Oh my God. "Of course. Right."

"Yeah," he continued. "So I just, like, made my landlord a little mad, which I felt really bad about, but then I was like no I'm gonna for sure pay rent every month, except then I didn't know that when you write a check, you had to have *all* the money in your bank account, so..."

Oh my *God*.

"Where are you living right now?" I asked.

"In my car," he said, and it came out cheerfully. "Just for a while."

I had no idea what to say. When I didn't speak, he looked back at me.

"It's all good, Tess," he said. "Really."

"Does Julie know?" I asked.

He shook his head. "She would feel bad and it's not that big a deal. It's been an adventure. Like, it'll be a cool story one day, you know?"

Again, he said it like he was done talking, and again, I waited because I knew he wasn't finished. And again, he eventually forced another laugh.

"It's not without its issues, obviously. Like I kind of have to rush after work because the doggie daycare closes and I have to go get Alfie. And he has to go every day 'cause I can't just leave him in the car, of course. It's too hot and what if someone took him, you know? But it's fine." He smiled again. "If I drop him off right when they open, I usually have time to go to the gym so I can shower before work and if I don't shave, I can get to work a little early so I can leave a little early. Though I can't go on the weekends, of course. 'Cause the daycare is closed. I keep wanting to try another daycare that might be open Saturdays at least, but Alf can be a handful and a lot of them have waiting lists and stuff. But it's okay. It's totally okay."

I told myself not to get involved.

It wasn't my problem. This was not my circus. Finn was not my monkey. He was more like a golden retriever, anyway. Or an otter, like he'd said when we first met. Or one of those quokkas who have no natural predators so they trust everyone and would go extinct if they lost their home and got put into the wrong ecosystem because they're just too nice for their own good and—

"Finn, come home with me."

His lips parted. "What?"

I sighed. "Come stay at my place. Just until you find a place to live. It's easier to house hunt when you're not living out of your car."

He stared at me, confusion on his face, but beneath it was a wary sort of fear that made my heart feel weird. Like it was kind of aching or something.

"That's gotta be against one of your rules," he said.

"Probably," I agreed. "But you and Julie aren't together anymore, so maybe the rules are different."

He smiled, but a moment later, shook his head. "I can't, Tess. I appreciate it, but I don't want to be—I don't want to make things, like, hard for you."

Even though he'd cut himself off, I knew what he'd stopped himself from saying, and that made the weird heart ache even worse.

"You're not a burden, Finn," I said, and when he blinked rapidly a few times, I knew I was right. "Come to my place. At least for tonight. You can crash on the couch. Shower. Shave. Get a decent sleep before work tomorrow. I mean, not to be an asshole, but you'd be doing everyone a favour. You kinda look like you'd be sticky if I touched you and it's completely unfair that the world can't see your gorgeous face beneath that beard."

He laughed, the sound dry but sad, but didn't say anything. At his feet, Alfie whimpered and Millie nosed him. I reached out and touched Finn's arm, which was not actually sticky.

"The dogs are having so much fun," I said. "You can let them hang out while you clean up. And then Alfie can get a good night's sleep outside the car, too."

I think he almost said no again, but Alfie picked that moment to nuzzle Millie and Finn was one hundred percent the type of person who would do anything for their dog.

Two

Usually when I got back from walking Millie, I brought her straight back upstairs to Dottie's. Dottie would acknowledge our return from her bedroom, where she was curled up with her totally-not-porn novels, by hollering something like she was going to call the cops on the hooligan breaking into her house. Millie would excitedly rush through the house and hop into Dottie's bed, where Dottie would accuse her of being a rabid beast. I would tell Dottie she was a senile old bat, then say goodnight and lock the door behind me before going down to the garden suite.

But that night, I didn't.

That night, Finn parked his car in my spot on the driveway and I figured it made more sense to get him settled at my place first. So with the dogs circling our feet, I let him in and showed him where the towels were and told him to make himself at home while I brought Millie upstairs.

And that was where I met the crypt keeper.

"Jesus Christ!" I gasped as Dottie's door swung open before I even touched the knob, then almost recoiled as a shadowed figure wearing a ratty burgundy bathrobe and dark grey silk bonnet emerged. "Dottie?"

"Who else would it be, you moron?" she asked.

"I don't know," I said. "I didn't realize you went to bed looking like a zombie that got turned after a failed cremation."

She cackled, slapping her thigh. "No offense taken. I know it must be hard when you're uglier than the ass end of a moose with hemorrhoids."

I laughed because that was fucking hilarious. "What are you doing out of bed, old lady?"

I thought she'd respond with another jab, but Dottie just folded her arms.

"What?" I asked.

"Don't *what* me," she said. "I would like the tea now, please."

"Oh, damn. I didn't realize your mental faculties had gotten so bad that you can't even boil the kettle for yourself," I said. "Do I need to hire you a caretaker?"

"Do I need to remind you there's an overnight-guest clause in your lease?"

I scoffed. "You would use the terms of our lease against me?"

"To get that good gossip? Hell yes I would." She leaned against the door frame. "Who'd you just drive up with? Because it looked like a tall Norwegian Viking and if he's not yours, I want you to put in a good word for the SENILF upstairs."

"The SENILF?" I repeated.

"It's like a MILF but it's your Sexy Elderly Neighbour," she replied.

"It sounds like it's a single line away from senile, you old bat," I said.

"Maybe he's into that."

"Maybe. I'll ask for you."

She raised her eyebrows. "So? Who is he?"

"He's a—" I hesitated, trying to think of how to explain who Finn was. "—a friend. Who needs a couch to crash on."

She looked skeptical. "That's it?" I nodded and she snorted. "Well, that's boring. I have a couch he can use if that's all that's happening."

"It's kind of complicated."

"What's so complicated about a tall hunky blonde finally taking you to poundtown?"

I wrinkled my nose at her. "Don't say poundtown. And what do you mean, finally? I get laid."

"You never bring anyone back here."

"Yeah, because I don't want to offend your delicate eardrums with my escapades."

"Maybe my eardrums could use some offensive escapades," she said. "I keep trying to get those audiobooks from the library but they're too complicated for me to figure out."

"Perv," I said.

"Thanks, hoe," she replied. "But you *are* okay, dear?"

The sudden solemness on her face surprised me. "Yeah. Why wouldn't I be?"

"You showed up with a scruffy Viking in the middle of the night. I'm gonna be a tad worried."

I was oddly touched. Emotionally, not physically, which would have gotten a very different reaction from me. "Well, thanks, but I promise it's okay. I do know him. He's a friend who's going through a rough patch right now."

"Hmm. That is uncharacteristically nice of you," she said. "But let me know if you and your friend need anything."

"We won't. Have a good night and don't die in your sleep, please."

When I went downstairs, the shower was running. Alfie had nestled himself onto my couch, but his ears perked up as I walked in. Sighing, I joined him, scratching his ears as he snuggled up on my legs and trying to process what the hell just happened

I mean, I knew what *happened*, at least in a literal sense. Finn said Alfie had jumped out of the car and ran off, and he'd been in such a panic that he hadn't grabbed his leash as he chased after him.

But we hadn't talked much more about Julie or what had happened. Not that there was much else to say. I knew Finn well enough to believe he not only didn't know about what Julie had done, but that he also didn't hold anything against her. I believed he was happy for her, that he wanted her to be true to herself, that he was sad it hadn't worked for them but excited to see her flourish.

I couldn't say I would've felt the same, but Finn was a far better person than I was. Although I felt like choosing to live in his car so she felt more comfortable was a step too far, even for the best of people.

Part of me hated he did that for her. Another part wondered how Julie could let him. But as angry as I was at her for ghosting me—and not just that, but for lying to Finn about it—I knew she had no idea.

At her core, Julie was a sweet person. She wouldn't have let Finn suffer, and from what little Finn had said about it, there really had been a lot of pain on her part when it came to their breakup. And I could understand that. Realizing you couldn't be attracted to someone like Finn? Gorgeous, loving, and who didn't have a mean or hateful bone in his body?

The guilt of ending things must have eaten at her.

I frowned as I kept petting Alfie. I wasn't sure why I had any sympathy for her. Hard time or not, she didn't have to handle things the way she did. But then, I'd always had an inconvenient soft spot for Julie.

When the bathroom door opened, I jumped. I'd been so deep in thought I hadn't heard the shower turn off, but it must have, since Finn walked into the room a moment later.

And fuck.

Fuck.

Finn's dirty line cook aesthetic was gone. And even though it hadn't been that long since I'd last seen him, somehow even my memories hadn't done justice to how fucking hot he was. His hair was still wet, though it had the tousled shininess of just-washed cleanliness. And he'd shaved away the scruffy not-quite-a-beard, so his skin was smooth and the cut of his jaw was as chiselled as ever.

And then there was his body.

Not just the niceness of it, which I knew intimately. But the way he was holding himself. His forehead wasn't crinkled with stress and his shoulders were less tense. Even his lips were playing up into a hint of the smile I knew so well.

Oh, and he was also wearing one of my bath towels wrapped around his waist and nothing else.

"Damn, he looks cozy," Finn said, looking at Alfie fondly.

I looked down at the little brown dog, whose head was resting on my thigh as he let out the cutest snores, snoozing away without a care in the world. "I think he was tired after his escapades with Millie."

Finn chuckled. "Probably. Um, but I was wondering…"

"What's wrong?"

"Nothing." He shrugged, a bashful look on his face. "I just wondered if you had a washing machine I could borrow. I'm, uh, running a little short on clothes that don't smell like my car."

Fuck, I hoped that didn't mean he was going to be wrapped in that little towel for the next hour or so while he did laundry.

Or maybe I did hope that.

"Of course, yeah," I said. "In the utility room. It's the door on the right."

"Got it," he said, then immediately turned around and opened the door on his left.

"No, the other right!" I said, startling Alfie awake, but it was too late.

"Holy crap!" Finn said, distracted from his clothes washing mission. "This is so cool! What is this?"

I winced as Alfie stood, using my legs as a platform to launch himself off the couch as he reacted to Finn's voice. Sighing, I followed him to the hall, where Finn was standing as he clutched the towel around his waist.

"It's my art studio," I said.

Finn's eyes were practically circles. "Wow. I knew you were an artist, but I didn't know you were, like, an *artist*-artist." He stepped into the room without asking, looking around at the various half-finished paintings I had sitting around the room. "These are amazing."

It was sweet of him, even if I didn't agree. "They're okay."

He studied the painting on my easel, which was an unfinished field of wildflowers for one of Kira's interior design clients she'd signed a contract with before realizing she was about to have a baby.

"Can you draw me?" he asked.

"Like one of my French girls?" I asked.

He tilted his head. "What's that mean?"

"Nothing," I said. "I just..."

I should have said no. I should have told him that I didn't draw on command just because someone asked me to. I mean, I did, but it was usually because someone gave me money when they were asking me to.

But Finn looked so excited and he was smiling and I just...

"Yeah," I said. "Okay. I'll do a quick drawing of you while you wash your clothes."

I got a sketchbook and a pencil while he loaded the washing machine with his clothes, then asked him to sit on the couch with Alfie while I settled at the small kitchen table that only sat four if I pulled it away from the wall. Not that it mattered, since I never had company anymore, but once upon a time, Kira and Jackson used to come over to hang out regularly.

For a while, the only sound was my pencil dragging along the paper as I focused on creating the lines of Finn's face and body. He sat still, occasionally brushing his fingers along Alfie's back or scratching his head.

But it was quiet.

Too quiet.

I wasn't used to Finn being silent. I was used to him asking me where I'd put a third ear if I had one or how many cookies I thought I could steal from a fancy party without anyone noticing.

I shouldn't have cared. He was going through some stuff and I was letting him stay on my couch because it was the right thing to do. It wasn't up to me to make him feel better, not when I was already far too involved in this. Doing anything more would make it complicated.

And yet...

"What's your favourite form of potato?"

I didn't look at him as I asked, but from the corner of my eye, I saw Finn tilt his head.

"What?" he asked.

"Your favourite form of potato," I repeated. "Like I want to say fries, but I'm a total slut for scalloped, you know?"

He chuckled. "Okay. Yeah. Um... I think I'd say pancakes."

That got me to look up. "What?"

"Potato pancakes," he said. "My mom used to make them all the time when I was a kid. She'd make homemade applesauce to serve with them but I liked it better with sour cream. So I'd alway eat one with applesauce, one with sour cream, one with applesauce..."

"I didn't know you could pancake potatoes," I said. "Although I guess it would be like a hashbrown?"

"Yeah. You can pancake anything if you try hard enough."

"Yeah? Can you pancake bacon?"

He made a *pfft* noise. "Easy. You just pour pancake batter over bacon."

"Fair. What about, like, broccoli?"

He thought for a moment. "I mean, you could, but that would be better as a waffle."

"Waffles are better in general, though."

"Yeah, but that wasn't the question."

"True." I added some shading on his nose. "Okay, it's your turn."

"My turn for what?"

"Ask me something."

"Um... what kind of ice cream do you wish existed?"

It wasn't a great question as far as Finn questions went, but it was better than not talking. But after inventing a flavour of ice cream so sweet that Chuck may not have even eaten it, featuring peanut butter, waffles, and—controversially, perhaps—both strawberry and maple syrup, I couldn't think of another weird question to ask.

So instead, I just made it awkward.

"You grew up in Richmond, right?" I asked.

"I did," he replied.

"Didn't you say once that your family is still there?"

He didn't reply right away. When I glanced up to see why, his face turned pink.

"Yeah," he said. "They are."

So clearly something was going on there, too. I told myself not to ask, then immediately ignored myself because apparently I was a nosy bitch.

"Why couldn't you stay with them instead of in your car?"

He looked like he didn't want to answer and I was about to tell him it was okay to not tell me, but he finally sighed.

"My dad is—well, my stepdad, but he's... he's my *dad*, you know? He's sick right now."

He wasn't looking at me when he said it, instead scratching Alfie's ears as that uncharacteristic crease appeared on his forehead.

"I'm sorry," I said. "Is he going to be okay?"

"Yeah, of course," he said. "I think." He glanced up, trying to smile. "He has cancer. But he's gonna beat it."

"Of course he is."

"He needs surgery and they don't know when it's going to be," he continued. "So it's just a lot right now. My sister—well, my stepsister, like his daughter, but we grew up together obviously—she's living there right now. Like, to help them. But they moved into a townhouse a few years ago since my sisters and I had all moved out and there's not enough rooms and I just didn't want to stress him and my mom out more."

My heart did that aching thing again. "They don't know you're staying in your car?"

"They don't know Julie and I broke up, either," he said. "Mom went on stress leave from the hospital because of all this so it's not like she sees Julie there anymore." He looked up at me, his eyes guarded. "I *am* going to tell them. When I find a new place to live. Just so they don't have to worry."

He seemed to think I was going to lecture him about keeping things from his family. Probably because he didn't know that would make me a giant hypocrite.

Three

I RUED THE DAY that I thought dog snores were cute, which was the same day that I discovered that dog snores were not, in fact, cute.

They were worse than sleeping next to someone who was snoring. When that happened, you could just kick the person until they rolled over, as Brad could have attested to many times throughout our marriage.

But you can't kick a dog.

That's just wrong.

So instead, you had to put up with Alfie while he was snoring loud enough to shake your bedroom window. Which wasn't even that much of an exaggeration because he was sleeping on a pile of clothes next to the window and every so often the curtain shifted, sending a streak of golden light across the room.

And yes, that could have been because there was a fan blowing in the room, but I was holding Alfie responsible for it anyway. Just like I was holding him responsible for the fact that I couldn't sleep. It had absolutely nothing to do with the fact that Finn was lying next to me.

In my bed.

In the dark.

It had taken an embarrassingly long amount of time for me to realize the flaw in my plan to have Finn sleep on the couch. It wasn't while I was drawing him sitting on said couch. It wasn't when he got up to switch his clothes to the dryer and I had to scold my body for reacting to the sight of an entirely-naked-except-for-a-towel Finn. It wasn't when I showed him the drawing and he'd declared it the best thing he'd ever seen, which was sweet even if it was wrong.

No, it wasn't until I'd dug out the spare blankets and a pillow from my closet and handed them to Finn that I remembered he was stupidly tall.

"You're not going to fit, are you?" I asked.

He shrugged. "It's fine. My legs bend."

"It's barely more room than in your car."

"Yeah, but it's a lot softer." He smiled. "And a lot less scary than sleeping outside. Like, your neighbourhood is nice, but it's still kinda creepy out there, you know? So this is more than fine, Tess. Really."

Don't do it, I told myself. He said it's fine, don't do it, don't say it, don't you dare—

"Just come share my bed with me," I blurted.

His eyes widened in surprise. "I... really? Are you sure?"

Not at all, my inner voice screamed. Tell him you changed your mind, say you—

"Of course I am," I said. "It's not like it's anything we haven't done before."

He glanced back down at the couch, biting his lip, and since I'd already committed myself to saying stupid shit, I kept going.

"It'll be more comfortable, Finn. And I won't be able to sleep knowing you're squished up on the couch."

Which may or may not have been true. I wouldn't know. Because Alfie had insisted on accompanying us to the bedroom, which I said was fine, and Alfie was snoring like a pug with a head cold, which was less fine. But at least he was on the ground. I only had a queen-size bed. And seeing as I was delightfully chunky and Finn was broad-shouldered, I was doing my best not to brush against him so I didn't wake him up as we lay there.

Though as it turned out, I didn't need to worry about that.

"Are you still awake?" Finn whispered after I'd been staring at the ceiling for God knows how long.

"Yeah," I said. "Are you?"

"I think so," he said. "I guess I could be dreaming, but I'm pretty sure I'm not."

"Want me to pinch you to find out?"

He chuckled. "Nah, I'm good. Is Alfie keeping you up?"

"I mean, he does snore really loud for such a little guy."

Finn shifted on the bed, turning to the side. "I can take him out. We can sleep on the couch."

"That wasn't me kicking you out, Finn. It's okay."

"Oh. Okay."

There was a weird sort of inflection in his voice and I frowned. "Did you want to go sleep on the couch?"

"No, no," he said quickly. "I'm good. I just didn't want to keep you up."

"It's fine. He'll quiet down eventually, right?"

"Probably, yeah."

An awkward sort of silence fell. I glanced at Finn out of the corner of my eye. "Is everything okay?"

"Yeah, of course. I'm great."

Just like earlier, his voice made it sound like that was the end of the statement, but something about it wasn't convincing. I waited and, just like before, he let out an awkward chuckle a few moments later.

"Although," he said. "Would it be weird if I took another shower?"

I almost laughed at the randomness of the question, but that would have bothered Finn, so I just pressed my lips together for a moment.

"Not weird at all," I said. "But you're sure everything's okay?"

"Totally."

"So you just... feel like showering again?"

"Something like that."

He was an awful liar.

"You can tell me what's wrong, Finn," I said. "I don't want you to be uncomfortable."

"Nothing's *wrong*, really, it's—" He sighed and I could almost hear him blushing. "Okay. I've been, uh, showering at the gym, right? And it's not very... *private*."

Oh.

Oh.

"And then earlier tonight I was kinda overwhelmed so I was maybe crying in the shower a little."

My realization was interrupted by another aching feeling in my chest. "You were upset?"

"No, just overwhelmed." He rolled onto his back again, the blankets tugging slightly as he relaxed on the pillow. "I'm not used to letting people do things for me and it's been a rough couple weeks and it bothers me that you were hurt because of Julie and me. And like, I always feel better after crying. I guess I'm not supposed to tell people that."

"Fuck anyone who says you shouldn't," I said. "I feel better after crying too. Crying in the shower is normal. And eco-friendly. You definitely save on Kleenex."

He let out a soft laugh. "Okay. So yeah, I was kinda focused on that earlier, so I didn't feel like... um... you know?"

I'd known what he was trying to say for a while, so I finally took pity on him. "Are you saying you're horny, Finn?"

"I mean, it's kinda hard to, like, do anything when you're in the car and your dog is right there," he said, soft embarrassment in his voice. "So, uh... I guess so?"

I didn't bother trying to talk myself out of it that time. It wasn't like I'd succeeded at it any of the other times that night.

"Okay, fine," I said, sighing with fake resignation as I rolled on my side to face him. "I'll give you a blowjob."

His neck snapped to face me. At the same time, Alfie let out a particularly loud snore and the curtain moved, the shaft of streetlight just bright enough for me to see Finn's eyes wide with surprise.

"What?" he asked.

"A blowjob," I repeated. "Like when someone puts another person's dick in their mouth? I'm pretty sure you've had one before. Unless I'm really misremembering things."

"No, I have," he said, completely missing the joke. "I just, I mean, I—"

"If it's too weird after everything, it's fine," I said, trying not to smile. "You can go take another shower. I won't be offended."

"No, it's not that," he said, and I almost felt bad about how distressed he sounded. "You're just already doing way too much for me. Like, you literally took me off the street, Tess. I don't want you to think you have to do *that* too. You didn't have to do any of this."

It was almost unreal how nice and thoughtful Finn was. And also how hard it was for him to accept help, apparently. I'd always known he was a people pleaser, but I was quickly realizing he was a people pleaser to a fault. To a point where he was hurting himself so he didn't risk upsetting anyone else.

Which sounded familiar, but I wasn't in the mood for self reflection.

"Are you saying you don't want a blowjob, Finn?" I asked.

"Not if you feel like you have to."

"What if I want to?"

The curtain shifted again and I saw him frown. "What?"

"What if I really, really want to suck your dick? Would you want to then?"

"I mean, yeah," he said. "But only if it's beca—*mmph*."

The rest of his sentence fell off his lips and onto mine as I used a kiss to cut him off.

"Finn," I whispered. "Shut up and let me put your cock in my mouth."

He groaned quietly, but there was a familiar spark of excitement in it. "Yes, ma'am."

Before he could do something stupid like roll towards me when I wanted him to stay on his back, I shook the blankets away and got to my knees. Leaning in, I placed a hand on his chest, kissing him again and absorbing the soft sigh he let out as I did.

Once his clothes had dried, Finn had dressed in his grey sweatpants again. *Just* the grey sweatpants, I was discovering, because even in the mostly dark room, I could see the outline of his cock pressed into the fabric. His chest was bare, skin warm beneath my fingertips as I reacquainted myself with the landscape of his muscles. As I did, I slipped my tongue in Finn's mouth, eliciting another one of those sighs and a noise of appreciation as I flicked it against his.

Then, once I was ready, I pulled away and focused on what I said I wanted.

Which was his cock.

In my mouth.

Because I'd been telling the truth. I *really* wanted his dick. I would have preferred it in my pussy, but that wasn't an option given that I didn't keep condoms in the house. Which seemed stupid, but Dottie's comment about me never bringing anyone here was true. And whenever I met with couples, I made them buy the condoms, because why should I pay for them when I was the one doing them a favour?

And then there was Zain, which... well.

Zain was a special circumstance, and one I didn't want to think about when I had Finn in my bed.

So oral would have to do, which was not all that bad a consolation prize. Not when I tugged Finn's sweats down and he sighed in relief, and not when I trailed a finger up his thigh to his groin and made him squirm delightfully beneath me. I smiled as he whined softly. I'd almost forgotten how vocal he was in bed and how much I'd loved it.

He wasn't a talker like Zain was. The words Zain could come up with practically caressed me themselves. He could make my breath catch and panties go damp just from growling things in my ear. Finn, on the other hand, liked to moan and groan and whimper, punctuated with the occasional utterance of "Oh my God" or "Oh fuck" or "Yes, ma'am" or *"Please."*

And that got me going in a completely different yet entirely similar way.

Because I loved making him come undone. I loved the breathless noise he made when I wrapped my fingers around his cock, the smooth skin searing hot.

I loved the way his stomach hollowed when I leaned in, looking up at the hint of light shining off his eyes as my breath brushed the head of his cock.

I loved the moment of teasing anticipation, the tension and excitement as my mouth hovered just above him, close enough that I could almost taste the saltiness already. I loved feeling his cock twitch needily once, then again, then almost a third time before I took him into my mouth.

"Fuckkk," he groaned, a sound of relief underscored by a need for more. I sucked on his tip gently before letting it fall from my mouth for a moment.

"You okay?" I asked.

"Uh-huh," he said. "I'm great. My dick really likes your mouth."

"Well, good thing my mouth likes your dick."

Before he could respond, I took him in my mouth again, sliding my lips down inch by inch until I had the most I could take without him stuffed in the back of my throat. Wrapping my fingers around the base, I stroked his shaft a few times, then took a breath and bobbed my head forward in an attempt to take more.

It wasn't going to be a long blowjob. I'd known that from the moment I positioned myself between his legs and he'd drawn in a sharp breath before I even touched him. And then there was the tension of his muscles as I put his cock in my mouth, the clench of his fist on the bedsheets that told me he was fighting to control himself.

But that was okay. I didn't need long to make it incredible.

He panted as I ran my tongue along the underside of his shaft, dragging it against the sensitive spot on his crown. Then I sucked again, gently at first, increasing the pressure until he was gasping. After licking him up and down so his cock was slick, I wrapped both hands around him and stroked firmly while circling my tongue around the tip.

"Fuck, Tess," he whimpered. "You're gonna make me embarrass myself."

I lifted my head, though I didn't stop moving my hands. "Embarrass yourself how?"

He laughed. "Coming way too fast."

"Pretty sure I've seen you hold out for ages before," I said. "And also that I can make you come a few times in a night if I really want to. You have nothing to prove to me, Finn."

I didn't mean it as anything more than what I said. It was just reassurance that I wasn't going to judge him for coming too fast. But Finn paused, his eyes on mine and his head tilting to the side as he took those words in.

"I don't," he said, almost more to himself than to me.

"You don't," I repeated. "I know you're a sex god who can make me forget my own name. One quick blowjob isn't going to change that."

He smiled, but didn't say anything else. He just leaned against the pillow as I returned his cock to my mouth. Another soft sigh fell from his mouth, the sound relaxed as he reached down to stroke my hair.

And that.

That was what I wanted.

I couldn't say why. I didn't know why I was so eager for him to relax, to be calmed, to make it clear to him he was in a place where he was safe and unjudged. It shouldn't have mattered to me. Not when I hadn't seen him in weeks and, up until a few hours earlier, had been upset that he'd walked out of my life without so much as a word, even though I now knew that wasn't what happened.

But God, something about him. Something about him and that day and I just... I needed to be that person for him.

Which didn't make sense at all, so I stopped thinking about it and focused on swallowing as much of him as I could.

It wasn't long until I had the taste of his pre-cum in my mouth, and not much longer after that when he murmured a warning he was about to come. His hand tightened on my hair, not quite pulling it, but more like he was tensing before the first spurt of cum spilled into my mouth. I kept sucking and working his cock until I was sure I had every last drop. Only then did I pull back, swallowing as I sat back on my knees and looked up at him.

His eyes were closed and his head rested heavily on the pillow. But before I could crawl back over his leg and return to my spot on the bed, his eyes opened and for the first time that night, he looked like Finn. Fully like Finn, like the happy, optimistic, and bubbly airhead who could make anyone his friend. He sat up, lunging forward and battering my mouth with heated kisses.

"Is it bad for me to say I missed that?" he asked between kisses. "Like, I missed *you* more, but I really, really missed the way you do that."

The words made a warm wave roll over my body and a soft noise escaped my lips, just loud enough that Finn heard it. I felt him smile against my mouth, then he nipped my bottom lip.

"My turn now," he murmured.

And yeah, I could've mirrored his actions. I could've insisted it was fine. I could've even told him I'd had my pussy eaten earlier that day, actually, by my brother's best friend before I left Kelowna.

Maybe I *should* have told him that last part.

But I really, really missed the way Finn ate pussy.

So I let him lift my top over my head and urge me onto my back. I let him slide my pyjama pants down and nuzzle my fabric-covered mound before he stripped my panties off, too, then put a large hand on each of my thighs to hold me wide open for him. I wound my fingers through his squeaky-clean hair as he dove in, spoiling my clit with his tongue, lapping eagerly at my folds and indulging in me as much as I was indulging in him.

And after I came, trying to stifle my cries as I held his head against my core until I was quivering and panting for breath, I let him draw me into his arms, both of us still naked as we curled into each other and tucked the blankets around us.

"Tess?" he murmured as I faded towards sleep.

"Hmm?"

"If you got cloned, would you have sex with your clone?"

"Yeah. But only a couple of times. I feel like one of us would get bored because we would both know all my moves."

"Mmm. Good point."

"Would you?"

"I'd have sex with whatever version of you would have me."

I laughed. "Yeah, but would you have sex with your clone?"

"I think we'd both be down to try it."

I laughed sleepily, then we fell silent again.

"Tess," he said again a few minutes later.

"Yeah?"

He cuddled in closer and buried his nose in my hair. "Thanks for letting me and Alfie stay over."

Four

"He is a damn fine man," Dottie muttered as she sipped her lemonade.

"He's pretty alright," I said.

She snorted into her glass. "*Pretty alright*? What kind of tail are you pulling that *he* is just 'pretty alright'?"

I shrugged noncommittally, sipping my own lemonade as my eyes followed Finn's shirtless form crossing the lawn with the pushmower.

"I didn't think you'd need to watch this version of the show," Dottie continued when I didn't say anything. "Aren't you getting your own private one?"

"Jealous?" I asked.

"A little," she said. "Have you seen that man?"

"Yep."

"Mmm," she said. "So he's your...?"

"Friend."

"You're full of shit, skittle tits."

"How am I full of shit?" I asked, then frowned. "And *skittle tits*?!"

She shrugged, her eyes still fixed to Finn. "I'm just sayin', those noises you were making last night sounded a little more than just 'friendly' to me."

"You were listening to me get laid, you rusty old nipple?"

"The whole neighbourhood listened to you get laid, Screamy McGee."

"I wasn't screaming," I scoffed.

"Millie thought you were being murdered."

Millie's ears perked up at the mention of her name, which allowed Alfie to get the upper hand in the wrestling match they were having at our feet. And by upper hand, I meant more like upper-entire-body, since he managed to mount her again. Sighing, I put my lemonade down and reached down to separate them.

"Little Guy, you gotta do that kind of thing in private," I said.

"Not like you and Finn set a great example for him," Dottie muttered.

I nudged Alfie away from Millie. "I'll keep it down next time, Pervy O'Toole."

"Next time?" she said lightly.

"Next time my *friend* and I decide to have a *friendly* little hookup that means nothing except that two *friends* need to get laid."

She let out a derisive sigh. "Crazy bitch."

"What?!"

She turned to me, disbelief on her face. "You got a man who looks like him, getting you to make noises like *that* last night, mowing my lawn, offering to cook you dinner, and you're calling him a friend?"

"I'd say that's friendly behaviour," I said.

She shook her head. "Let me tell you, if I was ten years younger..."

"I'm sure Finn would be fine with you the age you are now."

"Of course he would." She sipped her lemonade. "But if I was ten years younger, I'd be able to overpower you and lock you in the closet so I could get my turn with him."

I had to laugh, shaking my head before drinking more of my lemonade. Both of us fell silent, eyes glued to the sun-kissed glow of Finn's skin reflecting gold in the evening sun.

He stopped near the end of the yard, which wasn't all that far from where Dottie and I were sitting on the porch. That was both fortunate and unfortunate. It was fortunate because I could drink in the sight of him as he used the long-discarded t-shirt to wipe his hands and face, my eyes trailing down his bare chest and stomach to the v-lines disappearing into the boxer-briefs peeking out above the waistband of his shorts.

And it was unfortunate because it meant the yard wasn't very big and Finn was done mowing it.

But even the unfortunate was sort of fortunate, since Finn caught sight of me and Dottie looking at him and a bright smile spread across his face, completing the picture of perfection as he ran a hand through his shaggy blonde hair.

And also because it meant Finn was about to make dinner, because of course the man was a kitchen god along with being a sex god and a yardwork god, apparently.

"Well, that should do you for a few days, Ms. Price," he called across the yard after putting the lawnmower back in the garage and pulling his shirt on.

"Just call me Dottie, sweet thing," she said.

He smiled bashfully. "Sorry, Dottie. Force of habit. My mom always told me to be respectful to people I just met."

"Well, your mom was right," Dottie said. "But since your little guy Alfie and my sweet Millie are so *friendly* now, I think we're *friends* too, aren't we?"

I tried not to laugh as she held out a glass of lemonade and he took it gratefully.

"Yeah, of course," he said.

"Perfect. And since Tessa here told me just now how *friendly* you are—"

"And that's enough of that," I said, setting my empty glass down on the table.

Dottie cackled as she rose from the bench and began clearing the lemonade. "Either way, you did a great job on the lawn, Finn."

"Thanks," Finn said. "But it was nothing. I'm happy to help. Especially to thank you for watching Alfie all day."

"He should be tuckered out with all the humping he had going on," she said.

Finn grimaced. "Yeah, sorry. He's a little... you know. The vet said he'd grow out of it, but it hasn't happened yet."

"Nah, sweet thing," Dottie said. "It's fine. Millie wasn't complaining. She looked like she could maybe use a cigarette after they were done the third or fourth round, but she wasn't *complaining*." She took Finn's empty glass from him. "Now, if you want to leave him here again tomorrow, I'm more than happy to let him tucker himself out again. But you know, I have some lightbulbs that are a little high and with my old knee, getting on the stepladder is a tad iffy. So if you wouldn't mind giving me a hand with that when you pick him up..."

"Uh, yeah," Finn said. "Of course. If I'm back tomorrow, I'd be happy to."

And there it was.

Proof that Chuck was *wrong*.

I mean, I'd known he was wrong that morning after I'd finished telling him about running into Finn the previous night. But Chuck had been insistent that Finn staying with me had to *mean* something.

"How in the hell do you end up in these situations, Tessa Breanna Lane?"

"Pure talent, I guess."

"Or a complete lack of survival instincts."

"Excuse you," I said. "I am surviving just fine. It's thriving I have a problem with."

"You took home a man who was living on the streets."

"I knew him before he was living on the streets. And he wasn't—that's oversimplifying things way too much."

"Oh my God, Tessa," he said. "He was living in his car and you took him home and made him your boytoy. That *means* something."

"Oh my God, Chuck," I mocked. "It's not that serious. He needed help and someone to talk to. And it's Finn. He's like if a ray of sunshine and a golden retriever had a baby."

"Your point?"

"I'm more like—"

"Oh my God," Chuck interrupted. "Don't you dare say you're like the sound of darkness or something like that, you walking cliché."

"I was going to say I was more like a mix of a raccoon and a rainy day."

He frowned. "What does that even mean?"

I shrugged, sipping my coffee. "You're the one reading way more into this than you need to."

Which was absolutely true.

If it wasn't for the fact that Finn had slept so soundly that he'd woken up late and started worrying about getting Alfie to daycare on time, I doubt he would have come back that night without a hell of a lot more convincing. Instead, I'd told him we could ask Dottie if she'd watch Alfie for him.

And of course, Dottie took one look at Finn and would've probably agreed to subject herself to risky experimental medical tests to have his babies for him, so she said yes. But when Finn had dropped me off at work—because of course he insisted on driving me to work that morning—he'd seemed uncertain.

"I'll see you tonight," I said before getting out of his car.

"Yeah, of course," he said, an easy smile on his face. "I gotta come get my dog."

I paused with the door partially open. "You're not staying again?"

Something flickered on his face. I didn't think it was hesitancy at the idea of staying with *me* again, but the vulnerability of accepting help in general.

"I would love to," he said. "But you need to let me do something for you."

"Finn—"

"Please?" he asked, his voice firm. "Let me make you dinner?"

And I mean, I wasn't going to say no to that. Not when I was pretty sure I'd had sexy dreams about the brown butter gnocchi he'd made the one and only time I'd agreed to have dinner with him and Julie.

So I didn't say no, and Finn smiled, tapping his fingers on the steering wheel.

"Awesome," he said. "Now I just gotta think of something for Dottie to thank her for watching Alfie."

"You should get him to cut the lawn," Chuck said after I refuted his statement to him yet again. "And if you talk him into doing it shirtless, I wouldn't say no to you calling me so I can drop by and join your lechery."

"Oh, of course," I said. "I'm sure your boyfriend wouldn't mind at all."

Chuck snorted. "Of course he wouldn't. I'd bring Charles with me."

"I thought you two were dedicated to the concept of monogamy."

He gave me a dirty look. "We are. But no one says we can't look. It's a fun couple activity for us. We've even gone out to Wreck Beach a couple of times now."

I gaped at him. "Seriously? With *Charles*? To check people out?"

"Well, yes and no," he said. "It's not really to check people out. It's more to help Charles learn to embrace the beauty of naked time."

"The... what?"

"Naked time. I like being naked in front of other people. He likes giving me whatever I like. And you of all people don't get to judge us for our weekend activities."

"Just because I'm surprised doesn't mean I'm judging you. You do whatever floats your boats."

"Don't you worry about our boats," he said. "They're floating fine. Frequently and with youthful vigor." He crossed one leg over the other and tapped a finger to his chin. "Though, that does bring up another point about our dear, sweet Finn."

"He's not even *my* Finn, Chuck," I said. "There's no way he can be *our* Finn."

He waved a hand at me. "What about Zain?"

"What about him?"

Chuck gave me an incredulous look. "I mean, you and Zain are..." He lifted his hand and rolled his wrist until I spoke.

"Fucking when we see each other once in a while?" I asked. "That has nothing to do with this."

He pressed his lips into a line. "Tessa."

"What?"

"You and Finn—"

"—have nothing serious."

"He's living with you!" he exclaimed.

"Temporarily."

He snorted. "Sure. Tell me that again in a few weeks when you've stocked up on condoms and he's still sleeping in your bed and cooking for you every night as he does yardwork for your SENILF."

"You would not like to F my SEN," I said. "And it's not a big deal. It's the same for me and Zain." Inspiration hit and I pointed a finger at him. "And see, it can't be serious with Finn. Zain asked me yesterday if he could stay over Friday night because he's in town for a—" I stopped myself before saying "job interview," since Chuck would jump on that like it was Charles on a nude beach. "—a business thing. So Finn will have to find somewhere to stay by then."

Unfortunately, saying Zain was staying over for a night was just as juicy to Chuck as the job interview portion would have been. His eyes went wide and he spread his hands in front of him.

"He's coming to spend the night with you? Mr. High Maintenance is choosing to stay with *you* instead of in a five-star?"

"He's coming to a business thing. I just have a pussy worth sleeping in an old queen-size bed for."

"Hmph," he said. "And does he know?"

"What?"

"That he's not the only one tapping that worthy pussy?"

I wrinkled my nose. "That was the weirdest way to say that. And yes, he does know. I'll remind him again, but he's always been aware we're not exclusive."

"So he knows about you and Claire?"

"Claire and I have stated multiple times that we are just friends."

"Who fuck."

"Yes."

He huffed. "I don't get it."

"I don't need you to get it," I said. "You just need to respect that I don't have anything serious with any of them."

"Because you're still maintaining a fake marriage to your asshole ex."

"Not *just* that."

"Sure." He uncrossed his legs and turned towards his desk. "I just hate to see you give up your happiness because of Brad Schubert, of all people."

I glared at the back of his head. "Brad doesn't control my life. I do."

"Sure. Just like this thing with Finn isn't serious."

"It's not," I insisted.

And Finn proved it after he finished cutting the grass that night, uncertain yet again if he'd be welcome to stay at my place the next night.

While I helped Dottie bring the lemonade back into her house, Finn parted a slightly unwilling but mostly exhausted Alfie and Millie from each other. After Finn thanked Dottie again for watching Alfie, the three of us went down the porch stairs to the basement entrance.

It was muscle memory for me to reach up the back of my shirt to unhook my bra as soon as I walked in so I could hang it on the hook by the door. My hand was halfway behind me before my muscles remembered that, unlike most days, there was someone with me. I tried to correct myself, but Finn caught the movement.

"You can take your bra off," he said. "I don't mind."

"How did you know that's what I was doing?" I asked.

"You told me and Julie about it one time," he said. "You said you always took your bra off as soon as you got home. Then you undressed next to our front door..."

"Oh yeah," I said. "I forgot about that."

He smiled. "I didn't. That was so fucking hot."

"It was," I agreed, though I looked at him carefully. "It doesn't bother you?"

"No. Your boobs should be free if you want them to be free. It's your house."

"No, I mean, it doesn't bother you to think about Julie?"

He shrugged, opening the fridge and pulling out the ingredients he'd bought on his way home from work. "I mean, it makes me sad that things didn't work out, but it's okay. I always worried a little that I wasn't... you know." He set a carton of chicken broth on the counter, his cheeks turning pink. "Like, I wasn't smart enough to keep up with her."

I had no idea how to respond to that. It hurt, somehow, to hear him say that about himself. To say it like he didn't know what a catch he was.

Finn glanced over and must have seen the surprise on my face because he smiled again. "Not because she'd ever said anything. But like, you know how smart Julie is. Things were great with us, but I think she'll be happy with someone who can challenge her that way, you know? Like, she loves museums and art galleries and wants to travel all over the world to learn shit. And that's totally cool and stuff, but it's a lot of reading and examining and I just... it's not my jam. I'm not that good at it."

"So you thought you weren't going to last?" I asked.

He shook his head. "No, not at all. I'm just saying I kind of get it."

"But that's not why you broke up."

"No, of course not. And I'm not upset that we broke up because she realized something like that about herself." He looked at me again, something pleading in his sincere eyes. "I know you're still probably pissed at her because of what she did. That's fair. I'm kinda mad about it, too."

"She blocked me out of nowhere after promising to come to my event," I said. "Yeah, Finn. I get she had other stuff going on, but to not even say anything?"

He nodded as I spoke. "I get it. Totally. Just, like, I want you to know she wasn't thinking normally at the time. She was scared and worried and then she came to terms with it, but that meant she was gonna have to tell her family and they don't really, uh... support that kind of thing, I guess?" His eyebrows pinched together in an imploring expression. "I know it probably sounds like an excuse, but it's not. I just want to help explain that she's still a good person, even if she did something shitty."

"Are you still friends?" I asked.

He shrugged. "Sort of. We don't talk much or anything though."

"But you moved out and started living in your car for her, which she doesn't even know about."

"Well, yeah." He moved something on the counter idly. "I just thought if there was one thing she didn't feel bad about, it might help."

"What do you mean?"

He sighed. "Like, she was scared to tell her family. She felt bad about us breaking up. Everything changed for her really fast and in my head, if she knew I thought she was doing the right thing, it would make it easier for her."

"Don't you think she'd want to know, though?" I asked. "I mean, I might be upset about what she did, but I don't think she'd want you to sacrifice as much as you did for her, Finn."

He was still looking down at the counter, but I could see the odd expression on his face. After a tense, uncomfortable moment, I walked forward to join him.

"Why don't we talk about dinner instead?" I asked. "Do you need a hand with anything?"

Just like that, brightness returned to his face.

"Right," he said. "Okay. So, I know you said you liked the gnocchi and brown butter mushrooms, so I figured I'd treat you to another one of my specialities that's kinda like that." He motioned at the ingredients on the counter, including a giant bag of scallops.

"Well, colour me intrigued," I said, trying not to wince.

"What colour is that?" he asked. "Like, a kind of purple or...?"

I tried not to laugh. "No, it's just a saying. But if anything, I think intrigue would probably be a type of green."

"Oh." He frowned. "So you don't like scallops?"

I blinked and looked up at him, wondering how he'd figured that out. "What makes you say that?"

"Well, if intrigue is green and they make you feel green, that might be like sick, so..."

I couldn't fault his logic, especially since he was right about me not liking them. "Well, I'm not a huge seafood fan, but I'll try them."

His face fell. "I don't want to make something you won't like."

"Finn," I said. "Let me try them. I know you're an awesome cook, so maybe I've just never had them done right."

A sweet smile spread on his lips. "Well, then I'm looking forward to the chance to show you how delicious scallops are."

"Do you think it's bad I haven't told my family what happened with me and Julie?" Finn asked as we sat on the couch later that night.

I couldn't say the question was unexpected. Despite acting like his usual cheerful self, Finn had been introspective all evening. I'd thought he might ask something like that while we were eating, but I'd been so taken aback by the deliciousness of the brown butter scallops and parmesan risotto served with a side of sauteed kale and bacon that he couldn't stop grinning.

"Seriously," I said, poking at the squishy round disc with a perfectly seared crust on it as Finn's cheeks turned pink. "I don't understand. What the hell was I eating that people were calling seafood if this is actually seafood? Why is this so delicious?"

"It's pretty easy," Finn said. "First, you gotta get fresh seafood. If it's not fresh, it's just not as good. Second, the worst thing you can do is overcook it. No one likes eating rubber. I don't think so, anyway." He sliced a scallop in half. "Third, you gotta get 'em really dry before you cook them, like patting them down with a paper towel. And then you just put salt, pepper, make sure the pan is super hot, get your butter all melted and pop 'em on for like two minutes. Then when it's all crispy on the one side, flip it over and keep pouring butter over it while the other side gets crispy." He popped the scallop in his mouth. "Ian taught me that."

"Who's Ian?" I asked.

"My step-dad," he said. "He's an awesome cook. But he mostly likes to do barbecue now. He makes a mean Carolina barbecue sauce." He chewed the rest of his scallop and swallowed it. "I should get him to show me the recipe."

I waited for him to say more, but he was quiet for a moment before looking at me.

"Okay," he said. "If a wizard magically turned you into a condiment of your choice, which condiment would you be? I'd be butter, I think."

That question morphed into what the sexiest condiment is, but there was no more mention of Julie or his family or what had happened while we ate. Once we were done, Finn shooed me out of the kitchen, insisting he would clean up. And far be it from me to clean the kitchen when I didn't have to, so I took Alfie outside for a bathroom break before the two of us settled on the couch to catch up on the latest episodes of *Secret Rednecks* while Finn did the dishes.

When he finished, he joined us. Alfie stirred as Finn sat, lifting his head to watch Finn fold his tall body onto the cushion next to mine, but put it back down with a heavy huff.

Finn laughed. "Normally I take him for a walk after dinner, but I think he's pretty much exhausted."

"A humping marathon tends to do that," I said.

"Maybe he needs a Gatorade."

I snorted and Finn smiled, leaning against the armrest of the couch. We chatted a bit as we watched, mostly about the antics of the secret rednecks and what we thought would happen next, but there was nothing of consequence until the episode ended.

Then, in typical Finn fashion, he dropped the question about if I thought it was bad he hadn't told his family about what happened with little to no lead-in.

"I'm the last person to judge you, Finn," I answered.

He reached over to scratch Alfie's ears idly as the little brown dog kept snoozing. "Yeah, but like... is it *really* bad of me? 'Cause you might just be saying that and—"

"I haven't told my family I'm divorced even though it's been five years," I said.

Finn looked from Alfie to me, blinking once as he processed my statement.

"Wait," he said. "You were married before?"

"Uh... yeah," I said.

"Why didn't I know that?"

"I... don't know," I said.

But that was a lie.

Because I did know. I knew exactly why he wouldn't know and it was because I never brought it up with him or Julie. I had never told them about Brad or that part of my life. Or about Nathan and Mel.

I'd barely told them anything, because why? I'd always said it wasn't serious.

"Well, I was," I said. "We got married just after I finished university. His name was Brad and he just believed in me when no one else did, I guess."

"What do you mean?"

I shrugged. "My family always kind of treated me like a joke. They thought being an artist was stupid."

"That's stupid," Finn said. "Didn't they ever see how good you are?"

I felt something warm rise from my chest up my neck. "They aren't really, uh, artsy kinds of people. I was starting to feel like they were right when I first met Brad and he didn't think I was a joke. So much so that when I brought him home to meet everyone, it started making the rest of them take me more seriously."

He nodded in understanding. "Why did you break up?"

"He was cheating on me the entire time."

I couldn't recall a time I'd seen Finn angry. Up until then, I wouldn't have said it was possible for his face to darken with anger the way it did just then. And honestly, it was a good thing Brad wasn't around. Finn was one of those people who was beyond nice. Beyond friendly. Beyond kind. Which meant that he was also one of those people who was downright terrifying when he was angry, since it took a lot to get him there.

Including, apparently, cheating.

"What an asshole," he said. "I don't know why anyone would do that in the first place, but especially to *you*." He glared down at his hands. "Why doesn't your family know?"

"A few reasons," I said. "Like when it was happening, I couldn't bring myself to admit I'd been wrong about him. I didn't want people to know I'd failed at yet another thing. And part of me was worried they'd try to talk me out of it." I sighed. "He's charming. People liked him a lot more than me most of the time, and I felt like my family did, too. So I kept telling myself I'd wait until the divorce was finished before telling them. Then my parents' house burnt down."

His lips parted in shock and all the anger that had been there dissipated. "What?"

"My parents' house burned down. Like, just after my divorce was finalized."

"Oh my God," he said. "Were they okay?"

I nodded. "No one was hurt. They lost the house and almost everything in it, though. Like, the least damaged room was their bedroom, but between the water and the smoke, it wasn't like they could salvage much in there. Most of the photos, keepsakes, heirlooms and all that kind of stuff... gone. My mom had to beg people for copies of their wedding photos and old school pictures for me and my brothers. All... all the sketchbooks and paintings and stuff I'd left there from when I was a kid were gone."

"I'm so sorry," he said.

I swallowed back a lump in my throat, almost surprised at myself for getting choked up as I thought about the stacks of stuff I'd had in my parents' basement. A lifetime of things gone because there was always some reason I couldn't bring them to Vancouver. I didn't have space at my apartment. Or there wasn't room in my suitcase. Or we were moving and would get them once we were settled in.

"So once that happened, I didn't want to tell them about the divorce," I said. "Like, I figured I'd wait until things were taken care of and they had a place to live and all that. Why add stress, right? But of course, then they expected that Brad would be there with me when I went back to help them and stuff. So I... I asked him. If he would pretend we weren't divorced. Just until it was taken care of. And since he's in real estate, he had connections to things that could help my parents. Plus he gave them money, since insurance doesn't actually cover as much as you think it will."

"Why did he do that?"

"He wanted me back. So he played along because he figured I'd change my mind about leaving him. And of course I wasn't going to. I still planned to tell everyone once it was all taken care of. But then the house was rebuilt and he was everyone's hero and I just... I couldn't. So I kept lying and he kept playing along."

"What do you mean, playing along?"

"Like, he comes to my family's events once in a while." I bit my lip. "Remember the second time we got together? When I came to your and Julie's apartment for the first time?"

He nodded.

"I'd spent the weekend with him and my family. It was my parents' anniversary and they wanted everyone there. So he came along, pretended we were still together. My mom calls him sometimes and he pretends we still live together even though he's been living in Seattle for a few years now." I tried to laugh. "So, trust me. I'm definitely not judging you for not telling your parents that you and Julie broke up. I understand why you'd decide to do that. And I know that you will tell them eventually. If anything, you should be judging me."

He shook his head. "Not at all. I'm just sorry that you *do* understand it, you know? It sucks."

"It sucks," I agreed solemnly.

"Like, I know I should tell them," he said. "It's just that Ian—my dad... well, my step-dad, but he's my dad in every single way except genetically. He's always done so much for me when he didn't have to. Like—" He shifted, leaning down to rest his elbows on his knees. "My actual dad, not Ian, used to take me for a weekend once in a while when I was growing up. And he *hated* Ian. He thought Ian wasn't raising me right and it was his fault I was, like... stupid."

I couldn't stop my jaw from dropping. "Your dad called you stupid?"

"Not, like, specifically. But he had a lot of thoughts about how I should act and stuff. To be 'manly.'" He half-laughed. "He always said Ian wasn't a good example of that and I'd kind of get it into my head that my dad didn't want me around because I acted like Ian. So I'd go back home and try to act like how my dad said. And it would always take Ian a bit to help me get back to normal after that, but he never gave up on me. He always, *always* made sure I knew he'd be there for me, and he never said a bad word about my dad. It took until I was a teenager before I realized how awful my dad was."

"Do you still talk to him?"

Finn shook his head. "Not after what he said about Hailey."

"Hailey?"

"My step-sister. One of my step-sisters." He sat back, clearing his throat. "Abby is my other step-sister. They're twins and they always took care of me growing up. Like, spoiled me rotten 'cause they're like eight years older than me. So they're my step-sisters, but I'm close with them."

"Of course," I said.

"And Hailey," he continued. "She's always been my sister, ever since Mom and Ian got married. Just like she's always been Ian's daughter."

"Right," I said, though I was a bit confused.

"We just didn't know she was a sister or a daughter at the time," he said. "And after she told us she was a girl, my dad found out, obviously. He was still picking me up at my mom's place once a month or whatever. And he saw me hug Hailey goodbye one day after she'd started transitioning. When I got in the car, he just started going off about how Ian was a shitty dad and that it was his fault Hailey turned out 'like that' and that I better not think I could do what Hailey was doing, except he didn't call her *Hailey*, he was using the wrong name and I just—"

His voice hitched with anger, shaking as the words spilled out faster and his cheeks turned red. He swallowed, then cleared his throat again.

"I was done," he said. "I told him he had no right to talk about my sister like that and that Ian was a better role model than he'd ever been and some other stuff I probably shouldn't repeat because it was pretty mean. But he ended up kicking me out of the car. Which would've been fine except we were almost at his place in Surrey and he wouldn't let me get my backpack out of the trunk, so I didn't have my phone or any money and it took me like four hours to walk home."

"Oh my God," I said. "That's horrible. I'm so sorry."

He shrugged. "It was for the best. I realized how much shit my dad was putting in my head that didn't need to be there and how much Ian had always helped me out. How he always treated me the same as my sisters even though he was my step-dad. And like, when I said I didn't want to go to college or anything because I'm bad at school and I hated it, he didn't judge me. He helped me get a job I liked and that I was good at. He really loves my mom, which like, I also really love my mom so I'm glad he treats her right."

He smiled, though it wasn't his usual smile. It was more the kind of smile that's holding something back.

"And now he's sick," he said. "He's got cancer. Mom's having a hard time with it. Hailey moved back in with them to help and so this thing with Julie and not having a place to stay... it's not fair." He looked up at me. "I didn't want to give them more to worry about if I didn't have to. Like, once they have some answers or his surgery gets scheduled or something, it'll be different. But for me... I was getting by, you know?"

"I know," I said. "I understand."

"I will tell them," he said again. "I just wanted you to know all this 'cause I don't know, like... when."

He didn't say anything else, but the implication was clear enough.

"I'm not going to make you leave," I said. "I wouldn't have told you to stay here if I wasn't okay with it."

"Yeah?" he said, though his voice was uncertain.

"Of course."

"And do you want me to, like, sleep here on the couch?"

I raised my eyebrows. "Do you not want to sleep in the bed?"

Finn's cheeks started turning pink. "I mean, I'd rather do that. But I don't want you to feel like I'm pressuring you to do stuff like, um, last night."

Somewhere deep in my mind, a voice that sounded suspiciously like Chuck's started to echo.

"You know it doesn't have to mean anything if we do, right?" I asked. "It's like before. We're friends."

He nodded. "Yeah. Of course."

"And if I have other similar friends that I sometimes hook up with, that wouldn't bother you?"

"Not even a little."

And of course, that was when I remembered the thing about Zain staying with me that weekend. But it felt like it'd be a dick move to tell

Finn I wasn't going to make him leave and then immediately inform him he'd have to find somewhere else to stay Friday night.

That was fine. I'd just tell Zain he needed to get a hotel. And then I would join Zain in said hotel for the night.

"Alright," I said. "So you're okay with us being friends that share a bed and sometimes fool around without it having to mean anything else?"

Finn nodded, though his forehead creased with confusion. "I mean, yeah. Why?"

Chuck wasn't there for me to scream "I told you so" at, so I mentally yelled it at the voice that sounded like his in my head before standing and going into the kitchen. Digging into the reusable bag I used to haul my things to and from work, I withdrew the box of condoms I'd stopped to buy at Shoppers Drug Mart on my way home. I brought them to the coffee table and set them down in front of Finn. He looked at the box, then up at me, the corners of his eyes crinkling.

"You can stay as long as you like, Finn," I said, then turned and walked to the bedroom. Behind me, I heard Alfie whine in protest as Finn stood to follow me.

Six

"I swear you're living the dream," Claire said from between my legs.

I squirmed, trying not to gasp as her tongue circled my clit. "It is pretty awesome."

"Seriously." She paused to suck on the swollen little bud and I couldn't hold back a moan. She chuckled as she released it from her mouth, then slipped a finger inside of me. "You should buy some shares of a condom company if he's gonna keep fucking you like that."

"You're not wrong." A shudder of pleasure ran through me. "He's been at my place since Sunday and even though it's only Wednesday, I swear we've fucked ten times."

"Really?"

"Well, no, now that I say it out loud, it seems like an exaggeration. But it's definitely more than…"

"More than three?" she asked as I trailed off into a moan.

"More than six," I managed to say.

"He must be really backed up after those couple weeks of car-and-dog-induced celibacy, huh?"

"I'm not complaining," I said, squirming beneath her touch. "I mean, there's a good chance I won't be able to walk straight ever again in my life. But I'm not complaining."

"You definitely won't be walking straight if I have anything to do about it." She curled her finger inside of me and I moaned again. "What did he say when you said you were going out with me tonight? You did tell him, right?"

"Of course I did. He was doing the dishes when I went to leave. Turned around and told me to have fun and have lots of orgasms like I was on my way to summer camp or something."

Despite the distraction of Claire's tongue, I had to smile at the memory. Finn had found an apron in my pantry that I must have accidentally stolen from Kira back when I was living with her, which he kept putting on every time he cooked. The sight of that six-foot-whatever man in a teal cotton apron with lace ruffles on the edges *killed* me. And by killed me, I meant killed my panties, because it was both unexpected and unreasonable how hot that mix of broad-shouldered muscles and femininity was.

"That reminds me," I said. "I have to tell Zain to book a hotel for Friday."

"Finn knows about that too?"

"Mm-hmm. I told him the entire story, actually. With hooking up at the work dinner thing and all that."

"What did he think of that?"

"He liked it, if the way he bent me over the couch before I could finish talking was any indication."

She raised her eyebrows as she looked up at me, an amused smirk on her lips. "Right there in the living room?"

"Ye-*esss*," I hissed as she added a second finger to my pussy.

"In front of his dog?"

I could barely bring myself to nod. "It's no wonder Alfie thinks it's okay to keep humping Millie whenever he wants. His dad has so little shame doing the same thing that Alfie doesn't even react to it anymore."

Claire cackled, the sound like the screech of two pieces of Styrofoam rubbing against each other. "Wow. I love this man, which are four words I never thought I'd say, especially about one that I haven't met."

"I think you'd get along with him."

"I feel like he's the kind of guy I'd go out with to pick up chicks together."

"Not that I've ever seen him pick up chicks, but I feel like he would be genuinely amazing at the 'have you met Claire' type of wingmanning. Mostly because he wouldn't even realize he was doing it."

"Perfect. If you ever decide you're done with him, let me know so I can take him to The Place or something."

"Don't let me hold you back. You could take him now if he wanted to go."

"And would he want to go?"

I tried to legitimately consider the question, but that was very difficult on account of Claire beginning to work my clit even harder with her tongue. It was all I could do to keep my eyes from rolling back in my head, let alone come up with words. She chuckled against my pussy and another warm shiver rushed through my body, that hungry place in my core beginning to ache with the need for release.

This had been our way of catching up for weeks now. It had started as a challenge; Claire still didn't have the easiest time coming, but we'd been experimenting with different things that might get her there. One day, I'd had the brilliant idea that if she was distracted by something like telling me about her day while I ate her out, it might help her come.

She'd been skeptical at first, but forcing her to focus on our conversation had worked. It was one of the few times she'd shattered beneath me, thighs clenched around my ears as her hips bucked against my face, and I'd definitely thought about that moment once or twice since then.

Once or twice a day, that is.

It was so good that Claire had decided I should have the same experience, and now it was almost routine. I'd get to Claire's, she'd ask me how my day was, and then suddenly I was naked with her head between my legs as my answers took longer and longer to give.

"Well?" she asked, reaching up and cupping a hand around my breast so she could pinch my nipple when I didn't manage to answer her. "Would Finn be into that?"

"Not sure," I gasped. "He's generally up for anything. But if you'd asked me yesterday, I would've said no, since he was still kinda fucked up about Julie."

"He's hung up on her?"

"No, not really. I mean, he hasn't said anything about that and Finn is pretty open about what's going through his head."

"That's fair. Any guy who tells you he didn't have time to jack off in the shower because he needed to have a good cry is probably not gonna bother trying to hide much."

"Yeah. But I guess what I said got to him because he called her yesterday."

She stopped and looked up, making me squirm in discomfort as she took the friction away from my clit. "He did? What did she say?"

"Dunno. He just said they had a good talk and didn't offer much more than that."

She scoffed. "How dare you? You should've known I'd want the details."

"Sorry. Can you ever forgive me?"

"Mmm..." she said, then teased her fingertips along my folds. "We'll see. But he's doing better now?"

I nodded. "He's the same old Finn now. The attitude of a golden retriever and the memory span of one too, apparently." I held my breath as she cackled, then squirmed again. "Now will you *please* make me come?"

She smirked and lowered her mouth to my clit.

"Maybe," she said. "After you tell me what's new with Kira."

I whined, closing my eyes and tilting my head back on the pillow. "Do you know how red she'd turn if she knew I was talking about her in the middle of fucking?"

"I'm assuming about as red as the flush on your chest, darling. How's her baby doing?"

I tensed. "Nope. No way. Hard pass on that."

"What?" Claire asked, her eyebrows wrinkling in concern.

"Not talking about babies during sex."

She rolled her eyes. "You do with Zain."

"I—*ah*—talk about *making* a baby during sex with Zain. Not a specific baby."

She shook her head as she slipped a slick finger into my ass, making me tremble beneath her. "I will never understand what you two think is so hot about that."

"I wouldn't expect you to. It has to do with a part of sex you don't enjoy because it involves men."

"I mean, fair, but fantasy's fantasy. I still wouldn't enjoy the fantasy of it if we were pretending you could get me pregnant."

"What about if the fantasy was of *you* getting me pregnant?"

Funnily enough, Claire went silent. Unfunnily enough, her tongue stopped lapping at my clit and I whimpered before clawing at her head.

"Why are you stopping?"

"I think you might have just awakened something in me." She lowered her head, but didn't press her lips back to my clit. "Like, I know it's not possible, but the idea of it..." She frowned. "Do I want to be a dad?"

"I don't know. Do you?" I asked desperately as I tried to push my hips up to meet her mouth.

Her head tilted to the side. "I'm going to have to do some self reflection on why the idea of me knocking you up is so fucking hot. Maybe I do want you to call me Daddy."

"I don't know," I said again. "Think about it later. I'm so fucking close."

"Try it," she said. "Let's see if I'm into it."

Fuck. She could have probably asked me to do anything just then and I would have because I was so desperate to come.

"Okay, uh... please don't stop," I said. "I'm so close... Daddy."

It felt all sorts of wrong, which we unanimously agreed on when we both burst out laughing the second I finished speaking. Luckily for me, Claire muffled her laughter by shoving her face against my pussy again, and my laughter morphed into a desperate cry as she flicked the tip of her tongue against my swollen clit. I braced myself, waiting for the disappointment of her pulling back again, but she curled the fingers she had inside me and my legs began to shake. Moments later, my orgasm hit, and my back arched as I came uncontrollably on Claire's tongue.

When my breathing had steadied and my thighs fell away from her ears, she placed a final gentle kiss against my mound. Sitting up, she wiped the back of her hand across her mouth

"Your turn?" I asked, shifting to change places with her.

"Nope," she said cheerfully. "Not today. The lady bits are closed for business this week. Something about renovations."

I frowned at her, confused in the haziness of my recent orgasm.

"They're, you know, stripping the paint off the walls at the moment," she continued.

It took another second, but when I got it, I rolled my eyes. "You sure? I don't mind using my hands or something."

"It's not you, darling, I promise. I'm just not into it when I'm on my period. You can owe me one for next time."

"Deal," I said, sighing as I reclined back on her pillow.

She moved up, pressing a kiss to my lips before stretching her long body out to lounge beside me. A hand ended up on my head, fingertips gently scratching my scalp as I rested against her.

"So Kira," she said.

"Kira," I repeated. "She's doing about as well as can be expected given the situation."

"That sounds like it's not very well at all."

I shrugged. "Velma's a little colicky, I guess, so she's crying a lot. And Kira still has to finish some work stuff from before she realized she was actually about to go on mat leave, so that's stressing her out. Not to mention Jackson's stuff. He's trying to be home as much as possible, but there's some stuff he has to be at the lab for."

"Mmm. The downsides of being the only expert for a very niche type of science."

"Exactly. So they're scrambling from the chaos of having a child unexpectedly. I know Kira wouldn't trade Velma for the world, but trying to balance everything is hard on her."

"Poor girl," Claire said sympathetically.

I nodded. "What about you?"

"I believe 'poor girl' is only fifty percent accurate as a descriptor of me."

I rolled my eyes. "I mean, what's new?"

"Oh, the usual. I spent most of this week in meetings with people who are more than happy to spend my family's money but less than happy about having to explain how they're spending it."

"Sounds boring."

"It is. Which is why I was really looking forward to Paris Fashion Week, but then Paige had to go and ruin everything."

"How'd she ruin it?"

Claire sighed, her usual sassy but good-natured demeanour fading into something more solemn. "She decided she also wants to go to Paris Fashion Week."

"Can't you ignore her the whole time you're there?"

"You'd think," she said bitterly. "But then Mom got wind of the fact that both her precious daughters would be attending and figured it would be excellent publicity for us to make some appearances together. And Paige decided since she was the older sister that she was going to stay in the apartment even though I very clearly dibsed it, so now I have to stay in a hotel with a scotch selection that's not even half of what we had at the apartment."

I twisted my head to look at her. "You understand I had sympathy for you until the scotch complaint, right?"

She smiled, though it still wasn't quite her usual mischievous one. "I do. But to counter that, Paige is the worst and I'm going to complain about literally every inconvenience this causes me, regardless of if it's a 'let them eat cake' problem or a legitimate issue."

"Fair. As long as you realize it's a 'let them eat cake' problem."

"Very much so. But it's a legitimate complaint, too. I mean, she waited until this week to make this decision and most of the hotels are already booked. I'm literally flying out on Friday."

"That does suck."

"It does. But it would suck a lot less if I had someone there to liven things up." She traced a finger up my arm. "You know, piss off Paige so much that she refuses to be around me. So maybe you should come with me."

"To Paris?" I asked.

"Why not?" she said. "It'll be fun."

"As much as I love being used to piss people off—and I do—one, I have to work," I said. "And I also have Kira's baby shower this weekend. Two, Paige will be there. Remember that whole thing where my boss is her nemesis?"

"Oh yeah." She sighed heavily. "Damn. I can't believe I can't talk you into a free trip to Paris."

"I can't believe I'm turning it down," I said. "What the fuck is wrong with me?"

"Plenty of things, darling, but you more than make up for it with your excellent qualities."

"Like what?

"That ass, for one."

Both of us started laughing. It took a moment to quiet down, but we did, falling into an easy and comfortable silence. Claire ran her fingers through my hair and my eyes fluttered closed.

"I just hate how being around her makes me feel," she said after a while.

"Who? Paige?"

"Mm-hmm."

"How does it make you feel?"

She was quiet for long enough that I reopened my eyes and looked up at her. Claire's forehead was wrinkled in thought and she was looking at some distant spot in her room, contemplating what I'd asked.

"Unsettled," she finally said. "Paige is exhausting. I don't enjoy being around her because she doesn't enjoy being around me, and that wears on a person after a while."

And that...

That made one of those prickling alarm bells go off in my head

"Maybe I can figure something out," I said as casually as I could. "I just saw Zain last weekend and Finn'll be fine on his own and Kira—"

"No," Claire said.

I sighed. "Claire, I—"

"No," she repeated. "You already told me why you can't and I don't want to guilt you into coming just because you think I can't handle my sister for a week."

"You're not guilting me," I said. "But if it's something that bothers you, I can—"

"Tessa, I've lived my whole life with depression," she snapped. "I can handle being in situations like this on my own."

And that.

That was *not* like Claire.

Frowning, I sat up so her hand fell away from my head. "What is going on with you?"

"Nothing's going on with me," she said, sounding insulted. "I just don't like being told I'm some delicate child who can't handle things."

"At no point did I say you couldn't handle it," I said. "I never even implied that. Or that you're a delicate child."

"You changed your tune completely the moment I said Paige makes me feel unsettled."

"Because you're my friend and I want to make sure you're okay," I said. "I've never heard you admit to something that makes you feel that way and yeah, it worried me. Because if you were reaching out for support and I turned it down, I'd feel awful."

"And I'd feel awful if you started getting resentful because you felt guilted into giving things up for me," she said.

I gave her an unimpressed look. "Like that would actually happen."

"It has," she said coldly.

I blinked. "What?"

Claire's throat flexed and she looked down. "It has happened. I had an ex who... It was what ended us, okay? She felt like she couldn't leave because she was scared I'd hurt myself and I felt like absolute trash when I found out she was only with me because she didn't want the guilt of that on her hands. It sucks both ways and I never want to be like that again."

Once upon a time, my instinct would've been to be mad. To be offended that my friend would think I could do that to her. But looking at Claire, at the heat in her eyes masquerading the fear behind them, there was no anger. There was no insult.

There was my girl-friend-not-girlfriend, a woman I cared deeply about in a way that was both platonic and physical, showing me a part of her that didn't often see the light. A part of her I knew about.

A part of her that wasn't really *her*.

"I don't feel like you're guilting me into anything," I said. "I want to make sure if you're asking for help, I'm there for you, because that's what friends do. Two, I'm not your girlfriend. We're not together like that."

"Yet you matter to me more than she ever did," Claire said. "Girlfriends come and go, but you're like... you're my friend, Tess. I don't want to push you away."

"Then stop trying to," I said. "I can change my plans this weekend and—"

"No," she said, but it was gentler that time and she put a hand over mine. "Please don't, okay? I... I'm sorry I just, you know. Overreacted. But I truly, honestly don't want you to change your plans for this."

"What if I want to go to Paris, though?" I asked. "I mean, Brad and I went once while we were married, but I feel like I'd enjoy it a lot more with you."

"I will take you to Paris another time. In the fall. That's my favourite time to be there. And we'll be able to enjoy ourselves and do whatever we want because we won't have my stupid sister annoying us." She leaned in, kissing me softly. "This trip would be infinitely better if I wasn't going by myself, but not so much better that I can take you away from Kira's baby shower. That girl needs you right now, darling. I want you to be there for her."

And yeah, I protested a bit more, but as usual, Claire was right.

I needed to be here for Kira, which she proved not even ten minutes after Claire and I discussed Paris when my phone started vibrating on the bedside table

"Tess?" came a high-pitched, watery voice as soon as I answered.

I sat up. There was no hesitation, no frowning, no moment of me not understanding that Kira was at anxiety level eight thousand and calling me out of desperation. In the background, I could hear Velma screaming, the high-pitched wails piercing even though it sounded like they might be coming from another room

"What's wrong?" I asked.

"I'm s-so sorry to bother you, but I just, I..."

"You're not bothering me. Tell me what's going on."

"I... Velma... I just... I need help," she said, then started sobbing.

Seven

THERE'S NOTHING QUITE LIKE knocking on a door and being greeted by a shrieking, squalling, inconsolable baby.

Or maybe there is. Maybe if you were to knock on the door of a house where a particularly vocal opera singer was being tortured by another opera singer who took delight in narrating the situation by singing in whistle tones.

But that seemed like an unlikely scenario. People don't generally answer the door in the middle of torturing someone.

So I would argue there was nothing quite like the sound that greeted me when Kira opened the door that night. Nor was there anything like the sight: Velma writhing in her mother's arms, wrinkled and red-faced, tears staining her cheeks, and the gaping maw of her toothless mouth spread wide. Then Kira, a sheen of sweat on her forehead, her normally tidy pixie cut sticking up on one side, with matching tear stains coating her cheeks.

"I don't know what else to do," she said by way of greeting, her voice wavering more than usual. "I've tried everything that usually works. Every way I'm supposed to hold her, walking, swaying. I'm starting to feel seasick, I think. But it's not working and I didn't know who to call or what to Google or... it's been hours. I think?" She looked confused and her eyes started watering again. "Since dinner. I don't... I don't know what time it is."

"Kira," I said, reaching towards her. "Give me the baby."

She did so instantly, without protest or pause. A moment later, a look of guilt flashed across her face, likely because she *was* so eager to hand Velma off. Not that she had a reason to feel guilty, but considering she probably couldn't have told me what day it was or how long it had been since she'd washed her hair, it was understandable, if unjustified.

Velma continued screaming as I took her in my arms, back arching as she let out a particularly horrific shriek. One of the brimming tears in Kira's eyes breached her eyelid and trickled down her face, then another. Then she started sobbing.

Though admittedly, her cries were far less annoying than Velma's.

I tried to comfort both of them, but like mother, like daughter. Kira was as resistant to my efforts as Velma was. Granted, I was not a baby whisperer. I didn't know very many babies. I'd always liked them, but I wasn't a mom or even an aunt. So why I thought repeating the things Kira had already tried—swaying, walking around, cuddling her, and trying to soothe her with soft hushes—would work, I didn't know.

But I'd been pretty confident my methods of trying to soothe a grown woman would work, though Kira resisted them too. I told her to go upstairs and sit for a while, but the guilt of handing off her daughter without hesitation seemed to have wormed itself into her exhausted mind and wouldn't leave. I tried to tell her to cry about it, to go sob until she felt better, but she couldn't bring herself to leave the room or focus on herself.

"Isn't there anyone you can call? Like a... I dunno." I tried to think. "Isn't there anyone that new parents can call for help? Like, I'm going to help you as best I can, but someone who knows what they're doing?"

She sniffled, wiping her hands across her face. "Most of them are for people who have given birth. But the ones I've had time to find, they're really booked up and... and what if they think I'm a bad mom?"

My heart ached for her. "You're not a bad mom."

She choked on another sob. "What if they take her away from me?"

"They won't do that, Kira."

"You don't know that."

"Do you even know who 'they' are?"

She thought for a moment, then frowned, but didn't say anything.

"Where's Jackson and when's he coming back?" I asked.

"He's giving a k-keynote speech at this conference," she said, running a hand through her hair. "And he wanted to cancel but I told him it was fine because I could handle it. I should be able to do this. I should be able to help her, Tess, and I can't... I'm failing."

Her voice cracked. That probably wasn't the cause of Velma's sudden screech in my ear, but the timing of it was spot on. Kira stifled another sob and plunked herself down on the couch, cradling her head in her hands, the despair rolling off her in waves.

Now, I was willing to admit and own the fact that I was an asshole. Sometimes. But sometimes it wasn't clear what the asshole move would be.

Because I wasn't quite as stuck as Kira was on what to do. Sure, I didn't know what resources there were for adoptive parents. Kira had only been back in my life for a short amount of time and I'd barely had time to reconnect with her before she was a mom, let alone learn how to help her with that. And before she'd known she was going to be a mom, she'd cut out the only other person who might've known what to do.

Because Mel Mauldin did some kind of social work or something. She might not have known exactly what to do, but she would've had more resources in this situation than I did. She'd been helping them find other adoption agencies at one point.

But Kira had ended any semblance of friendship she had with Mel.

Because of me.

Because of what Mel and Nathan had done to me.

But I knew someone else who might be able to help.

It took me a long moment to decide if it would make me an asshole not to tell Kira about her. Or at least, to decide if I could live with how much of an asshole I would be if I didn't at least try to call her, especially knowing... well.

Knowing I had a way of getting a hold of her now.

"Kira," I said. "I have an idea."

She looked up at me, her red-rimmed eyes wide with hope. "What?"

"I can't promise anything, but if you can hold Velma for two minutes for me so I can make a call, I might know someone."

Despite only taking a couple of minutes like I said it would, Kira wouldn't hand Velma back to me when I got off the phone. Instead, she paced the living room, her eyes still watering as Velma screamed, her face twisted into one of empathetic pain that I was certain all mothers wore at some point. That expression stayed on her face until a short time later, when three gentle knocks on the front door cut through the shrieking baby cries. With my throat dry, I took a deep breath, then let it out before going to open it.

For a moment, neither of us spoke.

"Well, I guess I've got the right house," Julie finally said.

"Was the tip off the fact that I'm here or the screaming baby?" I asked.

The bridge of her nose wrinkled adorably as she cringed. "That was stupid. I just—"

"It was a joke," I said.

"—had no idea... oh." She let out a breath. "I figured this would be awkward."

"I did too," I said. "And thank you for coming anyway. Can you please help my friend and we can deal with the awkward thing after? Or, alternatively, I'm open to continuing to ignore it for the rest of our lives."

Her cheek twitched, almost as if she was about to laugh, but she just nodded. I stepped to the side to let her in, closing the door as she kicked off her shoes.

She looked the same as the last time I'd seen her, only in different clothes. Her blondish-brownish hair was tied back in its typical ponytail and she was dressed casually in leggings and a cardigan sweater. She was holding what looked like a small purple duffle bag and also looked approximately eight thousand times more nervous than usual.

Though, that wasn't for long.

After taking her shoes off, she took a breath and stopped chewing on her bottom lip. As she let it out, the nerves fell off her face and were replaced by a calm, understanding look. An entirely different version of the Julie I'd seen at the door walked into the living room, everything about her giving off gentle and caring waves as she set her warm eyes on Kira and Velma.

"Hi Kira," she said in a steady, confident voice over the sound of Velma's shrieks. "My name is Julie. I'm a midwife."

Instead of reassuring her, a distressed line deepened on Kira's forehead. "A midwife? But I... I didn't give birth to her."

"That's okay." Julie set her bag down on the floor. "All new moms need support and we do lots of checks for babies after they're born, too. I can't promise to figure out what's going on, but I can try."

Kira stared at her, then she blinked as her eyes watered. "Really?"

"Of course. I'm here to help. What's your little munchkin's name, Kira?"

"V...Velma. Velma Clark."

"Oh, that's so lovely! Can I hold her?"

I had no idea what Julie did. I caught bits and pieces of it as Kira explained what was going on and what she'd tried, but I busied myself by tidying the room and giving them as much space as possible. I was folding a stack of small, soft baby blankets when my phone buzzed in my pocket. Putting the final blanket on the stack, I pulled it out as stealthy as I could to see yet another message from Zain.

I know you're busy, kitten, but can you just let me know if me staying there for two nights works for you so I can book my plane tickets?

I rolled my eyes. I'd half-assumed he would end up staying in Vancouver for two nights anyway, so it wasn't exactly a surprise. I did still need to tell him about the hotel, though, but just as I started to respond, Julie asked if I could grab her the blanket I'd just folded.

"Yeah, of course," I said, then tapped on one of the auto-fill responses to Zain's message—*Yes, that works*—and shoved my phone back in my pocket.

After directing me to spread the blanket on the floor, Julie set Velma on top of it and beckoned Kira over.

"So, you know she's got colic," Julie said over Velma's wails.

"Yes," Kira said. "And I know it'll... it's not forever."

"That doesn't make it any easier in the moment," Julie said. "It's okay for that to feel very, very overwhelming. But you're managing it really well."

Kira's chin trembled. "Thank you."

"But what I *think* is going on here is a baby who is having a very unlucky night," she continued. "From what you said about her spitting up and such, it sounds like she might have a touch of reflux. And I think that's led her to have some very uncomfortable gas."

Kira looked bewildered. "You think it's just gas?"

Julie nodded and began doing some magical kind of baby massage or something. I don't know. I couldn't really see what she was doing, since Kira was leaning in to watch as Julie showed her how to rub Velma's tummy to get things moving. Then she took a chunky little leg into each hand and began pumping them as if Velma was pedalling a tiny invisible bicycle.

"I think it's best for you to talk to her pediatrician because I don't know you or her or the history here," Julie said as she repeated the massages and little bicycles pumps. "I'm here to help get you through today, but you need to check with her doctor, alright?"

Kira nodded. "I understand."

"But if it is reflux or gas, they might suggest something like gas drops. In the meantime, you can help get her a bit of relief by doing this a few times, then—" She finished another round of little bicycle movements, then lifted both of Velma's legs in unison and tilted her back.

What followed was one of the longest, loudest, most raucous farts I'd ever heard.

And considering it was coming from a child not much bigger than a slightly overweight housecat, muffled through the thick padding of her diaper, and over the sound of her veritably *shrieking* as it came out, that was saying something. Kira recoiled and even Julie looked surprised at the force of that fart.

But for the first time since I'd been there—and the first time since dinner, based on what Kira said—there was a break in the wailing.

Just a small one. Velma let out another shriek a moment later, but Julie took her legs and bicycled them a few more times, then repeated the tilt back. Another, albeit quieter, trumpeting sound came from Velma's diaper, and the cries staggered again.

"Yep," Julie said. "Gassy baby."

Kira's lips were parted as she stared at her daughter. "That's it?"

"Seems to be." Julie rubbed Velma's tummy again, then cycled her legs again. "Just a very, very unlucky combination of things happening all at once."

"I can't believe it," Kira said. "After all that... I thought... I keep feeling like I'm doing something wrong and like I'm a terrible mom."

"Well, that's untrue," Julie said. "But it's also a very common, very normal feeling. You're doing the best you can and you know what? You reached out for help when you needed it. Do you know how hard that is for some moms to do? You recognized you were getting overwhelmed and scared and you called for help. You're doing good, mama."

Kira blinked, but there was no holding in the tears that were breaching her lashline. "Thank you. Thank you so much. I... how can I repay you for this?"

"I'll accept gratitude in baby cuddles," Julie said. "Why don't you go take a few minutes to yourself so I can get those in?"

Which left me and Julie—and yes, Velma, but Velma had some bigger concerns going on, like how she didn't float away like a freakin' balloon with that much gas in her, so she wasn't paying attention—sitting awkwardly in the living room.

"Tess," Julie said after a few moments of quiet tension. "Can we take the option where we don't ignore this for the rest of our lives and talk about what... what I did?"

Fuck.

"Right now?" I asked.

"Maybe we can grab a drink or a coffee or something after this?"

My instinct was to say no because I didn't want to. But considering she'd just helped my best friend and gotten an impressive amount of gas out of a baby, it felt like a total dick move to decline.

After all of it, she'd shown up for me.

"Alright," I said.

Eight

"I THOUGHT MAYBE YOU weren't going to come," Julie said.

I smiled wryly as I slid into the booth across from her. "I wouldn't do that."

Which was true, even if I'd considered doing exactly that.

Down the street from Kira and Jackson's house was a small neighbourhood pub that should have gone bankrupt years ago, if not for the desire of people to have a reasonably priced place to get alcohol while avoiding a DUI. It was called something, but I'd only ever heard it referred to as The Dive, and although there was a sign on the door with the name on it, I'd never bothered to read it. That had made it semi-difficult to tell Julie where I would meet her, since I wanted to stay with Kira longer to make sure she was okay.

It was after Julie had left and Kira had calmed down with Velma nuzzling against her mom's chest that I considered not going. I mean, an eye for an eye, right? She ghosted me, so it only made sense to ghost her right back.

And honestly, once upon a time, that's what I would've done. Once upon a time, I would go through messages from couples and reject them based on vibes instead of facts. I would block, delete, and not think twice about it.

But disgustingly enough, it seemed like I may have experienced some sort of personal growth in the last couple of months and learned how to take the high road.

So even though I loitered at Kira's for a bit, texted Claire back to let her know everything was okay, then Finn to thank him for sending Julie and that I'd be home later, then a middle finger emoji to Z Biggest Asshole who had messaged me thanking me for replying to his message sooner than the three to five business days he expected and that he was excited to see me, I didn't ghost Julie.

There was a half-full glass of what was probably vinegary wine in front of her when I sat down and a full beer sitting on the table across from her.

"I figured you could use that," she said, motioning at the beer. "But if you want something else, I can get it."

"This is fine," I said. "Thanks."

Then, silence.

"How have you been?" she asked

I sipped my beer. "Are we really doing small talk?"

She grimaced, looking down. "No. I just don't know what to say."

"Neither do I, Julie."

She nodded, looking down at her hands. "So I guess you heard, um, pretty much all of what happened? Because you and Finn are..."

"Finn is staying with me now, yes," I said, my words guarded. "He's been at my place since Sunday."

Her throat flexed and she almost had to force her head up to look at me. Once she did, I wished she hadn't.

"I had no idea about any of it," she said, the pain in her voice matching the genuine torment in her eyes. "I swear to God that I didn't know. He told me he had a place to stay and that it wasn't a problem. If I'd known... I thought it wouldn't hurt to ask because he might stay with his mom. And I had *no* idea his dad was sick."

I frowned. "How did you not know about his dad?"

"Ian got diagnosed the week before we broke up, I guess, but Finn... I don't know if he wasn't ready or he didn't want to upset me or something. But he didn't say a word about it."

"Jesus," I muttered.

"I know. He went to his mom's for dinner one night, but I got called for a delivery. When I got home, he was quiet, but I didn't think..." She sighed. "I know I was going through my own stuff but I swear he didn't tell me. And I never would've thought he'd keep something like that from me. I didn't want to hurt anyone."

I raised my eyebrows and Julie's face turned red.

"I didn't want to hurt you, either," she said softly. "I did, and I'm sorry for it. But I didn't *want* to. I just panicked."

"What did you panic about?"

"Being a zombie," she said.

I almost laughed. I mean, I'd suspected as much, but hearing her say it, especially like that, was arguably hilarious. But her voice was soft and her eyes were downcast and somehow the inconvenient soft spot I'd always had for Julie came roaring back.

"So when I asked you that last time we saw each other—"

"I lied," she said. "Of course I had feelings for you. And I have no excuse. I knew the rules. But I didn't know what to do, Tess. I mean, I was with this man who was sweet and funny and so, so good to me. And I was supposed to be attracted to him and suddenly I wasn't anymore." She sighed and took a sip of wine. "I told myself it was because I was into you and that my feelings were making everything more complicated and that it would be less painful for everyone if I just cut us all off. But I was scared because part of me knew it wasn't just you, you know? And I wanted to make that part go away because it meant..."

She trailed off, but I knew what she was going to say. Even if Finn hadn't told me as much, it was one of those things that people just understood in these situations.

"I'm sorry," she said again. "I knew it was wrong. I knew it would hurt you and I still did it. I am a really, really shitty person."

"I mean, you did a shitty thing," I said. "You're not a shitty person, though."

Her mouth twitched. "God, I wish I could believe that right now."

"Why wouldn't you? Doing shitty things doesn't mean you're unequivocally bad." I tapped my fingers against my beer. "I won't pretend it didn't suck. And, yeah, I was pissed until Finn told me all this stuff. And okay, I might still be a bit annoyed. But you're not a shitty person, Julie."

"I don't know what I am," she whispered.

To my horror, there were tears in her eyes, and I almost dove out of The Dive. I'd dealt with enough crying that night.

"What's going on, Jules?" I asked.

"I feel so fucked up. I feel like I fucked up. Like—" She sat up a bit, though her eyes were trained to her wine glass. "When the whole thing with me being bi came out, my family struggled with it. They're not the most open-minded people. But I thought they accepted it until I realized it was just the fact that I was dating a man that made it 'okay' with them because they could pretend I wasn't what I said I was. So then, telling them I'm a lesbian... it changed everything." She toyed with the glass. "Some days, I think it would be easier if I dropped it and started dating a guy again."

"Don't change who you are to make other people comfortable," I said. "Making yourself miserable isn't the answer."

Which was great advice, even if it was coming from a fucking hypocrite like me. But Julie didn't know I was a hypocrite, so it was okay.

"I know," she said. "But I feel lost. Like, I was thinking a couple of weeks ago, when was the last time I did anything for me? And you know what my solution to that was?"

"What?"

"I decided to take a few weeks off. My solution was to take the vacation time I was owed." She laughed, shaking her head. "And now I've been sitting around for four days not doing anything because I don't know *what* to do. Because everything in my life is for someone else."

She picked up her wine glass, taking a sip before continuing.

"With my ex, I tried to change who I was so he would love me. I was a dancer growing up because my mom wanted to be a dance mom. Even with you, Tess."

"Me?" I said, surprised.

"Not that it's your fault," she said. "You never asked me to be anything but myself. But it was such an instinct to make what *you* wanted a priority over what *I* wanted that I lied to you when you asked me to my face if I had feelings for you. I could've said yes. I could've told you what I wanted. But I'm so focused on not upsetting other people, I go against the things I want and need."

"That's relatable," I said.

She smiled sadly. "I just want to be myself for once. I want to stop trying to be what other people think I am. But I don't even know how. I thought about quitting my job, actually."

That was also a surprise. "Why?"

"I became a midwife because my mom wanted me to be a nurse," she said. "Not that I don't enjoy it, but I wouldn't have ever chosen this career if I'd been allowed to make my own decisions. "

"What would you have picked?"

"I don't know," she said with one of those laughs that made it clear she didn't think it was that funny. "Even when I was a kid, I knew my mom wanted me to be a nurse. If it had been up to me, I wouldn't have gone to school right away. I would've travelled and seen the world. But I never got to have any adventures like that."

And here's the thing.

I owed Julie nothing.

I didn't owe her my time. My energy. My ears while she broke down. I didn't owe her shit.

But Julie always had this way of worming into my heart and making me feel things I didn't want to feel. Like empathy. And softness. And the desire to keep her safe. She was like a fucking baby deer, small and unsteady and nervous, but so endearing that you couldn't help but be captivated by her.

I didn't know if she still had feelings for me, but it didn't matter. I might have cared for her, but I didn't feel *that* way about her. Even if I did, I didn't think I could get past what she'd done. Not on that level, anyway.

But as friends?

For the second time in recent memory, a memory of Zain's words echoed in my mind. Which was very annoying, frankly, because it was ridiculous that his voice was living in my mind like that. But that didn't change the fact that what he'd said was right.

People fuck up. People do things that cause pain and say things that hurt and sometimes you can't forgive those things.

But if you don't try, you end up pretty fucking lonely.

"You said you're on vacation right now?" I asked.

She nodded.

"For how long?"

"Another two weeks."

"Cool." I took a gulp of beer. "This is going to sound weird and sketchy as fuck, but do you want to go to Paris Fashion Week?"

A bewildered look crossed her face. "Like… in France?"

"Yeah."

"Paris," she repeated. "With you?"

"Oh, no," I said. "I have this friend who's going to Paris and would probably be totally up for taking you, as long as you would be willing to mess with her sister while you're there."

Julie's mouth opened, then closed, then opened again. "...what?"

"Look, you wanna go on an adventure, Claire will give you an adventure." I took another sip of beer. "I can't go with her because of some stuff I've got going on but trust me. You'd like her."

"You have a random friend who would potentially take me to Paris," she said. "With what money?"

"Her mom's, mostly."

"So she's rich," she said, her voice pitching up.

"Well, she gets by," I said. "And I haven't talked to her, but I'm willing to bet you a ride on her private jet she says yes. So, you interested?"

"I... I... yes," she said. "But why?"

"Why what?"

"Why are you doing this?" There was something painful on her face again. "After I did what I did, I was hoping you'd let me apologize. I wasn't even expecting forgiveness, Tess. I just wanted you to know I was sorry. So this is... I don't deserve this."

I looked down at my beer, twisting my mouth to the side. "I spent a long time convincing myself and everyone else that what you did didn't bother me because we were just friends. I said it was a dick move, but that it didn't matter that much because there was nothing there."

She inhaled a shallow breath. "W-Was there anything there?"

I pressed my lips together but didn't say anything. Even though I could continually lie to everyone else and to myself, for some reason, I couldn't lie to Julie.

"Look, you'd be doing me a favour," I said, and she nodded, understanding that I couldn't answer her. "I know Claire doesn't want to go on this trip by herself and I can't be there. But you could. Keep her company, have a good time... you know."

Julie's shoulders tensed. "Would I have to, like, have sex with her?"

"Oh, God no," I said. "I mean, she *is* a lesbian, but she wouldn't expect you to sleep with her. I wouldn't have even suggested this if I thought she would."

"So you don't think she'll be attracted to me?"

I gave her an unimpressed look. "That's not what I said. I just mean she wouldn't make you fuck her in exchange for something."

She nodded, a million thoughts rushing through her mind so fast that I could almost hear them. Finally, she looked up.

"Okay," she said.

"Okay?"

"Ask her. If I can go."

I nodded. "I'll check with her and give her your number if she's interested."

She nodded, glancing down at her glass.

"One more thing," she said.

"What's that?"

She licked her lips. "I know you didn't want to answer what I just asked about feelings and stuff. But I want to make it clear, I was only asking for me."

I frowned. "What do you mean?"

"I was asking if there was anything there for me specifically. But if there's something there for Finn..."

My shoulders tensed. "What do you mean, something there? He's just living with me."

She raised her eyebrows at me. "Tess, you'd have to be willfully ignorant to miss how into each other you guys were. And I don't know about you, but most people don't take in a guy from the streets to live with them if they don't care at least a little."

She wanted to know if I had feelings for Finn?

Sweet, hilarious, fucks-like-a-god Finn?

Finn, with his gorgeous smile and muscular body.

Finn standing in my kitchen wearing a teal ruffled apron, cooking me dinner when I walked in after work.

Finn cutting the grass, sun reflecting off his hair as Alfie played on the porch with Millie.

Finn drawing out a begrudging smile from my face, his infinite positivity and optimism something so foreign to my life that I hadn't known I'd been missing it.

Finn lying in my bed.

Finn holding me as we fell asleep.

Finn making me feel like it was okay to just be. To just have fun. To walk away from the heavy things in my life that never seemed to end and think about what would happen if vegetables had theme songs.

"He's a great guy," Julie said. "And I know he likes you. He always has. So if you like him back... I just mean, don't punish him for me fucking up. Don't punish *yourself* for me fucking up."

"I'm not punishing anyone," I said. "I'm not punishing you, either."

She bit her lip. "But *is* there something there for Finn?"

And wasn't that just the fucking question.

Nine

"So you are sending Julie on an intercontinental trip with a woman she's never met because she's craving adventure after ghosting you, coming out as a lesbian, and accidentally making her ex-boyfriend homeless?" Chuck asked as he ran the blackout roller stamp across a list of donor names from the Recycl-Ball.

"Pretty much," I replied, feeding a stack of papers he'd finished blacking out into the shredder.

It was one of the best, most productive days I'd ever had at CARE. Chuck and I had been working on this since Loni had burst in with a crazed glint in her eyes first thing that morning.

"She is *stealing* our *donors*," Loni screeched from the lobby. Chuck and I had looked at each other, then scurried out of our office and towards the noise.

"Who is?!" Dinah gasped as she mirrored our actions, bursting out of her office.

"Who *else*, Dinah?! Paige 'The Absolute Rat' Martelle!"

It took a few minutes, but we managed to corral Loni into the boardroom, where she spent the next fifteen minutes subjecting us to the chaotic rambles of a mad billionaire. From my understanding, Loni had received word that some of the donors who attended the Recycl-Ball had been approached by employees of ArtCycle and invited to their imminent gala. Said gala had already stolen our date auction idea and, apparently, the trashy love theme none of us really understood.

"Someone had to have leaked it," Loni spat. "Someone in this office is—" She paused for dramatic effect. "—a mouse."

We stared at her in silence.

"Do you mean a mole?" Dinah asked.

"Of course not! I mean a mouse. Sneaking in here and spying on us and sharing confidential information." Loni slammed her hand on the table. "I want it found. I want it crushed. I want whoever the mouse is to be arrested for corporate espionage. In the meantime, we're upping security."

"We have security?" I asked, legitimately surprised.

Dinah shot a fiery look at me. "We can absolutely up security, Loni. As your longest serving and most trustworthy employees, Chuck and I can take care of this. Tessa, you're no longer required for this meeting."

"Nonsense," Loni said. "Tessa's insight is imperative for this meeting."

"Foiled again," I muttered in Dinah's direction, and her face flushed so red that I almost heard the blood rushing in her veins.

When all was said and done, we talked Loni down from a plot that sounded like it was taken from an Austin Powers movie and into doing just two ridiculous things. Dinah was in charge of going through the employee records, Recycl-Ball guest list, and master donor list and cross-referencing it to people who liked ArtCycle on social media, since we had no way to access ArtCycle's gala guest list. I was a little worried that Claire's name would pop up on the guest list and flag something, but a quick text to her calmed that fear.

CM

Nothing to worry about, darling. Claire Martelle didn't attend that event. My alter ego, Violet "I Go By Vi" Brayder attended, though her ticket purchase is likely under her personal assistant, Michael Torris.

That left me and Chuck to go page by page and line by line through old meeting notes, plans, and contracts from the Recycl-Ball, first blacking out the information with Chuck's handy-dandy blackout roller stamp, then shredding the documents, then shredding the shreds. No one bothered telling Loni that these were just the printouts and like any modern business, all of it was saved digitally, though Chuck had to remind Dinah of that so she'd calm down after Loni left.

Then we'd started working on our task, which was pointless and somehow relaxing at the same time. The gentle schick-schick sound of Chuck's roller stamp was rhythmically broken by the occasional shrill of the shredder as we chatted.

"Julie is getting on a plane with a woman she's never met to go to Paris," Chuck continued after the shredder finished the stack I'd just fed it. "Are you kidding me, Tessa Adam Sandler Lane?"

"I know, right?" I grumbled. "I can't believe Julie might get to join the mile high club before I do."

"Are you not worried about either of them?"

"Not really. Julie will either have the time of her life or come back and realize she's not as into adventure as she thought." I fed a stack of papers through the shredder. "Claire will take care of her either way, even if it's crazy."

"And the reason I wasn't given the option to take Claire up on her free trip to Paris was...?"

"You'd want to bring Charles and the entire purpose is for Claire to piss off her sister?"

Normally, bringing up Charles put Chuck into The Charles Zone. That was the name I'd given to the sudden shift in his mood, where he got a dopey little smile on his face and started looking like he was going to melt into a puddle on the floor.

That time, though, mentioning Charles put a line between Chuck's dark eyebrows and he couldn't quite meet my eye.

"Well, obviously," he said, trying to cover the fact that he'd set off about eight thousand alarm bells.

"What's wrong?" I demanded.

"Nothing's wrong," he said haughtily.

"You got sad when I mentioned Charles."

"How dare you?" he scoffed. "I did not get sad at the mention of my wonderful, amazing boyfriend."

"You're frowning. It's going to give you a wrinkle."

His hand flew to his forehead instinctively, then he glared at me. "It will not. My skin is impeccable."

"Chuck."

"Tessa."

"What's going on?"

"Nothing's going on."

"How come I have to tell you everything about my life and you sit there thinking you don't have to tell me everything about yours?"

"Because that's the way it is, Tessa Celine Lane."

"Fine." I turned to my desk and grabbed my phone out of the drawer. "I guess I'll call up Charles and ask—"

But I didn't even get the sentence out before Chuck lunged across the room and snatched my phone out of my hand.

"Do not. You even. Dare," he said pointedly. "He cannot know about this."

"About what? The 'nothing' that you're insisting is going on?"

He opened his mouth, probably to hurl something snarky back at me, then sighed and looked down at my phone. "I'm meeting his parents."

"I know. You told me. You're going to a barbecue."

"Yeah, that was the plan. But instead we're doing it tonight."

"Really? Since when?"

He sighed again. "Since last night, when he casually mentioned it's his mom's birthday and they always go out to dinner at Maki Lounge because his mom loves sushi. And I said if she really loves sushi they should take her to Umai Sushi Bar because that's the best sushi in Vancouver. Then he said that was a good idea and he trusted my opinions on sushi because I have the best opinions on sushi and that maybe I should just come with him to dinner so I could tell them what the best things to order were since they'd never been there before and, well, long story short I'm meeting his parents tonight."

Neither of us spoke for a moment after Chuck's ramble. For Chuck, it was probably because of the drama of the whole thing. For me, it was because it took my brain a second longer to process his words on account of how fast he was speaking those clipped, panicked words.

"Well... isn't this kind of good?" I finally asked.

He stared at me, lips parted. "Are you for real?"

"What? He's your boyfriend. You're gonna have to meet them eventually."

"Oh my God." Chuck looked up at the ceiling. "I can't believe you're saying that. *You*, Miss One-Time-Thing, are acting like me meeting his parents isn't that big of a deal?"

"Just because you had a couple of bad experiences in the past doesn't mean this is going to be like that," I said.

"You have got to be—" He stopped and took a breath, then let it out. "Tessa, I am the first man Charles is bringing home. Ever. He has not dated since he came out. Meaning that this is not only the first time I'm meeting them but the first time they are seeing, with their own eyes, tangible proof their son is gay. And as open-minded and wonderful and accepting as he's made them sound, you never know."

"This coming from the guy who came out as pan by not telling your parents before bringing a guy home?" I asked.

"That was different," he said.

"How was that different?"

"I was not the one being brought home."

I had to laugh. "So it's okay when it's someone else suffering?"

He gave me a disgusted look. "Do you think I'm some kind of asshole who thinks my suffering matters more than the suffering of others?"

"Uh, yeah. Aren't you?"

"Well, yes, but that's not the point."

I shook my head, trying not to laugh again. "Look, the only way that you don't end up being the first guy Charles brings home to his parents is if you break up with him and let him bring someone else home first. Is that what you want?"

He looked horrified. "Of course not."

"So this is going to have to happen sometime."

"I know, but what if it changes everything? I'm not ready to... to risk him."

Chuck and I were close friends. Very close friends. I'd been naked with him before in an entirely non-sexual way and it's hard to imagine friends can get any closer than that. But I wasn't used to seeing him being this vulnerable. I wasn't used to being the level-headed one in the room. But beneath Chuck's lightweight knit sweater, his shoulders were tense, and his eyes were cast down.

"Has he said anything that makes you think his parents aren't supportive?" I asked.

Chuck shook his head.

"Has he done anything that's made you think it's not worth taking this step with him?"

"No. No, of course not. He is worth it."

"And is Charles going to treat you to a long session of him showing off his impressive throating skills after you leave the dinner to thank you for making such a good impression on his parents?"

Chuck snorted. "Well, obviously. That's just a given."

"Do you think he deserves your support and encouragement in going through this big moment together?"

"Yes. Yes, of course."

"Then so what if it changes things, Chuck? It's not going to *ruin* things. Charles adores you."

"He does," Chuck admitted. "He—"

And then his voice caught. I waited for him to continue, but his cheeks began to go steadily redder.

"He what?" I pressed.

"He... might've told me he loved me last night after I agreed to go," Chuck said, his words rushed.

I gaped at him. "How did you not lead with that?! What did you say?"

Chuck's face was fully red now. "Uhh... nothing."

I stared at him. "You did not. You didn't do that to him."

"No, I did." Chuck's voice was high-pitched. "I said nothing."

"You weren't ready to say it back?"

"Well, it seemed kind of pointless to say it back since I sort of said 'Of course I'll come to your mother's birthday dinner' and he said 'Are you sure, I know you're nervous about this' and I said 'I'm very sure. I'm in love with you, Charles' and he was responding to me. So I just kissed him.'"

"That's unbearably sweet," I said.

"I know. Even for me." He sighed. "And now I'm panicking because I want to impress his parents."

"You will," I said. "With your killer sushi knowledge."

He didn't laugh. "And what if they don't like me and that changes how Charles feels about me?"

"Aside from the fact that he literally just told you he's in love with you, I don't think Charles could change the way he felt about you without going through some severe Clockwork Orange type shit, and even then it'd be iffy."

Chuck was quiet for another moment, but when he looked back up, the usual sparkle in his eye had returned. "You think so?"

"I know so," I said. "You two are disgusting. Make sure you come up with some bullshit task for Dinah to deal with all morning so you can tell me all about it tomorrow."

The rest of the day passed by quickly, at least until Chuck snuck out early so he could get ready for dinner with Charles's parents. I promised to cover for him as long as he promised to tell me all the details of his night, which he said he would, then stole away looking uncharacteristically nervous. Once he was gone, I took over the roller stamp duties, but didn't get much more done before calling it a day myself. It was surprising how tiring a full day of actually doing work could be.

When I got home, garlic and cheese slapped me right in the face. Metaphorically, of course. But the scent of it was so strong my stomach growled, and that growl was loud enough that Alfie looked confused, even as he rushed up to greet me.

"Hey Little Guy," I said as I reached down to pet him, though I couldn't quite take my eyes off the sight in my kitchen.

Finn was standing at the stove, hovering over two different pots. He'd changed into baggy grey shorts and a wonderfully fitted t-shirt after work, and of course he was also wearing the teal apron that was just a little too short for him. There was an oven mitt on one hand and he looked over his shoulder at me with a grin.

"Hey, Tess," he said excitedly. "How does four cheese fettuccine Alfredo sound for dinner? I made the pasta myself and there's asiago, parmesan, and romano in the sauce. Well, and one more, but it's a secret ingredient."

"Sounds like you want another blowjob tonight." My stomach growled again and Alfie let out a soft, confused boofing sound. "Maybe two, actually."

"Not gonna say not to that," he said. "But you're gonna have to let me go down on you first."

I held back a smile as I reached up my shirt and unhooked my bra. Finn paused his stirring to watch appreciatively as I slid it down and hung it on the hook near the door.

"Wanna come taste the sauce?" he asked when I was done. "Make sure it's cheesy enough for you?"

"If I ever say no to that, please take me to a hospital," I said.

He looked concerned. "Really? Why?"

"It's a joke," I said. "Because if I ever don't want to taste sauces containing one or more types of cheese, I'm obviously sick."

His dimple appeared in his cheek as a lopsided smile returned to his face. "Oh, okay. I'll ask as often as I can then, just to make sure."

He dipped a spoon into the sauce and passed it to me to taste, then leaned down to kiss me hello.

And yeah, it was horrible.

The scenario, I mean. Not the sauce. The sauce was orgasmic, as expected, and if I could've filled a bathtub with it and just eaten it with a ladle, I would've.

It was the disgusting domesticity of it all. Of coming home to see this man in my kitchen, cooking dinner as I cuddled with his dog. Of hearing Julie's question echo in my head, wondering if there was something there for that man, and not quite being able to say no, but in no way, shape, or form being able to say yes.

But there was that man, making me smile as he told me about his day and how he'd seen three ducks crossing the road while fighting over an entire loaf of bread, and how he'd gotten home early and went up to see if Dottie needed help with anything and she'd asked him to take out her recycling.

"I think we should get her a new organizer for her recycling," he said as he stirred the sauce. "The one she's got has a step on it and with her knee, it puts her off balance. But if we got her one that was open so she could separate it all in the kitchen, it might—"

Three loud knocks on the door cut him off. Alfie started barking and I frowned. Being in the basement, I didn't get a lot of random solicitors or anything, and Dottie usually banged a broom on her floor if she needed my attention since it was easier than doing the stairs with her knee. I followed Alfie to the door, bending down to scoop him up so he didn't run outside.

Then I opened the door to see Zain standing there, one eyebrow raised, a suitcase sitting beside him.

"Hey, Teacup," he said. "I didn't know you had a dog."

Part 2

Confession: A queen bed is
roomier than it seems.

Ten

I had no reason to feel guilty.

None at all.

Feeling guilty would have implied that I felt bad that Zain showed up and discovered another man in my house. And why would I feel bad about that? Zain and I weren't exclusive. I was very clear about it.

And okay, maybe I could have felt guilty about the fact that I promised him a place to stay and then promptly ended up trying to figure out how two grown-ass men and a delightfully chunky woman were going to stay in a technically-two-bedrooms-but-really-one-bedroom-and-one-art-studio garden suite with a single couch. I'd *had* a solution to that—a hotel—but then Zain had to go and show up a day earlier than intended.

And yes, perhaps it was my fault that I forgot to read the text he'd sent me the previous night telling me his interview had been changed from Friday afternoon to Friday morning so he'd changed his flight to Thursday night. Maybe if I hadn't just responded to it with a "yes, that works," he would have realized I didn't actually know he was coming a day early instead of staying Saturday night like I'd assumed.

But to be fair, I'd been in the middle of helping my new-mom friend with her shrieking potato of a child when he'd texted, so I was a little preoccupied. Then there was the whole thing with Julie after, so I'd forgotten.

It was a miscommunication, plain and simple, exacerbated by me trying to help people by comforting colicky babies and forgiving ghosts and giving hot guys a place to stay.

This is why it was so much easier to be an asshole. Which is why I shouldn't have felt guilty about any of it, since I was *trying* to do nice things and they were just backfiring spectacularly.

Yet as Zain glanced past me and realized there was a tall, blonde, apron-clad man cooking dinner in my kitchen, my cheeks flared red.

"It's fine," Zain said, his voice so flat that it sounded like it wasn't fine at all. "Shit happens, Teacup. I'm sure I can find a hotel or something."

Yes, I told myself to say as Alfie squirmed in my arms. That's a great idea. That was actually going to be my idea anyway. You go get a hotel and I'll come stay in it with you tomorrow night like I planned. Or even tonight, maybe, but after dinner, because as much as I like your dick, Finn made four cheese Alfredo and also I have a lot of thinking to do because there's a chance I like him more than I want to, but also you're here and that's... that's complicated because I think I might like you more than I want to, too.

But apparently, the part of me that shouldn't have felt guilty was in control of my mouth at the moment, which was probably both a good and bad thing.

"Of course not," I said, even as part of my brain screamed at me to shut up. "There's plenty of room here." Which was a lie. "I've been looking forward to you staying over."

At least that part was true.

Zain raised his eyebrows. "If you're sure."

"Of course I'm sure." Also a lie.

"Alright, kitten," he said, his mouth twitching into a smile. "Sorry. I didn't realize your friend was sleeping on the couch."

Ah, fuck.

I tried to think of a response, but all that managed to come out was a grimace. Luckily—or maybe not luckily, depending on how you looked at it—it said everything it needed to.

"Or not." The smile on Zain's lips faded into a guarded smirk I recognized all too well as the expression he usually made before some kind of clever, biting remark.

"Zain—"

"It's all good," he said lightly. "This is perfect, actually. I was worried about listening to your snoring all night when I have an interview early tomorrow."

"I don't snore," I said, insulted.

He let out a short huff of laughter. "Sure you don't, Teacup. Either way, I'll put my earplugs in—" He glanced over my shoulder at Finn again. "—just in case."

"Zain," I said again, but even though it was far more exasperated that time, he ignored me as he walked into the house.

"So who's this, then?" he asked loudly.

Finn, being Finn, turned away from the stove, a friendly grin on his face as he waved his oven-mitt-clad hand in greeting.

"Hey, I'm Finn!" he said. "Sorry, I didn't know we were having someone over for dinner."

"I'm Zain," Zain said as I shut the door behind him and put Alfie on the ground. "And yeah, it was a bit of a surprise. But I can order something in."

Finn shook his head. "Not a chance. I made *so* much pasta. And there's garlic bread in the oven. You like garlic bread, right?"

"Do I look like the kind of person who doesn't like garlic bread?" Zain said. Alfie shot forward to greet him excitedly, jumping at Zain's knee.

"Nah, you seem pretty normal to me," Finn said. "And any friend of Tessa's is a friend of mine."

Zain looked amused. "How long have you and Tess known each other?"

"A couple of months, I think?" Finn frowned slightly. "If you count the whole time."

"Why wouldn't you count the whole time?" Zain asked.

"Well, like, does it count if you don't see each other for a bit?"

"I think so," Zain said. "I wouldn't expect you to see each other every day. Although I guess if you're living together, it's kind of a different story."

"We're not living together," I muttered, but neither of them paid any attention to me.

"That's only been since, like, Sunday," Finn said, turning back to the stove so he could stir the sauce again. "How long have you known Tessa?"

"Most of her life," Zain said.

"Are you her brother or something?"

Zain glanced at me incredulously. "Do you think we... look... alike?"

"You don't have to look like family to be family," Finn said. "I look nothing like my sisters. And not even just because they're girls."

"Right, of course," Zain said. "But no. Her brother and I are friends."

"Oh, cool! You must have some crazy stories about her, then."

"Do I ever," Zain said.

Finn seemed to expect him to tell one of those crazy stories, but asshole though he was, Zain didn't elaborate. Instead, an awkward silence fell through my kitchen as I glared at Zain and he stared back, a challenge in his eyes.

Fuck, I wish I'd told him to get a hotel.

"Alright, cool," Finn finally said. "So I have a question for you, Zain."

"What's that?" Zain asked.

"So imagine pasta starting to grow on your head instead of hair. What kind of pasta do you think would be best?"

"What pasta... what?" Zain repeated, tearing his gaze from mine.

"What pasta would make the best hair?" Finn turned slightly, pointing a wooden spoon at Zain. "And you can't say angel hair. That's cheating."

Zain looked at me, partly stunned and partly amused and completely baffled. "Holy hell, Tessa. Where did you find this guy?"

"At the park," Finn said before I could respond. "I was living in my car."

For some reason, that seemed to raise more questions in Zain's mind, even though I thought it was fairly straightforward. But Zain didn't have time to give me much more than an alarmed and incredulous look before Finn started talking again.

"I'd probably pick fusilli," he said. "Because it would look kind of like curly hair, maybe. I like my hair a little longer, but fusilli wouldn't get tangled the same way something like spaghetti would."

Zain's mouth opened, then closed. A moment passed and then he couldn't seem to help himself any longer and turned to Finn. "Wait, so the pasta that's growing instead of hair is cooked pasta?"

"For sure. Hard pasta would be painful. Unless it was fresh pasta. That might be okay."

Zain tilted his head to the side thoughtfully. From his feet, Alfie boofed in frustration and Zain crouched down to give him the attention he wanted so badly.

"Okay," he said. "So can you eat the pasta? Because if it's your own personal pasta garden, that changes the answer."

"Oooo," Finn said, his eyes going round. "I never thought of that! Let's say yeah, you can eat it."

"Okay, well, I'm picking function over form, then," Zain said. "Tortellini, for sure."

"That would still look okay, though," Finn said. "Like if it was all kinda close to the head and stuff?"

Of all the people I expected to have a serious and thoughtful discussion with Finn about the pros and cons of pasta hair, Zain was not one of them. But that was just another one of those things that was so amazing about Finn. With anyone else, there might have been a fight. There might have been tension. Anger. But Finn just rolled with it. He seemed to be able to take any situation and make it... well...

Enjoyable probably wasn't the right word, since I couldn't say I was enjoying the way Zain was ignoring me but talking animatedly with Finn. But it was, at the very least, tolerable. Manageable. Less intense in a way I both admired and appreciated.

I wished I knew how he did that. Especially since Finn got *Zain* talking *animatedly*. I didn't know if I'd ever witnessed Zain do anything animatedly before.

But there he was, making Finn thoughtfully consider which dessert he'd train a hypothetical falcon to steal for him, given that the falcon's claws would need to grip said dessert tightly enough to get it from point A to point B.

"I'd train it to get crème brûlée," Zain said as Finn put a bowl of pasta in front of him. "The ramekin should be able to protect the dessert itself."

"Smart," Finn said.

"I try occasionally," Zain said. "What's your next question?"

"Wait," Finn said as he sat down. "Tessa didn't answer."

"I'd go with donuts," I said. "Sturdy enough to hold up to the claws and the ones with the holes in the middle would be easier for it to grip, I think."

"Mmm, right," Zain said, but he didn't look at me as he brought a forkful of fettuccine Alfredo to his mouth. "Actually, can I change my pasta answer? I'd pick this specific pasta to be my hair."

Finn laughed. "It's good?"

"Fucking amazing," Zain said through a mouthful of food. "You're a damn good cook, bud."

Finn's face turned a bit red, but he grinned.

"It's delicious," I agreed. "Thanks, Finn."

"Okay, if you had to pick a favourite smell, what would you pick?" Zain asked, because apparently he was in a gigantic pissy baby mood and thought if he focused on keeping Finn talking, it would be less obvious that he was being a passive aggressive asshole.

Though in fairness, he was being a passive aggressive asshole who was currently benefiting me.

Because I didn't really want to talk about what was going on, either.

But even if he was only doing it to avoid talking to me, Zain couldn't hide his amusement at Finn's responses. And Finn liked that; each time he made Zain laugh, his lips spread into a proud smile.

The two of them were as different as could be—at least, I thought they were—but somehow, they clicked. Sure, Finn could probably make friends with anyone, but Zain was grumpy and stuck up and seemed far too serious to entertain a hypothetical question about what he'd have to warn someone about if he swapped bodies with them for a few months.

Zain's plan to avoid talking to me didn't work forever, of course. After we finished eating, I collected the plates off the table.

"I can get this so you and Zain can visit," Finn said, rising to help me.

"Don't worry about it," I said. "You cooked. The least I can do is clean."

He thought for a moment, then clapped his hands together. "Well then, I'll take Alfie out for a walk."

"What?" I said, trying not to sound alarmed.

He had already grabbed Alfie's leash from the front door. Between that action and the W-word, Alfie had started losing his mind, nearly tripping Zain as he bolted for the door.

"I'll see if Dottie wants me to take Millie out with us," he said, bending down to put Alfie's leash on. "You'd like that, hey, boy?"

Alfie's entire body wiggled.

The room felt very empty when Finn closed the door with a resounding bang a few moments later. I was still standing at the sink, my back to the table and my hopes up that Zain would just go to the living room and... I don't know. Do something else. But apparently that was when he decided he'd had enough of being a gigantic pissy baby and it was time for us to act like adults.

"He seems nice," he said.

"He is nice," I replied.

The chair scraped against the floor as he pushed it back from the table, then crossed the kitchen and picked up a tea towel as he joined me.

"That whole 'I found him in the park living in his car' thing, though..."

"I didn't find him in the park," I said.

"No?"

"We'd already left the park. He was on the sidewalk."

Zain snorted back a laugh. "Okay, so you took a homeless guy home, is that it?"

"Of course not. I knew him before that."

"How'd you know him?"

"I fucked him and his girlfriend. Ex-girlfriend, now. Obviously."

"Of course." He picked up the plate I'd just washed and wiped it. "Well, nice of you to help him out. Take him in. Give him a nice warm bed to sleep in and in exchange you get dinner cooked for you and... hmm. Anything else?"

"I don't have to justify helping out a friend to you."

"Wasn't asking you to. I'm just making conversation."

I rolled my eyes. "Oh, *now* you're making conversation."

"What was I supposed to say before?" he asked. "I don't know him or what the situation is. I don't know if he knows you and I have fucked before. I was simply trying to keep yet another secret for you, Teacup."

"I didn't ask you to keep a secret, for the record. And yes, he does know we've fucked."

I left out the part where Finn got so turned on hearing about it that he'd bent me over the living room couch and fucked me from behind until I'd come on his cock twice. Zain didn't need that ego boost.

"Well, now I know," Zain said.

"Now you know," I agreed. "I'm just helping a friend, who's a really nice person that's down on his luck, and it's been a bit of a crazy week, and I didn't tell you about it for understandable reasons, and everything is fine."

"Everything is completely fine," he said. "You found him in a park on... Sunday. After you and I were together when you were in Kelowna earlier that day?"

"Yep. That would be the same day."

"And now he's living with you. And... sleeping with you."

"Casually."

"Casually, but he's living with you."

I put a plate on the drying rack a bit harder than necessary. "It can be both."

"Of course it can. There's no reason it can't be that. It makes complete and total sense."

"Exactly. So there's no reason for you to be upset about it."

"Why would you think I'm upset about it?"

"I don't." I put the final plate on the rack. "I'm just telling you that you shouldn't be. Unless you thought you and I were something more than secret casual fuck buddies."

"Of course I didn't," he said, but it came out a bit more pointedly than his previous sentence. "I know what this is."

"Good. I'm glad."

"Honestly, I'm relieved," he said.

My shoulders tensed, but I pretended it was for reasons other than the unexpected sting of his words. "Relieved?"

"Yeah. You're a little less high-strung when you're getting dicked down regularly."

"Fuck you," I muttered.

"Nah, I think he'll be back soon," Zain said. "And besides, Teacup, I have eyes. Frankly, if you weren't fucking him, I'd be insulted."

"Why?"

"Because I'd be very concerned why you were fucking me when you clearly have no taste."

There was another little jab of pain in those words. "Were?"

"What?" he asked.

"You said 'were.' Instead of 'are.'"

He shrugged. "I wasn't sure if that was still on the table."

"Well, it is. And I have great taste. And you have no reason to be jealous."

"Why would I be jealous?"

"I don't know." I scrubbed at an already-clean spot on the pot I'd put in the sink. "You have no right to be."

"Well, I guess it's a good thing I'm not," Zain said.

"Exactly. Good."

"Good. Glad we agree."

"Yep. You're damn right we agree."

"Good."

And maybe if it wasn't the most aggressive session of agreeing I'd ever been part of, I would've believed it more.

Maybe if I could have convinced myself more, I wouldn't have gone to bed that night only to stare up at my ceiling, listening to Finn's breath as I imagined Zain's.

Maybe I wouldn't have wondered why the hell I felt so guilty about what was supposed to be two different casual things with two different men who had, somehow, ended up in my home at the same time.

Eleven

"YOU NEED TO TALK some sense into her."

"How am I supposed to talk sense into her?"

"I dunno, but she seems to listen when you do it while you're eating her out, so maybe you can sneak into the bathroom and make her smarten up."

I glared at my Caesar salad and poked it with my fork. "I knew I should've never let you two meet."

Claire and Chuck looked at each other with scarily similar expressions of exasperation on their faces.

"I'm pretty sure *you* were the one who was like, 'Chuck, you'll have to wait until lunch to find out what happened on the latest episode of the insanity that is the Tessa Lane Show because Claire said she could meet for lunch today and I don't want to tell this story twice,'" Chuck said.

"And because I wanted to hear about your dinner with Charles's parents first," I said. "It wasn't entirely selfish."

"He makes a good point, darling," Claire said, sipping her wine. "You're the one who suggested lunch."

"Because *someone* said she couldn't give me an excuse to not go home after work so I could avoid the mess that is my life," I muttered.

"Because *someone* is taking your sweet little ex-not-a-girlfriend to Paris for a week and they're leaving tonight," she replied.

"Yeah, well... I thought I needed both your opinions on this." I put a forkful of salad in my mouth. "Though for the record, you're the one who insisted on eating at Beaujolais Park. Chuck and I would've been perfectly fine going to, like, Olive Garden."

"Speak for yourself," Chuck said as he reached for another piece of the freshly baked bread to slather in whipped garlic butter.

"I have a standing arrangement for a semi-private booth here," Claire said, patting her mouth before sipping her wine again. "Which seemed appropriate given the subject matter you wanted to discuss."

"Oh my God. It's not that serious," I said.

"That's why you're trying to avoid going home so you don't have to face another evening of awkwardness between the two men you're totally into?"

I ate another bite of salad, then continued speaking through a mouth full of croutons. "I'm not avoiding them. I'm just... purposely trying not to see them."

Chuck and Claire shared another look of unimpressed exasperation before turning back to me.

"I cannot believe you're doing this," Chuck said.

"What? Eating a salad? I happen to love Caesar salad."

"Oh, of course. You're definitely not sitting here doing the whole 'Oh my God, how can I possibly choose between these two hunky men who both want to take me to poundtown on the regular' thing?"

"Of course I'm not," I said, stabbing a crouton indignantly. "I'm doing the whole 'Oh no, why is this happening to me, I'm not supposed to feel anything about *either* of them in any capacity except the capacity of my vagina' thing."

"In fairness, your vagina has a pretty significant capacity," Claire said.

My mouth dropped open, the crouton on my fork forgotten as I paused. "What did you just—"

"Not like that," she said. "I meant like..." She stopped and thought. "Well, maybe like that."

"You're calling me a slut?" I asked.

"Aren't you?"

"Yeah, but you don't have to say it."

Chuck lifted his pristine white cloth napkin to his mouth to muffle his burst of laughter.

"I didn't say it, actually," Claire said. "I just said you have a large capacity vagina."

"I cannot believe you're implying I have a loose vag," I said.

"I'm not implying that. Trust me, I know your vag is not loose at all. It's a metaphor."

I glared down at my plate. "For what?"

"For the fact that I think your vagina has the capacity to handle at least two dicks from hunky men who want to take you to poundtown and one sparkly dildo attached to the not-hunky-so-much-as-stunningly-attractive woman who also wants to take you to poundtown."

"Vaginal capacity aside," Chuck said, "I think we need to circle back to that whole 'feel something about them' thing, because *that's* new."

"What's new?" I asked blankly.

"You admitting you have feelings for either and/or both of them," Chuck said.

"I didn't admit shit! I'm just... I don't know. Zain was jealous or upset or something even though he had no right to be, and—"

"Are you sure about that?" Chuck asked. "Or are you projecting those emotions onto him because you feel weird about wanting both of them?"

"I don't feel weird about that!"

"What do you feel weird about, then?" Claire asked.

"I... don't know," I said. "That's the problem. They both knew about each other. Sort of. I just feel bad, I guess. Because I told Zain he could stay and messed up. I don't like letting people down. That's it. Obviously."

"You're such a liar," Chuck said, then looked at Claire. "Back me up here because she's spiralling."

"I don't think she's wrong, though," Claire said. "She's not lying. I think she's willfully and purposefully trying to stay ignorant. Because it's not them she feels guilty about."

"What is it, then?" I asked.

"Tess. You like them."

"I like their dicks."

"You *like* them. You like *them*. And you're feeling guilty because you don't want to let yourself be happy about it."

"Happy about what? Both these assholes were supposed to be one-time things and now—"

"Now you like them. Now you're into them."

I was starting to regret inviting Claire even though she was footing the bill. She had this horrendous way of pinpointing things, then holding them up and shoving them in my face until I couldn't ignore them anymore.

Because she was right. I poked at my Caesar salad again, my throat suddenly feeling too tight to swallow.

"Tess?" Chuck asked when I didn't say anything.

"I don't want to like them."

"But you do?" he pressed.

I sighed and put my fork down. "Fuck. This was never supposed to mean anything. With either of them."

"I think the problem here is that you're expecting it to," Claire said.

Chuck's thick, dark eyebrows furrowing. "What?"

"It doesn't have to mean anything," Claire said. "And if it does, you don't need to know what it means right now. So what if one's your brother's best friend? So what if you met one at a threesome and took him in off the streets? So what if you don't think it can be anything more than what it is now because your family thinks you're married? They're not here, Tessa."

"But—"

"*You* are. You are, and Zain is, and Finn is. You're allowed to enjoy that for what it is."

"And what about when they want more?" I asked. "Because there's no planet, universe, or timeline where I want to have that conversation with my parents. 'Hey Mom, hey Dad, by the way, I'm not married to that guy you adore anymore. Instead I'm taking two dicks at the same time and one belongs to your oldest son's best friend and the other is this guy I met during a totally separate threesome than the current threesome.' Do you know how disgusted my dad would be?"

"I swear," Chuck said exasperatedly. "You can lead the unicorn to the bridge but you can't make her burn it down."

I stared at him. "What the fuck is that supposed to mean?"

He pursed his lips as he stared back. "It's another metaphor, Tessa Belinda Lane. Usually it's leading a horse but I figured since you're our resident unicorn..."

"It is not a metaphor. It's nonsense."

"Regardless," Claire said before Chuck could try to explain what the hell he'd said. "Darling, it's almost insulting that with our friendship being the way it is, you're still looking at this like your options are 'one night only' levels of casual or 'turn my life upside down and tell my father I like taking multiple cocks at once instead of doing the normal thing and just telling him you have two boyfriends' levels of serious. We're the perfect example. Would you say we're casual?"

"We casually have sex, yes," I said.

"But we're seriously friends, right?"

She had a point. I fidgeted with my fork and didn't say anything.

"We're girl friends who fuck, not girlfriends," she said. "It's not casual, but it's not serious. You and I simply enjoy each other for what we are."

"But this is different," I said.

"How? There are different levels of casual and serious. If you like them… like them. Enjoy it for what it is."

I pushed a piece of lettuce around my plate, another uncertain thought popping into my mind. "And what about you and me?"

She lifted her wine glass to her lips, pausing to sip before speaking. "I know you probably think I'll say that I'll be supportive either way and understand if that's where your heart lies. But frankly, if either of them has a problem with the fact that you hook up with your bestie on the regular, they're not the right guy for you."

"So you wouldn't give this up?" I asked.

"I think it's more that you wouldn't be able to give me up, darling."

"Good," I said, trying to sound a lot less relieved than I actually was, as if I'd totally known that would be the answer. "Because even if Julie gets in first, I still want to join the mile high club and you're the only person I know with a private plane."

Claire looked amused. "You seem very certain that she and I are going to hook up on this trip. I've spoken with her on the phone one time."

"You paid ten grand for a date with me when you didn't even know my name and then fingerbanged me in a nightclub the same day we met."

"Yes, but what are the odds I get lucky like that twice?"

I snorted back a laugh. "Whatever. I just know that Julie's hot and you're hot and picturing two hot girls going at it on a round bed with satin sheets and a leopard-print blanket thirty thousand feet in the air is really doing it for me."

"You think my plane has a round bed with satin sheets on it?" she asked.

"Don't tell me if it doesn't. I'm enjoying my imagined visual."

"I'm not," Chuck grumbled.

"Why are you visualizing my visual?"

"I'm not doing it on purpose," he said. "*You're* the one planting images in my head that I feel guilty for picturing because it feels problematically male gaze-y for me to enjoy fantasizing about that scenario, especially when one of the people in said fantasy is sitting right here and I'm also in a very serious committed relationship with a man whose parents I just met and would not give up for anything."

"That was the most respectful way I think anyone's ever told me they're currently picturing me naked," Claire said, her fae-like smirk crossing her face. "And for that, you have my permission to continue imagining it."

Chuck looked horrified. "That's not what I—"

But Claire's horrific cackle cut him off. He sighed, shaking his head, though there was a hint of laughter on his lips.

"Either way, I think you and Julie are going to have fun," I said. "I wouldn't have suggested it if I didn't."

"You don't think I'm going to be too much for a sweet, kind, newly-out woman whose only sapphic experience is with you?"

"Oh, you'll for sure overwhelm her," I said. "But she'll be fine."

"Are you honestly saying that or are you secretly hoping Julie gets overwhelmed as a bit of payback for the whole ghosting thing?" Chuck asked.

"What do you think I am, some kind of vindictive asshole?"

"Uh... Yes. I do."

I shrugged. "Fair. But not in this case. If they hook up, great. If not, great." I looked at Claire. "Just remember Julie's track record with keeping things casual is abysmal."

The topic was interesting enough to push the conversation away from Finn and Zain and the feelings I didn't want to have. I was thankful for that, despite it being the reason I'd asked Claire and Chuck out for lunch.

Of course, that meant after Claire paid the bill and we were waiting outside the restaurant because Chuck had eaten half his weight in caramelized cheesecake and needed to use the bathroom before we walked back to work, Claire brought up the fact that I still had no idea what I was fucking doing.

And, in typical Claire fashion, she did it after notching her fingers under my chin and lifting my head up to plant a sweet, heated kiss against my lips.

"What was that for?" I asked.

"To remind you how fucking hot I think you are," she said, then leaned in and kissed me again.

"Mmm. And what was that for?"

"To butter you up when I ask you what you're going to do about your boys."

I pulled away from her. "They're not *my* boys." I paused, then tilted my head in amusement. "And they're a collective now?"

"Your concerns seem to be about them as a collective rather than individually, so yes. They're your boys."

I sighed, focusing on an elderly tourist couple holding hands on the other side of the street, the woman leaning heavily on a cane and the man gripping his large camera as they walked by a panhandler. "It's not anything serious."

Claire's voice was exasperated. "Tessa. Darling."

"What?"

"You're so fucking stubborn."

"So I've heard," I said.

"You're so stubborn that you're more willing to lie to yourself than to just face the fact that you want them both. Or—" She reached up, pulling her long brown hair over one shoulder thoughtfully. "You're scared."

I let out a loud scoff. "I'm not *scared*. What would I be scared of?"

"Opening your heart again," she said. "The aforementioned telling your dad how many dicks you like at once. Risking your excellent sexual arrangement with your rich, spunky best friend."

"Considering you're not into guys, you are probably my least spunky friend."

She cackled. "But that's it, isn't it?"

I almost said she was wrong.

Almost.

But then something weird happened and...

I almost didn't lie.

"It's not... *not* that," I said.

Claire's face softened. "You deserve to be happy, Tess. You're allowed to go after the things you want."

I looked across the street again, feeling heat rise up my neck and onto my cheeks. "I barely know what I want."

"You want Finn. You want Zain. You want me."

"Yeah, and if Zain has a problem with that? And Finn has nowhere else to go. And—"

"You're overthinking this when you don't even know how they'll react," she said.

"Yeah, but how do I figure that out?"

She gave me an unimpressed look. "You are far smarter than this."

"I'm... I didn't sleep well last night," I said stiffly.

"Darling," she said. "Just talk to them."

"'Just talk to them,'" I repeated flatly. "That's great advice. Thanks."

"I strive to fulfill your needs every time."

I rolled my eyes. "Seriously, what am I supposed to do? Just walk in after work today and go 'I want to fuck both of you'?"

Twelve

"I want to fuck both of you."

Zain and Finn looked as different as different could be. Zain's skin was brown and tattooed and his hair was dark. He wasn't muscular or toned or broad shouldered and he was at least six inches shorter than Finn. And Finn's skin was a warm shade of tan spotted only by the occasional freckle, his blonde hair long and shaggy, blue eyes bright and lively and eager.

Yet there they sat on my living room couch, side by side, both wearing identical expressions as they turned their heads and blinked in unison at me standing just inside the front door.

"Yeah, the interview went great, thanks for asking," Zain finally said. "The company seems like a good fit and they sounded impressed with my resume. I'm hoping I'll get a callback for the second round of interviews, but they won't be deciding for a while yet. I'm feeling confident, though. But what about you, Teacup? How was your day?"

I gave him a dirty look and set my work bag down. "Shut up. I've been planning out what to say since lunch."

"Clearly, since you didn't even take your shoes off before dropping that on us. What do you mean, you want—"

I waved a hand, shushing him as I went into the speech I'd planned instead of shredding more pointless documents with Chuck.

"I should be able to fuck both of you and not have it be a problem. Both of you were clear about that going into this whole situation. I never

"

said I was exclusive to anyone and that means no one can be mad about it because it was just supposed to be a casual thing."

"Someone was mad about it?" Finn asked, but I ignored him, too.

"So I'm not choosing. We're not doing that. And if that's a problem, one or both of you can leave. I don't care. I don't want to give up what I have with either of you—or with Claire either, because I'm fucking her too and I am *not* stopping that—and I don't know what that means for any of this but that's how it's going to be."

Zain turned his head and Finn glanced at him, both silent as they exchanged a look I couldn't read.

"Uh, well, we kinda figured, Teacup," Zain finally said. "We already talked about it."

I looked from one to the other, stunned. "You did?"

"Were you expecting that we sit around in silence when you're not here?" Zain asked, dry amusement on his face. "We were talking after I got back from my interview. Like you said, he knew about me—in detail, it would seem—"

My face burned red.

"—and I didn't know about him specifically, but I knew you were seeing other people. You've told me about Claire before," he finished.

"Exactly," I said. "I have."

He glanced at Finn again, that amused smirk still playing on his lips. "Did you think we were going to have some kind of jealous battle for your affections or something?"

"We can if you want," Finn said. "I'm okay with trying roleplay."

"No," I said quickly. "No, I... that's what I don't want. So it's good, then. That you talked and... and nothing's changing."

"Not so fast," Zain said. "I mean, we knew going into this that you like to fuck around. But the whole part where you said it's not a casual thing anymore—"

"I didn't say that."

"No? You didn't burst in here with a whole spiel about how it was *supposed* to be casual and you're not choosing between us because you like what we have and you don't want to give it up?"

Panic was rising up my throat. "Yeah, I don't want to give up what we had. Which was casual."

"It was supposed to be casual. But now you're saying—"

"Nothing. I'm... I'm saying nothing."

"Teacup, are you—"

"Shut up."

"No." His voice was firm but gentle and he rose from the couch. "I'm not dropping this. Not if you're standing here telling me this isn't just about fucking around anymore."

"That's not... I didn't say that," I said. My palms started sweating and I pressed them to my hips.

"Don't you lie to me, Tessa Lane," he said. "Not about this."

"Tess, do you want, like, something... more?" Finn asked softly. "'Cause if you do... like, I know we've always said we're just friends and that, but if you're feeling something different—"

Great. My palms were sweating and my shoulders were curling forward as my muscles tensed, preparing for the rejection I didn't know I was fearing.

"—that'd be so awesome," Finn finished. "I just... I never wanted to say anything because you said we couldn't be more than friends, but I really *like* you." He looked down at his hands. "You make me want to be a better version of myself, but you don't act like I need to change. You don't make me feel stupid. I can just be relaxed around you and... and I just like that. I like you. And like, Alfie adores you, and I trust his opinion."

Fuck.

Fuck.

My heartbeat was not supposed to be speeding up when he said something like that.

"I don't know what I want right now," I said. "And if you need a better answer than that, you're not going to get one because it's the only answer I have. Obviously these things weren't the 'one time things' I said they were. Obviously I like being... around you and stuff. I started this conversation because I don't want to feel like I can't be with both of you because someone's going to take things the wrong way or get their feelings hurt or something. I don't know what this is, but I like it. I want to keep doing it."

"So... you want things to continue the same way they were before you stormed in here and blurted out that you want to fuck both of us," Zain said. "Because again, Teacup, we kinda both already knew that. I mean, he's living with you and I have a fucking pet name for you."

"It's a cute pet name," Finn said, and I tried not to blush.

"Yeah," I said. "That's it. But it's not like I knew that before I walked in."

"I want you to do what makes you happy," Zain said. "And honestly, I'm not just okay with it, Tess. I... I really like the idea of it, actually. If that's what you're wanting."

I raised my eyebrows, but before I could process that, Finn spoke up.

"Same," Finn said. "I like what we have. I like what you have with him, especially if you keep telling me about it."

Zain snorted and I felt my cheeks burn again. "Even if you're not the only ones? Because I'm not giving up Claire."

"I wouldn't ask you to give up your sugar mama," Zain said.

"She's your sugar mama?" Finn asked, managing to look both bewildered and impressed. "Wait, I guess that explains why she's taking Julie to Paris."

"She's not my sugar mama," I said. "That's not how it is."

"She's rich, spoils you, and you have sex with her," Zain said. "That's basically the definition of a sugar mama."

"She's my friend," I said. "That's it."

He smirked but dropped it. "Okay, so you want to fuck me, him, and Claire. Anyone else?"

"I don't know. I might want to keep my options open."

He chuckled. "Then go for it."

"You'd be okay with that?"

"Teacup, I'm not joking." He folded his arms across his chest. "What you do and what you need from other people doesn't concern me. What matters is that I get you, too."

"I wanted to say something like what he said but he said it way better, so like... also that for me," said Finn.

I couldn't have stopped the smile that spread on my face if I'd wanted to. And I kind of did want to because for some reason, showing that I was happy felt weird. But there was a warm feeling in my chest and a sudden sense of relief that I couldn't control.

"Okay," I said. "Awesome. And you know, if you wanted to hook up with other people too, I'm okay with it."

"How very equitable of you," Zain said, his voice dry but his eyes sparkling in the way they did when he was just teasing. "Though, that does... uh... lead to another question."

"What?"

"Do you..." He trailed off and thought for a moment. "Are you saying that you'd want to hook up with all of us at the same time?"

"I'm not... *not* saying that," I said. "I'd be open to it. I mean, obviously."

He half-laughed. "Yeah but is anyone else you're involved with, uh... not straight?"

"Claire is a lesbian," I said.

"I'm straight," Finn said.

Zain nodded, though he let out a jokingly sarcastic puff of air. "You couldn't have found at least *one* other person who was into fucking guys for your little group, Teacup?"

I laughed. Because it was funny. Because it was clearly a joke.

Finn, however, didn't laugh.

"I'd be into it," he said.

Zain turned to look at him, confusion wrinkling his forehead. "You just said you were straight."

"I am," Finn said. "But that doesn't mean I wouldn't hook up with a guy. Like, you're hot."

Zain looked at me as if I knew what the hell was going on. I half-shrugged and he turned back to Finn with an incredulous look on his face. "Finn, are you sure you're fully straight?"

"Yep."

"But you just said you'd have sex with another guy."

"Well, yeah," Finn said. "What does that have to do with it?"

Zain pressed his hands together and took a steadying breath. "Okay. Do you like fucking girls? You're attracted to them?"

Finn nodded. "Of course."

"And do you think you'd like fucking guys?"

"Yeah. I mean, it's still gonna feel good."

Zain nodded slowly. "Okay, and you think guys are attractive?"

"I mean, yeah. I just said you were hot."

"Alright," Zain said. "And what about a transman or a transwoman?"

I don't know if Zain noticed Finn's expression darken a bit, but I did.

"You mean a man or a woman," he said.

"Right," Zain said. "And what if someone said they were neither? Non-binary people?"

"Yeah, of course," Finn said.

Zain moved his hand to his mouth, propping his elbow up in the palm of his other hand. "So, you're attracted to and would fuck women, men, or anyone else."

"Well, yeah, if they're into it."

"Right." Zain nodded. "Bud, you're like... the opposite of straight."

Finn frowned and looked at me. "Really?"

"Straight people are only attracted to people of the opposite sex," I said. "So... yeah. I'd say you're probably not straight."

"Oh. I guess that makes sense." He looked back at Zain. "So what am I, then?"

Zain shrugged, something like sympathy on his face. "That's up to you, man. I say bisexual because that felt the most right, but I mean, I'm attracted to pretty much anyone. Or you could use pansexual. Some people just say queer. Whatever you want to call yourself, really. But you, my friend, are very much not a heterosexual. In my opinion, anyway."

"Oh," Finn said.

Both Zain and I watched warily as he processed this massive new piece of information he apparently hadn't known about himself. I didn't know if it was right for Zain to be the one to tell him he wasn't straight, but in fairness, I had a feeling Finn didn't actually know what "straight" was.

Either way, it was a big thing. A massive thing. When I first figured out there was a name for how I felt and accepted that I was attracted to more than just men, it shook me for days. The whole world seemed different, like my eyes had opened and so much had fallen into place and I'd caught up with how everyone else in the world must have felt all the time.

Not to mention that Finn... well. I couldn't help but see the similarities between him and Julie. I mean, no one told Julie she was bisexual, but she'd had her realization in a similar way to Finn: a statement they thought was one thing but revealed a whole side of them they hadn't known about. And that had to be confusing, to know that your ex went through nearly the same situation and you didn't realize it about yourself.

I waited for Finn to say something. I prepared myself to go to him, to hug him, to be the person he needed in that moment.

But when he finally looked up, first at me and then at Zain, he grinned.

"Well then," he said, and slapped his hands against his thighs. "Put me in the kitchen and turn on the stove."

Zain's mouth opened, but nothing came out. Finn's grin widened.

"'Cause I'm a pan, Zain. Get it?"

"Yes, unfortunately," Zain said.

And I couldn't help it. I couldn't hold the laughter in anymore. It burst out all at once, bubbling out as I lost it at the resigned sense of disgruntled amusement on Zain's face, and Finn's look of pride beaming off his face before he started chuckling, too.

"Okay," I said when I finally managed to stop laughing. "Are we doing this?"

"Doing what?" Zain asked.

I looked from him to Finn. "Fucking?"

"Right now?" Finn asked excitedly.

"You're both here, aren't you?"

It was a good day when I could throw Zain off. His lips parted and he blinked, an unusual expression of uncertainty crossing his face. "Like… together?"

"I assumed that's why you were asking if anyone else in my 'group' was into guys," I said. "And I mean, I wasn't expecting us to all do it together, but then you and Finn decided you want to fuck each other. So why not give it a go?"

"I never said—"

"You said last night you'd be insulted if I was fucking you but not him because you thought he was hot."

Zain's throat flexed as he swallowed and he looked at Finn. "Are you…"

"I mean, do you?" Finn asked.

Zain held up his hands. "You're the one who gets to decide what your first time with a guy is like. If this is how you want it—"

"Oh, hell yes," Finn said. "Do you know how fun threesomes are? Let's do it!"

"Yeah? Okay," Zain said, but his voice was higher than normal. I shook my head.

"Zain, we're not doing this if you don't want to," I said. "Threesomes are fun until someone doesn't want to be involved and then they suck."

"It's not that," he said. "I've just... never had a threesome before."

"And if you don't want to, that's fine," I said. "Don't let us pressure you. All I'll ask is one of you eat me out before you get busy with each other since you couldn't be bothered to figure this all out before I got home and now I'm kinda horny thinking about it."

"No, I do want to," he said, mouth twitching with quiet laughter. "It's just a first."

"Cool," Finn said. "So we both get some firsts. Sounds like fun."

Zain nodded as he seemed to consider it. His tongue poked out to wet his lips and then he looked at Finn, who was still sitting on the couch.

"Well," he said. "Let's get one of those firsts out of the way."

Then he closed the two-step gap between them, knelt with one knee on the couch, and pressed his mouth to Finn's.

Thirteen

There were rules we were supposed to follow.

There were things we needed to discuss.

Boundaries.

Limits.

Expectations.

The entire thing was supposed to start with a conversation that helped three people negotiate the terms of what we were about to do. That was how people kept from getting hurt. That was how things stayed casual. That was how I made sure that when I was with a couple, I wouldn't come between them when I came between them.

But Finn and Zain weren't a couple.

And it was damn hard to remember anything I was supposed to do or say or ask when I was watching Finn get his first kiss from another man.

I couldn't quite explain why. Maybe it was the excitement of knowing it was a first, that I was witnessing a moment. Maybe it was the stunned look of shock on Finn's face, the sharp inhale, the moment of surprise followed by the moment of relaxation a few seconds later. The way his hands fluttered for a moment, lifting off his thighs before settling back down, as if he wasn't sure what to do with them.

Or maybe it was because it was Zain.

Maybe it was seeing two sets of lips I knew intimately joining like that. Knowing how they felt, how they tasted, how they could each make me melt in such different ways. Hearing Finn's soft sigh, knowing that Zain was the one who made him make that noise, and watching Zain grip Finn's shoulder just a little less tenderly than he would have if it were me.

Or it could have been because I wasn't the newcomer.

I was always the third. The addition. The unicorn. The woman who wasn't part of what had already been established. But there was nothing established between them. These men had met the previous day and I was the one who connected them. I was the one who knew them.

I was in an entirely different position than I usually was.

Zain probably intended to give Finn a simple, straightforward kiss and then check on him. To press their lips together, then pull back and look into his eyes, to make sure that this man who had just realized he wasn't exactly straight was okay with what was happening. I watched as he pulled back, as he gave Finn one of his intense, soul-searching gazes, as his mouth started to form a word.

And then faster than I could catch it, I watched Finn finally decide what he was supposed to do with his hands, which was to let one dart up from his thigh and close around the front of Zain's shirt.

"Wait," he breathed, and then he jerked Zain forward to kiss him again.

And fuck.

Fuck.

A soft noise escaped my lips. I didn't mean for it to. But I couldn't help it. Not when the two of them were so fucking gorgeous together.

Zain cupped Finn's cheek, his tongue snaking out and slipping past Finn's lips. Finn groaned and the corners of Zain's eyes crinkled as a smile spread across his face.

"Oh, bud," he murmured as he pulled away from Finn. "I am gonna have so much fun with you."

"Well, yeah," Finn said as if it was the most obvious thing ever. "I pretty much always have fun."

Zain didn't correct him, just smiled and kissed Finn again before turning to me.

"Are you just going to stand there and objectify us by watching?" he asked.

"Maybe. You two are pretty hot together."

He smirked, but his eyes darkened. "Come here, kitten."

And damn if that low growl didn't compel me to close the distance between us. But as soon as I reached them, Zain's arm shot out and he grabbed my wrist.

"What are you do—" I started, but the words were lost into a pleased gasp as he yanked me towards him and pressed his lips to mine.

"You know what I thought about all fucking night?" he asked against my lips. "You, in bed with him, and I didn't even get to *taste* you. It was driving me crazy. So what I'm *doing*—" He nipped at my lip, making me cry out as his teeth sank into the tender skin. "—is getting my fucking kiss, Teacup."

A moan slipped past my lips, but a moment later, the warmth of his mouth disappeared. I blinked my eyes open, but before I could catch the breath he'd made hitch, Finn's hand slipped behind my neck.

"I would also like a kiss," he said, and pulled me in to capture me with his mouth.

Somehow, the intensity of Zain's kiss and the joy of Finn's were the perfect mix to make my legs go numb and my head feel light. Somehow, Finn working his tongue against mine as Zain urged me from my awkward hunched-over stance to straddling Finn's thigh was everything I hadn't known I'd been dreaming of.

"That's it," Zain murmured as I reached up to rest my hand on Finn's chest. He lifted one hand to brush Finn's hair back from his forehead while snaking the other arm around me. "Fuck, the two of you look good together."

"We'd look even better with you in here, too," Finn said.

In my experience, three-way kisses didn't really work. Mouths weren't designed that way; either everyone was going to get weird half-kisses or someone was going to be stuck kissing the corners of the other mouths while two people kissed properly. Or they might be the kind of socially awkward person who just waited for their turn with their face entirely too close to the others.

But with Finn and Zain… I don't know how we managed it. I don't know why it came naturally, how we came up with the instinctive choreography to tangle our kisses together like that.

But we did, and it was everything.

It was enough to make my head spin. Enough to make Zain moan. Enough to make Finn's cock harden more than it was, pressing against my thigh as Zain kept me steady on his lap.

Enough to do all that, and almost more, too fast.

"We… we missed a step," I whispered as Finn's lips moved away from mine, kissing down to my neck.

"Did we?" Zain murmured before taking his turn to slip his tongue into my mouth.

"Mmm," I said, then tried to blink the hazy arousal away. "I mean, yes. We… we didn't talk about this."

"Pretty sure we did," Zain said. "Remember the whole 'barging in and blurting that you wanted to fuck both of us' thing that led to an entire conversation about—"

"Not that," I said. "The rules."

He raised his eyebrows. "Okay. Tell me the rules, kitten."

"Well first, the safe…" I started, but my voice failed me as Zain traced a hypnotizing finger along my jaw and down the side of my neck that Finn wasn't kissing.

"The safe what?" he prompted.

"The safe word is probiotic," Finn said before I could collect myself enough to continue. He pressed another kiss to my neck, not looking up as he spoke. "No hitting, tying up, or spitting on or near Tessa. Get a hotel room so she doesn't feel like she's invading your personal space although—" He lifted his head, mouth twisted to the side "—I think that probably doesn't apply here 'cause it's her house. We bring the condoms, plural, non-negotiable, although, uh... she already bought some so that might not apply either. And don't fall in love with her."

His words hung in the room. Part of it was because I was impressed with how precisely he'd remembered the rules, even though if, as he mentioned, a couple of them didn't quite apply the same way they had when I'd been fucking him and Julie.

But most of it was because Zain's eyes met mine after Finn said the last rule and I wasn't sure if they were full of understanding for why I had that rule, or if it was pity because I'd had to make it in the first place.

"Oh," Finn said, his voice bright. "And Tessa likes the blue Gatorade."

It was enough to break that tense moment. Zain looked at Finn and raised his eyebrows.

"For after," Finn explained. "That's not a rule, though. But I bought a twelve pack and put it in the pantry on Tuesday. I think there's still a couple left."

Zain looked back at me. "Any other rules I should know, Teacup?"

"Not from me, but this is Finn's first time with a guy," I said. "Shouldn't you figure that out?"

"I'm going to take it easy on him tonight," Zain said, speaking to me but looking at Finn as he touched his cheek. "Partly because of the first time thing but mostly because I think I'm going to die if we keep stalling this. So we're going to stick with the basics and if Finn doesn't like something that's happening, he's going to tell me and we're going to back off."

"Yeah," Finn said like they'd discussed it before. "But also, what are the basics?"

Zain smirked. "Well, obviously some kissing. Some touching. I'm thinking I might put your cock in my mouth."

Finn grinned. "Nice. Okay."

"And I might want to put mine in yours, if you want that."

"You better," Finn said. "I'm stoked to try sucking cock."

A few things had shaken Zain's cool demeanor that day, but that statement seemed to make his brain stall. He inhaled, trying to cover the sharpness by forcing his breath to be steady, and I shared a devilish look with Finn.

Well, I looked at Finn with what I thought was a devilish look, and Finn looked back at me with a not-quite-blank expression in his eyes and a smile on his face.

"I think that's where we should start," I said. "Wanna work on that together?"

"Hell yes," Finn said.

Of course, that meant we had to change the way we were positioned on the couch, and Zain took that opportunity to demand our clothes come off. As much as it was my instinct to do the opposite of what Zain demanded because I liked annoying him, Finn shrugged and started lifting his shirt.

"Damn," Zain said, his eyes flicking down Finn's body and back up once he was naked.

"Insane, right?" I said.

"What's insane?" Finn asked

"How fucking hot you are, bud," Zain said.

"Thanks," Finn said cheerfully. "You're pretty hot, too. Maybe you should get naked now so you can show it off."

Zain spread his arms to the side. "Maybe you should come help me."

"Lazy ass," I said, and Zain burst out laughing.

"You know I think you're fucking delicious, Teacup," he said. "Every inch of you."

And since that made my stomach feel fluttery and my chest feel warm, I decided to help Finn undress Zain, even though he was lazy. Finn revealed the mural of tattoos on Zain's chest while I pulled his jeans and boxers down, freeing his incredibly hard cock.

I loved how hard he was. How he throbbed beneath my palm when I wrapped my fingers around him, his shaft wonderfully warm, the cool sense of confidence he was putting on betrayed by the excited way he shifted his hips. How there was a drop of pre-cum on his tip and how I wanted to run my hand over it so I could spread it along his shaft or lean down to lick it off.

But I wasn't going to. I was going to leave that drop right where it was, because it wasn't for me.

I wanted Finn to have it.

I wanted to taste it on his lips after he spoiled Zain with his mouth.

"Ready?" I asked as Finn dropped Zain's shirt to the floor and settled on his knees beside me.

I'd expected to see something nervous flash across his face. Some kind of hesitancy, maybe, or something worried. Something showing that this man was about to have a moment most would consider huge.

But like the easy and unconcerned way he'd accepted he wasn't straight, Finn nonchalantly looked down at Zain's weeping cock, then up at me with sparkling excitement in his eyes.

"Hell yeah I am," he said, and that was that.

I smiled and reached forward, wrapping my hand around the base of Zain's cock and directing it towards Finn.

"Lick the pre-cum off him," I said, and seconds later Zain was gasping as Finn's tongue lapped up the sticky fluid on his tip.

Then he was trying not to pant as I instructed Finn to circle the head of Zain's cock with his tongue. He tried to bite back a moan when I told Finn to open his mouth and stick out his tongue so I could tap Zain's cock on it teasingly, but failed at holding that moan when I gave Finn permission to take the entirety of Zain's tip in his mouth.

"Suck gently," I said. "Kind of from the back of your mouth, if that makes sense. So your cheeks kind of push in, then slowly move your head down and—"

"Fuck," Zain hissed, and his hand found the top of Finn's head. "Fuck, that's good. You learn quick."

Which was true. He was an excellent student, for the most part. The hardest part of the whole thing was trying to get Finn to stop smiling, since smiling and sucking weren't really compatible actions. The problem was that every time Zain groaned, every time he inhaled sharply, every time his hand tightened in Finn's hair or he murmured anything that could be considered even slightly tangential to praise, Finn wanted to grin.

But that was okay. We'd work on that. In the meantime, I decided I'd make up for that very minor shortfall by dipping my head and joining him.

"Holy fu-*uhhh*," Zain said when I kissed the base of his cock before licking my way up to the crown, where Finn was teasing the sensitive spot on the underside of the head with the tip of his tongue. I couldn't help but smile too, especially when Finn stopped to quickly kiss me before focusing on Zain's cock again.

For a while, the two of us alternated between licking Zain and kissing each other. It was only when Zain let out an almost-frustrated noise that I reached up and tucked Finn's hair behind his ear.

"Wanna make him come?" I asked.

"Yes," Finn said.

"In your mouth or in my mouth?" I asked.

"Mine."

God, I'd been hoping for that.

Not because I didn't want Zain's cum in my mouth. No, I wanted Finn to take it because of the moment right at the beginning of the blowjob where he'd stuck his tongue out so I could rub Zain's cock against it. That moment had done something to me, the sight of Finn with his mouth open wide and his eyes trained up, enraptured as he looked at the man whose cock was on his tongue.

I wanted to see that exact moment again and again, and I wanted to jack Zain's cock until he spilled his cum all over Finn's tongue.

"Fuck," Zain swore as his cock rested against Finn's tongue. "Fuck, you look so good like that. Stick your tongue out a little more and—*unghh*." He groaned loudly as Finn stuck out his tongue. "Yes. Your mouth is fucking perfect, Finn. You're such a good little cocksucker, you know that? Just fucking fantastic."

Finn made a pleading noise. I thought it was pleading for Zain to come until I saw his hand move between his legs and grip his cock. He stroked it firmly, his chest rising and falling as he breathed relief around Zain's cock. I couldn't help but squirm where I knelt as I kept stroking Zain. If he noticed, he didn't say anything, but that was probably because he'd also caught Finn reaching down to touch himself and that visual was enough to push him over the edge.

"I'm gonna come," he rushed to say, though it was a little late; the first spurt had already spilled onto Finn's tongue, and the last part of his sentence faded into a series of quiet, restrained moans as his cock pulsed in my hand. Finn watched, absorbed in the sight of Zain coming, and I almost wasn't sure if he even registered the puddle of cum collecting on his tongue until Zain heaved that final satisfied sigh. Looking up at me, Finn pulled away from Zain's cock and went to swallow.

"You looked good with cum in your mouth, Finn," I said, and I swear he almost choked on it.

Which maybe made me a bit of an asshole, but it was totally worth it to make Finn's cheeks turn pink as he swallowed while his hand was still wrapped around his stiff cock.

"Thanks," he said, his voice hoarse, and I smiled as I pulled him in for a kiss.

"You did so good," I murmured.

He groaned. "Can we please fuck? I need it so bad, Tess."

"Yes," Zain said. "I want you to fuck her, Finn."

Finn nodded eagerly and rose from his knees, his eyes on Zain as he held his hand out to help me up. "How do you want her?"

"The way you fucked her when she told you about me and her. And I want you to do it nice and slow so I can see her take every inch of that gorgeous cock of yours."

A moment after I was on my feet, Finn had me bent over the armrest. Then he pressed a kiss to the spot on my back between my shoulders and caressed my ass.

"Be right back," he murmured.

"Where are you going?" Zain asked.

"Uh... to get a condom from the nightstand?" Finn replied.

"Oh," Zain said. "I forgot you're using them."

Fuck.

I closed my eyes, trying not to grimace as a sense of awkwardness filled the room.

"Are you not?" Finn asked, his voice almost innocently confused.

"We haven't been," I forced myself to say. "I didn't think to tell you, but I swear, I got tested... after Claire got back from Tahiti. So like a month ago. And she's the only other person I've been with other than you two."

"I did too," Zain said. "I went after I was in Victoria with Tess and I haven't been with anyone else since."

I blinked, surprised. Considering Zain spent basically the whole time he was in Victoria getting laid, it was a little shocking to hear he'd only been with me since then.

"Alright," Finn said.

"I'm sorry," I said. "I didn't even think to say anything and... well. I promise, I don't have anything."

"It's cool," Finn said, and I could hear the smile in his voice. "I trust you. Though I mean, if we're sharing, I haven't been tested since Julie and I did it the first time. But also, I haven't been with anyone but you since."

There was another moment of silence, and while it was as charged with tension as the previous one, it was a different kind of tension.

"Okay," I finally said. "So if Finn got tested, didn't have anything, and then was with Julie, who was a virgin... and then me, who wasn't, but I got tested and didn't have anything, and I also have an IUD so like, that's not an issue, but I was with Zain and Claire, but Zain got tested and so did Claire and—"

"None of us have anything, Teacup," Zain said. "And if you keep trying to do fucking algebra or whatever to figure it out, it's gonna make me insane. Are you okay with both of us fucking you raw or not?"

"Yes," I said.

"Finn, you wanna do it without a condom?"

"Yes," Finn said.

"Fuck her, then," Zain ordered.

And barely a second later, Finn's cock was inside me.

Fourteen

I CRIED OUT AS Finn entered me. Not because it hurt—I was as turned on as I'd ever been in my life and my pussy was absolutely soaked—or because he went too fast. No, Finn worked his cock in slowly. Part of it was because Zain had told him to, I'm sure, but from the noise he made, part of it was also because if he went any faster, he was going to blow his load within seconds.

It was the relief of it all that pushed that noise from my mouth. It wasn't until he was inside me that I realized how hard I needed it. I was beyond just having someone make me come; I needed the intensity of taking something inside of me, of my walls stretching around the cock being stuffed inside my pussy. I needed Finn's fingers digging into my hips and the sound of his body slapping against my ass and the sensation of breath being pushed from my lungs as he shoved himself inside me again and again.

I needed to be *fucked*, and after that first thrust inside me and subsequent pause as he took a deep, steadying breath, Finn was more than happy to deliver.

"Oh, hell yes," Zain said. He adjusted on the couch, moving forward and getting to his knees so he could slide a hand beneath me and cup my breast as it swayed. His fingers found my nipples, pinching as he murmured wonderfully dirty things while Finn fucked me in front of him.

"Do you know how hot it is to see you get fucked like this, kitten?" he asked after a while. "Watching him disappear inside you, to see your body take that dick so fucking good? Your ass shakes every time he buries himself in you and all I can think about is—" He stopped, interrupting himself with a slow, husky laugh. "Well."

"What?" I gasped. "Tell me."

"You sure you want to hear it?"

"Yes."

"Yes, what?"

I fought back a smile. Zain didn't have a Daddy kink, my *ass*. "Yes, Daddy."

He leaned in so his lips were beside my ear and the deep rumble of his voice felt like it was vibrating inside me.

"All I can think about is how bad I want to fuck you when he's done." His hand moved off my breast and slid down my stomach, caressing it before he moved his fingers down further and further until he reached my clit. "How badly I want to get my cock in that messy little pussy and fuck his cum back inside you, then fill you up myself so when one of us puts a baby in you, you have no fucking idea who it was. I can't fucking wait to see your pussy dripping with all that cum, kitten, and—"

He said something else, but I didn't care what it was. My orgasm hit, hard and intense, as he fingered my clit while Finn fucked me. I cried out, handfuls of couch cushion fabric nowhere near strong enough to keep me grounded as ecstasy burst through me. I felt Zain laugh, his breath warm on my ear a moment before he kissed my cheek. As soon as the waves of pleasure faded enough for me to relax and slump forward, he moved his hand to my chin and forced me to lift my head. Dipping down, he kissed me one more time before moving away so I could catch my breath.

Once I had, I looked up at him. He was still kneeling on the couch in front of me, watching with heavy lidded eyes as Finn kept moving inside me. His cock was half-hard and he didn't have to say a word before I reached forward, touching his thigh, and opened my mouth.

"Good girl," he said, and even though that wasn't really my thing, I moaned as he stuck his cock in my mouth.

"Oh, God," Finn groaned behind me.

"Does she feel good?" Zain asked.

"Of course she does," Finn said, his voice strained. "But that… watching you fuck her face while I fuck her like this…"

"But I'm not fucking her face," Zain said. "That would look more like this."

Thank God he wasn't fully hard yet, because as good as I was at taking a cock down my throat, I was not ready for the moment he grabbed my hair and thrust himself as deep as he could go. I gagged and glared at up at him, but Zain just smiled

"Relax your throat, kitten. Don't you want Finn to see how well you can take a cock in your mouth?"

Finn already knew how well I could take a cock in my mouth, I wanted to say, but in fairness, I did want him to see me do it to someone else, too. So even though I was still glaring at him, I relaxed my throat, taking a deep breath before Zain thrust forward again.

"Oh my God," Finn murmured, and his next thrust inside me was even deeper than before.

It didn't take long for Zain to start matching Finn's pace. My breathing came in loud gasps through my nose, punctuated by the wet sound of Zain's cock hitting the back of my throat. His hand was on my head, pulling my hair back from my forehead as he whispered how good it felt, how he loved how his cock fit in my throat, how he thought about this view all the time and still couldn't get enough of it.

He kept talking in that low, husky voice until I felt Finn shift behind me.

"What are you—" I heard Zain start to say, but if he finished the sentence, he was an idiot. Because I figured out what Finn was doing the moment his long body hunched over and his chest pressed against my back. Zain's hand loosened on my head and I pulled back, letting his cock go with a soft pop.

Finn was tall enough that he could lean all the way forward and still be able to bury himself inside me while he opened his mouth to take Zain's cock again. I caught my breath as Zain groaned, his other hand moving to pull back Finn's blonde hair.

"So fucking hot," he mumbled. "Bud, you are so fucking hot, it's killing me."

Finn tried to not to smile around Zain's cock, but he still hadn't quite mastered that. He let Zain's cock fall from his mouth, but before I could replace his mouth with mine, he groaned loudly and squeezed his eyes shut.

"Fuck," he said. "I'm so fucking close."

"Good. Because as soon as you fill up that pretty little pussy of Tessa's, it's my turn." Zain's voice was thick and heavy again. "And I'm gonna make you sit here and hold her while I fuck her. I want her back to you, sitting between your legs with your arms around her so you can feel her shake while I make her come all over my cock with both our loads inside her. Sound good, bud?"

"Yes," Finn said. "Yes, fuck, yes, just... fuck. I'm gonna come."

"Good boy," Zain said, and I swear to God, if I didn't know it was physically impossible, I would've sworn Finn came so hard that it ended up in the base of my throat. His cock twitched and throbbed, sending spikes of pleasure through my body as warm cum spilled inside me. He leaned forward, his breath hot against my skin, choked sounds of overwhelmed pleasure muffled against my shoulder. It was only when he finally let out a quiet groan that I heard Zain chuckle.

"Sit up, bud," Zain said. "Hold her for me while I take my turn."

"Jeez, Zain," I said. "Give him a second to—"

But a surprised gasp cut the rest of my concern for Finn off as he put his arms around me and pulled me up. He moved us onto the couch, leaning against the backrest and bringing me between his spread legs so his half-hard cock pressed against the small of my back. Blinking, I looked at Zain, who had his hand around his cock and an almost evil smirk on his face.

"Hold her open for me, baby," he ordered, and Finn didn't hesitate before sliding his strong arms between my thighs and wrenching my legs apart, displaying my leaking pussy for Zain.

"Fuck, yes," Zain hissed, his voice low as he crawled onto the bed. "Look at you, kitten. Look at you all full of cum and spread wide for me." He dipped his head down unexpectedly and in one smooth movement, ran his tongue along my slit, tasting the cum Finn had just left there.

"Oh, yes," Finn whispered behind me. "Fuck, that's hot."

"I thought you wanted my pussy full of cum from both of you," I asked, trying to squirm beneath the firm grip both of them had on my legs.

"There's plenty left," Zain said, then lapped at me again before letting go of my legs so he could inch forward again. "I'm pretty sure we drained every last drop out of Finn's balls."

"And then some," Finn muttered.

Zain laughed as he positioned himself at my pussy. "Ready, Teacup?"

"You're the one who's wasting time being all—*ahhh*."

Zain groaned as he thrust inside me. Suddenly his body was pressed to mine and I was surrounded, Finn on one side holding me wide open and Zain on the other, belly to belly and hip to hip, his cock buried in me as deep as it would go.

"Perfect," he groaned. "Fuck, kitten. I thought your greedy little pussy was the sweetest thing I'd ever felt as it was, but now with his cum inside you... fuck."

He pulled back, then shoved inside me again. I let out another cry and he leaned in, covering my mouth in his as he did it again and again, wet, sloppy sounds filling the room as he found a deep and intense rhythm to fuck me. I moaned, trying to shift my hips so his pelvis would rub against my clit each time he pushed inside me, but the angle wasn't quite right.

"What do you need, kitten?" Zain asked as I whimpered.

"My clit," I gasped. "I wanna come again."

"Let go of her leg and finger her," he ordered, and Finn's hand slid between our bodies a second later. He fumbled for a moment or two, mostly because Zain's body kept trapping his hand since he didn't stop rutting against me while Finn tried to find my clit. Once his thick fingertips were on it, though, it wasn't long before I was teetering on the edge of bliss.

What set me over the edge, though, wasn't Zain's cock or Finn's fingers.

It wasn't the moment Zain kissed me, either. And it wasn't the moment he stopped kissing me so he could move his head past mine and capture Finn's lips again, although it was close. It wasn't the soft noise of appreciation Finn made or the muffled moan Zain responded with.

No, it was what he said.

"I cannot wait until I can fuck your mouth good and proper," he whispered to Finn. "You're going to look so good with my cock in your throat, baby."

And like, Zain's mouth was so good that he wasn't even dirty talking to me and it could make me come.

Which it did. I wailed as my orgasm hit me, my body desperate to writhe and squirm within the uncontrollable bliss exploding out from my core, but I couldn't. Not with Finn's strong hands holding me in place and Zain's body heavy against mine as he kept pounding me. So instead, that almost torturous intensity dragged out, the muscles in my core tensing as I shook in their arms, so consumed by my orgasm that I didn't even hear what Zain said as he started coming.

Which was too bad, because knowing Zain, it was something wonderfully filthy.

Just as the last surges of ecstasy wracked my body, Zain finished, too. He held still for a moment before heaving a huge breath and slowly, carefully pulling out so he could look at the cum dripping out of me.

My couch wasn't particularly large, but the three of us managed to collapse against it comfortably as the hazy afterglow of exhaustion enveloped us. Finn didn't seem to mind that I was using his shoulder as a pillow, and Zain's fingers were absentmindedly tracing patterns on my thigh after I'd hooked my leg over his.

For a while, none of us spoke. I don't know that any of us knew what to say. I didn't, even as the most experienced threesome-haver in the room. Because that... that had been nothing like anything I'd ever done before. That had been... well.

For the first time in a very, very long time, I couldn't lie to myself.

That should've scared me, maybe. Lying to myself came as naturally as breathing sometimes. I didn't know what it said about me that I could recognize that fact as easily as I ignored it.

And I'd lied to myself about both of these boys before. I'd lied about Finn even back when it had been Finn-and-Julie instead of just Finn. I'd lied about it being a one-time thing, about staying the night, about him being just a friend. And I'd lied about Zain, about how he made me feel.

About being able to be just friends who also sometimes fucked.

But right then, the only lying I could do was what I was already doing: between them with our bodies intertwined, the entire area between my legs slick and sticky with part of each of them, my nerves still firing randomly after the two of them made me come so hard I saw stars.

I couldn't lie to myself, but that didn't mean I had to recognize what I was feeling. So instead of acknowledging it, instead of letting the realization that everything had changed wash over me, I just waited until we'd caught our breaths, then tilted my head towards Zain.

"So your job interview went well, then?" I asked.

He inhaled, paused, then let out a tired chuckle. "I'd say it was the second best part of my day, Teacup."

IN NO WAY, SHAPE, or form should two adult men and one adult woman be able to sleep comfortably in one queen-size bed.

A king-size bed was stretching it, honestly. Finn and Julie used to have a king-size bed, so I would know. Granted, Finn was Viking-esque in stature and I was a delightfully chunky ball of roundness and Julie was smack dab in the middle of midsized. Zain might've been a touch thinner than she was, but regardless, the fact remained that three adult humans should not have been comfortable in my queen-size bed with a mattress that should've probably been replaced three or four years earlier.

And yet, the sleep I had nestled between those two men was the best I'd had in years.

We hadn't gone to sleep right after fucking. I mean, obviously. Rehydration was very necessary, as was a little thing called food.

Though, if it wasn't for the fact that Finn's stomach rumbled so intensely that I'd felt it vibrate against my side, I'm not sure we would've gotten up from the couch. Even after the round of giggles that resulted from that epic stomach growl, we were reluctant to untangle ourselves.

Which was good.

I think.

It meant things weren't awkward. It meant that when we finally did get up and get dressed, there were casual touches and nonchalant kisses and laughter as Finn and I played rock-paper-scissors to see who would have to go upstairs and face Dottie in order to get Alfie back, since he'd been upstairs the entire time.

It meant we ordered food, since no one felt like cooking, and talked with a sort of homelike ease that shouldn't have come so naturally to us.

Not when Zain and Finn had only just met.

Not when this was all so new.

But that was how we spent most of the night: talking, joking, eating dinner, curling up on the couch to watch TV since we'd exhausted ourselves fucking. Zain had whined when Finn and I vetoed his suggestion of watching some action movie in favour of binging a few episodes of *Thirty-Year-Old Grandma*, but was placated when we let him sit in the middle of the couch so Finn's arm was around his shoulders as held me against his chest. Alfie joined us, settling on Finn's lap and snoozing away his exhaustion of yet another day "playing with" Millie.

It might not have seemed like much of an exciting night, but it was one of the best Friday nights I could remember.

The only moment of awkwardness came later in the evening, when Finn's breathing turned deep and steady, only for him to jolt a few moments later as his head fell forward.

"Tired, bud?" Zain asked.

Finn laughed, his face turning red and his voice hoarse. "Yeah, I think so."

"Same," I said with a yawn.

"The antics of the thirty-year-old grandmas aren't enough to keep you awake?" Zain asked. "Although, that one says she's thirty-seven, so I don't think she qualifies to be on the show."

"Yeah, I think they're running out of options," I said. "Soon it'll be forty-year-old grandmas, then fifty-year-old grandmas, then just... grandmas."

Zain snorted, but moved his arm so I could sit up and stretch. "So, time for bed, then?"

And the answer to that was yes.

But the answer to that was also silence.

Because none of us knew how to ask how this was going to work. I could feel Zain's eyes on me, but I couldn't bring myself to look at him. It didn't feel right to relegate anyone to the couch, but I didn't think my bed was going to be big enough for the three of us.

"It's fine," Zain said after an awkward moment of silence. "I'll take the couch again."

"No," Finn said. "I'm taking it tonight."

"Bud, it's not long enough for you to be comfortable," Zain said.

I bit my lip. "I mean, I could—"

"No," they said in unison.

"Why not?"

"I'm not kicking you out of your own bed," Zain said.

"What is it with you and insisting on sleeping on the couch?" I asked.

"In this case, it makes the most sense unless you want to have all three of us squished into a queen-size all night."

That statement was also answered with silence. I pressed my lips together and glanced at Finn. He blinked at me, then looked at Zain, his mouth twisted to the side. Zain looked at Finn, then at me, then raised his eyebrows.

"You think the three of us can share your bed?"

"I mean, we can try," I said. "Someone can always move if it doesn't work."

"It'll be cozy," Finn added.

"And Finn's a cuddler, so he doesn't take up as much space as you think he does."

"It's true," Finn said. "I mean, you could probably sleep on top of me and I'd be fine."

Which was also likely true, even though no one slept on top of Finn that night. We ended up curled up with Finn behind me, one arm slung over my body and resting against Zain's arm, who had his hand resting on my hip. I had one of my legs on top of Zain's, not quite hooked around him, but that was because he had one of his legs between mine.

It shouldn't have worked. I should've been overheated, pressed between their bodies like that. Or claustrophobic, even, not able to roll over or move during the night. I should've been annoyed by the feel of Finn breathing on the top of my head or the way my hair kept brushing against my face because of Zain's breath in front of me.

It shouldn't have worked, but I was asleep within minutes, and when soft, deep voices stirred me out of sleep the following morning, I was still in the same spot, cozy and warm and safe in their arms.

It was a gentle kind of wake up, the kind where my mind slowly took on awareness, my eyes still closed as I floated up into consciousness. For a moment, I couldn't tell what the voices were saying, just heard they were there, as indistinct as waves washing up on the shore. But slowly, they became more defined, hushed words being murmured somewhere over my head, and I blinked my eyes open.

I was looking at the lines of one of Zain's tattoos scrawling across his collarbone near the base of his neck. My head was tilted, forehead not quite pressed against him, but close. The weight of Finn's arm was still heavy across my body and for a moment, I lay there, listening to the two of them talk.

"…best sleep I've had in a while," Finn was saying.

"I mean, you've been sleeping in your car," Zain replied. "So that's not saying much."

"Not in the last week, though," Finn said. "I've been here."

"True," Zain admitted.

It sounded like they'd only just woken up. Zain's voice was still hoarse with sleepiness and Finn's words were looped together in a gentle murmur. They were quiet for a moment, not moving, until Zain's fingertip twitched against my hip.

"How are you feeling about last night?" he asked.

"About the same as I always do."

"Really?"

"Yeah. I mean, nights are okay but I'm more of a morning person."

"I mean about what we did last night," Zain patiently said.

"Oh. I feel pretty good about it. Do you not?"

"No, I do. I just wanted to check in. See if you were having any second thoughts."

I felt Finn chuckle. "Zain, I barely have first thoughts sometimes."

Zain didn't laugh, but there was a smile in his voice when he spoke again. "Well, I like how your thoughts work. But it was also your first time doing anything like this with another guy. And, like, you... you came out, bud. Those are some pretty big things."

"Yeah, I guess," Finn said. "But I still feel good about it. I mean, I came so hard I thought my dick might explode but it didn't, so that's a good thing."

"Alright, good." There was another pause, then Zain shifted before speaking again. "Can I ask you something kinda personal?"

"Your dick's been in my mouth. You can ask me anything you want."

That time, Zain chuckled. "Okay, well... I just... what did you think 'straight' meant?"

"What?"

"You said you were straight but that you were into guys. I'm just trying to figure out the... the way you thought of that."

"Oh," Finn said. "I thought it meant that you'd only been with people who weren't the same gender or whatever. And like, I've never met a guy who wanted to hook up with me, so I just, like, didn't, I guess."

"I find it hard to believe no guys wanted to hook up with you."

"They didn't say anything, if they did." Finn paused. "Or maybe they did and I just didn't notice. That happens sometimes."

That seemed more likely to me, but Zain didn't say anything about it.

"Well, either way, I just... you know. Wanted to make sure you were okay with what happened."

"I am," Finn said, his voice warm.

"Good."

There was a pause.

"I mean, it was just the basics though," Finn said.

"It was," Zain agreed.

"Which means there's probably non-basic stuff that would be possible."

"There is," Zain said.

Neither of them spoke for a moment

"Are you wanting to talk about what that non-basic stuff might be?" Zain asked, his voice amused.

Behind me, Finn's cock twitched.

"Yeah," he said. "I think I wanna do more."

"Like what?"

"I mean, I'm pretty much good with anything."

"Anything," Zain repeated. "You're gonna let me do anything I want to you?"

"I think so," Finn said. "It depends on what it is. But I dunno what I don't know, right?"

"Well, you let me put my cock in your mouth. And you said I could put yours in mine," Zain said. "I'm guessing that means I can do things like stroke your cock or get Tessa to press both of us together and jack us off at the same time."

"I'd be up for trying that," Finn said.

"And what about your ass? Have you ever done anything there?"

"Tess and I have talked about it, but we haven't done anything." There was another pause and when Finn spoke again, I could almost picture his face, his eyes round as realization dawned on it. "Are you gonna fuck me? Like that?"

Zain's chest rose as he took a deep breath. I bit my lip, heat rushing through my body as I waited for him to respond.

"No," he said.

That surprised me as much as it seemed to surprise Finn. "Oh. Okay."

"Not yet," he said. "Not today. Another time, we can see where things go. But like, when you first started fooling around with girls, you didn't jump right into full sex. It's the same thing here. We'll... build up to that."

Finn didn't seem phased by the implication that they would be doing this again, even though I kind of was. I mean, I shouldn't have been, considering I'd said last night that I wanted to keep doing this, but it still seemed like a foreign concept.

"Okay," Finn said. "I get that. It probably takes like, some work and stuff, right?"

"Some," Zain said. "It's worth it, though."

"Have you ever...?"

"Yeah," Zain said. "Plenty of times. I'll let you do it to me at some point, if you want."

Finn's cock nudged against my ass and I almost moaned.

"Yeah, probably," Finn said. "I just, like... what does it feel like?"

"Worried it'll hurt?"

"Yeah."

"It might at first," Zain said. "A little, anyway. I mean, we'd try to make it not hurt, of course, but if it does, it usually only lasts for a moment. Then..." He trailed off, pausing, and his cock pressed against my thigh.

"Then what?"

"Then if you're with the right kind of person, it feels incredible. Someone who's fucking you to make you feel good as much as they are themself. 'Cause there are definitely guys out there who just want to use your ass to get off. But then there are the guys who want to make sure their cock is at the perfect angle to hit your spot every single time. The ones who jack you off while they're fucking you. The ones who want you to come like you've never come before."

"Please tell me you're one of those guys," Finn said

Zain laughed. "Bud, I don't even want to think about finishing until I've fucked every drop of cum out of your body."

Both of them were hard as stone. Finn was trying not to move, even though I could tell from the tension of his body that he wanted to grind against me. Zain wasn't as still, his hips moving forward every couple of moments, so gently that it wouldn't have woken me even if I'd been asleep.

"Damn," Finn breathed. "You're gonna say that and then make me wait for it?"

"It'll be worth it," Zain promised. "But in the meantime, I might not be able to stay away completely. Like maybe I'm gonna have to explore a bit, see how tight you are, you know? So I can imagine just how good it'll be to have my cock inside you. Or maybe while Tessa has your cock in her mouth, I'll have my fingers inside you, making you drip pre-cum down her throat."

"Right," Finn said, clearing his throat. "When, uh, could we like... try that?"

"I mean, I don't have to leave for a while, so if you want, we can try it as soon as Teacup stops pretending to be asleep."

The asshole.

"I'm not faking being asleep," I said. "You two were talking and I was politely letting you finish your conversation."

"Sure you were," Zain said.

"I was." I shifted back, sliding my hand between my body and his. "On what planet would you think anyone could still be asleep when I had these pressing into me?"

I cupped the bulge in his boxers while simultaneously pushing my ass back against Finn's erection. Both men groaned and Finn's arm tightened around me.

"Sorry," he said. "I was trying not to... you know. While you were sleeping."

"Don't apologize," I said. "I liked it. And I wasn't sleeping."

Finn groaned again, then pushed forward so he could rub his cock against me. I smiled, looking up at Zain, who had a glimmer in his eye as he leaned in to kiss me.

"Morning, Teacup," he said against my lips. "Were you getting all horny listening to me tell Finn about the things I'm going to do to his ass?"

"I think you know the answer to that."

"I think you should tell me."

"I think you should find out for yourself."

He smirked, then he moved his hand between my legs. Even through the fabric of my panties, I knew he could feel the heat and wetness pooling there.

"Oh, kitten," he whispered. "Fuck. You're so wet already."

"I am," I said. "And it's entirely your fault, so you better do something about it."

And oh, he did... not.

But only because he made Finn do it for him.

Sixteen

Some people may have thought that an unplanned pansexual awakening and subsequent threesome could have made things weird with me and Finn.

Those people did not know Finn.

I had thought Zain would stay in Vancouver the whole weekend, too, but he'd apparently promised his mom he'd go to Burnsley for dinner on Sunday, so he'd booked his flight for Saturday afternoon. It ended up working out since I had Kira's baby shower in the afternoon and Finn had planned to go over to his parents' place for a visit. So he offered to bring Zain to the airport before he visited them while Chuck stopped by to pick me up for Kira's baby shower.

When I got home after the baby shower and subsequent sangria-drinking with Chuck and Kira, who had never met before but got along as well as I'd hoped they would, Finn was already back and was vacuuming the living room. The sight of that was as sexy as when he was in my kitchen wearing the teal ruffled apron, but I held myself back as I closed the door behind me. It was the first time he and I had been alone since everything had gone down, and I wasn't sure how he was feeling.

But the moment he saw me, he switched off the vacuum and smiled brightly.

"Hey, Tess!" he said. "I hope you don't mind, but I saw your vacuum in the closet and thought I'd get some cleaning done. I didn't know what to do with the clothes you had on the floor in the bedroom so I put them through the wash, but don't worry. I checked the tags and made sure nothing was going to get messed up in the dryer." He grimaced almost bashfully. "I made that mistake on Julie once. She was nice about it, but I still felt bad about the sweater. It was her favourite cardigan."

"You vacuumed and did my laundry?" I repeated.

"Most of it," he said. "I didn't fold the second load yet."

"Would you like a blowjob?" I asked.

He frowned. "Is that a trick question?"

"No," I said. "I am literally offering you a blowjob because I can't think of a better way to express how amazing it was for you to do all that for me."

He grinned. "You don't need to give me a blowjob for that. I wasn't doing much anyway and I like helping out. Although..."

"Although what?"

He bit his lip. "Look, I'm not one for turning a blowjob down, but could we, like, go for a walk or something together? Like take Alfie and Millie out, or maybe even go to Spanish Banks?"

Something warm and fuzzy spread through my chest at the realization that Finn wanted to hang out with me. Something that triggered a spark of worry that I didn't want to address. So I ignored it and smiled at Finn.

"For sure. Let me get changed and I'll run upstairs and get Millie."

Which was a bad idea, since the moment Dottie saw me, she clasped a surprisingly strong hand around my forearm and tugged me into her entrance way.

"What are you doing, you deranged old hag?" I gasped, nearly tripping on the threshold as Millie bounded forward and jumped on my shins.

"Not letting you escape, you lucky little hoe," Dottie said, closing the door behind her. "I want details, and I want them now."

"Details of what?"

She gave me an unimpressed look. "Am I old? Yes. Are my eyes what they used to be? No. But I didn't spend a stupid amount of money for these progressive lenses to have you imply I couldn't see that *second* fine young man coming and going from your place over the past two days."

"Oh," I said. "That."

"Yes, that!"

"He's just a friend."

"Oh, of course," she said. "And this 'friend' causes you to make the same noises as that other 'friend'…"

"Jesus, do you press a glass up to the floor and listen in or something?"

"Of course not. I drilled a hole in my bedroom floor so I could hear what's going on in yours better," she said. "Not that I needed to because you're like a bobcat in heat, but—"

"I am not!"

"Which one are you calling Daddy?" she asked pointedly.

I rarely got embarrassed easily, but that made my face go red. "Oh my God. Did you actually drill a hole in the floor?"

Dottie rolled her eyes. "No, dumbass. But it's not like my husband soundproofed the house thinking one day I'd have to renovate the downstairs and start renting it out to a little hoe who keeps pulling in the finest damn men I've seen since said husband passed on."

"I can't believe you heard me call him Daddy," I said.

She shrugged. "Whatever chickens your nugget, small fry."

"Whatever… are you hungry or something?"

"Not the point." She folded her arms across her chest. "So? Details. Tell me everything. Do the boys… do things together? Or just with you? Because I know Finn's car was parked in the driveway all night and I didn't see that other one leave until both of them went out today."

There was no getting out of the conversation without giving Dottie at least a bit of information, so I told her that yes, Zain was incredibly hot, and yes, his name was Zain and he was my brother's best friend and yes, I called him Daddy and it started as a joke but he liked it so it stuck. By then, Millie started whining at my feet and pawing at the door, so I said

I'd stop by later that week with more details and to stop putting her ears up to the vents and listening to me and Finn fuck.

I thought maybe the reason Finn wanted to go for a walk together was that he wanted to talk, but when we got to the dog beach, he was his typical Finn self. He seemed to have as much fun as Millie and Alfie did as he played with them, throwing a tennis ball and laughing as they chased each other across the sand. It was only once the dogs had gotten most of their excitement out and were exploring and sniffing every branch and rock they came across that I managed to get him to focus long enough to ask a question.

"How are you feeling about last night and this morning?" I asked as we walked along the beach.

"Still good," he said. "Honestly, Tess, I know you and Zain seem to think I should be freaking out about things, but I'm not. I feel good about all of it." He laughed. "Although, I guess I do feel a bit silly for not knowing what 'straight' was for so long. I'm gonna have to tell Julie about this because it's kinda funny, don't you think? That we both didn't know even though it was probably kinda obvious?"

I smiled. "It is a little funny."

He grinned. "Right? But like, it's okay. I'm okay. Are you okay?"

"I'm okay," I said. "And how did your visit with your family go?"

Some of the brightness faded off Finn's face, but his smile didn't disappear. "They're alright. My dad's in good spirits. Still no surgery date or anything yet but they just said to be ready because it might be a couple of weeks, it might be a couple of months, it'll just depend on when they can get him in. Which like, silver linings, right? 'Cause it's not so severe that he needs surgery right this second. And they're keeping an eye on things so if it does get worse, they'll reevaluate. Waiting just sucks 'cause there's not much else we can do in the meantime, you know? But actually, I was wondering something."

"What's that?"

"Like, I know this me living with you thing isn't permanent or whatever, but since Dottie said she's cool with watching Alfie if I help around the house and stuff, would you be cool with me spending Fridays over at my parents? Then I can go over and help my dad a bit and give Hailey a day off from helping out or whatever."

"Of course," I said. "That's not an issue at all."

"It means I might not be around to cook that night," he said. "Except I will this week 'cause Ian's got an appointment that Mom is taking him to."

"You don't have to cook for me every night, Finn."

"Yeah, but I like to," he said. "And I wanna give you some rent money. So you need to tell me what that costs and stuff."

I told him it wasn't a huge deal, but he insisted. Part of me worried. I mean, it was natural, wasn't it? Because cooking for me was one thing, but him giving me rent money meant he wasn't just staying with me. He was living with me.

But it was only a small part of me that was worried. The rest was oddly okay with it in a way that was almost scary.

My life fell into something over the next week. Not a routine, since nothing about it was routine at all, but whatever it was, it felt good. Chuck spent most of Monday telling me about the barbecue he'd had with Charles's parents and how Charles's dad sometimes got hockey tickets from work and said he'd love to go to a game, the three of them. And how Charles's mom had made a huge tray of this layered cake thing for dessert that he'd love so much, she'd insisted on sending the leftovers home with him, which he'd brought for lunch.

Just the cake leftovers. Nothing else. And it had to be at least half of a large lasagna tray that had been leftover because Chuck couldn't even eat the entire thing, despite having nothing else for lunch that day.

Loni continued going insane in her quest to find the office mole-mouse. On Wednesday, she burst into the office unexpectedly and

Dinah nearly faceplanted in the hallway in her rush to get all of us into the boardroom. Once we were there, Loni waited until the door was closed before slamming her hands onto the table.

"Brenda McClane," she declared, then looked at us expectantly.

There was a long pause as we all stared back at her.

"What?" Chuck finally said.

"Bren-da," Loni said slowly. "*Mc-Cla-ne.*"

"Is she... is she the mole?" Dinah guessed.

"What?" Loni asked.

"The mouse," Chuck said. "Is Brenda the betrayal mouse?"

"What? Of *course* not!" Loni scoffed. "Brenda McClane can be *trusted.*"

"Oh, good," Dinah said, her voice high.

"And do you know why?" Loni continued.

"I mean, I guess because she—"

"Because she is *loyal,*" Loni interrupted. "Because she was approached by the Martelle witch with a contract for a project and she turned. It. Down!" She emphasized each word by slapping her hand on the table. "*That* is the kind of loyalty we need from the people we work with. And that is why she would be the perfect double agent."

We spent the next fifteen minutes talking Loni out of approaching Brenda to ask her to "spy on ArtCycle" and report back to CARE. Especially since after she left, Chuck told us that he knew Brenda had been approached by Paige, and that she'd turned the contract down because she was retired and Paige wasn't offering nearly enough money for her to come out of said retirement.

After Loni left, I texted Claire to tell her about it and ask if Paige had approached Brenda for a real project or solely to piss Loni off, but unusually for Claire, she didn't get back to me right away. It wasn't until I got home from work that she texted me back, which I thought was odd since it would've been around three in the morning in Paris.

But it made more sense when she told me why.

CM

To answer your question, yes, it was totally an attempt by Paige to piss Loni off. She was talking about it at one of the runway shows a couple of days ago. In unrelated news, remember how Julie's here?

Me

No, I totally forgot that I suggested you take Julie to Paris with you. It seriously took you both this long to fuck?

CM

…yes

Me

So you did?

CM

Also yes.

I frowned at my phone. Claire wasn't a one or two word texter.

Me

Are you feeling okay?

It took her a while to message me back. Long enough that I almost considered calling her, despite knowing it would run my phone bill up a ridiculous amount.

CM

I am. It's been a weird week. I wasn't going to. Like, with being around Paige all week and everything you said about Julie not being able to do casual, I thought we could be friends and have a fun time. Go to the bars and stuff.

But she… I don't even know, Tess.

I think I like her.

Holy shit.

Me

That's amazing.

CM

Is it? Or is it terrifying? Because I barely want serious and I definitely don't want monogamy. But I also want to fall asleep every night with this chubby goddess who happens to be the sweetest person alive sitting on my face.

Me

I mean, I'm here to talk about it if you want, but it's ultimately up to you if it's terrifying or not.

CM

I'm not giving up what we have. That's a dealbreaker.

I raised my eyebrows at that.

Me

That sounds almost serious.

CM

> Because you're seriously my best friend. And I seriously don't think I've ever had a friend like you. And I seriously adore your pussy. I like her, but you're part of my package now.

Holy shit. It was a good thing Finn wasn't home from work yet because I was stunned, standing in the kitchen and staring at Claire's message. I mean, I thought Julie and Claire might hook up, but this… well.

There was a battle happening in my chest. Not one featuring upset or jealousy; no part of this involved jealousy, which I guess was a good sign. Because part of me was screaming, wanting to be ecstatic and thrilled for Claire. Wanting to celebrate that she was happy, that she was enjoying herself, that she and Julie had found something together, even if it wasn't clear what that something was.

But part of me remembered that final message on MatchMi, the one that wasn't even from Julie but from an automated system informing me I'd been blocked.

I didn't want Julie to hurt Claire.

But that was the risk I'd taken, I told myself. By suggesting they go to Paris together in the first place, I'd left it up to them to figure out. Claire knew what Julie had done to me. It wasn't like it was hidden. If she still liked her like that, it wasn't up to me to question her trust.

A nauseous sense of pride in myself hit me. I wasn't sure I was a fan of the feeling, but apparently I was having a week of personal growth or something.

I heard from Zain a couple of times that week, though that wasn't unusual. We texted semi-regularly, usually about stupid things. Zain loved a good meme and I loved a good video featuring puppies, so that was most of what we sent back and forth. But that week, I'd sent him the same question I'd asked Finn about how he was feeling with what had happened with the three of us.

Z Biggest Asshole

> Physically, a bit tired still. Making the two of you come like that takes a lot out of a guy.

Me

> And emotionally?

Z Biggest Asshole

> Emotionally wishing Vancouver was a lot closer to Vernon than it is.

I pretended that didn't make me smile, but it did. That he wished he was closer, I mean. Because the fact that Vancouver wasn't close to Vernon was not something to smile about, but there was also nothing any of us could do about that.

Or so I thought.

"Ugh, what a fucking nightmare," I groaned as soon as I opened the door when I got home on Friday. Finn was in the kitchen wearing his teal apron and a sweet-and-sticky garlicky scent was filling the house.

"What was a nightmare?" Finn asked.

"The bus," I grumbled, dropping my work bag on the floor for Alfie to sniff as I reached up my shirt to unhook my bra. "I'm pretty sure it was a new driver. Like, a new-new driver who probably just got their license or something because they drove so freaking slow." I hung up my bra on the hook and turned around. "And then there was construction on the—"

And then I stopped, my mouth half open as I saw Zain sitting on the couch.

"Wha—"

"Surprise!" Finn said.

"Hey Teacup," Zain said.

I waited for him to say, you know, something more, but his gaze was firmly glued to my now-braless chest. I waited for another moment, thinking he'd look up, but he didn't.

"Um, hello?" I said, half-amused. "My eyes are up here."

"What good does that do me when your tits are down there?" he asked, still staring.

"You're horrible," I said.

"What? You're the one who walked in and immediately started taking clothes off." He finally looked up, a smirk on his face hiding the excited smile in his eyes. "I'm just appreciating the view, kitten."

"Don't *kitten* me," I said, mostly because there was no way we had time for him to do what that word made me want him to do before dinner was ready. "What are you doing here?"

He shrugged, then stood up. "I'm trying to use some of my built up vacation time before I quit, so I decided to take Fridays off for the rest of the summer. Helps for scheduling interviews since I don't have to book a day off and make them suspicious. And Finn and I were talking a couple days ago—"

"You were?" I asked.

"Uh... yeah?" Zain said. "Why wouldn't we?"

"I didn't know you had each other's numbers."

"Well, we did this thing where we exchanged them after we slept together last weekend," he said. "We didn't think to include you in said exchange since we both already had your numbers."

"Yeah, but you could've made a group chat with me or something," I grumbled.

Finn laughed from behind me. "I told you, man!"

"You did," Zain said, shaking his head with a resigned look on his face. "Told you what?" I asked.

"I said we shouldn't make one until after this weekend because this way, we could surprise you with me showing up," Zain said. "Finn said you'd be upset you weren't in our chat."

"I'm not upset," I said. "Just... annoyed."

"Pretty sure those are synonyms," Zain said, stepping towards me as his voice lowered. "But we both agreed that if you were, it would be entirely my fault. Can you forgive me, Teacup?"

"No," I muttered, folding my arms.

"Not even if I promise to, I dunno, use my tongue on your clit while Finn fucks you?"

I twisted my mouth to the side. "Well..."

He knew he'd won long before that moment, but smiled as if he was relieved all the same. "Do you forgive me enough to kiss me hello?"

And of course I did. Him and Finn both.

Seventeen

"I THINK THE DISHES need to soak," Zain said, coming up behind me after dinner.

I looked down at the mostly clean plates I'd put in the sink while the tap was running. "Is that so?"

"Yeah." His lips pressed against my neck and it took everything in me not to shiver. "I think we've waited long enough to get started."

"You two didn't start without me while I was at work?"

"You think we'd start without you, Teacup?" he asked.

"Why not?" I replied. "It's not like Finn and I didn't touch each other all week."

"I mean, we kissed a little," Finn said as he brought the rest of the dishes over. "But that was it."

I bit my lip, trying not to let on how much the image of the two of them making out got me going. "You could have done more. I wouldn't have been mad."

"Noted for next time," Zain said before kissing my neck again. "But this time, both of us have been sitting around thinking about how good that hot, wet pussy is going to feel when we take turns fucking it. And how you make the most delicious, sloppy sounds when we fuck your throat. I was hoping to find out if I make those same sounds when Finn fucks mine."

Fuck.

Fucking Zain and his fucking mouth.

"But if you'd rather do the dishes," he said, letting go of my waist. "Finn and I can entertain ourselves."

"We can?" Finn said.

"Of course, bud. Come here."

Finn's breath hitched as Zain kissed him. There was a pause, then he let out a soft exhale that wasn't quite a moan but was vocal enough to make me want to shiver in excitement.

"Good boy," Zain murmured, and Finn moaned in earnest that time. And I couldn't take it anymore.

Drying my hands, I turned around. Zain drew me in naturally, shifting from kissing Finn to kissing me not like he'd been waiting for me to join them but like I was simply meant to be there at that moment. As we kissed, I put a hand on Finn's chest and he leaned in, his lips finding the side of my head and pressing a kiss there, too.

"Fuck, I missed you," Zain said against my lips. "Both of you."

I didn't respond. I couldn't. I didn't know what to say to that because the truth was that I'd missed them too. And that didn't make sense, at least not completely, because Finn had been here with me the whole time.

But I'd missed *them*. Together.

My ass hit the counter behind me as Zain nudged me forward. I kept my eyes closed, sighing as anonymous hands slipped up my shirt and down my ribs, tracing little patterns along my skin that made me shiver. Finn tucked himself in close, leaning down as Zain alternated between kissing him and kissing me, and I could feel his thick bulge on my hip. At the same time, I could feel Zain's erection pressed against my pelvis, his body resting heavily on mine as his kisses grew deeper.

And God, I wanted to touch them.

I slipped my hands between our bodies, moving them down slowly until I had their clothed cocks against my palms. It was almost funny, the twin noises they made, sighs of relief as I cupped them through their pants, and both of them ground their hips forward like they couldn't control it.

Okay, I lied. It was actually funny, and I couldn't stop myself from giggling.

"What?" Zain asked.

"I think we should move to the bedroom," I said.

To no one's surprise, both men agreed with me.

I was naked by the time we got there. I mean, it wasn't like I could walk and take my jeans off, so technically I was in the room when those came off, but the point was that by the time Finn and Zain entered the room, I was naked. Finn followed my lead, his shirt long gone and his pants on the floor seconds later.

Then it was just Zain who still had clothes on like a fucking heathen.

"This seems incredibly unfair and inconvenient," I said as he closed the door behind us.

"Inconvenient?" he repeated.

"How are you going to fuck me if you don't even take your pants off?"

"Begging me to fuck you already?" Zain asked.

"I'm not begging, I'm—"

It only took one smooth movement for him to step forward and slip his hand between my legs, using a gentle push forward to guide me to the bed and force me to sit. A thick finger nudged its way into my slit and I looked up at him as he hovered over me.

"Ask me nicely, kitten," he said.

"Or what?" I replied.

"Or I won't fuck you."

I grimaced, then huffed out an annoyed breath as the craving for friction grew to be too much. "Fuck me, *please*."

"Hmm," he said, making his finger dance along my slit again. "I don't know if you really want it. You didn't even throw a 'Daddy' in there."

"That's because I don't care which of you fucks me," I said. "But hey, if you want me to call Finn Daddy too—"

"Not a fucking chance," he growled. He took his hand from between my legs and unzipped his jeans. "Wanna hold her for me, Finn?"

"God, yes," Finn said, his voice heavy with arousal. "I love holding her while you fuck her."

"And I love fucking her while you hold her," Zain said. "Lie on your side with her ass in your lap for me. I want you to grind your cock against that perfect, thick ass of hers while I fuck her so you're nice and ready when I'm done and it's your turn."

"Yes, sir," Finn said, moving to the bed.

"Don't worry," Zain said, looking at me as I raised my eyebrows. "I know it'll be too much for you today, but if you ask nicely, maybe one day I'll let him take your ass while I take your pussy, kitten."

I blinked, my lips parted as I processed what he said—they were going to fuck me together, holding me between them as they both buried their cocks in me—but before I could react, Finn had guided me to lie down and was spooning me from behind. Zain joined us half a second later, pulling me in for a kiss as Finn pushed my ass cheeks apart and nestled his cock between them, letting out a pleased groan as he did.

"Perfect," Zain murmured, and then he reached down and lifted my leg over his hip so he could bring his body flush against mine.

His cock nudged against my center and I was sure that brief amount of contact had soaked him. I was dripping for them, dripping from the feel of their cocks and Zain's words and Finn's groans. Zain's mouth was twisted into a smirk as he gripped his cock, sliding the tip of it up and down my slit.

"Why aren't you fucking me?" I asked.

"You didn't ask properly," he said, then pushed forward and let just the head of his cock breach my entrance. "I mean, you said please, so I guess you can have the tip, but you knew what I wanted to hear, kitten."

"How is it that I'm in bed with two of you and yet neither of you want to fuck me right now?" I groaned.

"Whoa now," Zain said. "It's not that I *don't* want to fuck you, Teacup. I do, very much. I just also want to hear—"

"Daddy," I blurted. "You want me to call you Daddy because you pretend you don't, but you fucking love it when I call you Daddy and make you think about how badly you want me to make you one because all you can think about is putting a baby in me. So for fuck's sake, Daddy, just fuck me alread—*ahh*!"

I cried out, stars appearing in my vision as Zain pushed forward, burying as much of himself in me in one thrust as he could. It wasn't the whole thing, not when we were on our sides and I had a belly and my leg only went so high and there was another person behind me with his cock sandwiched in my ass cheeks, but it was enough.

I clutched at him as he moved, the tip of his cock at the perfect angle to hit my g-spot each time he sheathed himself in me. It was that odd sensation of relief but not quite satisfaction, of wanting more than what Zain was currently doing because I wanted it harder and faster and deeper so I could erupt in ecstasy all over his cock, but not *needing* it. Because even though he wasn't fully buried in me, even though he was matching the same slow, intense pace that Finn was as he rubbed against my ass, even though he was kissing me and holding me tight against his body in a way that made me feel dear and precious and wanted, it was slowly building up that sensation of overwhelming pleasure.

As was the way he was looking at me.

Because his eyes were on mine, deep and dark and full of something as vulnerable as it was exhilarated, holding my gaze as he pushed his cock inside me.

"Tessa," he breathed. "Fuck, Tessa, I..."

I kissed him.

It wasn't to cut him off. His words had trailed off before my lips met his. But there were words there, terrifying and true but unspoken.

And they had to stay that way.

"Don't stop, Daddy," I said against his lips.

The corners of his lips flicked up. "Don't you dare come, Teacup. Not yet."

I scoffed in offense. "But—"

"Nope." He kissed me harder. "I need you to hold onto it."

"For what?"

"For Finn," he said. "Because we're going to blow his fucking mind, Teacup. Together."

"But—" I protested again, but Zain cut me off with another kiss and thrust into me deeper.

"Don't you want to do that for Finn?" he asked.

"Yeah, but—"

"Don't you trust me yet, kitten?"

And God help me, but I did.

I trusted him enough to do what he said, even though it was almost torture to tell him to stop fucking me because I was too close to coming. And I trusted him enough not to sob as he pulled his dick out of me, stretching over my shoulder so he could give Finn one of his heated kisses before telling me to get on my back so Finn could take his turn with my pussy. I trusted him enough that I fought against coming as soon as Finn was inside me, gripping the sheets hard as Finn's cock stretched me even more than Zain's had.

"Keep fucking her, Finn," Zain ordered, and then he moved away.

I frowned, looking over Finn's shoulder to watch him. "Where are you going?"

Zain smirked. "I think Finn should see what it's like to have someone play with his asshole while he's fucking someone, don't you?"

"Yes, please," Finn gasped.

His thrusts slowed for a moment and despite knowing it would do nothing, I craned my neck, trying to see as much as I could happening over his shoulder. I could see Zain's face and chest, but not what his hands were doing. But that ended up being fine, since my mind insisted on filling the blanks in itself.

In my head, he had one hand on Finn's perfect ass, spreading him open as he ran his fingers along his crack. His fingers were glistening, probably with spit because he hadn't asked me where the lube was, and he was about to press the tip of one finger to Finn's puckered hole so that Finn—

"Oh, fuck," Finn groaned, and his pelvis pressed against mine as he filled my pussy completely.

"Relax, baby," Zain murmured, his eyes trained on Finn's gorgeous ass. "Hold still and relax. It's gonna feel so good."

"I know," Finn breathed. "It's just—"

"—something you haven't done before, I know." Suddenly Zain dipped down so I could only see the top of his head, and between my imagination and the sound Finn made, I knew he'd just pressed his lips against Finn's ass. "I promise you, it's gonna be so good, though."

"I can vouch for that," I whispered into Finn's ear. "I don't even have the same magic spot that guys have and it feels amazing."

"And I'm gonna make sure you're ready," Zain added.

"How?" Finn asked, a mix of interest and concern in his voice.

Zain didn't answer, but a second later, Finn inhaled sharply.

"What's he doing, Finn?" I said.

"Oh my God," Finn grunted. "His tongue is… he's… he's licking my butt, Tess."

"Do you like it?" I asked.

"I… I-I love it," he said. "Fuck, that's… that's…"

And whatever came out next was unintelligible. He ground his hips forward, his cock still buried deep inside me, and for a while that was how we stayed, Finn gently pumping his hips forward to grind against me, moaning and occasionally murmuring his disbelief that Zain's tongue was in his ass.

"Fuck," Zain muttered after a bit. A moment later, his voice was less muffled. "I can't believe this, but I can't hold on anymore. I need to come before I explode."

"Just from eating his ass?" I asked, confused.

"Yes, Tessa," Zain said in his dry, sarcastic voice. "It's definitely *just* from eating his ass and not the fact that I'm stroking my cock while I do it."

"Well I can't see that," I said.

"So you thought the thing that made the most sense was me needing to come because I was eating his ass?"

"Do what I was doing to Tessa," Finn said, ignoring both of us.

Zain's eyebrow flicked up. "I was going to get Tessa to—"

"No." Finn's voice cracked. "Fuck, Zain just... just rub it against me. Please."

"Fuck," Zain breathed. He hesitated, but a moment later he climbed on the bed behind Finn. I watched as he gripped Finn's hip, his eyes dark and heavy lidded as he pressed his body to Finn's. They both sighed and Finn's arms trembled a moment before he pulled out a bit. Zain groaned, his head tilting back, then Finn pushed his cock deeper inside me again. He moved slowly, grinding his ass back against Zain's cock before pushing forward, his eyes flickering closed as a look of bliss crossed his face.

"Look at this ass," Zain groaned. "It's so fucking good, bud. If you and Tessa put your asses in front of me and made me pick a favourite, I'd be there until I fucking died." He paused, his hand moving to Finn's lower back before disappearing from view. After a moment, Finn whimpered.

"And this pretty little hole," Zain continued. "So fucking tight and needy. I want to fuck this so bad, baby."

Finn groaned and I swore I felt his cock throb inside me. "Do it."

Zain looked up, his expression pained. "Finn, I—"

"*Please.*" Finn's voice broke again and his eyes opened. "Please, Zain, I don't want to wait. I want it. So much."

"But—"

Finn's body shifted, grinding back again, and Zain inhaled sharply. His eyes met mine, uncertain but wild with need. I glanced at Finn, who looked just as desperate, then looked back at Zain and nodded as subtly as I could. Zain took a breath, then let it out and caressed Finn's ass.

"Are you completely sure, bud?" he asked.

"Hundred percent," Finn grunted. "I want it. I've wanted it since you brought it up the first time."

"Lube's in the nightstand drawer," I said.

Zain's throat flexed as he swallowed, then he reached for the nightstand. Finn's face was flushed with excitement as he moved in and out of me slowly, like we both knew we weren't fucking to come just yet, but that we couldn't help ourselves from indulging.

"Can I stay like this?" he asked in a hushed voice.

"Inside me, you mean?" I asked.

He nodded.

"You fucking better," Zain said, and Finn half-laughed, half-groaned as Zain returned to the bed. "You better have that big cock buried in Tessa the whole time, because she doesn't get to come until you're going to. I want her to come all over that dick while I'm inside you, bud."

Oh, God

Zain needed to hurry up with the lube. The feel of Finn was already driving my body crazy, like my nerves were screaming out their frustration to find out why he was in me but not moving the way I needed. But the enjoyment of the whole thing drowned that out. I couldn't deny how much I loved the closeness of him, the connection, the way my pussy was dripping knowing how fucking good we were all about to feel.

And the wait was worth it.

It was worth it from the moment Zain breathed that Finn's ass was ready for him. From the moment Zain pressed the head of his cock to Finn's ass and Finn drew in a breath. From the way Finn's body tensed, then relaxed, as a low groan escaped his slightly parted lips.

"Good job, baby," Zain said. "You're taking it so good."

"Th-thanks," Finn gasped.

"That's just the tip," Zain said. "Think you can take more?"

"Uh-huh."

"You sure? Because I can—"

"More, Zain," Finn demanded, and even I had to chuckle that time.

"Whatever you say, boss," Zain murmured.

The noise Finn made just then was low and throaty. I felt his whole body tremble, quivering with tense pleasure, and a moment later, his hips started grinding forward against me.

"Fuck," he groaned. "Fuck, fuck... fuck... don't stop. Please don't stop, Zain."

"I'm not gonna stop, bud. Not till you fill our girl up with cum."

"Not gonna take long," Finn said, half-gasping and half-laughing.

And that was the fucking truth for all of us.

Because I couldn't have imagined how amazing it would feel. I hadn't gone into this thinking it was about me. I knew I'd get off eventually, but this was about Finn. But every thrust pushed Finn's cock deeper inside of me and it was like my mind couldn't keep track of what was happening. The cock inside me felt like Finn's, it stretched me like Finn's, the body spreading my hips wide open felt like Finn, but the way he moved—that was Zain. The rhythm was Zain. The intensity was Zain. Finn was moving too, but he was letting Zain control him, guide him, possess him as they fucked me together.

And the noises?

That was both of them.

That was all of us.

"I... I think..." Finn interrupted himself with an unintentional moan. He took a deep breath before he could continue, his voice coming out high-pitched. "I think I'm getting close."

"You think?" Zain asked, his voice strained.

"It's... it's kinda... different, I think. Something feels different."

"Oh, fuck yes," Zain groaned.

"Is that good?"

"So good. You're doing so good, baby." He started moving faster, his hips slapping against Finn's ass. "Teacup, start fingering that pretty little clit of yours. You're gonna come at the same time as him."

I shoved my hand between mine and Finn's bodies, rubbing my clit urgently. Finn's lips parted and his already pink cheeks began to turn red. I was fairly sure the way his body was trembling was the same as the third pattern setting on my favourite vibrator.

"Tell me when you're gonna come," I whispered. "I'm so close, Finn."

"Almost there," he gasped. "I'm... I'm... fuck, I'm gonna... T-Tess, I'm... Zain, I..."

And then he made a sound like I'd never heard before and I was lost.

I writhed beneath him, control of my body surrendered to pure elation in an agonizingly wonderful way. My back arched and I felt Finn's cock start to spasm, spilling inside me as he cried out his own bliss.

"Fuck," Zain swore suddenly. "I'm gonna come, baby. I'm gonna come in your ass."

"F-F-Fuck," Finn said, and his words were practically a sob. "Fuck, I-I... God, I can't stop c-c-*coming*."

"That's it," Zain said. "Give our girl every last drop, baby. Her pussy is so hungry for it, isn't it? Doesn't she feel so good to fill up like this?"

"Yes," Finn gasped. "Fuck, yes, it's... fuck."

I heard it all from the haze of my own orgasm. When I finally blinked myself back to reality, Finn was nearly keeled over and hunched against me. His breath was hot against my skin, choked sounds of overwhelmed pleasure muffled against my shoulder. It was only when he finally let out a quiet groan that I heard Zain chuckle, then felt Finn squirm and whimper slightly as Zain pulled out of Finn's ass. Finn rolled to the side shakily, though he wrapped his arms around me as he lay down. I held him close, feeling his breath heavy on my skin and the slick sweat on his shoulders as Zain joined us. He curled up behind Finn and leaned over him, kissing me gently.

"You okay?" he asked.

"Mm-hmm," I replied.

He kissed me again, then nuzzled against Finn's cheek. "You okay, bud?"

"Ungh," Finn replied.

Zain laughed almost nervously. "Did we break you?"

Finn nodded.

"Sorry," I said.

"Don't be sorry," he murmured, cuddling in closer to me as he reached back to pull Zain towards him. "Please just never stop breaking me."

And those words stuck with me for a long, long time.

Part 3

Confession: Bring her
flowers on the first date.

Eighteen

"You know, you might be a greedy little taint licker, but I don't think I've ever seen you so happy as I have these past couple months," Dottie said.

"Taint licker has turned into one of your go-to insults, eh?" I asked.

She shrugged as she sipped her iced tea. "Not my fault it's so accurate for you."

"You don't think I'm insulted you think I'm a taint licker?"

"You expect me to believe you're putting your mouth all over the junk of that tall drink of water there and that slightly shorter drink of water over there and not giving either of their taints attention?"

I looked at Finn, who was pushing the lawnmower across the yard, then to Zain, who was pulling weeds out of Dottie's flowerbed. "I mean, yeah, but not usually with my tongue."

Dottie cackled loud enough to catch Zain's attention. He glanced up, eyebrows raised, but she just waved at him nonchalantly.

"Don't mind me, sweet thing. Alfie's getting his freak on over here again and Millie gave him the what-for."

Zain smirked and shook his head, turning back to the weeding. In fairness, Dottie wasn't lying, though we'd stopped laughing about it a while ago since there was usually about a sixty percent chance that Alfie was trying to hump Millie at any given time.

"What a world," Dottie said, sighing as she sat back against her chair.

"What do you mean?"

"Sitting on my porch with the hoe downstairs, drinking iced tea, watching her boys care for my lawn like it's my own personal Chippendales show..." She laughed. "My dear husband wouldn't have believed it."

"That you're such a perv?"

"That you kids these days just do that." She motioned towards Finn and Zain again. "That you can openly be with whoever you want now."

I didn't tell Dottie the truth, which was that a lot of people couldn't openly be with whoever they wanted. Or that the three of us weren't openly with each other because my family still thought I was married and Zain's family didn't know he was bisexual and Finn's family... well. He was confident that they'd be accepting of him no matter what, but he was still waiting until he'd found a permanent place to live to tell them he was pansexual and polyamorous and also was no longer with Julie and hadn't been for months.

God, we were a bunch of liars.

And that didn't even begin to address that the only reason Finn was able to keep his breakup a secret from his mom, who had worked out of the same hospital that Julie had, was because Julie had come back from Paris and promptly quit her job. Now she was pursuing her new passion: travelling the world as Claire's "live-in personal assistant" because "sugar baby" wouldn't look as good on a potential future resume.

Not that she actually was a sugar baby. She and Claire did truly like each other. And that was a shock as much as it wasn't. I'd thought they would get along, but it wasn't until we got together after they got back that I really saw how much sense it made.

Claire had told me about it a few days after she got back from Paris. I knew something was up when, unlike most days, she didn't want to have the conversation while one of us was eating out the other.

"I need to tell you something," she'd said when I asked what was going on.

"What's that?"

Her throat had flexed as she swallowed and she couldn't look at me. "Julie and I are together. We're... dating."

I nodded as if I'd known that all along. "Exclusively?"

That got her to look at me. "Fuck no. I told you, you're part of my package. And I told her that, too. I mean, given your history, I would never ask or expect you to talk to her or have anything to do with her if you didn't want to. And the same goes for her, too, obviously. But I'm not losing my best friend over this. If it's an issue, I'll tell her—"

"You'll tell her nothing," I said. Claire's chin trembled, a mix of panic and fear sitting in her eyes, and I couldn't help myself from scooting closer to her on the bed. "It's not an issue."

"Tess, I'm feeling things about that girl," she said, her voice wavering. "If it bothers you—"

"It doesn't," I said. "You're my friend, Claire. I want you to be happy, more than anything. If Julie makes you happy, fucking go for it."

And that, surprisingly or not, was the truth.

Because yeah, I could have let it bother me. I could've held that grudge against Julie. I could've warned Claire yet again about what Julie had done to me, as though she'd forgotten and as though that one decision made in a moment of emotional terror should follow her for the rest of her life. I could've said forgive but never forget, that a tiger can't change its stripes, that once a ghoster, always a ghoster.

But why?

Julie and I had talked. She'd apologized. And I was apparently turning into the kind of person who had empathy and feelings and shit, so I was going to take the high road.

And when Claire took me to the VIP room at The Place for drinks with Julie and the infatuation between the two of them was so strong that I could almost taste it, I knew it was the right thing to do. Especially when Julie went to the bathroom and Claire took the opportunity to finger me furiously before she got back, the impish glimmer in her eyes and wicked smile on her face almost enough on their own to make me gush all over her hand.

But I didn't. Not until Julie was back in the room and folded her arms across her chest, watching with amusement as Claire worked my pussy beneath the table. She didn't move until I came on her girlfriend's fingers. Only once I was gasping for breath did she come forward, kissing Claire lightly before joining us on the bench.

"I hope you saved some energy for later, because that was hot as hell," she said.

"Princess, I always have energy for you," Claire said, and cheesy as it was, I couldn't stop myself from smiling as they kissed again.

Because the thing was, Dottie was right. I may have sidetracked the conversation by my inability to let her say the words "taint licker" without commenting on them, but the fact remained that I was happy.

Happier than I'd been for a long time.

And it wasn't just because of Claire or Finn or Zain. It was the casual after-work walks to grab coffee with Kira, sometimes with Velma in the stroller and sometimes just the two of us while Jackson watched the baby.

It was seeing Kira's joy and confidence as a mom grow as the shock and suddenness of Velma's arrival gave way to routine.

It was the snuggles with said baby as Velma's colic began going away and her inordinate gassiness gave way to countless giggles.

It was going for drinks with Chuck and Charles. And, after I'd brought Finn with me one time, it was Chuck demanding that Finn come with me every time not just because he wanted to stare longingly at Finn's ass whenever he could but because Finn and Charles got along like two labs at a dog park.

"Did you have any idea we have the same type?" Chuck had asked as we watched Charles and Finn with almost morbid fascination. They were about to launch into what felt like the third hour of discussing the intricacies of that year's NHL draft like they'd been friends for years instead of the aforementioned three hours.

"Hot and good in bed?" I replied. "I think a lot of people have that type."

"Hot, blonde, sporty sweethearts with puppy dog eyes, firm asses, and big di—"

"Babe, d'you remember which guy it was who scored the two goals when we went to the hockey game a while ago?" Charles asked suddenly, oblivious to the fact that Chuck had just revealed he had a big dick.

"Why, in any world, would I remember that?" Chuck asked.

"Because he was the one you said you'd let crush your head with his thighs if you saw him in a jockstrap."

"Oh, right," Chuck said. "I don't know his name. He was number twenty-nine."

"Shit," Charles said, shaking his head as he turned back to Finn. "You're right. It was game one."

"I told you he didn't score two in the second," Finn said, laughing as he sipped his piña colada.

"Yeah, I guess I should've known. We didn't see him get injured and that was game two, so—"

Chuck and I glanced at each other as Charles and Finn went back to their conversation.

"Exact same type," Chuck said.

"Apparently," I replied. "Though, Zain doesn't fit that profile."

"No? You don't think moody broody tattooed kings with thick hair and dirty mouths are also my type?"

"Your type seems to be anyone legal and consenting," I said.

"Not true. We both know you're not my type."

"Asshole," I said, but I was laughing.

Despite Chuck's accurate description of Zain, they hadn't met yet. It wasn't that I was trying to hide Zain from him or anything, but seeing as Zain didn't live in Vancouver, the three of us usually stayed in and enjoyed our limited time together.

We didn't see Zain every weekend, but it was close. He hadn't gotten a new job yet, unfortunately, so while sometimes he came just to hang out with me and Finn for a couple of days, other times he was there because he was attending another interview in Vancouver. Other weeks, he couldn't make it at all, sometimes because he was interviewing for a job in Calgary or as far as Toronto and Ottawa, and other times because flying into Vancouver every weekend wasn't exactly cheap.

But when he was there... fuck.

It had scared me how easy things felt when Finn first started staying with me, how comfortable he seemed in my home and how naturally we'd fallen into a routine. And that was nothing compared to how much it scared me that Zain fit into that little routine as if he'd always been meant to be part of it. How Fridays felt like the longest day of the week because half the time, I knew they were together and I was stuck listening to Loni as she went into full-on conspiracy mode about the betrayal mouse.

And how I knew they were fooling around. How I knew there was a good chance I'd come home to both of them in my bed, already naked, already sweaty, already having given in to each other, and that meant they'd both turn their attention on me and I'd have two tongues and four hands spoiling me until whoever got it up first slid his cock inside me.

It wasn't just the sex, either. It was eating Finn's delicious dinners together. Washing up the dishes and chatting about our days and weeks. Watching stupid action movies on nights when Zain convinced us he should get a say in what we watched and great reality television on all the other nights when Finn and I won him over.

It was the moments I sat back and realized how entirely different and yet perfectly complementary we all were. It was Zain trying not to let on how frustrated he was that he hadn't got a job offer yet and the different approaches Finn and I had to comforting him. Because yeah, getting a blowjob would definitely make Zain feel better, but it was Finn's bright smile and unwavering optimism that actually cheered him up.

"It just sucks," Zain was saying as we ate dinner one Friday night after he'd gotten a rejection letter from a job he'd really been hoping for. "This would have been so great. The hours. The pay. Even some travel, but not too much. The teams I interviewed with were great. It would've been such a good fit."

"Well, it's a good thing you didn't get it," Finn said.

Both Zain and I looked at him skeptically. Finn put his fork in his mouth and chewed, then swallowed, then smiled at Zain.

"Like, think of how awesome the *perfect* fit will be if the good fit was that good," he said. "And all you gotta do is wait a little longer before you find it? It's gonna be so worth it when you do."

Zain was quiet for a moment, looking down at his plate before lifting his eyes to Finn's. Finn was chewing another bite of food, a blank but sunny look on his face, and a smile spread across Zain's lips.

"I bet you end up at one of those jobs that has, like, a ping pong table in the lunch room," Finn said. "And free ice cream and onsite yoga and stuff. You know what I mean?"

"I do, bud," Zain said. "Thank you."

"No problem," Finn said. "But, uh, for what?"

And that was just it. Finn didn't even know how much Zain needed someone like him. *I* hadn't even known how much I needed someone like him. Not until I realized I'd started looking forward to being at home. Until I'd made an off-hand remark about having a shitty day because Dinah was up to her usual bullshit and got home that night to my favourite meal on the stove, clean and fresh sheets on the bed, and a bouquet of flowers on the end table next to the couch, which had a pile of blankets and a full season of *Thirty-Year-Old Grandmas* queued up.

I'd had people take care of me before. Brad might have been a total dirtbag, but when we'd been married, he'd showered me with attention and presents and trips around the world.

But the way Finn took care of me was different. It came from a different place. And I don't know that he ever realized how special he made me feel.

How much it meant to me that he cared so unwaveringly.

Then there were things like the way Zain and Finn interacted with Dottie.

By the third time Zain had come to visit, Dottie had him wrapped around her wrinkly little finger. She'd coerced him and Finn into helping in the yard on Saturdays when we all needed a bit of time to let our sex drives recover and both agreed without complaint. Zain enjoyed gardening, he said, and he didn't get to it much anymore because he lived in a condo without a balcony in Vernon. And Finn loved mowing the lawn because... well, I didn't really know why, but he always looked like he was having a blast doing it. So even though I'd offered to help out because it felt a little weird to make them do all the work while I sat around drinking lemonade with Dottie, they'd both said not to worry about it.

Sort of. Finn said not to worry about it and Zain said I could make it up to him with my mouth later. The joke was on him because I would've done that anyway.

And that was how we got to where we were that Saturday when Dottie told me I looked happy.

"He would've liked you all, too," Dottie said.

"Huh?" I replied.

"My husband," Dottie said. "Keep up, you dingleberry. He would've been out there with the boys, showing Finn how to cut stripes into the lawn and making sure Zain knew the difference between a dandelion and a potato sprout." She shook her head, a smile on her face. "Thirty years ago, this kind of arrangement or whatever you have going on would be hush-hush and hidden away. Now they write books about it and it's happening right under my nose. Hell, even in the seventies when we were all about free love and all that, I didn't think it'd ever be like this."

"I'm going to pretend you were talking about the royal 'we' when you said that so I don't have to think about you being involved in the free love movement."

"I was a stunner back in the day, you know."

"You're still a stunner, Dottie, but that doesn't mean I want to think of you like that."

She didn't respond right away. When I looked over to see why a moment later, Dottie was staring back at me, lips parted and a look of suspicion on her face.

"What?" I said.

"That might be the nicest thing you've ever said about me, dipshit," she said. "Your boys really have changed you."

"They're not my boys," I said, feeling my face start to go red.

"You don't see any future with this?" she asked. "Even when you can get away with having relationships like this now?"

"It's not that," I said. "And it's a lot more complicated than you think. We all have... I don't know. Other stuff that affects whatever this is. But we can still enjoy what we have now."

Dottie opened her mouth to say more, but was distracted by Finn turning the lawnmower off, even though he hadn't finished the lawn. Zain turned to look at him, too, just as Finn dug into the pocket of his shorts and pulled out his phone.

"Hey, Mom," he said with a huge smile. "How's it going?"

"Look at that," Dottie said. "He's even good to his mother. It's always a good sign when a man is good to his mother."

"Do you think Finn is capable of not being good to anyone?" I asked.

"Doesn't matter." She gave me a significant look. "If he treats his mother right, he'll treat all the important women in his life right."

I didn't know how true that was because frankly, I'd met some God-awful mama's boys in my days, but I didn't get a chance to respond to Dottie. Not when I was still looking at Finn, and not when the bright smile on his face began to fade and his eyebrows began to crease into a frown.

"Oh, fuck," I breathed.

"What?" Dottie said.

"His dad," I said like that would answer her question, even though Dottie had no reason to know about Finn's dad. Or, well, stepdad. But that had to be it; that was about the only thing I could think of that would make Finn look like that.

His stepdad.

Who had cancer.

Nineteen

I DIDN'T REMEMBER PUTTING my glass down, just that I was suddenly moving across the lawn towards Finn, who was nodding as if his mom could see him through the phone

"Right," he said, his voice shaking a bit. "Of course. Yeah. No, I'm fine. I'm fine. Are you okay? And he... okay. Good. Do you want me to come by?"

I was still looking at Finn, hovering like I could do something to help him, when I felt a hand on my lower back.

"What's wrong?" Zain breathed.

I shrugged and felt him stand a little closer as we waited.

"It's not a problem," said Finn. "I can... I'll bring dinner. I'll get the fried chicken he likes. Okay. See you soon. I love you."

He hung up slowly, taking a deep breath and letting it out as he slid his phone into his pocket. When he turned to look at me and Zain, his eyes were wet, tears barely holding on behind his lashes.

"What's going on, bud?" Zain asked.

"Are you okay?" I added.

Finn nodded, then an uncertain laugh burst out of his mouth.

"He's scheduled," he said.

"For surgery?" I asked.

Finn nodded. "It's the weirdest thing to be happy about. Especially 'cause, like... it's surgery."

"That's fair," Zain said. "Surgery is a big deal. Good news can still be scary news."

Finn nodded, then exhaled loudly. I didn't know what to say, so I did the only thing I could think of and wrapped my arms around him. One of his arms went around me, but I felt him reach out with the other. A moment later, Zain brushed against me, and from my spot squished between them, I could hear Finn's shaky breaths and Zain's steady ones and the comforting beat of both their hearts.

"I said I'd bring dinner over for them," Finn said, his voice sounding almost distant. "I'm sorry to miss some time together, but I—"

"Don't apologize," Zain said. "We get it."

"Of course," I agreed. "And we'll both still be here when you get home."

Zain shooed Finn away from the lawnmower and said he'd finish up and I told Finn not to worry about Alfie, I'd seen him get his dinner enough times to know how he liked it. Finn nodded, then grabbed his keys and kissed us each goodbye, waved at Dottie with a reassuring smile, and headed to his car.

And then it was just me and Zain.

"Think he'll be okay?" Zain asked. His voice was the same even tone it usually was, but there was worry in it all the same.

I nodded. "He'll feel better after he checks on them. Make sure they're eating. You know."

"Mother them a little," he said.

"He's got great maternal instincts."

It could have been weird. Finn and I were alone together all the time, and Finn and Zain spent most of the day on Friday with each other while I wasn't there. But Zain and I hadn't been together like this since his first trip to Vancouver when Finn had walked the dogs while we aggressively agreed with each other.

So it could have been weird.

Maybe it should have been weird.

All of this was fucking weird, after all.

But it wasn't. There was no moment where we weren't sure how to act with each other anymore, just like there was no moment where we fell into each other, giving in to the way things used to be like there were four separate connections in this strange little situation we were in.

Because there wasn't. It wasn't that there was me-and-Zain and me-and-Finn and Finn-and-Zain and then me-and-Finn-and-Zain.

It was just the last one.

It was all of us, together.

Metaphorically, of course. Physically, that night it was just me and Zain. But as weird as it wasn't, Finn's absence was still conspicuous. Partially because Finn was by far the best cook of the three of us.

"You're already hungry?" I asked when we went inside after Zain finished mowing the lawn.

"Some of us spent our Saturday afternoon doing manual labour instead of lounging on the porch and drinking lemonade while leering at those of us doing said labour, Teacup."

"I offered to help."

"You know as well as I do that you would've whined the whole time."

"I would not," I said. "It would've been eighty percent of the time, max."

"And you would've spent the other twenty percent half-assing everything so we knew it would be pointless to ask you next time."

"You think I'd weaponize my incompetence like that?"

He smirked. "Wouldn't you?"

"Not the point." I opened the fridge and twisted my mouth to the side. "I can make us something, but I'm no Finn. How do you feel about sandwiches?"

He came up behind me, hands slipping around my waist and lips pressing against my neck. "I prefer the kind that contains you in the middle."

"Of course you do."

"Preferably stuffed with twice the meat and extra mayo."

I groaned, but only so he couldn't tell how hard I was laughing. "You're the worst."

"Well, I'm not German, but Finn might be. You'd have to ask him."

"What?"

"To figure out which of us is the wurst."

"Oh my God," I huffed, trying to wriggle out of Zain's arms as he dissolved into laughter. "You're terrible. Awful. Horrendous."

"Not what you said last night," he said, loosening his grip just enough that I thought I'd gotten away. But of course, it was Zain, and he was actually just letting me go long enough to close the fridge door before he pinned me against it. "I believe last night it was, 'Oh Daddy, you fuck me so good, give me more of that thick meaty sausage—'"

"I said maybe seven of those words," I said. "And they weren't the ones in the second half."

He was smiling as he kissed me, laughter brushing against my face in warm puffs until it wasn't, until the laughter faded into quiet sighs as he worked his lips against mine. I relaxed against the fridge, my head tilted up and my eyes closed, just enjoying the moment of quiet indulgence in his mouth.

"Tess?" he murmured.

"Hmm?"

"About those sandwiches..."

I groaned and opened my eyes, reaching up to push on his chest. "Way to ruin the moment, asshole. 'Hey, Tessa, kissing's nice and all, but can you go make me a sandwich?'"

"Actually, I was going to ask you if we could take a raincheck on the sandwiches."

"Oh. So we can go fuck?"

"Not that I'll ever turn that down, but it was more so that I could take you out to dinner."

I raised my eyebrows. "Like at a restaurant?"

"That's generally where they serve food, yes."

I didn't laugh. "You want to take me out to dinner. Like... a date?"

I expected him to say no. Honestly. I expected Zain to shake his head and roll his eyes and say no, he just didn't feel like eating sandwiches or ordering takeout.

So I was surprised when he nodded solemnly.

"Yeah," he said. "A date."

"But—"

"But we're not dating," he said before I could. "And even if we were, wouldn't that also include Finn, and should we go on a 'date' without him even though we both know damn well that he'd be fine with it. I know, Teacup. But you and I have been doing whatever this is for months now and dating or not, I want us to have a first date."

I stared into his dark eyes for a moment. They were as resolutely determined as they were vulnerable, and I just...

Something about his eyes made me want to melt.

"But," I said as if I was continuing my thought from before, "if it's our first date, shouldn't you have brought me flowers or something?"

His mouth twitched. "How many times have you gotten flowers on a first date?"

"Well, zero, now," I scoffed.

"I guess we're even," he said. A few months ago, I would've thought the way he said it was with biting snark, but now, I knew he was joking. I rolled my eyes and reached up to kiss him again.

"You need to shower first, though," I said. "You smell like fertilizer."

"Thanks, kitten," he said. "You always know just what to say to make a guy feel good."

"Hey, I didn't say you smell like shit, even though I'm pretty sure that's what the fertilizer is," I said, and even though he'd already turned away to head to the bathroom, I heard him laugh.

Despite not having participated in the manual labour, I took a quick shower once Zain was done, since sitting on my ass in the sun all day had made me a little sweaty. I put on some lipstick and mascara and dressed in a pair of jeans and a flowy, sleeveless top that I loved, figuring we weren't going to be going anywhere particularly fancy.

When I finished, I'd expected Zain to be ready to go and waiting in the living room, but he wasn't there. He wasn't in the bedroom or the kitchen either and I frowned.

"Where'd he go, Alf?" I asked.

Alfie, however, wasn't in the room either. Not that it mattered, because his absence sort of answered my question.

Well, it did, until a couple of minutes later when there was a knock on the door, at which point I was just confused.

I opened it to see Zain standing there. He'd shaved and styled his hair, brushing the thick black strands back off his face. He had on jeans and the dress shirt he'd been wearing when he arrived on Thursday, since he'd flown straight from work. Now, though, he'd rolled up the sleeves, showing off the tattoos inked on his forearms and the Viole watch he had on his left wrist.

And in his hand, a small bouquet of the pink garden roses he'd been tending for Dottie every week.

"Dottie said I could," he said as I opened my mouth. "Trust me, I wasn't committed enough to this to risk making her mad. Pretty sure she would've used it as an opportunity to legitimately spank me."

"You would've been bare-ass across her knee before we could even leave the yard," I said.

"And you would've been right there taking pictures, wouldn't you?"

"Don't be stupid. I would've livestreamed it."

He smiled as he held the flowers out to me. "Ready for our date, kitten?"

And if the way my heart was fluttering was any indication, I definitely was.

Twenty

"You're sleeping in tents the whole time?" I asked.

Zain nodded, a resigned look on his face as he helped himself to another salad roll. "That's what Josh wanted, so that's what Josh is getting."

"You," I said as he dipped the roll in the peanut sauce. "*You're* sleeping in a tent?"

"I'm sleeping in his tent," Zain said. "Since as the best man, it's my responsibility to both plan a bachelor party that could theoretically kill him and also keep him alive during said bachelor party."

I took a bite of my salad roll. "Is that going to be weird for you?"

"Why would it be? Josh and I have shared a tent a bunch of times."

"Yeah, but you haven't done it since you started fucking his sister behind his back."

It was kind of a mean thing to say, but Zain just considered it as he took a thoughtful bite of his salad roll.

"It might be," he said after he swallowed. "But it hasn't been weird all the times I've seen him since we started doing this."

"Really?"

He shrugged. "Maybe I should be worried about what this says about me, but not really. If it wasn't for the whole Brad thing, I'd straight up tell him."

"You don't have the whole 'but she's my best friend's sister' guilt thing anymore?"

He snorted. "No. I barely had it to begin with, but I was trying to justify shit in the moment. You're an adult and I know I'm not gonna hurt you, so I have nothing to worry about."

My face started to feel warm, but before I had to think of a response or let Zain see the effect his words had on me, the server returned with two steaming bowls of pho and a plate of toppings. For a few minutes, we busied ourselves with our meals, taking the first delightful sips of broth in relative silence.

"Speaking of Brad, though," Zain said once we were a few bites in.

"Ugh," I grunted. "Isn't it bad form to talk about exes while on a date?"

"Yeah, but unfortunately, you're still pretending that yours isn't an ex."

Sighing, I put my chopsticks down. "Fine. What about Brad?"

"You've barely mentioned having to see him next weekend."

I sipped my water before picking my chopsticks back up. "Probably because it's working out pretty well. He shows up to a family event so my mom stops harassing me, but I don't actually have to see him all weekend. Well, except during the flight there."

Which I'd thought was stupid, but Brad insisted it would look suspicious if we didn't fly in together and it was a small price to pay for not having to see him the rest of the weekend.

But then Zain gave me a concerned look. "And on Sunday."

I frowned. "Why would I see him Sunday? We don't fly out until Monday. I thought the whole reason you were doing it on the September long weekend was so we had the extra day."

"Aren't you in the wedding party?"

"I'm basically Leslie's stand-in for the ceremony but she's doing most of the planning and stuff with Shenae and Jeanie. Part of the perks of being the B-list bridesmaid."

He looked worried. "Do you have any idea what's happening at the bachelorette party?"

"Of course," I said. "Friday night, we check into the estate house at the winery and we're doing dinner or something chill with the bridal party. Saturday is a wine tour and luncheon at the winery with all the moms and aunts and stuff, then dinner and dancing with the non-old-people. Sunday is a spa day and more dinner and dancing that night."

Proud of myself for remembering it all, I took a big bite of pho.

"With the guys," Zain said.

"Wuh," I said with noodles in my mouth.

"I can't believe no one told you," he said. "No wonder you weren't freaking out."

"Freaking out about what?!"

He sighed. "Josh and Audrey decided they wanted to merge the parties on Sunday night, so the guys are all going back to Kelowna in the afternoon and then out to Tidal Beats for a club night. And then the guys who are in or have partners in the bridal party were going to stay at the estate house."

I stared at him blankly.

"Which would include you," he said. "And Brad."

I stared at him more.

"Teacup?"

I swallowed my mouthful of noodles. "No."

"What?"

"No. I'm not sharing a room with him. He can get his own room."

Zain shrugged and ate some of his pho. "I'm not gonna argue with you. It's your secret, Teacup."

"How did no one tell me this?" I asked. "When was this decided? What... what?!"

"I mean, I emailed the guys about it two days ago," he said. "But I guess they would have assumed you'd know or that Brad would tell you."

"And you thought he would?" I asked. "You didn't think to warn me because you know he'd for sure use this as an opportunity to force me to stay in a room with him?"

"I am warning you," he said. "Right now. During this conversation."

"You've got to be fucking kidding me," I muttered. "I can't believe you didn't tell me about this sooner."

"I thought I'd give Brad a chance to prove he's not actually a piece of garbage," he said.

"You know as well as I do that he is."

"Yeah, well, sometimes I like to think better of people who don't deserve it for some reason." He stirred his soup with his chopsticks. "He doesn't know, right?"

"Know what? How to not be a piece of garbage?"

"About us."

I looked at him, partly incredulous and partly insulted. "Why in the hell would I tell him that?"

"Because I would have," he said. "If it were me."

My chest suddenly felt hollow. "You would?"

The fear and betrayal in my voice was enough to make Zain look up. When he did, his eyes were burning with anger, but when he spoke, his voice was cold.

"Teacup, give me some credit," he said. "I meant if I were you. I might try to be a good person most of the time, but when it comes to him... If I was hooking up with someone I knew he hated as much as he hates me, I would rub it in his face just to fucking hurt him."

My heart started beating again and I felt tension release in my shoulders. "Sure you would. And then he'd immediately tell your whole family you're divorced and have been lying to them for five years."

He shrugged. "Knowing how much it would piss him off, it might be worth it. Do you know how hard it's going to be seeing you with him that weekend?"

"I'm not with him, though."

He gave me another one of those burning looks and his voice went so low, I had to lean in to hear him.

"The fact that I'll have to be in the same bar as you and pretend I don't know what it's like to be inside you, that I'll have to watch you sit next to him and know what you look like with my dick in your throat, what it's like to fuck you while Finn holds you down, how hard I get when I'm sucking the taste of your pussy off his cock..." He shook his head, holding my gaze and refusing to look away. "It's going to take everything in me to keep my hands off you when I'm sitting there being jealous of that absolute shitstain of a human."

My mouth was suddenly dry, probably because my lips had parted as he spoke and my breath had caught as he whispered in that low, rough voice. I swallowed hard and looked down at my bowl of pho.

"I'm surprised you'd say you're jealous," I said.

"When another person is pretending to be yours? When everyone else in the world thinks he's still with you when I'm the one who deserves to be yours? Why wouldn't I be jealous?"

I raised my eyebrows at him. "Seriously? I regularly fuck two other people. Are you saying you're jealous of Finn and Claire?"

"That's completely different," he said. "Claire and Finn respect you. They treat you how I want you to be treated. They didn't take you away from me. Brad did. And then he hurt you."

"That doesn't explain why you're jealous of him."

He half-laughed. "Because seeing you with him pisses me off, Teacup. Because even though you're not with him anymore, I still can't stop myself from thinking that it should've been me. I should be the one who comes up to you when those parties merge together and kisses you, dances with you, takes you back to that estate house and fucks you until you can't see straight. And if I'd done something about it sooner, I would've been the one on your arm and in your bed and trying to put a baby in you instead of him."

"And you think I would've just gone along with that?" I said. "If you'd told me back then? You think I would've chosen you?"

"Yes," he said.

"You seem pretty confident."

His eyes flashed dark again. "Teacup, I would've done anything—anything—to get you. You could've told me to bring you unicorn tears on a platter made of clouds and I would've found a way. So yeah, I think you would've chosen me." His eyes flicked down, taking in my body, before meeting mine again. "Just like you've chosen me now."

"You can't say that," I breathed.

"I can," he replied.

"Zain—"

"I know," he said. "It is what it is, and what it is isn't serious, and I'm not going to pressure you to make it more. But back then... don't deny that I would've been yours, Teacup. Just like you would've been mine."

And fuck him, but he was right.

And fuck me, but I was almost starting to wish we had that.

Not just us, either. I was starting to wish that what we had here, what we had with Finn, was it.

And fuck.

Fuck.

That was terrifying.

Luckily, Zain had also said it in a way that was very, very hot, so not only was I terrified, I was also turned on. My panties were already starting to cling to my pussy and I could feel my nipples pressing against the fabric of my bra.

And Zain, being Zain, could tell how much I wanted him.

"Take the rest to go?" he asked.

I nodded and he flagged the server down.

We barely made it home. I could see the bulge of Zain's cock in his jeans as we sat in the Uber and every bump we hit on the road sent a shock of need coursing through me. When the driver pulled up to my place and we got out, Zain took my hand in one of his while he tipped and rated the driver on his phone in the other so that as soon as I unlocked the door, he could slam it behind us and press me up against it.

Urgency was part of being with Zain. Urgency defined us; impatience and desperation driving us forward and forward and forward until we exploded and shattered into each other. Heat and need were what I knew with him, his lips and hands and cock building up the pleasure that would eventually overtake my body.

That time together was no different.

Passionate was never a word I would have used to describe Zain before, but now it was the first one I associated with the thought of him. It was something he kept from most people, only releasing it when he deemed something important enough to share it.

Something, or someone.

Or, in our case, someones.

Because he had passion for me. He had passion for Finn. But it had been a while since I'd been the sole recipient of Zain's passion and I'd almost—not quite, but almost—forgotten how intense it could be.

And how much I loved it.

He held me against the door, devouring my mouth with his and rubbing his body against mine. I could barely keep up with his kisses or the demand of his hands, hardly able to lift my arms in time for him to tear my shirt off my body. He didn't bother unhooking my bra, just shoved the straps down my arms and tugged the cups beneath my tits so he had access to my aching nipples.

"Fuck, kitten," he growled as he grabbed one breast, squeezing just hard enough to make me whimper. "How the fuck do you do this to me? How do you drive me crazy like this?"

"Practice," I gasped.

He shoved his face into the crook of my neck and sank his teeth in. I cried out, but it didn't stop him from sucking on that tender spot.

"Are you marking me?" I asked.

"Fuck yes I am," he said, then traced his tongue along what I assumed was the mark he'd left. "Because you're mine, Teacup, and since I'm not allowed to tell the whole fucking world that, I'm going to put this mark here every time I see you. The rest of the world might not know who put it there when they see it, but I will." A teasing finger traced up the other side of my throat, leaving a trail that made me shiver. "And when Finn gets home, I'm going to make him put his mark over here. Because you're ours."

"But—"

"I know," he said, then nipped at my neck again. "For now. But that doesn't matter, kitten. For now or forever, you're fucking ours."

And I don't know who I thought I was kidding by protesting. Especially not when he pushed his hand into my jeans and groaned as he slid a finger along my dripping pussy. Especially not when he put two fingers on my clit and began to rub with the confidence of someone who knew exactly how to make me come.

Because he did know. And he did make me come, standing right there against the front door, his lips on my neck and his hand between my legs and his words echoing in my ears.

That I was his.

That I was theirs.

Because fuck him, but he was right.

For now.

Twenty-One

WHEN FINN GOT HOME a few hours later, Zain and I were in bed. Not because it was particularly late, but after he made me come against the door, I'd dropped to my knees and let him fuck my face.

And he had.

Hard.

But like, good hard. The kind of hard that I knew I was going to remember for the rest of my life and would probably get myself off to on a regular basis. Because it had been so fucking hot, my back to the wall as he rested one hand against it, his other hand on the back of my head as he thrust into my mouth. Wet, sloppy sounds had filled the room, punctuated by Zain's groans and his words because of course he was talking as he shoved his cock down my throat.

He kept his cock in my mouth longer than usual after he came. It was long enough that I'd squirmed, confused as to why he hadn't let go of my head.

"Sorry," he'd panted. "Give me just a sec, Teacup. I came so hard that I think if I move right now I'm gonna pass out."

It had been hard enough that once he did pull out of my mouth, he barely had the energy to pull up his jeans and go upstairs to get Alfie. But he did, and once he got back with the dog, we'd gone to my room and climbed into bed.

The intent hadn't been to fall asleep. I'd brought my laptop and thrown an old episode of *Secret Rednecks* on while Zain had pulled out whatever the latest nerdy science fiction novel he was reading. But somehow, when Finn got back, it wasn't until he crawled into bed behind me I opened my eyes and realized my laptop was gone, the only light being the golden glow of my cheap IKEA bedside lamp. I was facing Zain, who was sitting up against the headboard and looking past me, his book closed with a crumpled receipt marking his spot.

"You're back?" I murmured as Finn curled his tall body around mine.

"Sorry," Finn whispered. "I was trying not to wake you up."

"S'okay," I said. "I wasn't trying to sleep."

"You were sleeping," Zain said. "For at least an hour."

"Yeah, but I wasn't trying to."

A puff of laughter brushed against my hair as Finn kissed the top of my head. "Zain said you guys went for dinner. Did you have fun?"

"Mm-hmm," I said, then frowned and tried to sit up. "Wait, how did... are you okay? How were your parents?"

He moved back so I could sit. When I turned to look at him, the first thing I noticed was how red his eyes were. The second was the almost drawn look on his face. And the third was that he was smiling, though it was softer and more resigned than usual.

"They're okay," he said. "Everything's okay. Ian's happy he finally has a date. He started a countdown on the whiteboard my mom keeps on the fridge. Like 'thirty-whatever days until my ass surgery.'"

Zain let out a surprised laugh. "His what surgery?"

Finn's smile widened in amusement. "His ass surgery. 'Cause it's prostate cancer?"

"Oh," Zain said, trying to stifle the laugh. "Sorry. I don't think I actually knew that. But don't they, uh, go in... like, through his stomach?"

"Yeah," Finn said. "But Ian says it's in his butt so it's ass surgery. He thinks it's funny. You and him would... would get along, I think. He'd like you."

Something about the way he said it set off one of those instinctive alarm bells. Or maybe the alarm bell had been going off ever since I saw the redness of his eyes but I'd still been waking up and had only just noticed it.

"What's wrong, Finn?" I asked.

I half-expected him to deny anything was wrong, since Finn didn't like to "bother" people with his problems. But Finn just took a breath and let it out.

"So, I told them," he said. "That I'm, um, pan."

Holy shit.

"How did they take that?" Zain asked.

"Really good," he said. "Mom was like, 'You know we love you no matter what and Ian was like, 'Okay, cool' and Hailey was like, 'I knew it.'" He laughed. "Abby was like, 'No you didn't, you're just excited you're not the only LGBTQ+ person in this family anymore' and Hailey was like, 'Well yeah, obviously that too.'" The smile faded off his face. "So it was more the, uh, finding out that Julie and I broke up ages ago and that I was living in my car until a friend gave me a place to stay that they didn't take well."

"You told them everything?" I asked.

"Sort of," Finn said. "I didn't tell them about the three of us. I just figured that might be a little much once my mom started crying."

"She cried?" I repeated.

His mouth twitched. "Yeah. When I said I'd, um, lived in the car. She was upset that I didn't ask for help. And when I said I didn't want to make things harder for them because of everything with the cancer and that, then Ian got upset and just…" He sighed. "I didn't want to make them feel bad. But I did. So I kinda felt like a fucked-up disappointment and then I apologized for that and then Mom said I can't think about myself like that because that's what my dad would've said about me and—"

"She said what?" Zain said, his voice cold.

"She didn't mean it like that," Finn said. "I know that. And she apologized and so did Ian and she said it was just that she worries and doesn't want me to feel like I can't ask for help when I need it and all that. Then Hailey started getting mad because she said they were turning me coming out into a negative thing and that wasn't fair and Abby took her side, of course, and now I feel like everyone's fighting with each other and this is the worst time for all this to happen because we should be focused on Ian." He leaned against the headboard. "I shouldn't have said anything. But Mom asked why Julie didn't come with me and I didn't want to lie to her."

"You had every right to say something," Zain said. "It's not your fault they're upset."

Finn's throat flexed as he swallowed, but he nodded.

"I know," he said. "And I think I just have to give them some space and time to like, hopefully understand? I know it'll be fine. I'm just sad about it right now. But like, hopefully it's all good by the long weekend."

"Why's that?" I asked.

"Because Ian's surgery is a couple days before it," he said. "And before all that happened, I told them I'd stay with them for a few days since if Ian needs help, like, walking or in the bathroom or something. Hailey doesn't want to be the one to do that kind of stuff and Mom would need the help."

I felt Zain's eyes on me.

"The September long weekend?" I asked.

"Yeah," Finn said. "Why?"

"Tess and I are supposed to be at her brother and sister-in-law's parties that weekend," Zain said. "But I can be here if—"

"You absolutely can't," I said. "You're the best man. But I'm sure if I told Audrey—"

"Your ex-husband is going to be there," he said. "How are you going to come up with a story that covers all those bases, Teacup?"

"If you give me a minute, I'm sure I can—"

"It's okay," Finn said quickly. "I appreciate it, but I'll be at my parents' all weekend at least. Please don't miss this because of me."

I studied Finn, worried he was just saying it because of the whole not wanting to be a bother thing, but he had an earnest, pleading look on his face

"Okay," I said. "If you're sure. But you know if you need anything..."

"I know," Finn said. "And that's why you're the best. Both of you."

Zain and I wrapped him in hugs and comforting words that night, but it took a couple of days for Finn to feel like Finn again. I couldn't blame him for that. Finn was a people pleaser, so knowing that he had upset someone—especially when those someones were his family—was hard. Not to mention the comment his mom made about his dad saying he'd be a disappointment. She hadn't meant it to be hurtful; she'd meant to point out that those were words his dad put into his head, that Finn *wasn't* a disappointment or a fuck up or any of those horrible things and that he only thought that about himself because his dad had been a God-awful person.

But sometimes, things come out twisted. Sometimes, the message between the lines is louder than the words are. And in moments where emotions were high and people were hurting, it was easy for things to come out wrong.

Still, Finn was resilient. When we drove Zain to the airport the following day, Finn kissed him goodbye right there in the front seat of the car, which I was pretty sure they'd never done before if the unfading smile on Zain's face was any indication. And in the group chat we had for the three of us, he shared his usual funny stories from work and asked his daily weird question that got the three of us talking for hours. At night, he still made dinner for us, and we walked Alfie and Millie together like we usually did, and we watched trashy reality TV together if Dottie hadn't come up with some chore for him to help with.

The following weekend, Zain didn't come to Vancouver because it was his nephew's birthday, and his parents expected him to be at the birthday party. It ended up working out because on Saturday, Finn's mom called and asked if he would come over for dinner again. When he got home, he was back to his usual sunshiney self.

"Everything went okay?" I asked as Alfie bounded off the couch and to the door to greet him.

"It went great," Finn said. "We talked things out and Mom apologized. So did Ian. I don't think Hailey threatened them into it but she's being pretty protective right now. But all's good."

He was in such a good mood, apparently, that he came over to the couch and got to his knees in front of me. But he wasn't fast enough to do it before a quiet thought had started to creep through my mind: that if he could admit to what he'd been keeping from his family and have it be all good when he was done, maybe...

But then he stripped off my leggings and moved his head between my legs so he could help himself to my pussy, and that thought got pushed far, far away until the next time we saw Zain.

Which was not when we expected it to be.

"Jesus Christ!" Finn exclaimed the following Wednesday, nearly dropping the plate of chicken tikka masala he was about to put on the table as the front door banged open.

Alfie let out a loud, delayed bark that turned into an excited yelp.

"Zain?" I said as he walked in the door.

"It's not Friday," Finn said. "Is it? No. I worked today."

"It's not Friday," Zain agreed. He was wearing grey slacks and a light blue dress shirt, the collar unbuttoned and tie undone. The sleeves were rolled up to his elbows and he had a blazer over one arm and his rolling suitcase in the other.

"So you just decided to play hooky for the day and come see us?" I asked.

"Nope," he said, reaching down to scoop up Alfie so the little brown dog would stop jumping on his leg. "But I happened to be in town and thought I'd drop by."

"Oh, you just *happened* to be in town," I said.

"But what brought you to town?" Finn asked. "And you're staying for dinner, right? There's lots."

"I'd love dinner," Zain said. "And I was just here to sign some paperwork."

It took me a second. I heard the word clear as day and it didn't stick out, but the guarded expression on his face that made me reconsider it.

"Paperwork," I repeated.

"Paperwork for what?" Finn asked.

Zain scratched Alfie's ears, then set him down on the floor. "My new job."

I stared at him. Finn turned around, his eyes wide and his mouth open. "Your... what?"

Zain's guarded expression cracked, revealing something vulnerable and nervous.

"My new job," he said, answering Finn but looking at me. "I'm moving to Vancouver."

I had never been so happy—so fucking elated and thrilled and ecstatic—and so terrified at the same time.

I'd never felt my heart lift in excitement as my stomach dropped.

And I'd never, never flown into someone's arms faster than I did into Zain's just then.

Part 4

Confession: Bad things
come in threes.

Twenty-Two

"You're fired."

The boardroom was silent. I was looking at Chuck, who was staring at me with an oddly wide-eyed expression for some reason. Confused, I glanced at Dinah, who was frozen but also staring at me with her mouth hanging open.

Finally, I looked at Loni, who was standing on the other side of the boardroom, her palms flat on the surface of the table, and who was also staring at me.

"What?" I said.

"You," she said slowly. "Are. Fired."

I half-laughed. "For what? I didn't do anything."

"There's your answer," Dinah said. "You've never done anything."

"Didn't do anything?" Loni repeated, her voice almost scarily flat as she ignored Dinah. "You have the audacity—the *audacity*—to sit there and... The nerve. The gall of you, to sit there and—" She straightened up, taking her hands off the table and raising a finger to shake it at me. "We trusted you. *I* trusted you. And you betrayed us."

"I don't know what you're talking about," I said.

The foundation caked on Loni's face did nothing to hide the way her cheeks turned blotchy and red. "And you're going to continue to *lie* to me? How dare you, Tessa? We took you in, we gave you a job, we gave you everything, and you—"

"Loni," Chuck said. "Could you please share with me and Dinah why you want to fire Tessa? Even if Tessa knows, we don't know what happened."

It was risky on his part. I think we all knew that, given the wave of intense anger that spilled from Loni's eyes as she set her murderous glare on Chuck. But seeing as Chuck actually was integral to the operation of CARE, he must have had some brownie points in the bank or something, because Loni just grabbed her purse.

"Why tell you," she said, digging into the boxy colour-block bag, "when I can show you?"

She whipped her hand out of the bag with a flourish and threw a small stack of printer paper on the table, and that's when I knew.

I was fucked.

Completely and thoroughly fucked.

"Loni, I can explain—" I started.

"I don't want to hear it!" she screeched, startling Dinah enough to make her jump. Plucking a piece of paper off the table, she brandished it at me, showing off a large and unfortunately clear black-and-white photo of me.

And Claire.

Kissing.

"How do you explain this?" she shouted. "You are sleeping with the enemy!"

"I'm not," I said. "I swear, she's—"

"Who is that?" Dinah asked.

"None other than one Claire Elaine Shaughnessy *Martelle*," Loni spat dramatically.

"Who?" Dinah said.

Loni's eyes flared again. "How do you not know who—"

"Paige Martelle's younger sister," Chuck said, his voice resigned.

Dinah's head whipped towards me, her eyes almost bugging out of her head. "You did *what*?!"

"I can explain," I said loudly. "Just let me—"

"All these months I thought you were helping me find the mouse," Loni said. "And instead, you've thrown a dagger in my spine. You've wounded me, Tessa. How *could* you?"

"She's been helping us!" I said. "Remember when you wanted Brenda McClane to be a double agent? She's like that, but—"

"I would never suggest such an inane proposition," Loni said. "A double agent? That's ridiculous. Preposterous. Absolutely idiotic, which is exactly what I'd expect from a *traitor*."

"She's not trying to spy on CARE. She's been giving me information about ArtCycle," I said.

"And why would she do that?" Loni spat. "What could *you* possibly offer her?"

"The opportunity to piss off Paige since the only person who hates Paige as much or maybe even more than you is Claire?" I said.

For some reason, Loni didn't buy that, nor did she bother responding to it. Instead, she picked up another paper from the stack she'd thrown on the table, which contained another photo of me and Claire from the same day. We weren't kissing in that one, but she was touching my cheek, and I almost didn't recognize the vulnerable and tender look on my face. Were it not for the fact that it was proof of my so-called corporate betrayal, it would have been a lovely photo of us standing outside—

Oh fuck.

My mouth went dry. Dinah was reaching for the remaining photos and I lurched forward, snatching them away before she could touch them.

"Hey!" she snapped.

"Give me a chance here, Dinah. I just want to see what I apparently did," I lied, my heart racing.

Because I knew what I did, which was kiss Claire on the sidewalk outside of Beaujolais Park.

And I also knew that we'd been waiting there.

For Chuck.

Who had been in the bathroom after the three of us had lunch together.

And who seemed to realize it at the same moment that I did, given the sudden ashiness of his face.

I flipped through the photos quickly, my fingers trembling as I looked at each one. Me and Claire talking. Claire giving me an exasperated look. Me giving Claire an exasperated look. Three more almost identical photos of us kissing.

And that was it.

"How many photos of just me and her do you have?" I asked, then glanced at Chuck. He seemed to understand, his shoulders lowering as he let out a breath.

"I have more than enough proof," Loni said.

"How did you... find this out?" Chuck asked, his voice staggering.

"It must have been very clever," Dinah the suck-up said.

Loni pressed her lips together and lifted her chin almost proudly. "It was clever, Dinah. It was very clever of me to look down an avenue we hadn't checked before. Claire Martelle is an anomaly, after all."

"What's that supposed to mean?" I asked.

She glared at me. "Despite her status, she has no interest in being a public figure. If it wasn't for seeing her at Paris Fashion Week, I wouldn't have even recognized her, but my usual street photographer was complaining that he'd taken pictures of her outside Beaujolais Park before realizing there is no market whatsoever for photos of a reclusive little lesbian regardless of what her last name is. Imagine my surprise when he showed me them so I could see if there was anything to use against Paige Martelle and I saw my supposedly loyal artist-in-residence tongue-to-tongue with the enemy."

"My tongue wasn't in her mouth that time," I said.

"*That* time?" Dinah repeated with badly imitated shock. "You did this more than once?"

"It's probably been going on for months," Loni said. "Years, even."

"It has not," I said. "I met her at the Recycl-Ball."

Loni's face twisted into something almost monstrous. "She infiltrated the Recycl-Ball?!"

"That's where I know her from!" Chuck said. "Loni, this is the woman who donated ten thousand dollars to us."

"She is!" I said, suddenly hopeful. "And that was just at the date auction. She spent—"

"Chump change," Loni declared. "The Martelles may not be worth as much as my family, but that's practically an insult."

"Like leaving a one dollar tip on a hundred dollar meal," Dinah said.

"Not to normal people," I said. "That was our best Recycl-Ball ever and it was because of me."

"You nearly forgot about the date auction," Dinah said. "Even if you weren't a mouse, you're completely incompetent."

"She is not," Chuck said. "The auction was her idea and wouldn't have succeeded without her."

"No," Dinah said firmly. "No, I'm done. Loni, I have been saying for years that Tessa is a waste of our funds and this proves it. There was no reason to keep her on staff before. Now that we know she's actively trying to harm CARE? It's a liability to keep her around. Frankly, she should be escorted from the property."

"For what?!" I asked. "I never told Claire anything about CARE."

"You are lucky we aren't involving our lawyers," Loni said. "Or the police. Now, clear your desk out and go crawling back to the Martelles for help because you are no longer welcome in the CARE family."

And with that, she took her purse and stormed out of the boardroom, leaving me sitting there with Chuck and Dinah.

"Well, you heard the boss," Dinah said cheerfully. "Chuck, you can escort her to get her personal effects."

"No," Chuck said.

Her eyes flashed. "Excuse me?"

"I said no," Chuck said determinedly. "If she goes, I go."

"Chuck, no," I said. "Don't."

He looked at me desperately. "But—"

"You need this job," I said.

"Yeah, but if both me and Dinah talk to Loni once she's calmed down, we can get her to change her mind," he said.

"And why would I do that?" Dinah asked.

"Because—" Chuck started, then went quiet.

Dinah's mouth twisted into a smirk. "Tell you what, Tessa. Give me one reason. One thing you do that's worth keeping you around. One good reason that I should agree with Chuck and talk Loni into keeping you."

"Because it's... it's my birthday?" I said.

"Your birthday was last week," she said. "You made Jia order you cupcakes."

Shit.

"Because it was my birthday a week ago and I haven't worked off the investment CARE made into cupcakes for me?"

She rolled her eyes. "Get out."

"But—"

"Chuck, if you won't escort her to her desk, I'll get Jia to do it." She stood from the table. "Tessa, it's been a pleasure. Firing you, that is. The rest of it has been literal hell. Good luck."

"Dinah, wait," Chuck said.

"Bring it up again and you're fired too," she said, then walked out, leaving Chuck and I sitting there in silence.

"Well," I said when I found my voice again. "I guess my long weekend is starting two days early."

"Tess," Chuck said, his voice wavering. "This... they can't. I can fix this."

"I don't think you can," I said. "It was bound to happen eventually. If it wasn't this, someone would have eventually figured out I do approximately nothing—"

"You do not do nothing," Chuck said fiercely. "Yeah, we fuck around, but you have absolutely accomplished things here."

"There is nothing I do that couldn't easily be done by someone else," I said. "I'm a leech at best."

"Yes, but you're *my* emotional support leech."

"Most people just call that a work wife or something."

"You've always said you'll never get married again, though."

We both laughed. It wasn't all that funny, but we had to, otherwise we wouldn't have been able to lie to ourselves about what those wet, choked, sobbing sounds were. And frankly, Chuck and I were more of the laugh-and-hug type of friends than the cry-and-hug type of friends, so it just felt better to force a bit of laughter when he wrapped his arms around me in a comforting but resigned embrace.

Once we'd composed ourselves and wiped the tears that were obviously from laughter off our faces, I took a deep breath and walked out of the board room. Jia and Austin were standing at the reception desk, Jia's cheeks a light shade of pink as she twirled a piece of dark, shiny hair around her finger. They both looked up and a playful smile spread across Jia's face.

"Did you get fired this time?" she asked, like she always did.

"Yep," I replied, like I never had before.

She started to laugh, then stopped. "Wait, what?"

"I said yep," I repeated as I walked across the lobby. "Sorry it's a bit past the end of August, but if Austin has any sense, he'll still take you out for that date you had bet on it."

"You told her about the bet?" Austin said. "And it... it wasn't a date."

I rolled my eyes. "You two are so goddamn annoying. Everyone knows you're into each other. Stop playing these stupid games and just ask her out, you fucking coward."

Austin's mouth dropped open and from behind me, I almost heard Chuck wince, but I ignored them as I stormed down the hallway to my former office.

There wasn't much for me to collect. A mug I rarely used. A few pens. A drawer full of junk and cough drops and Advil and tampons that I hadn't used since getting my IUD. Stuff that I didn't care about but wasn't going to leave there for other people to use out of sheer spite.

And also a bunch of office supplies.

"Apply for EI," Chuck said as he tucked a box of mechanical pencils under my mug before grabbing a stack of multi-coloured Post-Its and trying to shove them in the bag, too. "As soon as you get home. I'll make sure your termination papers say it's without cause so you're eligible."

I took a final handful of highlighters, then struggled to zip my bulging bag closed. "Thanks. That'll at least cover rent for a while."

"Are you going to be okay, Tess?" he asked.

Finally managing to get the bag shut, I put it over my shoulder, then looked up at him.

"It'll be fine," I said. "It's not like things can get any worse."

And I know.

I shouldn't have said it.

I said out loud that things couldn't get any worse and the universe gave me a skeptical look and said, "Hold my beer, you ignorant fuck."

Twenty-Three

UNTIL THEN, I'D BEEN looking forward to having my place to myself for a couple of nights.

Not because I was tired of Finn staying with me or something. I wasn't. But it had been crowded with the two of us and adding a third person into the mix for the past week and a half had turned it from crowded to cramped.

Zain had been staying at my place since his last day at his old job. That hadn't been the original plan; as soon as they had offered him the position, he'd started looking for an apartment in Vancouver.

Which made sense. Like, I couldn't live with Zain. Eventually, my brother would come to visit him—he'd never visited me, but I wasn't Zain and more importantly, didn't want Josh to visit me—and that would raise some serious questions, like "Why is my sister living here and not with her husband?"

The problem was that finding something that suited Zain was proving to be difficult. It was hard enough to find a decent place to rent in Vancouver, but I'd had to bite back more than one comment about him being high maintenance when apartment after apartment didn't meet his standards. At one point, he'd tossed around the idea of getting a two-bedroom apartment so Finn could be his roommate—though we all know it would be more like his "and they were just 'roommates'" type of roommate—but that seemed more and more unlikely. On top of trying to find a dog-friendly apartment, Zain was too picky. He turned down one apartment because it was too dated, another didn't have a balcony, a third didn't have a big enough bedroom, a fourth wasn't close enough to his new job, a fifth didn't have enough parking spots available... and on it went.

So even though he'd hoped to have an apartment leased by his last day of work and use the three weeks he was taking off between jobs to move and settle in, as of the Wednesday before he was set to start his job, he was still at my place.

Which was way too fucking small for three people, not to mention three people where one of them was stressing about an impending family surgery and another was stressing about his lack of apartment, his job, and the impending bachelor party he was responsible for as best man. It was one thing to share a bed and a bathroom between the three of us for two nights. It was quite another to spend over a week stepping around two grown men and a dog and not being able to take a shower for longer than ten minutes, partly because someone always seemed to need the bathroom and partly because there was never enough hot water for all three of us.

So initially, Zain's plan of going to Kelowna a few days early to get ready for the bachelor party, see his family, and get his suit fitting done for the wedding in two weeks worked well. Finn's dad's surgery was first thing Thursday morning, so Finn had taken Wednesday and Thursday off and was planning on bringing Zain to the airport, then staying at his parents' Wednesday night.

Now that I'd been fired, though, I was kind of sad neither of them were going to be around.

But that was okay, I told myself as I got off the bus with my bulging bag of stolen office supplies. They both had their own stresses going on, but both of them were still probably home. Finn would pull me in for a rib-crushing hug that would make me feel like nothing could hurt me.

And there was likely enough time for Zain to cheer me up with an orgasm or two or three before he had to go.

Except then everything went to shit, because of course it did.

When I opened the door, Finn was pressed up against the counter with his face flushed pink and Zain was holding a fistful of Finn's t-shirt as he pressed his body against him. And that was fine, since it was one of my favourite sights in the world, especially when they both turned towards me with surprised expressions on their faces.

"Tess!" A wide grin spread across Finn's face as Zain let go of his t-shirt. "You picked the best day to come home early! Guess what?"

"Um... you saw a really cool frog today," I said.

"I did, actually," Finn said.

"Really?"

"Yeah. While I was walking Alfie earlier. He tried to eat it. But that's not it, though." He glanced at Zain and nudged him. "Go on, tell her!"

Zain looked significantly less excited than Finn, which was not unusual because Zain almost never looked excited. But there was a glimmer of happiness in his eyes.

"I found an apartment," he said. "Immediate possession. I can pick up the keys on the way to the airport."

"That's great!" I said. "I'm so glad you finally found a place."

"Yeah, and guess what?" Finn said.

And the thing is, I'd already guessed what. I'd guessed what the moment Zain spoke because Finn looked so damn excited and happy and I just...

I knew.

"What?" I asked.

"It's got two bedrooms," he said. "And guess what else?"

I forced the biggest smile I could. "Don't tell me it's dog friendly."

"It is!" Finn said. "And get this, there's even a little dog area right outside he can run around in, but there's also a dog park like super close by. So guess what?"

I laughed, mostly because if I didn't, I was going to cry and I could not let them see that. "Just tell me, Finn."

"We're gonna be roommates!" Finn said brightly. "I thought maybe we'd miss you because we're gonna leave for the airport early so we can get the keys. Then I can start moving my stuff this weekend."

"And the movers my company hired are going to bring my things in on Saturday," Zain said. "As long as you're still sure that's okay, Finn."

"It is," he said. "Ian'll be sleeping a lot, I'm sure. I can be away from their place for a few hours."

I kept smiling. I had to. Because I was happy for them. I don't know why that happiness hurt so much. We'd been talking about this ever since Zain got his new job. Finn was never meant to stay with me long-term. None of this was a surprise.

And yet I wanted to scream.

"Congratulations," I said. Instead of screaming, crying, and/or throwing up, I put down my heavy bag of office supplies and extended my arms. "Come here. I'm so... so happy for you both."

Finn hugged me with his usual amount of enthusiasm, though it wasn't enough to force out the tense air I'd filled my lungs with. Then it was Zain's turn. His hugs weren't as tight and energetic, but they were warm and comforting and sensual and usually left me dizzy as I inhaled the clean scent of his cologne.

That day, though, even though his body was pressed against mine and I could feel the half-hard bulge pressed against me from his make-out session with Finn, he felt far away.

Or maybe I was the one who was far away.

"I'm so glad you're here," he said. "I was stressing so much that we were going to miss you since we've gotta leave early now. Why'd you leave work so early?"

And here's the thing.

Yes, I could have told them.

Yes, I *should* have told them.

Yes, I fully understood that I was making one of those God-awful decisions to keep a vital bit of information to myself.

But I couldn't bring myself to do it. Not right then.

It wasn't like it would make any difference to the situation. Me being fired wouldn't make one of them stay. All it would do was bring their excitement crashing down and make both of them more stressed than they already were about the various things they had going on. And, more importantly, if I didn't tell them, I could ignore the crushing weight of panic that was starting to settle in my chest.

Because pretending everything was completely fine was my specialty, of course.

"Must've just been fate," I said to Zain. "So that I didn't miss you before you left."

Unfortunately, while my specialty was pretending everything was fine and lying out my ass to keep everyone believing it, Zain's specialty seemed to be flagging when that happened.

"What's wrong?" he asked.

"Nothing," I said. "What makes you think something's wrong?"

"Teacup," he said. "You're a terrible actor."

"And you're a terrible candlestick maker," I said.

"Maybe, but that has nothing to do with this."

I shrugged. "I thought we were just saying random things the other person was bad at since I don't see what your statement has to do with anything, either."

And maybe luck was on my side. Bad luck or good luck, I wasn't sure, but luck all the same. Normally, Zain would call me out. He'd ask and ask and ask until I admitted what was wrong.

He didn't, though. Maybe because he thought he knew the answer. That I was sad they were leaving. That they were living together without me. And maybe he thought giving me a bit of time and grace to process that was the best option.

Or maybe he was in a rush and they just really had to leave for the airport, so he didn't push the issue.

They left not too long after that. I kissed Zain goodbye, then Finn, then Zain again because he said the next time he saw me he wouldn't be able to so he deserved a second kiss. I told Finn to take good care of his dad and to let us know how everything went. I told Zain to try not to kill my brother before the wedding but also I wanted as many dirty details to use for blackmail as he could give me. Then they got into Finn's car and I waved as the boys drove.

And then I was alone.

Which was fine. It sucked, but it was fine. Just because I was alone didn't mean I was alone. Claire and I had talked multiple times about all the benefits of not being monogamous and this, this right here? That was one benefit.

Because yeah, I didn't get an orgasm or three from either of the boys to help cheer me up, but I could still call Claire. And not only would Claire probably be thrilled to help me with those orgasms, but I wouldn't have to waste time talking when I could be coming because she'd probably be more than happy to eat me out while I told her about my awful day.

I took off my bra, then flopped down on the couch with a sigh and pulled out my phone. Chuck had texted to make sure I got home okay, which was sweet but totally unnecessary, and I sent a quick "I'm fine" before pulling up my message thread with Claire.

Me

> Hey. You busy?

CM

> Wow. You must have a sixth sense or something.

Me

> Why's that?

CM

> I was just freaking out and thinking I desperately needed to talk to you.

And like, yeah, I was having a shitty day. But for Claire to say she needed to talk to me desperately was concerning.

Me

> What's wrong?

CM

> Julie and I are going to meet her parents tonight. And I feel like I'm walking into the lions' den.

Like "Hey, what's up super conservative parents who are apparently religious and homophobic, I'm the almost-a-decade-older woman who's fucking your newly-out lesbian daughter that is having a quarter-life crisis and just quit her job to be my totally-not-a-sugar-baby. Did she mention that I'm an incredible catch because I've struggled my whole life with severe depression and oh yeah, your daughter's not the only one I'm fucking because I don't believe in monogamy?"

"Oh and also she thinks I'm totally fine and chill with all of this because she's ALSO freaking out about this very big major step and is worried I'm going to hate her after all this so I'm pretending to be super chill about it when I am VERY CLEARLY NOT SUPER CHILL ABOUT IT."

Jesus. That was both serious and kind of insulting, since this was the first I was hearing about her and Julie getting to this point in their relationship. But I swallowed that back, along with my own bad day, as I responded.

Me

Well, if you want my advice, I would say maybe don't start with any of that.

CM

How am I supposed to start it, then?

Me

You could try "Hello, my name is Claire." And then maybe throw in a "By the way, I'm a billionaire heiress to a makeup empire who doesn't currently know any hitmen, but knows people who would know where to find them if someone were to piss me off too much."

CM

I'm not a billionaire.

Me

Yet. Also not the point.

CM

What IS the point, then? Why do I have to meet them at all?

Me

I mean, it's important to Julie, obviously.

CM

Fuck.

Me

Sorry.

CM

Don't be. You're right. I can do this for her. She deserves it and frankly, I'm incredibly impressive, so I have nothing to worry about.

Me

Of course you are.

Thanks, darling. You always know just what to say. Sorry I word-vomited all over this exchange. How are you doing?

And yeah, she was legitimately asking. Yeah, she actually cared what was going on in my life and was probably wondering why I'd texted in the first place.

But telling her what was up meant telling her that I'd gotten fired.

And telling her I'd gotten fired meant I'd have to tell her why.

And the absolute last thing she needed when she was about to walk herself into the lions' den, as she'd said, was to feel guilty about that.

So I took a deep breath and let it out, then replied.

I'm fine. I was bored and thought I'd see if you were around.

Then I turned my phone screen off and put it on the cushion beside me before flopping down on my side on the couch and staring at the TV across the room, which showed a girl I would have screamed at for being an uncommunicative idiot if I'd been watching her in a TV show instead of on a black screen.

Twenty-Four

I SPENT MOST OF Thursday job hunting. By that I mean that in between texts to Finn asking how his dad was doing and receiving periodic updates that included a hilarious guide to male kegels one of the nurses had taught him, I updated my resume. Then I texted Chuck to confirm he would be okay with me listing him as my supervisor at CARE so I could use him as a reference. Then I spent the rest of the day trying not to hyperventilate as I scrolled past job listing after job listing I wasn't qualified for. After spending the afternoon cursing myself out for following my heart and pursuing a career as an artist instead of whatever fucking degree I needed to be an investment associate since those guys made bank and everywhere seemed to be hiring them, I came up with a brilliant idea.

It was time.

I was going to paint again.

I hadn't been in my studio much in the past little while. I'd gone in a couple of times to finish up the work Kira had sent me before they adopted Velma, but seeing as she was my only regular client, there hadn't been much in the way of commissions since she went on parental leave. And the only thing I'd done other than that was the portrait I'd drawn of Finn the first night he stayed with me. It had been ages since I'd painted something because I wanted to.

Because I felt inspired.

Because there were thoughts and feelings and emotions swirling about in my mind and I needed to get them out, to splash them across a page or a canvas so I could process them.

It was time to process them.

Creating things used to come as easily as breathing. I used to fill pages with drawings in all different styles, everything from cartoons to realistic portraits to abstract interpretations of whatever was in my heart at that moment. When Brad and I were together, I had more paintings than I knew what to do with and more visions than I could ever bring to life. My studio had been full of an ever-rotating selection of canvases as I created and sold, created and showed, created and gave.

After the divorce, I would sit, a blank canvas in front of me on the easel or a sketchbook open to a new page and a sharpened pencil in my hand, and I would stare.

And stare.

And stare.

It made sense, looking back. I wanted to draw what was in my heart. At best, there were days when there was nothing there. At worst, the things going through my heart weren't things I wanted to bring into the physical world.

But, I thought as I opened the door to my studio and put the second-last canvas I had in the room on my easel, maybe I was ready.

Maybe this was a sign.

Maybe it was time.

Maybe I could go back to doing the thing I'd always felt I was born to do.

Or, I said to myself three hours and four morose beers later, maybe I was full of shit.

The blank canvas in front of me seemed to agree.

"What the fuck," I groaned after finishing the last gulp from my fourth beer and slamming the bottle on the table next to me. I'd been expecting it to make a satisfying thunk sound, but it caught on a splotch of dried acrylic paint that dulled the sound.

And that was the last thing I needed right then.

Angrily, I swatted the empty bottle off my table. It fell to the ground with an equally unsatisfying clatter. Plucking a medium-sized filbert brush from the table, I dunked it unprofessionally into the blot of green paint I'd poured onto my palette and brought it to the canvas, swiping it across the textured surface once, then twice, then again and again until my feelings were represented in simple but bold streaks on the canvas:

THIS

IS

BULLSHIT

I put the brush back down, then sighed and picked up the beer bottle I'd knocked over and went to throw it in the recycling bin. Then I looked at the fridge, tilting my head to the side as I contemplated the closed door for a moment as thoughts began to swim in my head.

"Well, there's no reason I can't get more drunk tonight," I muttered to myself, then went and grabbed another beer from the shelf.

I'd just popped the cap off and taken a sip when a vibrating sound nabbed my attention from across the room and I realized I'd left my phone sitting on the coffee table for the hours I'd been not-painting. Flopping on the couch, I picked it up to see way more messages than expected on the screen.

Chuck

> I know your boys aren't home. Wanna go for drinks tonight so I have an excuse to check on you and make sure you're okay?

I snorted. I was way ahead of the game on that one.

Another was from Claire:

CM

> I have good news and bad news.

> Bad news: Julie's parents are fucking awful.

> Good news: watching someone stand up to her awful parents makes Julie super horny and we definitely fucked in the car on the way back to my place.

Finn had sent the group chat with me and Zain a few more updates on his dad, who was in good spirits after his surgery.

Finn

> He kept being like "I need to pee" and Mom was like "Just go, you have a catheter"

> And he didn't seem to get what that was

> And when he finally did he was like WELL I CANT GO WITH ALL OF YOU WATCHING ME so we had to turn around

> But he didn't know that he actually doesn't control when he's peeing so by that point he'd already peed but we all just pretended he was doing it

And Zain had responded to those messages, of course, but had also sent me a series of texts just between me and him.

Z Biggest Asshole

> Just so you know, your brother is an idiot. At no point did anyone tell him that he had to bring his own alcohol this weekend, nor did anyone suggest he buy literal fucking moonshine.

> If we make it out of this without anyone ending up in the ER with alcohol poisoning, I'm considering it a success.

Then, since I apparently hadn't responded to his hilarious message fast enough:

Z Biggest Asshole

> Did your phone die or are you busy at work for once?

> Teacup? You home from work yet?

Shit.

Part of me had realized what time it was, but none of me had connected that time with the fact that on a normal day, I would have been home from work for a while already. And also would have eaten something, which probably explained why things looked like they were swimming. Blinking hard so I could focus on the screen, I carefully typed a response.

Me

> Yep, sorry. Was painting and lost track of time.

Z Biggest Asshole

> Can't wait to see what you painted. Wanna talk about yesterday?

Fuck.

I stumbled to the couch and plunked myself down so I didn't have to focus on standing and texting at the same time.

Me

What's there to tlak about?

"Shit," I muttered, realizing I'd sent it with a typo. As quickly as I could, I sent a second message, hoping he wouldn't notice.

Me

Why are you texting me? Don't you have strippers to hire or something?

Z Biggest Asshole

I'm back at the Mountainview now. And you really want to know if I'm hiring strippers for a party that both your brothers AND your dad will be attending?

I wrinkled my nose, then sent him back a middle finger emoji. His response included a laughing one, but my attempt to redirect the conversation didn't work.

Z Biggest Asshole

Teacup, I know you'll do almost anything to avoid giving me any credit whatsoever, but I can tell when you're not being yourself.

Me

No you cant

Z Biggest Asshole

Yes, I can. Like right now, for example.

Well your crazy because I am entirely myself right now

…not that you're a stickler for spelling or anything, but I don't think I've ever seen you use the wrong "your" before.

Ah, fuck.

I hadn't even started typing when my phone vibrated, and Z Biggest Asshole began flashing on my screen along with the selfie he'd sent me of himself at a gay bar in Victoria that I'd set as his contact photo.

"What the fuck," I said, then hesitated for half a second before hitting the Decline button.

Because yeah, I was trying to convince Zain he was full of shit. And yeah, I didn't think he knew me so well that he could tell when I wasn't myself.

But I also knew there was no way I'd be able to convince him I was sober. And then I'd have to explain why I was drunk. And I just…

I didn't want to.

Plain and simple. I didn't want to talk about it.

So I declined the call, then before he could be an asshole about it, I sent him another message

I'm in the middle of something. We can talk later

Are you sure you're not just avoiding talking to me?

His response took a while that time and I chewed on my lip, suddenly nervous.

And like, I knew that. I'd said it to myself a million times and probably to both Zain and Finn at least once or twice.

But that didn't mean I wanted to hear it.

That didn't mean I wanted to be reminded this was all my fault.

That I'd created the mess I was living in and that I was too fucking scared to crawl out of it because the potential mess when I did was even bigger.

And it didn't mean I was going to snap at Zain, though it did mean that I was glad no one was around to see the wateriness of my eyes as I typed my very mature and thoughtful response.

I am well aware of that but thakns for the reminder of the reason I've asid multiple times that I'm not mad or upset.

What is going ON with you?

What are you talking about?

My phone started vibrating, and again I declined the call.

Pick up.

No.

I just want to know you're okay.

I am fine.

Then pick up the phone and prove it.

He called again and I declined it, though my heart had started to pound in my chest.

Stop it. Stop calling me. And STOP ordering me around. You don't get to tell me what to do. You are not the boss of me and you need to get over the expectatation that you can try to control me liek that.

Z Biggest Asshole

I'm not trying to control you and I'm sorry you think that. I'm just fucking worried.

Me

Well, stop worrying.

And work on your fucking tone because I'm not putting up with this patriarchal toxic male bullshit.

And work on your fkuking apologies while you're at it because I'm not into this "Sorry you feel that way" bullshit, either.

Your being a prick.

He, wisely or not, didn't respond to that one right away. A few minutes later, my phone buzzed again, but instead of an actual apology from Zain, it was a message from Finn in our group chat:

He's sleeping again and Hailey and Abby came to take Mom to dinner so I'm just hanging out here. If hiccups suddenly got cured and completely stopped existing how long do you think it would take people to realize it?

It was a good question. It wasn't Finn's fault I was too drunk and angry to answer it well. So I just sent a short response—*I probably wouldn't ever notice*—before putting my phone back on the table and grabbing my beer. I went to take a sip, then paused, looking at the bottle queasily. Sighing, I pulled myself to my feet and went to the sink to dump the beer out, told myself I shouldn't order delivery for dinner because I had no paycheck anymore, then reasoned that I couldn't be trusted to use the oven right now and it was more important to actually eat something, so ordered delivery anyway. While I was waiting, I responded to Chuck—*No, not tonight. I'm already drunk and moping. Monday when I'm back from the bachelorette party?*—and then to Claire telling her to send me details of her and Julie fucking in the car.

I spent the rest of the night sobering up and watching TV on the couch with a throw blanket burritoed around me. My phone went off a few more times, but I ignored it until the swimming dizziness of my drunken vision turned to a resigned tiredness.

There were responses from Chuck and Claire, though neither seemed overly concerned with my lack of reply. Finn and Zain had kept messaging in the group chat, though it was mostly Finn. And then there was a message from Zain.

Z Biggest Asshole

You're right. I'm sorry for how I spoke to you.

I didn't message him back. It wasn't that I didn't believe him or something, but I just... I didn't have the capacity. I did message our group chat saying goodnight to both him and Finn, but I didn't text Zain directly.

And I probably should have. Because maybe if I had, I wouldn't have gotten ready for bed and tucked myself in, then stared blankly at the ceiling because my eyes refused to close.

Maybe I would have fallen into the dreamless void I was craving instead of letting my mind wander and wonder if I couldn't sleep because my queen-size mattress suddenly felt far too large for one person.

Maybe I wouldn't have started to worry about the next day, when I'd be flying out to Kelowna with none other than my stupid ex-husband. And then what would happen when said stupid ex-husband was spending the weekend around my stupid... Zain.

My stupid Zain.

I spent far longer than necessary convincing myself that sleep was just around the corner. When I couldn't lie to myself anymore, I got out of bed, sighing restlessly as I wandered to the kitchen for a glass of water.

Then brought that glass of water with me to my studio.

Then flicked the light on and replaced the *THIS IS BULLSHIT* canvas with my very last one, settled on my stool, and picked up a brush.

It wasn't finished when I finally dragged myself out of the studio after the sun rose the next morning. I hadn't quite captured the warmth of Finn's wide grin and there wasn't enough of a sparkle in Zain's eyes to turn the not-quite-accurate twist of his smirk into something less sarcastic, but that would have to wait until I could keep my eyes open and focused on something. As would the girl standing between them. She wasn't quite right, either.

But it was going to take a lot more than a few dabs of paint to fix that.

Twenty-Five

STAYING UP ALL NIGHT painting when I had a flight the next afternoon wasn't my best idea.

Nor was setting an alarm for an hour before I had to leave when I hadn't even started packing yet,

Or hitting the snooze button twice.

But I was not exactly renowned for my good ideas.

The first thing I packed was my phone charger, since I'd forgotten that the last time I'd gone somewhere. Then I packed six pairs of panties because of course I did. Then I frantically pulled clothes out of my closet and the pile of mostly-clean clothes near the window in a desperate attempt to find something cute enough to wear to a club for a bachelorette party. That was a waste of time, since I eventually grabbed my standard black leather pants and black satin top and black pumps because I didn't know where my other sort-of-sexy-but-in-an-I'm-not-nineteen-anymore-kind-of-way tops were.

I'd just shoved everything into my carry-on suitcase when there was a knock at the door. Before I could even turn around, it opened.

"Hello?" he called.

"Finn?" I said, abandoning my suitcase on the bed.

He was standing just inside the door dressed in a pair of grey shorts and a white t-shirt that set off the golden tanned glow of his skin. Given that his dad was in the hospital, I'd expected he would be tired, but he seemed better rested than I'd seen in a while. He looked at me, an almost abashed expression on his face.

"Sorry," he said. "I didn't know if I could just, like, come in now."

"Of course you can," I said. "You can let yourself in any time."

The abashed look changed into a lopsided smile. "Okay. Cool."

There was a quiet moment of awkwardness before I cleared my throat. "Um, what are you doing here?" I asked. "Did you forget something?"

"No," he said. "I'm here to take you to the airport."

"What?"

"For your flight. It's at two, right?"

"I mean, yeah, but I can take an Uber," I said. "You're supposed to be helping your dad. What if they discharge him or something?"

"They already did," he said.

"Wait, really?"

He nodded. "Yeah, he's home and napping. It was my turn for a break and Mom and Hailey can handle things for a bit. So I thought I'd drive you to the airport so I could see you before you go. If that's okay."

I tried to ignore the fluttery feeling in my chest. "It's definitely okay. Thank you."

There was another awkward moment and I frowned. I wasn't used to that kind of feeling with Finn; after living together for months, we were pretty in sync when it came to... well, a lot of things.

"Is everything okay?" I asked.

He glanced down, then back at me. "I mean, sort of. I was just kinda wondering though, are you mad that I'm going to live with Zain?"

It took everything in me not to growl in frustration. And by that I mean I took a deep breath and let it out as I internally screamed at Zain for dragging Finn into this.

"You know, the two of you teaming up on me is a lot more fun when it's in the bedroom," I said.

Finn frowned. "What?"

"You and Zain," I said.

"What team, though?" he asked, confusion still on his face. "Zain asked if I knew of any baseball leagues he could join in the spring or whatever and I said we could probably find a beer league and that I'd be totally up for playing too. But like, if you want to join, I'm sure there's a co-ed one we could—"

"No," I said quickly. "I don't do sports. I meant Zain telling you to ask me if I was mad about this."

The crease on Finn's forehead deepened. "He did?"

I studied him. Finn wasn't a good liar. Sure, he sometimes didn't tell people things because he didn't want to hurt them, but he wasn't great at lying about it. So it only took a moment of looking into his bright blue eyes to realize I was wrong.

"I guess he didn't," I said. "I'm sorry. He asked me the same thing and wouldn't drop it."

"Oh," he said. "That makes sense. He sounded kind of worried about it. But just, like, the other day you seemed kind of out of it and I didn't think much about it until last night, and I'm really sorry about that. I was just focused on—"

"Don't you dare apologize for focusing on your family right now," I said. "I'm sorry if I seemed upset but I really am not. You and Zain are going to have the best time living together."

That earned another smile. "Yeah, I think so. And Alfie's gonna love it too, I think."

"Of course he is."

"And you," he said. "'Cause you're going to come one day, right?"

And fuck.

Fuck.

"I'll come to visit," I said.

"Just visit?"

I swallowed back a lump in my throat, willing my eyes to stay dry. "Finn, even if things weren't complicated like they are, your apartment wouldn't be big enough for all of us. I mean, it's only two bedrooms and my painting stuff needs an extra room on its own."

"Right," he said.

I took a shallow breath and stepped towards him, reaching up and touching his cheek until his eyes met mine. Then slowly, softly, I kissed him.

He kissed me back, his mouth comforting and familiar and like home. For a moment, that was all that mattered: the taste of his lips and the feel of his breath and the smoothness of his cheek beneath my fingertips.

For a moment, I wondered what the fuck I was doing.

"You will still have to come here to let Alfie and Millie play," I said when we parted. "You can't just separate them now. And I'll come see you both."

"It's not the same, though."

"No, it's not," I agreed, and I hoped the smile I forced didn't look too sad. "But it'll be okay. It's still going to be good."

He leaned in for another kiss and I nearly lost my breath with how unintentionally sensual it was.

"I don't want you to be sad, Tess," he murmured.

"Don't you worry about me. I'm fine. I'm always fine."

I don't think that it was my imagination that Finn lingered in our embrace a little longer than usual. And even though he was his usual cheerful self as he loaded my suitcase in his car and asked me if I'd rather fight a herd of goats but the goats only had three legs each or one single goat but the goat was the size of a St. Bernard and had knives for hooves as we drove to the airport, I know I didn't imagine the way he wrapped his arms around me tighter than usual when we got there.

"You can just drop me off," I said as he put the car in park and put his hazards on. "I can get my suitcase out of the trunk."

He shot me one of those charming smiles. "How am I gonna hug you goodbye, then?"

It was a good point, and I would never turn down a hug from Finn. So I got out of the car as he grabbed my suitcase and put it on the sidewalk, then turned and opened his arms for a hug.

"Have a safe flight and an awesome time at the party," he said as he held me against his body. "I'll miss you both while you're gone."

Then he did that thing where he let go of me slowly. Where his arms loosened and we only parted just enough that we could look into each other's eyes. And his eyes flicked down to my lips, and I felt a shiver run through me.

And then, just before I could lean in, I saw something in my peripheral that stopped me.

Maybe I should have kissed him anyway. Maybe I should have done it to prove a point. Or because I knew it would hurt. Or just because I fucking wanted to.

But the reminder of what he could tell my family was too strong.

"I'll miss you too, Finn," I said. "Take good care of your dad and I'll see you next week, okay?"

He nodded and I forced a smile, then picked up my suitcase and walked towards the entrance, where Brad was standing with his eyebrows raised.

"Who was that?" he asked.

"A friend," I replied.

Brad glanced past me, where I assumed Finn was still getting into his car. "You hug all your friends like that?"

"He's having a bad day," I said. "So am I."

"Why?"

"Because I have to spend it with you, Brad," I said as I walked past him and through the sliding doors. "Why else?"

Part Five

Confession: The high road
is overrated.

Twenty-Six

MY MOM WAS UNNERVINGLY good at Pin The Cock On The Farmboy.

Seriously. It was worrying how accurately she could place a picture of a rooster on the enlarged—seriously enlarged—poster the maid of honour, Shenae, and Audrey's sister Jeanie had hung from the wall next to the pool. Where Audrey had almost tripped on an invisible crack in the concrete and I'd accidentally given the man chicken hands, Mom had nailed that cock right on the tip of the penis nobody had realized would be there.

"I'm sorry!" Shenae had gasped, tears in her eyes from laughing so hard after she and Jeanie unfolded the poster and Jeanie was so surprised by the picture that she'd fallen into the pool. "I thought it would have a star on his crotch like it did on the wrapper! Or that he'd be like a Ken doll or something!"

"That can't be real," Audrey's mom said. "He's gotta be wearing a prosthetic."

"I mean, it looks pretty real," Leslie, Audrey's pregnant sister, said.

"Yeah, right," scoffed Shenae. "They don't get that big."

There was silence around the pool. Obviously I didn't want to say anything because my mom was standing right there, but I would have said the Farmboy's dick was about the size of Finn's. But that didn't matter, because I wasn't the only one exchanging almost guilty looking glances with certain other women.

"I mean..." Leslie finally said.

"Don't you dare say Alex's looked like that," Jeanie said. "There's no way."

"You know as damn well as I do that I don't want to give that deadbeat any credit," Leslie said. "I might have married a bastard, but he was a bastard with a baseball bat down there."

It was more information than anyone probably wanted about Alex, Leslie's... well. Former husband might be the most accurate descriptor. Despite her being due to have her baby in the next three weeks, Alex had gotten cold feet and changed his mind about wanting to be a dad.

As much as I hated that for Leslie, it ended up working out well for me. Other than her, there were only two other single people involved in the bridal party: Zain and my other brother, Dylan. Once we'd divvied up the rooms in the estate house amongst everyone and their partners, there were two left: one featuring a king size bed and two singles, and another with two single beds. It didn't matter so much when it was just the girls and of course, we *could* have put a couple in the room with the single beds on the last night when everyone was staying there, but Leslie wasn't overly comfortable sharing a room with two men she didn't know very well.

So being the kind, compassionate, and selfless person I pretended to be, I volunteered to share the room with Leslie while Brad took a bed in the king-and-two-singles room with Dylan and Zain.

Zain wasn't especially pleased with the arrangement, of course, but because he was *actually* a compassionate person, he was happier with that arrangement than the one where I had to share a bed with my ex-husband, and so had barely complained about it.

"You're so full of shit," Shenae said to her sister. "Dicks do *not* get that big."

"They can," Audrey said casually. "There's a reason I'm finally getting married."

"Audrey!" her mom gasped.

A loud swell of hooting laughter rose from everyone, and it only got louder when she noticed I was standing there, frozen in place, and slapped a hand over her mouth.

"Oh, no, Tessa," she said. "I mean—"

"Please don't make this worse," I said.

She was laughing so hard she started crying and even I had to admit it was fucking hilarious. Although, I didn't admit that until I'd grabbed three of the Jello shots off the tray beside me and downed them in rapid succession. Mom, on the other hand, had been cackling at the original comment with everyone else, which was cause enough to take a fourth Jello shot.

I wasn't sure how we were all going to make it out that night. It was mid-afternoon, but after bottomless mimosas at the elegant brunch followed by the extensive wine tasting we'd done at the vineyard the estate house was on, it was safe to say we were all trashed. I don't think that had been the intent, given that a number of Audrey's older relatives, her mom, and my mom had been invited to the daytime portion of the Saturday activities, but damn if Audrey's family didn't know how to party.

And, apparently, damn if they hadn't influenced my mom to party with them.

I'd never seen this version of my mom before. "Lewd" wasn't a word I would have ever associated with her, but get her in the right company with a few mimosas and apparently, the same woman who had yanked an old Harlequin romance out of my hands as a young teenager and scolded me in a hushed tone about age-appropriate content also was first in line to pick her colour of penis-shaped tumbler to drink additional wine out of.

Well, second in line. She let Audrey go first because she was the bride, but Audrey's choice was obvious since there was only one white glitter-coated penis tumbler.

Mom picked the pink one.

It was extra surprising given that Mom wasn't even supposed to be there when we brought out the more salacious decor. But like I said, Audrey's family liked to party.

"Why aren't there any dicks here?" one of her aunts, who I thought might be named Marie but who everyone kept calling Bubbie, had asked.

"Because it's a bachelorette party," Leslie had replied. "And we've generally been referring to them as 'the men.'"

I had nearly spilled the prosecco I was pouring for myself and Jeanie as I laughed, but Bubbie waved a hand in the air.

"Not *men*," she said. "Although if you're looking for any entertainers, I might know a guy or two who—"

"No strippers," Audrey said. "Josh and I agreed no strippers for either of us."

"Pah," Bubbie said dismissively. "Either way, I meant *penises*. Where are the penis straws? The candy cocks? The dick decorations? Is this a bachelorette party or a… a… a nunnery?"

"Well, we were gonna put them up later," Shenae had slurred. "But we could break them out now."

There had been a cheer and I'd gone inside with her and Jeanie to grab the box of decorations they'd hidden. Along with the party guests, we'd started hanging things up by the pool, though I did down another Jello shot when I unveiled a large banner that read *SAME PENIS FOREVER* and my mom, of all people, shrugged and said "Unless you're swingers or something."

My mom.

My mom.

It was fine. I'd helped make the Jello shots the previous night and we'd purposely made them less boozy than usual for this exact reason. So my five shots were really more like two. Which was still a lot given how much wine I had in my system, but still. I was drunk enough to tolerate, again, my *mom* making sex jokes and comments about swingers like it was nothing, but not so drunk as to wonder if she was actually kind of okay with the concept of swingers.

It was my mom, after all.

It was just after I finished my fifth shot that Jeanie hooted with laughter and withdrew a flat plastic pouch and held it up.

"I forgot we bought this," she said. "Who wants to play Pin The Cock On The Farmboy?"

Which was a stupid question because of course we all did.

A corner of the large poster had ripped in the ensuing chaos of everyone realizing there was an actual picture of a naked farmboy with his bits on full display, but once Jeanie had climbed out of the pool, the three of us got it hung on the wall. One of Audrey's friends who was staying at the house ran inside to get the eye mask she slept in and as the bride, we'd made Audrey go first, then her mom, then each of the bridesmaids got a turn—Leslie bowed out, citing not wanting to wander around the pool blindfolded when she was nine months pregnant—and then, as Mother of the Groom, Mom wanted a turn.

"How the hell did you get it right there?" Shenae, who had pinned her cock to a section of wall three feet to the left of the poster, asked.

"When you're married for as long as I've been, you just know where these things are," Mom said as she slipped the blindfold off.

"Oh, God," I groaned. "How many Jello shots is it going to take for me to forget this?"

"It's payback for me having to hear exactly which of my son's attributes she's marrying him for," Mom said.

"So I get to be double scarred?" I asked. "Why would finding out—you know what, I'm not going there. I'm just going to drink more."

"That's my girl," Mom said. "Grab one for me, too."

"You know, that's what we should talk about," Bubbie said.

"Scarring Tessa?" Audrey asked.

"No! Marital tips." Bubbie lifted her glass. "The things every new bride needs."

"We did that at the bridal shower," said Audrey's mom.

Shenae snorted and waved her hand. "Yeah, in front of all the *proper* people."

"This is the real advice," Mom said. "Like how to find a dick in the dark."

Jeanie passed me a Jello shot without looking. "Actually yeah, that sounds fun. What advice do you have for the new bride, Bubbie?"

Bubbie walked—well, stumbled—over to Audrey, putting an arm around her shoulders.

"Well, dear," she said. "I know you're a good girl who's wearing white at her wedding, so I want you to know what's going to happen on your wedding night. You see, when two people love each other—"

She couldn't get the rest of the sentence out as everyone dissolved into laughter.

"No, no, for real," Jeanie said, flopping onto a lounger next to Audrey with her glass of wine and a loud squelching sound since she hadn't changed out of her wet clothes. "I have advice for you."

"Actual advice or more penis jokes?" Audrey said.

"Actual penis advice," Jeanie said. "You see, a good marriage always has the four F's."

"Is one of the Fs fucking?"

"Of course." She slung a dripping arm around Audrey's shoulders. "And the other three are Friendship, Fighting, and Fucking."

"You have fucking twice," Shenae said.

"You should definitely be doing it more than twice," Leslie muttered.

"No," Jeanie said, frowning. "I said Friendship, Fighting, Forgiveness, and Fucking."

"No, you said—well." Audrey laughed and leaned her head on Jeanie's wet shoulder. "Tell me about the four Fs."

Jeanie cleared her throat. "You need to be friends with your husband even though he's probably smelly. And when you fight, you need to forgive. And fuck. At least twice."

"That is excellent advice," Audrey said.

"And goes well with mine," said Bubbie.

"Which is?"

"Fight naked."

"What?!"

"Fight naked. Start taking your clothes off when you argue. That'll usually turn the fighting into one of the other Fs."

"Wait, do you both take your clothes off?" Audrey's mom asked. "Or just you?"

"Depends," Bubbie said. "If you wanna stop the fight, you tell him the rule and both of you strip. But if you wanna *win* the fight, you just start stripping down and he'll forget what he's saying."

For an impromptu advice session, it was pretty good. Some things were silly, some were practical, some hid practicality beneath ridiculousness in wonderful ways.

"Get a second TV," said one of Audrey's aunts. "No, seriously. Just get a second TV."

"Say I love you whenever you're parting so every goodbye is still a good one," Mom said. "And pick your battles. Compromise. If he wants to golf every weekend all summer, don't get mad. Get his credit card instead."

"Men like flowers too," Leslie said. "Alex sucks, but back when he didn't suck so much, he blushed like a teenager when I brought home lilies for him one day."

"If you want him to get you a little treat while he's at the store, tell him you want him to bring you home a little treat from the store."

"Don't tell him he's a dick when you're mad at him. Tell him he's *acting* like a dick. Complain about what he does, not who he is. Even if he's being a dick."

"Unless he walks out on you because he decides seven months into a pregnancy that he doesn't want to be a father," Leslie said. "Then he's a dick."

We all agreed with that exception.

"If he ever laughs at your choices, remind him that he was one of them," I said when it was my turn.

The others all laughed at that, though before the next person could speak, Audrey looked at me eagerly.

"Wait," she said. "Tess, you gotta have more than that for me."

"What?" I asked.

"You and Brad have such a great marriage," she said. "Brad is always so sweet and he'll do anything for you. I need all your secrets for success."

And fuck.

Fuck.

I was too drunk for that, but what the hell was I supposed to say? So I stalled, sipping my glass of prosecco as I tried to look thoughtful instead of panicked.

"Well," I finally said. "You won't always like each other."

Audrey looked both expectant and confused as everyone fell silent.

"You won't always like each other," I repeated. "But that's okay as long as you choose to love each other."

And as long as he doesn't cheat on you for your entire relationship, I thought, but I didn't say that part out loud.

"Good advice," Audrey's mom said.

"What else?" Jeanie asked, because apparently that wasn't good enough.

I took a deep breath, and then whoever the god or goddess of Jello shots was took over, because suddenly I was bullshitting my way through a list of marital advice.

"If something really bothers you, don't just let it go," I said.

Because sometimes there are some things the four Fs won't fix. Sometimes you can never forgive the fucker.

"Choose yourself first." Like when he begs and pleads for you not to leave, show yourself more respect than he does.

"Make sure your family likes him," I said. "But not *too* much." Otherwise when he inevitably fucks multiple other women, you'll get stuck faking a life you don't want to live because you're too afraid to find out for certain that they like him better than you.

"You each need your own space. And lots of it." Like living in different cities. Or... different apartments, maybe.

"Keep each other guessing," I continued. Like when he asks how far you'll go to keep a secret, get on your knees to show him.

"Recognize the big ways and the little ways he shows you love." Like giving up a promotion to defend you from your shitty ex or taking time away from his sick stepdad to drive you to the airport.

"Take care of each other." Like when you take him home so he doesn't have to live in his car. Or when he cooks you dinner every night. Or when he won't let something go because he knows you're lying to him about being okay even though it's super fucking annoying.

"And admit when you're wrong."

Like when he's rightfully worried about you because you're acting like an idiot and even though he apologized, you haven't come clean about losing your job and the way you're feeling and how you only realized how deep those feelings had gotten when they were taking the next step without you.

"That was beautiful, hon," Mom said, sounding like typical Mom as she spoke in a slightly stuffed-up voice and wiped a fake tear off her cheek. Then she took a loud sip from the straw of her penis-shaped tumbler.

"You can tell how much you care for him," Audrey's mom said.

I knew she meant well. And I knew she meant Brad because that's who everyone thought I was talking about.

But the image making my heart race right then was one of a smirking, dark-eyed man with tattoos and a beaming blonde with strong arms and soft lips.

Twenty-Seven

DESPITE SPENDING THE MORNING and afternoon polishing off most of the alcohol we'd purchased with the intent of it lasting the entire bachelorette weekend, everyone agreed we were in good enough shape to go out dancing that night.

Well, mostly everyone. Late that afternoon, the moms and aunts who weren't coming out clubbing that night bowed out to go back to their respective hotels, where I was sure my mom would pass out and eventually wake up wondering why she had a glittery gold penis shaped temporary tattoo in the center of her chest.

But the rest of us got ourselves ready to go out for dinner and dancing like we'd originally planned.

And it was fun, surprisingly. I didn't know many of the people there well since they were Audrey's friends and family and I'd also been sort of dreading anything to do with my brother's wedding because family obligations were stressful. But I spent a decent amount of time talking to Leslie who, despite her husband being a deadbeat, was excited to have her baby. And Shenae, the maid of honour, was as hilarious as Jeanie, the other bridesmaid, was recklessly chaotic. Dinner was delicious and after we were done, Shenae surprised Audrey with the hot pink limo we'd all pitched in to rent for the night to bring us from bar to bar, leading to a lot of squealing and woo-girling as we jumped in and popped a couple of bottles of champagne.

And yet, I couldn't bring myself to enjoy all of it.

I knew why. It's not like I was stupid. Willfully ignorant, yes. Straight up in denial, often. But stupid?

Well, also yes, but that wasn't the case this time.

It wasn't like I hadn't talked to Finn or Zain over the past two days. There was certainly tension there, but I wasn't giving Zain the silent treatment or ignoring Finn as he gave us updates on both his dad's condition—which was exceptionally good, apparently—and his progress of moving into his and Zain's apartment. I was responding to them both in our group chat, just like I always did, and had sent a few funny anecdotes of what was happening at the bachelorette party, including a stealth photo of the Farmboy.

Post-cock-pinning, of course. I wasn't about to send the boys an unsolicited dick pic. But after both of them demanded to see what the Farmboy was working with, I sent them a very solicited picture of him with the chickens removed.

But it was all very surface level. And I knew why. I knew why my own words from the advice-giving part of the bachelorette party were echoing in my head. I knew why things felt different than usual.

I was why.

Still, it took until we'd finished at the first bar for me to do anything about it, mostly because I needed a shot of tequila to calm myself. But once we got back into the limo, I settled myself in the corner while everyone else sang along to the pounding music and pulled out my phone.

I started with Finn because... well, Finn was the easier one to talk to.

Finn was sunshine. He was easygoing. He found the positive wherever he looked. Finn was the kind of person who made me want to be happier. And with Finn, there was understanding. Sure, sometimes it took a little effort to explain things because he had a habit of taking stuff way too literally and ended up thinking I wanted to join a baseball team when

I thought they were teaming up against me, but Finn understood the important things.

I envied his level of empathy. Finn would be sympathetic. He wouldn't get on my case about why I didn't tell him earlier; in fact, he'd probably commiserate about doing the same thing if he'd been in my shoes. If anything, he was just going to be sad that I hadn't told him in person because he wouldn't be able to give me a hug.

And that was exactly what happened.

Me

You know on Friday when you asked me if I was sad?

Finn

Yeah?

Me

I was. And I didn't tell you or Zain about it because you were both dealing with a lot of stuff and I didn't want to ruin how excited you both were about finding a place to live. Which I really am happy about for both of you. But I was sad because I got fired on Wednesday.

I'm sorry I didn't tell you sooner.

Despite my certainty that Finn would be understanding, I couldn't help but be nervous in those few moments between sending my texts and receiving his response. But it was, of course, for nothing.

Finn

Omg Tessa, I'm so sorry

That sucks so much

I totally get why you wouldn't have wanted to talk about it right away but thank you for telling me now

Are you okay?

I wish I could give you a hug

Did you tell Zain?

I waited until there was enough of a break between Finn's string of texts that I could tell he was done, which wasn't long; Finn was a quick texter, so when the last question came through and wasn't immediately followed by another one, I started typing.

Me

No, Zain doesn't know yet. I'm going to text him as soon as we're done talking.

Finn

He'll definitely want to know

I'm so sorry Tess
Everything's going to be okay though

If you want help finding a new job I can help

I'm not really sure how

Oh but like I go to a lot of businesses on my courier route so I can ask if people are hiring!

I couldn't help but laugh at his responses, and I definitely couldn't control that the sound was slightly watery. Hoping no one noticed me sniffle, I blinked hard a couple of times before sending another text.

Me

I'm not sure what I'm going to do yet, but I appreciate it. Thanks for understanding.

Finn

Of course. I'm here if you need anything at all

He followed that with a heart emoji that sent way too many emotions through me for something that was a cartoon symbol.

I didn't text Zain right away, but only because the limo pulled up to the next bar and I had to plaster a smile onto my face while we gave another set of bartenders a heart attack at the sight of a gaggle of women in their thirties descending upon their bar all at once. But as soon as we'd gotten our drinks and taken over a large booth near the back of the bar and took group selfies on three different phones, I texted him.

Me

How's the camping?

Maybe not the most telling opening line, but I wasn't sure Zain would get it right away since the reception near their campsite was spotty at best. Or maybe he was too close to one of my brothers or my dad to respond safely. Or maybe he would be too drunk to respond.

Of course, he responded less than a minute later.

Z Biggest Asshole

Miserable. What I wouldn't give for a shirt that doesn't smell like campfire and a mattress that doesn't collapse in the middle of the night so I end up sleeping on a tree root.

I bit back a smile.

Me

> You're the one who planned it, best man.

Z Biggest Asshole

> Yeah, well, you'd think I would've picked a place that at least had running water so I didn't feel like an unwashed mountain man or something.

Me

> I bet you look excellent grimed down.

Z Biggest Asshole

> What's that supposed to mean?

Me

> Yeah, like you know how people say someone cleans up well? You seem like the kind of guy who would grime down good.

He sent me back an eyeroll emoji and I had to cover another smile, knowing that meant he probably had that exasperated-but-not-actually-exasperated look on his face.

Z Biggest Asshole

> If by grime down good you mean I look like I smell and my hair hasn't been this greasy since I was going through puberty, then sure.

Me

> I don't believe you. Let me see.

Z Biggest Asshole

> You really think I'm gonna send you a pic when I'm literally surrounded by your family, "husband," and a bunch of guys who will for sure make fun of me for taking a selfie by the campfire?

Me

> Yes.

My phone buzzed a few minutes later and there was a photo of Zain taken in a way that made it clear he was trying not to be noticed. I wasn't sure if anyone had noticed or not; I was too busy gloating over the fact that I was right about how good Zain grimed down.

Because yeah, he did look like he smelled. Yes, his usually immaculately styled hair was messy. Yes, there was a layer of scruff on his chin thicker than I'd ever seen it since he generally shaved every day. And yes, he was wearing his glasses instead of his contacts, which was such a rare occurrence that I'd almost forgotten he even had them.

But holy hell, did he pull it off.

Z Biggest Asshole

> What you expected?

Me

> Better. Damn, you grime down really good.

Z Biggest Asshole

> You have the weirdest taste. I look like I'd give you a yeast infection.

Me

> Considering the last time I saw a greasy homeless-looking dude with a scruffy face and

> gross hair I took him home with me, I'm surprised you're just figuring that out.

He sent back a laughing emoji that time.

Z Biggest Asshole

> Where's mine?

Me

> Your what?

Z Biggest Asshole

> My pic. I miss your face.

Me

> You think I'm going to send you a pic when you're surrounded by my family and "husband"?

Z Biggest Asshole

> Don't worry, I'll make sure no one sees the screen.

I didn't bother making sure no one saw me taking the selfie. I figured no one would care if they saw me taking a selfie, which was proven when I couldn't send it to Zain immediately because Jeanie jumped into the booth beside me so we could take a set of selfies together. When she was done and we'd clinked our drinks, I waited until she'd gone off to dance more before sending the photo.

Z Biggest Asshole

> Fuck giving things up for a shirt and a mattress. What I wouldn't give to be in that bar with you right now.

I blushed, even though it was cheesy as fuck.

Me

> You will be tomorrow. Sort of.

Z Biggest Asshole

> **Not the way I want to be.**

Which was also true, although I had no idea how to respond to it. I also had no idea how to switch the conversation to what it was supposed to be about. But somehow, despite the fact that he was in the middle of the woods somewhere and I was in a loud, dark nightclub with pounding music, Zain could still read me like a book.

Z Biggest Asshole

> I know last time we texted, we didn't leave it on the best terms.

> I really am sorry, kitten.

I took a deep breath and let it out.

Me

> You were being an asshole, but you were right.

> Not about you and Finn moving, which I am appropriately bummed about but very aware that it's entirely my fault that things are the way they are.

> But I did have some stuff going on and I didn't tell you because you both seemed happy and stuff and so now I'm doing that because I should have told you before but I don't know how to appropriately transition from admitting that to what I actually need to say, so I'm just going to tell you I got fired on Wednesday.

I sent it, then tossed back the rest of my drink as I waited for his response.

Which was to call me. Like an absolute *idiot*.

And, also like an absolute idiot, I scrambled out of the booth and towards the entrance so I could answer it.

"What the fuck are you thinking?" I answered instead of saying hello.

"I said I was taking a walk to the bathroom," he said, though his voice was soft. "Are you okay? What happened?"

I glanced around. There was no one I knew nearby, but I still lowered my voice. "Loni found out about me and Claire."

"Like... that you're friends?"

"She had photos of us kissing."

He inhaled sharply. "Fuck."

"Yeah."

"Although..."

I frowned. "What?"

"Well, from a legal perspective, that's a questionable reason to fire an employee," he said.

"She thinks Claire was spying on CARE."

"And she has no proof of that because Claire wasn't."

"Well... yeah."

"So you could fight this."

"Sure, if I want it to get out that I'm hooking up with Claire," I said. "And if I want to risk everything I have to battle with a fucking billionaire who would never allow herself to have common sense because she thinks common things are for poor people."

"Doesn't Claire want to help?"

"I mean... maybe." My voice sounded small. "She might. When I... tell her."

He didn't say anything, but he didn't need to.

"I know, okay? I need to tell her. But she also had stuff going on last week and I know it's going to make her feel like shit. I don't need the lecture right now. I'm—"

"I'm not lecturing you," he said. "I just... I wish I could hug you right now."

And like, yeah, I expected that from Finn. But for some reason, hearing those words in Zain's low, deep voice almost broke me.

"I'll be okay," I said. "Everything is going to be fine."

And I know.

I know.

You think I'd have learned my lesson about even thinking things like "How could it possibly get any worse" or the falsely hopeful "It'll all work out" or using the fucking F word because everything was not F-I-N-E.

But I was nothing if not a gigantic idiot sometimes, which Claire kindly reminded me of the following day as I was trying to hide how much I was dreading going to Tidal Beats to meet up with the guys from the bachelor party.

CM

You are a gigantic idiot.

I raised my eyebrows at Claire's text message, abandoning my lipstick as I picked up my phone.

Me

In general or for a specific reason

CM

Ha fucking ha, Tessa. What the actual fuck?

My stomach dropped and my shoulders tensed. She couldn't have found out, not... not yet. Not before I had a chance to tell her.

Part of me agreeing to "give up" a night sharing a room with my "husband" so Leslie didn't have to sleep in a room with two men she didn't know was that everyone insisted I get one of the other rooms to myself for the other two nights. And that room had a private bathroom, which I decided I'd take full advantage of to get ready before moving all my stuff to the room with two single beds and no private bathroom.

And thank God I had, because if I hadn't been able to answer Claire's phone call, she would've probably gotten on her private jet and flown into Kelowna just to track me down and slap me.

"How fucking dare you make me learn this from my sister?" she said without even saying hello. Her voice was like dry ice, so cold it was almost heated, and I winced.

"I can explain," I started.

"How? How are you going to fucking explain this, Tessa?" she snapped back. "You got fired because of me and you didn't even have the decency to tell me?!"

"You were busy with Julie's parents and stuff," I said. "I wasn't trying to keep it from you, I was just—"

"You don't get to decide what information I can and can't handle!"

My face turned red. "It wasn't that I didn't think you could handle it—"

"No? What was it then? Because it sounds to me like you purposely didn't tell me this because I had other stuff going on and you made the call to not call me. Which sounds a lot like you thinking I couldn't handle it. You know that drives me crazy. You know that I had an ex who only stuck with me because she felt like I'd break down if she left and you fucking *know* I hate people trying to make that decision for me."

"That's not what I was trying to do," I said. "I was processing things and—"

"I should have been the first person to know," she said. "After you left, I should have been the *first* call you made. I was in that photo with you and you were fired directly because of me. But I got to find out by Paige thanking me for fucking with Loni because I was finally useful to her. You didn't think I'd want to know? That I'd want to help?! You thought hiding it from me—"

"I wasn't hiding it from you," I snapped, then lowered my voice to a hiss. "I was going to tell you, Claire, but I got fired, then I went home to find out that my... my... Zain and Finn got an apartment together and were leaving. And I texted you but you weren't around and I had eight thousand other things going on and I've been busy and drunk this entire weekend, so when exactly was I going to have time to tell you?"

"You could have made time."

"Just like you keep making time for me when you're busy with Julie all the fucking time these days?"

It was a low blow. It was an asshole thing to say. I mean, it was true, but it was also said as an attack, as a response to the anger and vitriol my supposed friend was sending through the phone at me as she screamed at me for getting fired.

Regardless, the intent of it was to hurt. And hurt it did. Because I was an asshole and when I was hurting, my reaction was to swing, to claw, to cause as much pain as I was being caused because somewhere along the way, I'd stopped taking the high road.

"So that's it, then," she said, her voice cold. "All this time you've been saying you're okay with me and Julie and now—"

"I *am* okay with you and Julie," I said. "But don't throw this 'making time for me' thing out when you've been as bad about it as I apparently am."

"Right, and you assuming that I can't handle hearing—"

"I knew you were busy with other stuff and decided to tell you about this at a later time," I said. "It's not like I fucking blame you, Claire."

She paused. "You don't?"

"Of course not! You're not some psycho fucking billionaire with a nemesis who thinks the epitome of betrayal is spying on the charity you started as a pissing contest with some other psycho fucking billionaire. I knew who you were. I knew what the risks were. I still wanted to be in your life. So why would you think I would blame you for this?"

"Because I..." she started, but trailed off. I didn't say anything and eventually she sighed. "I thought you would. I would."

"Yeah, well, I don't. But I'm glad you blame me for it."

"That's not what I—"

"You just said you would."

"If I was *you*, I mean."

"And what's the difference between you and me in this scenario?" I asked. "We're both in that photo. We're both kissing. The only difference is you work for a place you can't get fired from and I worked at one I could. So I guess it's my fucking fault, isn't it?"

"Tessa, I didn't mean—I'm sorry," she said.

"Yeah, well, me too," I replied, though it was probably a bit too aggressive to sound like an actual apology.

"Let's... let's talk about this when we calm down," she said. "When you're back from Kelowna. Tomorrow night?"

"I have plans tomorrow night," I said. "Tuesday I'm free."

"Okay. I can make Tuesday work."

"Cool. See you then."

"Tess, I'm—"

"I have to go," I said.

She sighed. "Okay. Bye."

I hung up, but it took a while before my hands stopped shaking enough for me to finish putting on my lipstick.

Twenty-Eight

"Oh my God, she's adorable," Leslie said, grabbing my phone so she could look at the photo Kira had just texted me. "Look at that messy little stinker."

It was a very accurate description of the photo, which featured Jackson holding Velma while they sat at the table, looking mildly amused as his daughter grasped a handful of spaghetti that was dangling off his fork. She didn't quite seem to realize it was food, but her tiny hand was covered in tomato sauce, as was Jackson's plaid button-down shirt.

Hope you don't mind some unsolicited "noods" was the accompanying message that Kira had sent, which was what had caught Leslie's attention as I snorted back a laugh. And of course, being at the about-to-pop level of pregnant that she was, she immediately wanted to know anything and everything about Velma.

It wasn't the conversation I'd expected to have in a place like Tidal Beats, which was the kind of trendy and pretentious club I would have loved going to when I was in university. As it stood, I was now the type of person who looked on in amusement at the early twenty-somethings acting exactly how I would have acted, like they were too cool for everything because they'd been to a far chicer place when they were in Vancouver or Toronto or, depending on just how pretentious they were, New York.

My go-to black outfit would have fit in perfectly at a place like this, seeing as there were at least four other people wearing something almost identical to it. But I wasn't wearing it that night. I'd wanted to, but the moment I stepped out of the bedroom, Audrey shook her head.

"You wore that last night," she said.

"I don't have anything else," I said. "Unless you want me to go in my bathing suit."

She grinned and grabbed my hand. "Nope. I have something for you."

Which was both good and bad.

Good because Audrey had a gorgeous wardrobe that I'd always envied and we wore nearly the same size. Bad because she picked out a skirt that wasn't nearly as short on her as it was on me because despite our height difference, I had a far more prominent ass than she did. Not to mention that I hated wearing skirts, but Audrey was so excited about how good it looked that I couldn't bring myself to ask for something else. Paired with a sheer long-sleeved top that I wore over a simple black camisole, I almost looked... well.

I don't know what I looked like. Like I regularly went out to clubs or something, maybe. Either way, Audrey had declared it the perfect outfit.

"It might be too perfect," Shenae said. "Brad's gonna want to bow out early so they can get back here and boink before they have to share their rooms with other people."

"Boink?!" Leslie had repeated.

"You know," Shenae said, then started pumping her hips forward as Leslie nearly collapsed with laughter.

"This has been one of the lewdest weekends ever and you decided using the word *boink* was the best course of action here?" Jeanie had asked.

I'd laughed my way through it, but the reminder that I was about to spend my evening pretending I was married to Brad made my stomach curl.

We went out for dinner before the guys got back from their camping trip so they had full access to all the bathrooms in the estate house.

Once we were done, we'd gone to Tidal Beats to wait for them. Audrey was dancing with some of her other friends, but I'd been distracted by the text from Kira and fell into conversation with Leslie as I sipped a far-too-trendy martini that wasn't getting me as belligerently drunk as I'd hoped and she sipped a virgin rum-and-coke at the large table reserved for our group.

So when the bachelor party walked in, we were the ones they saw first.

My brother was leading the pack. He wasn't looking in my direction as they walked in, instead scanning the dance floor as if he instinctively knew that was where Audrey would be. No one would have guessed any of them had been sleeping in tents for the past two nights. Most of them were dressed in jeans and t-shirts, some with a sports coat, but a few of them had worn polos or button-up shirts.

Like the one Zain was wearing.

My heart skipped a traitorous beat as I set my eyes on him. It had to be my imagination because he was still on the other side of the bar, but I swore I could smell the freshness of his cologne from where I sat. He looked like if I buried my face against the deep purple fabric of the dress shirt he wore, I'd be engulfed in something spicy and green and distinctly him. His hair was clean and styled in his usual way, pushed sort of back and to the side so it highlighted the strong lines of his face. His sleeves were rolled up to his elbows and there was a new watch on his left wrist, or at least one I hadn't seen him wear before. Then jeans, perfectly fitted but belted all the same, showing off his gorgeous ass and—

"God, he looks good," Leslie said.

"Yeah," I said as Zain's eyes met mine.

And fuck.

If he kept throwing looks like that in my direction, it was going to be a long fucking night.

"You are seriously the luckiest woman alive," Leslie said. "Girl, you hold on tight to him, because I think every woman in this room would consider nabbing him if you ever let him go."

It took me a second to realize she was talking about Brad. I looked back at the group of men. My eyes hadn't made it past Zain, but Brad was standing on Josh's other side as they all approached the table.

And he, of course, was looking right at me, too.

"There she is," he said as he walked up, an easy smile spreading across his face. "Hey, beautiful. Did you miss me this weekend?"

"Of course not," I said, and Leslie laughed loudly.

"You'll have to forgive me," Brad said, leaning in to greet Leslie. "But I don't remember if we've met."

"Oh, I'm Leslie," she said, sticking her hand out to shake Brad's. "Audrey's sister, the bridesmaid who had to pull out because her dumbass husband couldn't. And no, we haven't met. But I recognized you from the wedding picture."

"What wedding picture?" I asked.

"Yours!" she said. "Josh and Audrey have your thank-you card on their fridge. Your dress was gorgeous."

Well, that was news to me. Mom and Dad didn't even have the thank-you card from my wedding, though that was because it had burned in the fire along with everything else they owned. And Audrey hadn't been around when Brad and I got married, so that meant Josh was the one who had kept it all this time.

"That's so sweet of them," Brad said, then looked at me. "We really need to visit your brother more. I didn't even know that."

I tried not to grimace. "Me neither."

"Between you and me, I think it's because they look up to you two so much," Leslie said conspiratorially. "Because you have such a strong relationship. Josh wants to be that good of a husband for Audrey."

It was much, much harder to keep the grimace in that time. "Lucky Audrey."

Brad laughed brightly and, purposely or not, tightened his arm around my shoulders. I did everything I could not to project how uncomfortable I was. I probably would've succeeded, too, if Zain hadn't picked that exact moment to walk up to the table.

"How are you all doing?" he asked the three of us, though he was looking at me.

"Great," Brad said brightly. "Don't you worry about us. Go and have some fun, man."

"Oh, I will," Zain said. "But I need to borrow Tessa for a minute. Audrey mentioned wanting to do a group photo of the wedding party tonight and another one at the actual wedding, so I figured arranging that now instead of when everyone's too drunk to function might be for the best."

"Oh," I said. "Sure. And Leslie too, right?"

But Leslie shook her head. "As fun as that sounds, I feel like a photo of me nine months pregnant in a nightclub may be taken the wrong way by certain jerkwad husbands I'm potentially divorcing."

I could have kissed Zain for coming up with something to get me out of there. I mean, I couldn't have because Brad was right there along with everyone else who thought I was married. But tomorrow, when we were back in Vancouver.

Then I was going to kiss him.

And more, probably. But I couldn't think about that right now because I didn't know if my panties could handle those kinds of thoughts this early in the goddamn party.

"Thank you," I said after Brad let go of me so I could follow Zain.

"Anytime, kitten." His voice was low and he hit the pet name hard, like he was laying his claim to me even though no one was there to hear it. "Although I'm pretty sure this is proof that you're actually evil."

"What is?"

"The way you look tonight." He kept his voice steady, but I felt each word curl through me. "The see-through top. That fucking skirt. You're killing me."

"I borrowed it from Audrey, if that helps."

"Not really," he muttered. "Especially when I have to sit there and watch that fuckwit touch you like he owns you."

"You need to calm down," I murmured. "No one can find out. Least of all him."

"I know, Teacup. I won't do anything." He slipped a hand behind me, putting it on the small of my back and guiding me towards the spot where everyone was dancing. To anyone else, it would have looked like an innocent gesture, but it was like sparks danced through my spine and to all my extremities as he touched me. "But just so you know, when we get back tomorrow, I'm taking us both straight to your place and doing every filthy little thing I've been imagining doing to you since I walked in until the only word you know how to say anymore is Daddy—hey, Auds! You wanna do that group photo?"

"Oh my God," Audrey said over the music. "Yes! Thank you for remembering." She wrapped an arm around Zain and kissed him affectionately on the cheek. "What would we do without you?"

"That's why you're the best, man," Josh said, coming up and clapping his hand on Zain's shoulder before turning to me. "Teacup! How's it going?"

"Uh... good," I said as steadily as I could given that Zain had just unsettled me in the best way with his words. "How are you?"

"Drunk," Josh said firmly, and then proved it when he threw an arm around my shoulder. I almost fell over, not because he jostled me too hard or anything, but because I couldn't even remember when the last time I hugged my brother was. "You know, Teacup, we don't hang out enough."

Oh, God.

"Don't we?" I asked.

"Of course not." He took a sip from the beer he was holding. "You're too far away. It's stupid."

"Well, maybe you're the one who's too far away," I said.

I wasn't expecting him to nod solemnly. "Maybe. 'Specially since you're stealing this asshole from me!" He switched his beer to the hand that was still around my shoulder and threw his other arm around Zain.

My heart lurched. I knew that he meant Zain was moving to Vancouver and that Vancouver was a lot further from Burnsley than Kelowna was. But the way he phrased it, the moment that Zain and I made eye contact as Josh pulled Zain closer...

It wasn't exactly a good feeling.

"You'll come visit me though," Zain said in an even, warm voice.

"Yeah, but it's not the same, man." Josh sighed. "I already didn't see you enough. Now you're even farther."

"It'll be good, man," Zain said. "You're gonna be busy trying to knock up your hot new wife—"

Josh burst out laughing.

"—and then when you need a break, you've got the perfect place to escape to. Plus then you can see Teacup more often, too."

"Yeah," Josh said, brightening up. "The five of us can go for dinner and shit!"

I laughed, hoping it didn't sound too nervous. Because of course Josh thought Brad lived in Vancouver.

Of fucking course he did, and of fucking course I was going to have to deal with that eventually.

"And besides," Zain said, not quite ignoring what Josh said but also not acknowledging it. "You think my mother's gonna let me get away with not visiting them at least once a month? I might as well buy stock in Air Canada with how much I'm gonna be flying back and forth."

"Finally, your mom being super overprotective does something good for us," Josh said, then lifted his beer up. "To overbearing parents!"

Zain laughed, but I was fairly sure it was forced. "At least your dad didn't insist on coming tonight."

"You kidding?" Josh snorted. "He couldn't wait to get out of there so he could get a round of golf in. He's got another tee time tomorrow, apparently."

"Not going to join him?" I asked.

Josh laughed. "Teacup, I'm planning on being too hungover to even move tomorrow, let alone swing a club."

"Guys!" Shenae said, flapping her hand to beckon us forward. "Come on! Are we taking this picture or what?"

Josh reluctantly let go of me and Zain. I glanced at him, wondering if he felt as unsettled as I did, but his face was hidden behind a cool mask and the darkness of the club.

But as the bridal party huddled together for the photo, Zain moved in beside me. Then, hidden behind the forms of the celebrating people in the photo, he slid his hand around my waist again, holding me against him for a far-too-brief moment.

And I swear, that was the only reason I was smiling in the photo.

Once the photo was taken, I let Audrey drag me to the bar as her brother, Ben, insisted on buying a round of shots. My intention was to get myself a drink and go back to the table, but Dylan, of all people, suggested Audrey and Josh get muff dive shots.

"Isn't that the one with the glass full of whipped cream?" Audrey asked.

"And you have to find the shot in it," Dylan said. "Yeah."

"No way! It'll fuck up my makeup."

"Aw, babe," Josh said. "Are you too chicken to go against me? I know I'm damn good at muff dives, but—"

"TMI, man," Dylan muttered.

"Come on, babe," Josh said, ignoring him. "Muff dives, you and me." He leaned down and pressed a kiss to her lips. "I'll lick all the whipped cream off your face if you want me to."

"I fully regret making this suggestion," Dylan said, sighing.

His regret didn't change the fact that Josh talked Audrey into it, nor did it change the fact that Audrey definitely beat Josh at the muff dive competition. It did, however, get me another round of shots as Dylan and I agreed we deserved one after that, and by the time I finally got myself an actual drink rather than just a shot, I'd been away from Brad and the table for long enough that even I knew it was starting to look suspiciously like I didn't want to be around him.

Which I didn't, and I was starting to wonder why I was continuing to do this to myself when the person I wanted to be around was steadfastly refusing to do a muff dive with Josh, though Audrey was slowly but surely wearing him down.

But that was a thought for Sober Tessa to suppress. Bachelorette Party Tessa was a good amount of drinks in and didn't need to be dealing with those thoughts in the first place. So I procrastinated just a bit longer, just long enough to see Zain finally sigh and give in to the squealing excitement of everyone at the bar. And then a bit longer so I could see him shove his face into the whipped cream and also beat Josh's ass at finding the shot glass first. And then just before I could think about the fact that I wanted nothing more than to go and lick the whipped cream off Zain's lips, I excused myself and went back to the table.

Brad and Leslie weren't the only ones at the table anymore. One of Audrey's other friends was there, as was a cousin that I knew Leslie was close with. The two of them had their eyes focused on Brad like he was the only person in the room, even as he had an arm wrapped around Leslie's shoulder. She was holding a cocktail napkin, her cheeks red as she dabbed it under her eyes, and I was fairly sure from the position of Brad's other arm that he had it resting on her thigh.

None of the three women there knew it was an act, but I knew better. I knew he was falling into that old standby of his, the one where he was such a good guy and so sympathetic and just always there for whoever needed him. And that eventually, that would drown out the thoughts they had of "No, this man is married," and he would win.

Because it was a game to him. He'd said it was an addiction, a fixation, an irresistible compulsion that he'd fallen to again and again, but it wasn't. It was a fucking game of how much could he get away with, how far could he push things, how many women could he talk into his bed because sure, sex was good, but sex with a woman he wasn't supposed to be having it with was better.

And he was pulling that on Leslie, who was nine months pregnant and also kind of like my friend.

Which meant, as much as I wanted to run away and puke, then drink until my mind was foggy and I puked again, I felt obligated to at least check on her. So I drew in a breath, let it out, then casually walked behind the table so they wouldn't see me.

"...deserve more," Brad was saying. His words were intended for Leslie, but intentional or not, he was speaking loud enough that everyone could hear him over the thumping bass of the music. "You do what's best for you and your baby, but never forget that. You deserve more, Leslie."

Leslie made a blubbering sound and swiped the napkin across her eyes again. "I just don't understand why. Like, who waits until now t-to change his mind about being a father? What kind of person does that?"

"No real man would do that to you," Brad said. "No real man would walk away from the woman carrying his child."

"Yeah, but what am I supposed to do now that he has?"

"You want my honest answer?"

She nodded.

"Kick his ass to the curb. Take him for everything you can, make him pay you child support, and move on. You're a fucking catch, Leslie. You don't need a man like that."

I almost laughed. Almost. I mean, it would have been completely inappropriate and likely started a veritable war between me and Leslie because it would have sounded like I was laughing at Brad saying she was a catch. So I didn't, even though hearing Brad advise another woman to leave her husband was beyond ironic.

God, it was fucking hilarious.

Or heartbreaking.

I couldn't quite decide at that moment, but it didn't matter. Brad was distracted and that meant I could ignore him for a little longer. So I went to get myself another drink, being careful to avoid putting myself in the sightlines of Audrey and Shenae as they took over the dance floor.

Nearly everyone had joined them. Josh was a surprisingly good dancer, actually. Dylan less so, but he still swayed from side to side as he clutched a beer and chatted with one of the guys I didn't know. Ben was dancing with Shenae, Jeanie was doing what looked like the sprinkler much to the amusement of her husband, and Zain was walking up to the bar and sliding in beside me as he flagged down the bartender.

"Smooth," I said.

He smirked. "Just checking in. You okay?"

"Of course. I love watching my so-called husband put the moves on an overly emotional pregnant woman who keeps blubbering about how good a guy he is."

Zain's nose wrinkled. "Ugh."

"My thoughts exactly. So I decided to distract myself with more alcohol."

The bartender came up and Zain shouted his order across the bar.

"Why don't you go dance?" he asked after the bartender walked away to get his drink.

"I said I needed a distraction, not to torture myself and everyone else in the room," I said.

"I might have a distraction for you."

My heart thudded loudly. I wished it hadn't. I wished his words had made me nervous instead of excited. That they'd disgusted me instead of intriguing me.

Because we were in public. With over half my family. With people who didn't know about my divorce. With Brad.

I should've rolled my eyes and told him to calm down, that it was stupid to even hint at us being anything more than slightly less than strangers involved in the same wedding party.

"What kind of distraction?" I asked instead.

The bartender set a shot on the bar. Zain paid him and threw a healthy tip into the jar, then turned nonchalantly towards me.

"See those stairs over there?" he asked, nodding towards a large staircase across the room.

"Yes," I said.

"Those go upstairs."

I gave him an unimpressed look. "You don't say."

"Mm-hmm. In related news, did you know I used to work here when I was in school?"

"Really? I can't picture you working somewhere like this."

A smirk twisted his mouth. "Well, I didn't work *here*. This place didn't exist until about five years ago. Before that, there were two businesses. There was an awesome Mexican restaurant on one side, then the pub I worked at on the other. And they shared the second floor and rooftop patio."

"Wow," I said. "That's so distractingly interesting."

"If you think that's interesting, wait until you find out that those stairs didn't used to be there. It used to be that the only ways you could access the second floor were the staircase in the Mexican restaurant, which used to be over there—" He gestured to an area behind a large bar along the back wall. "—that I'm guessing they now use as a staff staircase or something. Or there were the outdoor stairs."

"I don't remember seeing any stairs outside."

"That's because it was cheaper to board them up than it was to remove them," he said. "But the thing is, with building codes and such, having a completely inaccessible staircase that someone could get trapped in is a really bad idea."

"I can imagine."

"Mm-hmm. So there's a set of stairs outside that you can't get to from the inside, but that you could access from the outside if you knew exactly where to look."

I sipped my drink, not looking at him and instead letting my eyes scan around the bar. "And if one wanted to know exactly where to look for those..."

Zain's tongue poked out, wetting his lips. "You know, I can't quite remember the exact spot they are. But if you're really interested, I guess I could run outside to remind myself."

"And what should I do to distract myself in the meantime?"

He took his shot, then leaned towards me under the guise of setting the glass on the bar, bringing his lips nearly to my ear.

"Just be patient, kitten," he murmured.

Twenty-Nine

"Wow, you sure know how to spoil a girl."

Zain grimaced. "They didn't used to be this, uh…"

"Gross?" I said, putting my small clutch purse on one of the less-gritty steps.

He laughed. "Look, it's been a few years since I've been here."

He'd been right about needing to know where to look to access the stairs. They were in the alley, not quite visible from the sidewalk, and the gap that was just big enough for us to squeeze through was opposite the alcove where the staff probably smoked in the winter. And it wasn't like I was expecting the stairs to be five-star luxury stairs or something, but I wasn't exactly expecting the dirty, barely lit, and slightly damp space that we ended up in.

"If anything this weekend is going to give me a yeast infection, it's this place," I said.

Zain chuckled again. "We don't have to mess around, Teacup. We could just, like, hang out for a few minutes. I mean, mostly I wanted to—"

And then his arms were around me.

I melted against him. I couldn't help it. Grimey as that staircase was, it was suddenly the place I wanted to be most in the world. Zain's arms were tight around me, holding me to his chest and confirming that I'd been right about how goddamn good he smelled.

Though, maybe it just seemed even better by comparison because the staircase was so musty.

Regardless, that hug was everything. The way his face was buried in my hair was everything. The beat of his heart against my cheek was everything I'd needed and more, and for the first time since... well, since at least the previous Wednesday, I felt settled.

Grounded.

Right.

"I'm sorry about your job," he said. "And about last week. I'm sorry I was an ass."

"It's not like you knew," I said.

"That doesn't mean I had the right to be an asshole." He pressed his lips to the side of my head, cradling me like I was precious, and something warm began sparking in the pit of my stomach. "I'm sorry I assumed it was all about me and Finn. That I didn't listen to you."

"Yeah, well..." I half shrugged in his arms. "You had some valid points. I mean, I see where you're coming from."

He loosened his grip a bit. "What do you mean?"

"Like, about it being my fault. That we can't all... you know. Be together or whatever."

"It's not your fault."

I sighed, pulling back, and he let his arms drop from around me. "It is, though. I'm the one who has all this fucking marriage and family baggage that I keep letting run my life. If it wasn't for me—"

"—then I'd be responsible for it."

I frowned in confusion. "What?"

He looked at me, something almost remorseful on his face. "If we didn't have this stopping us, Teacup, what do you think would happen? You think we'd all live happily ever after and everything would be fine? Finn's family would just accept that he's in a relationship with two people? Your family would be all hunky-dory about you and me being together?"

"I mean, maybe."

"Great," he said. "So then it would be me not being able to tell my fucking parents that I—"

The words seemed to get stuck in his throat and he fell silent.

And with anyone else, I might have just assumed this was something he'd thought of in a moment of self-reflection because we'd argued about it on Wednesday. I might have assumed he realized he was keeping secrets, too, and that he wasn't being fair to me by thinking it was my fault we had no future.

And sure, that might have been true. But something in the way he tore his eyes away from mine, something about the way he held his jaw, the slight crease on his forehead...

"What happened?" I asked.

"It doesn't matter."

"Zain."

"It's nothing I didn't expect."

Biting my lip, I reached out, weaving my fingers between his and pulling myself closer to him. He closed his eyes.

"Please tell me," I said.

He hesitated for another moment, then opened his eyes, but glanced down.

"I went to see my parents on Thursday," he said. "Because if I didn't, I'd be getting a guilt trip for the rest of my damn life over it. And they're pissed."

"About what?"

"Me moving." He sighed. "Dad's retiring. They want to move into Kelowna. Mom had this vision of her perfect little family all being near each other again, and now I'm ruining it because I'm leaving. That turned into my dad insinuating I had to change jobs because my lack of relationship meant I wasn't ever going to get promoted, since I couldn't show commitment to anything and what was the point in promoting someone who didn't have a family to support. And my mom lamenting about how I was going to find a girlfriend in Vancouver when I didn't know anyone or have any friends there.

"And I finally asked her. I finally fucking asked why it mattered so much, why I couldn't just do things on my own time. And I believe the exact response she had was 'If you don't start seriously thinking about settling down and finding a wife, people are going to start questioning what you are.'"

He punctuated the sentence with a dry little laugh.

"Zain..." I said softly.

He shook his head. "If it was just you and me, Tess... I mean, they'd be scandalized because you're 'married' and then again because you're divorced, but they'd be fine. They'd get over it. But it's not just you and me." He looked up at me, his eyes hurt. "I never, ever in my life thought this would be what I needed, but it is. And whenever I think of telling my parents, it's like my chest is fucking collapsing. There's... I dunno. Connotations to that kind of thing and yeah, my parents aren't as religious as others, but I figured it would still be an issue. But I thought they'd at least accept if I wasn't straight, you know? And they can't. But that first time with the three of us, I thought... I just thought it was gonna be fun and hot and that would be it. But now I need him as much as I need you. I need both of you."

I didn't know how to respond to that. I couldn't respond to that. Because yes, somewhere in my heart, I'd known that. I'd known it was something far deeper than I could admit.

But we couldn't.

"I can't tell them," he said. "I fucking... In the middle of that conversation, I thought, what if I just fucking said it? What if I just came out, right now, told them I'm bi and that I've probably been with more men than I have women at this point? And let me tell you, I just wanted to fucking say it, but I... couldn't. I couldn't face it. So even if I didn't need both of you the exact same amount, even if you never told your family about you and Brad, it's not like I could just pretend to be with Finn. I... I can't tell them."

I wished I didn't understand how he felt as much as I wished he didn't finally understand how I felt. I wished neither of us had to know what it was like to choose personal unhappiness because that was less painful than the alternative.

I wished, for what wasn't the first time but the first time that I'd acknowledged it, that he'd told me how he felt years earlier.

I wished things were different.

But they weren't. And there was no changing the past. There was only now, and there was only what we had. There was the strange little life we'd developed, one bound in secrecy, one that let us be happy with what we had even though we couldn't have everything.

Because yes, maybe one day I'd have come clean to my family. Maybe I would have told them what I'd done.

But I refused to ask Zain to do the same thing. Not when he wasn't ready. Not when I wasn't ready.

And between the two of us, I didn't know if we ever would be.

I didn't say anything before pressing my lips to his, but it didn't seem to matter. He accepted it, embraced it and embraced me, his breath warm and his lips comforting as we kissed away the hurt, at least for a while.

"Zain," I murmured.

"Hmm?" he replied.

"You smell like whipped cream."

He laughed, his breath soft against my mouth. "Do I taste like it, too?"

"No. You taste like beer. It's a weirdly delicious combination. Like... like an ice cream float, but with beer."

"If you like it, kitten, I'll make an effort to taste like this every time you kiss me," he said, pulling me in closer so our bodies were pressed together.

If one of us had been smart, we would've ended things there. One of us would have sensibly pulled away and reminded the other we were in a dirty staircase outside a club containing a ton of people who could never know about this.

But it was pointless; the moment he held me against him, I knew we weren't going to leave that little space until we'd given in and fucked. I didn't have the strength to say no, especially not when what I wanted to say was yes, and Zain...

Well.

It was almost like he needed it more than I did.

There should have been a sense of urgency to the way we touched each other. I guess there kind of was, but not in the way there should have been. We should've hurried, kissing frantically until I was wet enough for him to shove his cock inside me, which wouldn't take long because just being around him was enough to make my body react. We should've fucked hard and fast, filthy and nasty like the room we were in, and gone back to the party hoping no one had noticed we were gone.

But the urgency we had wasn't like that at all. It was an urgency for each other, an urgency that we couldn't get enough of. I couldn't seem to hold his body close enough to mine; he couldn't seem to touch enough of me at once, his hands going from cupping my cheek to sliding down my arms to pulling my hips towards him so I could feel the bulge in his pants.

Normally, Zain liked to talk. He would whisper dirty things in my ears, call me his kitten, tell me all the things he loved about my body and all the things he was going to do to me. But that night, his mouth barely left mine, too busy claiming my lips to do anything else.

Still, we managed to communicate through those kisses. It didn't take words for me to know he needed me to undo his pants, just like I didn't need to say anything for him to know he needed to lift my skirt and shove my panties to the side. Neither of us needed to say anything to know he was going to push my back against the dust-covered wall or that I was going to wrap a leg around his waist, my hands resting on his shoulders so I could balance carefully as he reached down to guide his hard cock into my pussy.

And neither of us needed to say anything to know what we were thinking as he stared into my eyes, not looking away for even a moment as my body accepted his cock inside it.

Neither of us should have said anything, but he tried.

"Tessa," he whispered. "I—"

"Don't," I said. "Don't say it."

So he didn't.

He just leaned in, kissing me as he fucked me slowly and sweetly and deeply against that wall.

As he made love to me.

Stupid as that sounded. Not just because it was corny but because it was stupid for us to fuck like that. It should have never gotten to that point. We should have stopped long, long before it had. We should have stopped before it was even a reality, back when this was nothing more than a heated moment in a hotel room, falling to my knees in front of him to show him how much I needed him to keep my secret for me.

But we didn't stop.

"You're getting close, kitten," he murmured. "Aren't you?"

"Yes," I gasped.

He smirked against my lips, slowing his thrusts. "Yes, what?"

It took everything in me not to whimper, which included clenching my muscles and tightening my pussy around his shaft and making him let out a staggered groan of a breath.

"Yes, Daddy," I whispered.

"Fuck," he said. "You feel so fucking good. You're gonna come for me and then I'm gonna come inside you, okay? I'm gonna fill this pretty little pussy up with all my cum. You want that?"

"Yes," I pleaded.

"Say it, kitten," he growled.

"I want your cum, Daddy," I whimpered, clutching him hard as I felt my body slowly but steadily climb to that euphoric peak. "I want you to cum in my pussy, fill me up, put your baby in there—"

He cut me off with a groan. "You don't know how bad I want that, kitten. You don't know how much I love coming inside you. The only thing I—" He interrupted himself with a shaky groan as he kept moving "—the only thing that comes close is when I'm inside Finn, when I'm fucking his ass while he fucks you, when I know you can feel the way I'm moving even though it's his cock inside you. I love the way he fucks you. But when we get home, I'm gonna make him change spots. I'm gonna make him fuck me while I fuck you. And trust me, kitten, you're going to be so full of cum it's going to be spilling out, it's going to be all over your goddamn pussy and thighs and then he's gonna clean it up with his tongue and—"

I tried as hard as I could not to cry out as I came, but it was futile. Zain hurriedly put a hand over my mouth, muffling the sound as I trembled, spasms of pleasure wracking every inch of me as he kept sheathing himself inside me. His own grunts were quiet, even as he reached his own peak, letting me feel him flood my pussy with rope after rope of cum.

He held himself in place as we both caught our breaths and came down from that high. His hand moved from covering my mouth to the side of my neck, caressing it as he kissed me. My eyes were closed as I rested against the wall, but I kissed him back, my body tired but satisfied, fulfilled and content and so perfectly right with his cock softening inside it.

But we couldn't stay there forever. We shouldn't have been there as long as we had been. So eventually, Zain pressed a final kiss against my lips, then carefully pulled out and put the crotch of my panties back over my mound.

"Sorry," he said. "Those are gonna probably be pretty messy for the rest of the night."

"I'll survive. I have some Kleenex in my purse," I said as he did his pants up. "Though, speaking of messes, can you make sure I'm not covered in dirt before we go back?"

He chuckled and made me turn around. I doubted there was actually any dirt on me, but he brushed his hands up and down my back and ass all the same.

"There," he said. "Perfect."

"I thought I was always perfect."

"You are." He kissed me a final time. "We can't go back in at the same time."

"I know. You go first."

"I'm not leaving you out here in the dark."

I rolled my eyes. "The entrance is around the corner. It's not that dark and I constantly walk Millie later than this."

"That's true," he said. "And also very different since Finn usually walks with you."

"Finn doesn't live with me anymore."

It wasn't meant to be a jab, but both of us felt those words.

"Teacup—"

"And I walked by myself long before I even knew him," I said. "Trust me, no one's going to kidnap me between here and the entrance of the bar. And even if they did, my ass is too big to kidnap efficiently. I'll be fine. You go and I'll follow in a few minutes."

"Yeah, but—"

"Oh my God," I said. "Just go so I can use the Kleenex in my purse to clean your cum off my pussy, okay?"

He opened his mouth, then pressed his lips together. There was a sparkle of laughter in his eyes.

"Okay," he said. "Just don't take too long."

"I won't."

He kissed me one last time, then went to the gap and poked his head out, checking to see if anyone was around. There wasn't, so he blew me another kiss, then slipped out of the staircase.

As soon as he was gone, I dug the Kleenex out of my purse and cleaned up, then used my phone screen to carefully reapply the lipstick that had gotten smeared while we'd been kissing. After taking some deep breaths in the hope that would help the pink flush on my cheeks and collarbone fade, I fixed my hair, then squeezed out of the staircase to leave.

Of course, I managed to rub against the side of it and when I looked down, there was a streak of dust across the front of Audrey's skirt.

"Fuck," I muttered. Pausing, I stopped to brush it off, then brushed my hands along my sides and back again. Once I was fairly certain there was nothing there, I turned to go back to Tidal Beats.

"That was one hell of a show, kitten," said a voice from behind me.

I had no thoughts. My heart jumped into my throat and I just reacted. Apparently my fight or flight response was heavy on the fight because I flung my arms out and batted in the direction of the voice.

I didn't hit him, of course. He was too far back, leaning against the brick wall near the alcove across from the staircase, but it wasn't like I had seen him in the shadows there.

Now, though.

Now I could see him.

"I think we need to have a little chat, beautiful," Brad said.

Thirty

SOMETIMES YOU JUST HAVE those moments where you know you fucked up.

Normally, there's a sense of panic. Anger. Regret or shame or fear.

But as I looked at my ex-husband standing there with a mix of disgust and anger on his face, I had the oddest sensation of something that was almost like relief.

Almost.

"What the fuck are you doing here?" I said.

"Honestly?" he said. "I was waiting for you to come back so I could get out of that fucking conversation with Leslie. But imagine how confused I was when I looked over and saw you walking out of the bar. And then when you didn't come back, I thought that being the kind, thoughtful, supportive husband you've apparently been bragging about all weekend, I should go check on you to make sure you were okay. Imagine how concerned I was when I didn't see you standing outside. How nervous I started to get that something had happened to you. And imagine my surprise, beautiful. Imagine my *fucking* surprise to walk down the alley looking for you, only to find you out here with him. What were you thinking?"

"It's none of your business," I said, my face turning red.

Brad raised his eyebrows. "You don't think so?"

"It's not," I said. "It's not any of your business who I fuck."

"In this particular case, I think it is, *kitten*," he said.

"Don't fucking call me that."

"What if it wasn't me, Tess?" he asked, ignoring me. "What if it was one of those women you've been bragging about me to?"

"I haven't been bragging about you," I said.

"Or what if it was Dylan? Or Audrey? Your future sister-in-law seeing her bridesmaid and her husband's best man fuck a few weeks before the wedding? What if Josh had come out here and saw his best friend fucking his married sister in a dirty goddamn stairwell at his own bachelor party?"

"I... I would... I'd..."

"What would you do, beautiful?"

"Oh, fuck off," I grumbled.

"No."

I looked at him, my lips parted. His eyes were like cement, heavy and toxic and grey, not an ounce of humour in them as he stared back at me.

"Excuse me?" I said.

"I said no. Not this time, Tess."

I laughed. I had to. "Are you fucking kidding me? The last time we went to Burnsley, you literally fucked another woman in your hotel room and got caught. So I did something like that and you're going to hold it against me?"

"Oh, I'm not holding it against you," he said. "But I've had enough. I've been doing everything you've asked for the last five years. I've more than proven that I can change. I want a second chance."

"Are you fucking delusional?" I asked. "I've told you multiple times that there's no second chance. I'm done."

"And yet you still pretend you're my wife."

"The second-worst mistake of my life was pretending we're still married," I said. "The first was marrying you in the first place."

Unlike most of the times I hurled words like that at Brad, he didn't sigh dejectedly or get that look of pain in his eyes. Instead, he smiled patiently, not quite looking at me.

"No," he said. "The worst mistake of your life would be choosing not to take me back right now."

I laughed. I had to. If I didn't, I would've screamed. As it stood, the sound came out almost warped, slightly psychotic, dry and frantic and disbelieving. "Excuse me? What makes you think I'm going to *take you back* right now?"

He didn't answer right away. Instead, he put his hand in his pocket, subtly withdrawing his phone, and idly twisted it in his hand.

"The same thing that's kept you from telling everyone we're divorced," he said.

I stared at the phone in his hand, a sense of dread boiling in the pit of my stomach. "Are you threatening me?"

"Never, beautiful." He twisted the phone again. "I'm just asking you to imagine what would happen, you know? What would people think if they found out you were fucking your brother's best man at said brother's bachelor party in a dirty staircase while your 'husband' was comforting a pregnant woman inside? Fake marriage or not, I can't imagine you would come across looking very good in that scenario."

"You think I wouldn't, I don't know, just tell them what happened? You don't think I'd tell them about the years of cheating?"

His lips curled into an amused smile. "Okay. Do it, then."

"What?"

"Do it. Go into that bar, right now, and explain to everyone that you've been lying." He used his phone to gesture towards the bar and stepped aside, which was stupid, because he wasn't blocking my path. But he was trying to be ominous and dramatic.

And unfortunately, it was working. I stared at him, lips parted and unsure of what to say.

"You can't, can you?" Brad said after a moment. "Because who would believe it, right? Who would *actually* believe that I put up with years of this charade because I'm trying to win you back after I—yes, admittedly—fucked everything up." He gestured towards the bar again. "Your little fuck buddy didn't even think of that as a possibility when he found out and he wanted anything to be true so he could finally get his grubby little hands on you."

"His hands aren't little," I said. "Or grubby."

"Not the point." He gave me a sympathetic look. "Tess. You know I love you. You know I think you're brilliant and beautiful and perfect in every way. And you know as well as I do that I fucked up. I fucked up *bad.* But I'm not the guy who's going to sit here and regret that for the rest of my life."

"Telling me you don't regret cheating on me is not helping your cause right now," I said.

He shook his head. "That's not what I'm saying. I *do* regret it and you know that, too. But I have never been the guy who was going to sit there and not do anything about it. I've spent five years showing you that I'll do what it takes."

"And you think blackmailing me is what it's going to take?" I asked.

He pretended to look shocked. "Blackmail? Who's blackmailing anyone?"

I gestured aggressively at his phone. "Oh, I don't know. Isn't this supposed to be implying that you took photos of us together or something like a fucking pervert?"

He toyed with the phone again. "You really think I'm the kind of person who would do something like that, beautiful?"

"You are absolutely the kind of person who would do that." I folded my arms. "And I sure as hell don't hear you denying it."

"Maybe I did and maybe I didn't, but it doesn't matter." He half-shrugged. "You'll believe what you want to believe either way."

"I believe you're an asshole," I said. "But I believe you're the kind of asshole who wouldn't be threatening me like this unless you could prove it because you know I'd deny it and you'd look like the idiot you are."

Another one of those sad, almost condescending smiles spread across his lips. "I'm not threatening you, beautiful."

I laughed. I had to. "Of course you are."

"Because I'm outright telling you that you backed yourself into a corner with this whole story?" he asked. "If I was the asshole you think I am, why would I *tell* you that? Why would I tell you what would happen if you finally came clean and told everyone you've been lying for years? That's not a threat, Tessa. That's me looking out for you."

"I don't need you to look out for me."

"Clearly, you do," he said, and his voice took on a level of heat I hadn't heard before. "You're not thinking this through. No one would believe I played along for five years just because I love you, so that means you're going to come across as the cheater. And your family wouldn't be okay with that. That's one of the things that matters most to you and it would be like an absolute car wreck." He stopped, shaking his head. "Tess, you'd lose so much."

"That would only happen if you lied about the whole situation."

"It's not just you, either," he continued. "What about Zain's family? Everyone would think he's a homewrecker. Then there's the whole 'ruining his relationship with his best friend two weeks before his wedding' thing to consider. And I can't imagine his family is going to look too kindly on it—"

And of course, I was already telling myself I wouldn't give in. Of course I was going to tell Brad to go fuck himself, that I'd live with it.

Because I was tired.

I'd been tired for a lot longer than I'd been willing to admit. I was tired of the complications. The lying. The double life. I was tired of working my ass off and getting nowhere because I'd made the choice to be stuck in my past.

And I was fucking *tired* of him.

I was done.

I was going to choose myself for once. And I was going to choose Zain. And Zain... Zain would choose me back.

I was sure he would choose me back.

"—especially once they find out about... Finn, was it?"

I blinked. "What?"

"Finn?" Brad repeated, like that name had any right to be in his mouth. "The guy you were talking about while you fucked? 'I love it so much when I'm fucking Finn's ass while he fucks you and when we get home, I'm gonna trade spots and make him fuck me while I fuck—'"

"How long were you standing there?" I asked.

He laughed. "Oh, long enough. I heard a lot, beautiful. I can't say the 'Daddy' thing ever did it for me, but we can talk about the baby thing if that gets you going. But—" He gestured at me with his phone again "—to be clear, I don't want to give it or take it in the ass from some other guy. And from what he said, it sounds like his family wouldn't be thrilled to hear that he does, you know?"

Every nerve and muscle and vein in my body seemed to be frozen as I stared at Brad. "Are you saying you'd out him?"

"You think I'd do that?" Brad asked.

"Yes."

He chuckled, shrugging again. "Look, maybe I just don't see the big deal. Everyone's been wondering about Zain for years anyway. I'm pretty sure the reason he ended up sharing a tent with Josh at the bachelor party was because half the other guys were worried about sleeping next to him."

"Oh, fuck you," I said. "That's such bullshit."

"I agree, but I can't control what other people think." He looked at me sympathetically. "Regardless, I want you to think it through, Tess. Think it through *really* well. In the middle of hooking up, Zain couldn't even focus on just you. He was talking about someone else. Fantasizing about someone else. He already knows he can't have you. That you've ended up so tangled in this fantasy world you created for your family that there's no getting out of it without everything falling apart."

"Stop," I said, my voice shaking. "Stop trying to manipulate me."

"I'm not manipulating you," he said gently. "I'm telling you that the only situation where you end up being someone's number one is with me. I want the chance to fix what I did. I'm the kind of person who wants you back because you mean more to me than anything else in the world. I don't want to hurt you, beautiful."

"Except you are," I said. "You're going to out Zain to everyone when he's not ready because I don't want you back."

"I'm not saying I would out him, Tess," he said.

"You're not saying you wouldn't."

He studied me for a moment, then shrugged almost reluctantly.

"No," he said. "I'm not saying I wouldn't."

"So instead of taking the high road, you're threatening me and threatening to ruin his life if I don't take you back."

"If I've learned one thing, Tess, it's that taking the high road just means you have farther to fall." He tilted his phone at me again. "Look, I'm willing to be reasonable—"

"Like hell you are."

He ignored me. "Think it over. Let's say until the end of the week. I'm sure that's more than enough time considering you apparently don't have a job anymore."

I didn't even bother reacting to the knowledge that he'd been there since... well.

He'd listened to the whole thing.

"I know you'll do the right thing," he said. "Break up with your little boyfriends. I strongly suggest you don't tell them what happened here because you know Zain will fuck everything up and, frankly, you were right about one thing." He shrugged. "I can't stand that fucker and I would really would prefer to see him suffer. Then you come back to the person who has always loved you. Who *will* always love you. And who is doing what it takes to get you back."

He didn't say "Or else," but I heard those words all the same as he tapped his phone against his palm. My throat felt swollen, choking back my breath as he looked at me. Then, before I could react, he stepped forward and pressed a kiss to my cheek that made acid rise up my throat.

"I'll see you inside, beautiful," he murmured, and then he was gone.

Thirty-One

BRAD TOLD ME NOT to tell Zain what happened, so I immediately told Zain what happened.

Sort of.

I mean, I didn't tell him after I walked back into Tidal Beats. It would look suspicious if I talked to him too much and there was no guarantee that Brad wouldn't just change his mind on everything he'd said and start showing everyone the pictures he probably took.

And I didn't tell him when we got back to the estate house later that night because how could I? There was no chance for me to be alone with Zain.

I mean, I guess I could have texted him, but there was that whole thing where Zain was sharing a room with Brad and I... well.

I'd seen Zain look at Brad with what seemed like murder in his eyes before, so I wasn't entirely convinced that Zain wouldn't just suffocate Brad in his sleep if I told him while they were in the same room. And while Brad's untimely death would ultimately solve all my problems, I didn't think it was worth Zain going to prison over.

So instead, I lay awake, trying not to wonder what was going on in the other room. If Brad was going to say something. If everything was going to go to shit before we even left the estate house the next morning. In between Leslie's snores, I listened for the sounds of a fight, of people yelling at each other, of any sort of roughhousing that might indicate I was fucked.

But there was nothing. Mainly because, as I found out the next morning, Zain had decided to sleep on the couch instead of in the same room as Brad, citing the couch being more comfortable than the single bed he'd been relegated to.

And I obviously couldn't tell him the next morning because the three of us were supposed to get a ride to the airport with my dad, who was driving back to Kelowna after his round of golf in the morning to bring us there before picking up Mom, Josh, and Audrey so they could all go back to Burnsley. But by some karmic miracle that clearly wanted to avoid the three of us having to be in an enclosed space for any period of time, there was an accident on the highway and Dad was stuck in traffic.

"I told him what time you had to leave," Mom said, a look of frustration on her face as she hung up her phone. "He says he might still make it."

"Look, no offense," Zain said, looking from Mom to Josh and Audrey and then to me. "I'd love to stick around and wait for Gary, but I can't risk missing this flight. I start my new job tomorrow."

"You can head to the airport without us," Brad said, no hint in his smooth voice about how much he'd prefer that option.

So Zain said goodbye to everyone and got an Uber to the airport while Brad and I waited at the hotel with Mom, Brad, and Audrey, only to end up ordering an Uber for ourselves when Dad still hadn't got there a while later.

"But you won't get to see your dad at all, then," Mom said with a fake sniffle in her voice.

I tried to appear disappointed. "It's okay. We'll be back for the wedding in a couple of weeks."

The Uber got us to the airport with just enough time for Brad to rush through security using his Nexus card. He wasn't flying back to Vancouver, of course; his flight to Seattle left about twenty minutes before the flight to Vancouver did. So I rushed through security slightly slower since I didn't have a Nexus card. Which was fine, because the less time I spent with Brad, the better, and if I missed my flight to Vancouver, I could avoid having to talk to Zain even longer.

Unfortunately, I got through security with time to spare. Brad had already boarded his flight, but Zain was sitting at the gate for the Vancouver flight, absorbed in whatever book it was he was reading that week.

And sure, I could have told him what happened then, when we were finally away from the prying eyes of everyone we knew and Brad was on a flight to a different place.

But I didn't, for the simple and selfish reason that I didn't want to spend an entire flight sitting next to Zain after dropping that bombshell on him.

So instead, I spent the entire flight sitting next to him, staring out the window, my heart racing as every mountain, every lake, every cloud brought us closer to the moment I had to tell him it was over.

If he noticed that something seemed wrong, he didn't say anything. I wasn't sure that he noticed. He wasn't in as rough of shape as my brother had been, but he hadn't bothered putting his contacts in that morning because his eyes were so red and his skin seemed a lighter brown than usual, making him look distinctly dehydrated even as he sipped a litre size bottle of water throughout the flight. If luck had been on my side, he would have looked even worse because at least that might have made things easier, but he didn't. He pulled that look off the way he pulled everything off; effortlessly and attractively, his glasses making him look somehow both a little younger and a little more mature.

Fuck him for being so goddamn beautiful, even when he was hungover.

But once we'd landed in Vancouver, collected our luggage, and were walking away from the baggage claim, I immediately told him what Brad had said the night before.

I mean, immediately after we walked outside.

"What are you doing?" he asked as I pulled out my phone.

"Getting an Uber."

"I've got it, Teacup."

"No you don't."

"Let me get it, kitten. Considering how hard I'm gonna take you when we get back to your place, it's the least I can do."

"You're not coming back to my place," I said.

He laughed, but it faded after a moment. I wasn't looking at him, but I could feel his eyes on me.

"Are you wanting to come to my place?" he asked.

"Why would I want to go to your place?"

"Because we talked about wanting to fool around after we got back home and you know damn well I'm going to take any opportunity to fuck you that I can," he said." If you don't want to, that's fine. But you're acting weird."

"I'm not acting weird."

"You are."

I sighed, aggravated, and unlocked my phone screen. "Whatever. Just, you're not coming over. And I'm not going to your place."

"What's going on?" he demanded.

"Nothing."

"Tessa, I swear—"

"What? You're going to order me to tell you?"

That hurt him. I knew it did without even looking at him, which I still couldn't bring myself to do, just like I apparently couldn't bring myself to tell him what was going on instead of acting like a total bitch. But even though I knew it was a low blow to use something I'd forgiven him for against him, he didn't react or lash out.

"Like I said, you were right about that, and I'm sorry," he said, his voice even and patient. "But that doesn't change that I'm worrying about you right now and would like to know what the fuck is going on."

"I..." I started, but my voice cracked and I had to swallow to clear my throat. "I just... I don't want to do this here."

"Do what here?" he asked.

I opened my mouth, then closed it as a shiver ran up my back.

"Do *what* here, Tessa?" he asked again, and that time his voice wasn't demanding.

It was desperate.

Urgent.

Scared in a way that made my heart creak and crack and it took everything in me not to burst into tears.

"It's over," I said.

I still couldn't look at him. I was looking at the cars driving by the pickup zone, listening to the whoosh of tires on pavement, the sounds of people calling for a taxi and greeting their loved ones and recounting what their flights were like.

But God, I knew exactly what his face looked like.

"What?" he said.

"It's over," I repeated. "We... we're over."

More silence from him.

More sounds of people surrounding us, oblivious to the way our worlds were falling apart.

"Like, you and me are over?" he asked. "Or—"

"Me and everyone," I said. "I... I'm over. I'm done."

"Why?"

Part of me instinctively thought I should come up with some lie to cover what was happening. Because that was my signature move, wasn't it? Lie, and lie, and lie some more, and then when that snowballed into something insane, lie about it again.

But I was starting to feel like I was all out of lies.

More importantly, I didn't want to lie to Zain.

So after an intense moment where I shoved those instinctive tendencies down, then steeled myself to say what I had to say, then chickened out until Zain asked me why again in an even more desperate voice that finally forced me to look at him and see the fear in his eyes, I immediately told him what happened.

"Brad caught us," I said. "Last night."

He blinked. "What?"

"He caught us fucking last night. At Tidal Beats." My chin trembled and I swallowed back the dryness in my throat again. "He told me not to tell you, so don't... don't tell him you know. But he saw us. He might have... recorded some of it. Or taken pictures."

I don't know how I was expecting Zain to react, but it wasn't like that. It wasn't the sudden visceral anger, the fire raising in his eyes and his nostrils flaring as he inhaled a sharp breath.

"He took photos of you?" he repeated.

"Maybe."

He let out a short bark of a laugh. "That fucker. That fucking—he's not going to get away with this, Tessa. I'll—"

"What?" I asked. "You'll do what?"

"I don't know yet. But I'll think of something."

"You won't," I said. "Because it's over. I'm going back to—"

"Don't you dare say that," he said. "Don't you fucking say you're giving him a second chance."

"I am. Otherwise he—"

"He *what*, Tessa?" Zain's voice pitched up. "He's going to tell people you were scared to admit you got divorced? He's going to spill your secret? People will understand, okay? It might suck for a bit, but I'll be there for you. Finn will be there for you. Claire too. Keeping this a secret isn't worth going back to that piece of shit, okay? No secret is worth that."

"He's going to tell everyone you're bisexual."

Silence.

Tires scraping pavement, then rolling into a whoosh as they pulled into the driving lane.

People chatting.

The sudden, shocking buzz of my phone vibrating in my hand.

I glanced down. The screen was lit up with an unrecognized number and I hit the decline button before looking back at Zain.

His lips were still parted. His eyes wide. It was almost innocent, how confused he looked. How stunned he was. His expression gave me the urge to smile, only to hold back how upset I was, but I fought it. A smile would just hurt both of us.

"It's not so easy, is it?" I asked, my voice soft. "To say just let him tell everyone what you've been hiding when it's your own secret."

"How..."

"He heard us talk about Finn, about what... what you wanted to do to him."

"I..." he said, then his throat flexed as he swallowed. "I'll tell them."

"No."

"Tessa—"

"*No*, Zain," I said. "I'm not letting you do that."

"You don't get to 'let' me do anything," he said. "If I want to come out, I will."

"You don't want to," I said.

"But I will."

"Literally last night you said you can't. That it'll mess things up for you. That your parents wouldn't understand. He heard that too, Zain."

His jaw clenched and he swallowed again, like he was trying to fight back a wave of nausea. "It doesn't matter. I'm going to tell them."

"No," I said. "We knew this was going to be a temporary thing, okay? We knew this wasn't going to last. So—"

"That isn't what I want," he said, his voice heated. "Especially not if you're going back to that fucking prick."

"I'd rather go back to him than have the guilt of this on me," I said. "This is the one... the one thing that I can't deal with, okay? I won't be responsible for you being forced to out yourself."

"I didn't ask you to do that for me," he said.

"And I never asked you to do anything for me either," I said. "I didn't ask you to give up your promotion for me, to quit your job for me, to move to fucking Vancouver for me. All I asked you to do was keep a secret."

"That's different," he said.

My phone started buzzing again, making me jump. Another unrecognized number. I tapped the decline button as anger flared through me. "Why? Because you're not the one in control?"

Zain's eyes looked dark as he glared at me. "You know damn well that's not—"

"Zain," I said. "It's over. We are over. Now you and Finn can go to your apartment and play house together until you actually want to come out and—"

"So that's it," he said. "That's what all this is about, isn't it? Me and Finn living together."

"It's not—"

"You're upset about us moving in together. Just admit it."

"Fuck off," I snapped. "It's not at all—"

"You're telling me you're walking away because Brad is doing exactly what Brad does like it's some big fucking shock that he'd do this," he snapped back. "So yeah, I think what you're actually pissed about is Finn and me living together, and you know what? We can fucking figure that out, Tess. We can work through that. It's not a reason to end things.

You're telling me it's over because you don't think we can work things out?"

The instinct to lie reared up again. I tried to fight it. I really did.

But it was too much.

I was too tired.

So I lied.

"I'm telling you it's over because I don't want this anymore," I said.

He blinked, his lips parting again. "What?"

"I don't want this," I repeated. "It's complicated. I'm tired. I'm sick of feeling like I've fucked everything up. I'm sick of not feeling normal. I don't... I thought I liked being with more than one person, but it turns out, I just like to fuck that way. What we have... it's too much. I hate it. So I'm going to go back to him and try again. And one day, maybe, I'll have the guts to end it properly, like a normal, sane person who won't hide it from everyone. But this... this is over. I'm done."

His jaw twitched. "You expect me to believe that?"

"I—" I said, then my phone went off again and I nearly threw it into traffic before declining the call. "Yes. I do."

"You expect me to believe that you don't want me? That you don't want Finn? Or Claire? Because I'm assuming Brad wouldn't let you have her, either. You think I'm going to believe that's what you want?"

"I don't give a shit what you believe," I said. "I'm telling you that's what I want."

"And I don't believe you," he said, his voice rough and low and angry. "I don't fucking believe you because you're a *liar*, Tessa Lane."

My throat felt tight. "Fuck you."

"What are you gonna tell Finn?" he asked. "Huh? How are you gonna look into his eyes and explain—"

"Don't you fucking guilt me," I said, but my voice cracked again.

"I'm not trying to guilt you. I'm trying to make you see some goddamn sense here."

"I'm not changing my mind, Zain. You need to accept that it's over and—"

And then my phone vibrated again with the same unknown number.

"What the fuck?" I snapped.

"What?" Zain said.

"Just a sec." I swiped up on the screen and lifted the phone to my ear. "Hello?"

"Tessa?" asked an unsteady voice that I didn't quite recognize.

"Yes? Who is this?"

"It's Josh."

That weird blood-draining-from-my-face sensation happened again.

My first thought was that Brad had already told them. That he'd lied, that he'd decided not to give me until the end of the week and had just called Josh and fucking told him. My shoulders tensed and I tried to play it cool, even as my hands began to shake.

"Oh," I said. "Um, hi. What... what's up?"

"You need to come back," he said.

I frowned, bewildered. "What?"

"You need to come to Burnsley," he said.

"But I just got to Vancouver."

That moment would live in my mind for the rest of my life. The sound of my brother choking on a sob. The confusion at his fear, at his shock, at the fact that I didn't even have his phone number saved in my phone. And the way his voice cracked when he spoke again.

"You need to come back home right away," he said.

"What's wrong?"

"I'm so sorry, Tess," he said, and there was another choking sound. "There's been an accident."

Part 6

Confession: I should have
said goodbye.

Thirty-Two

THERE ARE TWO WAYS to die: either you know it's coming, or you don't.

I don't know which way is better. I don't know which I'd prefer, if I had to make the choice about how I was going to go. Half of me thought knowing it was coming would be better. That if I knew, I could live out all those bucket list things because even though some Pinterest mom has a sign in her living room advising you to live every day like it's your last, it's simply not feasible to eat your weight in cheese and go to Disneyland every day.

But I don't know if I'd actually want to know. Because knowing it was coming would mean I'd probably be in pain. I'd be suffering.

I'd be scared.

But the thing is, when people say that they'd rather not know they're going to die, I think they imagine that they'll die peacefully. That they'll fall asleep one day and simply not wake up. Or that they'll have a heart attack that kills them before they even hit the ground. That whatever it is, it'll happen so suddenly that they won't know they're even dying.

That it'll be painless.

That it'll be quick.

That you won't have time to realize what's about to happen. That it's like the power going out, where all the lights turn off at once, instead of going around your house at the end of the night and turning off each room one by one, slowly shuttering yourself in darkness until that's all that's left.

I don't think people who say they'd rather not know they're about to die picture themselves in twisted scraps of metal. I don't think they imagine that there will be noise and screaming and pain. Still, they told us it was instant, whoever they were. The paramedics or doctors or... or whoever says those things. I don't know. I wasn't there when they said it.

All I know is that they said he probably didn't suffer because he died on impact.

Probably.

Like that was some kind of comfort.

I mean, it was, in a way. All things aside, all the years of pain and arguments and clashing of thoughts aside, I didn't want him to suffer.

But even as they said it—the *they* in this scenario being my mom and brother, who relayed whatever the original theys had said—I wondered if it was true. Or was it one of those things that they say to provide comfort. To take some of the scariness away. To give you those little shreds of hope that even though everything has just fallen apart, the last moments of his life weren't spent in pain.

But whether it was true or not, my dad was still gone.

ZAIN WAS ON HIS phone buying tickets back to Kelowna within seconds of me hanging up, an unspoken agreement between us that the fight we'd been in the middle of was over. That those moments hadn't existed. That regardless of me trying to end things, he was going to hold me, then touch my sullen cheek as he stared into my eyes, trying to read what was behind them.

The answer to that was nothing. A void where my mind had shut down to all but the most basic of functions.

I could breathe. I could walk.

But that was about it.

The flight back to Kelowna was roughly an hour after I hung up with Josh, which worked out. It gave me and Zain enough time to get to our gate. Just before we got to security, Zain's phone went off. Unlike me, his phone screen showed Josh's name, since he had Josh saved in his contacts. It was a good thing Josh called him. Neither Zain nor I had thought about what people would say when we flew back to Kelowna together. I guess we could have told people we ran into each other after our flight since they would've known we were on the same one.

But it was easier for him to just hear it from Josh.

He urged me to the side when his phone started ringing, telling me in a soft voice to wait there while he took the call. I did as he asked, staring blankly at the wall with my hand resting on the handle of my carry-on as Zain walked a few steps away and pretended he was hearing the news of his best friend's father's death for the first time. He wasn't far enough that I couldn't hear him, but I couldn't make out what he said. All I knew is when he came back, his eyes were wet.

"Josh asked me to find you," he said.

I just nodded.

By the time we got through security and to our gate, it was almost time to board. I asked Zain to watch my bags so I could go to the bathroom.

"Take all the time you need," he said. "If I have to make them hold the plane, I'll do it."

It was sweet of him to make that offer, even if it was pretty unrealistic. I think he said it because he thought I was going to cry in the bathroom, but I didn't.

My first message was to Chuck.

Me

> Sorry to cancel last minute but I can't make it to drinks tonight. I have to go back to Burnsley.

I sent it even though I knew it wasn't enough and Chuck would start blowing up my phone with message after message asking what was going on.

But I couldn't figure out how to send the second message.

> There was a—

No.

> My brother called and—

No.

> My dad d—

No.

> My dad was in an accident. He—

And then I couldn't figure out how to finish the message.

I sat there contemplating it long enough that Chuck did indeed start blowing up my phone. Two messages came through before I shakily typed the words.

Me

> My dad was in an accident. He didn't make it.

I copied the message before I hit send, then sent variations of it to everyone I could think of who needed to know. Finn, because obviously. Claire, since I'd made plans with her for the next night. Kira. Dottie, though I messaged Finn again as an afterthought and asked him to check in on her and Millie since I wasn't sure if the old bag knew how to reply to text messages.

Responses started coming through, but I ignored them. Instead, I took a deep breath and made a call.

He answered on the second ring.

"Hey, beautiful," Brad said, sounding amused. "You already have an answer for me?"

"I need you to go back to Burnsley," I said.

The amusement faded from his voice. "What?"

"You need to fly back. We need to go to Burnsley."

He laughed awkwardly. "Uh, I'd love to, Tess, but I just got back to Seattle and—"

"My dad died."

He stopped short. Maybe because of what I said or maybe because of the flat, monotonous way I said it. Somehow, the texts I'd sent had more emotion to them than my voice did.

Because as broken as I was, somehow, that was the only way I could say it.

"What?"

"There was an accident," I said in that same voice.

"Holy shit," he said. "Oh my God. What... are... are you okay?"

"I'm waiting for a flight. With Zain, for transparency's sake, since we were on the same flight back."

"Tess—"

"Just don't punish him right now."

"I was never—and I wouldn't," he said. "That doesn't matter right now."

"It does," I said, and that time I felt anger try to force its way into my mind, but all it did was make my voice sound more hollow. "Please just give me more time."

"Beautiful, I promise. I'm not some kind of monster who—"

"Yes, you are." My voice shook enough that I had to stop and swallow to loosen my throat. "Just please get yourself back to Burnsley."

"I will, but Tess, I—"

"Shut up, Brad," I said, then hung up.

Everyone but Dottie had responded to my texts while I was on the phone, though Chuck's and Claire's messages both came after they'd tried to call. I sent short, utilitarian responses to everyone explaining I was about to get on a plane again, declined a second call from Chuck, then took every remaining ounce of strength left to walk out of the bathroom.

I was in line to board when Brad sent me his flight details. Funnily enough, the earliest one he could get had a stopover in Vancouver. It wasn't on the same flight as me and Zain, since his flight from Seattle wouldn't make it in until long after ours had taken off, but I debated whether I should wait for him at the airport in Kelowna.

I decided against it. Not only would that mean we wouldn't get to Burnsley until early the next morning, but just because I was taking him back didn't mean I had to spend time with him. And I had a feeling that this time around, my mom wouldn't be getting on anyone's case about her whole family not being there at once.

Because we never would be again.

I PRETENDED TO SLEEP during the flight.

It didn't fool anyone, but Zain let me rest against the window with my eyes closed so I could shut the world out for a while.

I guess it didn't really matter if I fooled anyone else.

When we got to Kelowna, there was a car rental waiting for us. Zain must have arranged it. I wasn't sure. The entire sequence of events from the moment I answered my phone was like trying to do an eye test when you knew for sure you needed glasses. Things were hazy, and if I squinted, I could make out some details and make a guess of what might be happening, but most of it was a blur. Occasionally, brief moments of clarity peaked through, like when they flick the right lens in front of your eyes: recognizing that Zain had rented a car, for instance. But the plane tickets, boarding, the flight, the drive to Burnsley... I mean, it happened. I knew it happened because I ended up in Burnsley. But my mind was just...

I don't know.

It was blank and full at the same time.

It was quiet, save for the shouting.

But everything was muted. Everything was around me, static and chaos and confusion, but it was like a glass dome had surrounded me. I could hear the disarray of my thoughts banging on the dome. I could see indistinct shapes and pictures through the fogged-up glass. Underneath, though, it was just me. Just me and my breath and my heartbeat, broken though it was, and a numbness I couldn't shake off.

When we got to Burnsley, everyone was at my... my mom's house. I didn't knock, just let myself in, and Zain followed silently with our bags. The house was quiet, but I could see lights on in the kitchen. When I walked in, Mom looked up.

"Teacup," she said, her voice ragged, and she stood to hug me. Her eyes were red and swollen and lost, just so fucking lost, and she started crying again as she held me.

"Hey, man," I heard Josh say. From the corner of my eye, I saw movement as he stood up and hugged Zain. Over her shoulder, I could see Audrey sitting at the table, her cheeks wet. Beside her, Dylan sat with his phone in his hand but his eyes staring blankly ahead, red and unblinking and drained.

We must have looked alike just then. My eyes were so dry that I felt like I needed eyedrops, even though I wanted to cry so very, very badly.

But tears existed outside the dome.

"I know you and Brad usually prefer a hotel," Mom said. "But since he's not going to be here until the morning, can you... can you stay here tonight? Please?"

One of those clear moments came through as I blinked, realizing very suddenly that no one had asked me where Brad was. Which meant Zain...

Zain must have told them.

"Yeah," I said. "Yeah, of course. I can... I can stay. We can both stay once he's here, if no one else is in the guest room."

"Can I sleep on the couch?" Dylan asked from behind her. "I don't... don't want to stay at the hotel."

"Could we take the air mattress?" Josh asked. He looked at Audrey, his eyes pleading. "If that's okay, babe? I just... I want to be... here."

"Of course," Audrey said immediately. "If you'll have us, we'd like to stay."

Mom's chin trembled and she nodded. "Of course. Please."

I almost forgot Zain was in the room until he spoke.

"I'll head over to my parents, then," he said. "If no one needs anything or—"

"I'd love if you stayed too, sweetie," Mom said. "If you don't mind taking a couch."

"I... I mean..." Zain said.

"You're family, man," Josh said. "You've always been family."

Zain's throat flexed as he swallowed. "Okay. Yeah. I'd like to stay here."

I TOOK A LONG, hot shower in the guest room ensuite.

I thought maybe I'd cry in there. Finn and I had discussed the benefits of crying in the shower when he'd first come to stay with me and I thought maybe the dome would dissolve away for a bit.

But it didn't. I just stood under the water, numb as ever, staring at the white sheen of the wall as steam curled around me.

My hair was going to be a disaster the next day if I didn't dry it, but I decided that was a problem for future Tessa and just tied it up on top of my head, still wet. Everything else was automated. I brushed my teeth, put on lotion, got dressed, all of it without a single thought in my brain.

When I was done, I walked out and almost jumped in surprise. Mom was sitting on the bed, wrapped in a green bathrobe with her shoulders hunched and her hands folded on her lap. She looked up, her eyes full of embarrassment and fear.

"I hate to ask, sweetie," she started, and my first thought was that she was going to make me sleep on the air mattress so Josh and Audrey could take the guest room. I almost just turned to grab my stuff and vacate because that would be far easier than fighting, but Mom's voice hitched before I could.

"I just can't," she said, and her eyes filled with tears again. "I don't want to sleep in our... in m-my bedroom."

That was fair.

That was more than fair.

I nodded. "I can sleep in the living room. It's no problem."

But she shook her head vehemently.

"No," she said. "I want... can you stay?"

I stared at her, stunned.

"I don't want to be alone," she whispered.

And the dome cracked.

Just a bit. Not nearly enough. But enough that I felt my heart ache.

"Yeah, Mom," I said. "Of course."

I was sure she intended for us to just share the bed. I don't know that she expected us to curl up together. She didn't ask me to hug her as she cried. I just did.

But my eyes stayed dry.

Thirty-Three

I didn't sleep much that night.

It wasn't because Mom was there. She was probably the only reason I slept at all. The warmth of another person, the steady breathing as I replayed the details over and over in my head, helped me eventually drift into a fitful sleep.

They told me what happened the night before. I was sure they'd tell that story repeatedly, a sort of catharsis to help with the acceptance. And I'd be one of them; I was part of the *theys* now, another voice to answer when the chorus of questions came and asked what happened.

I'd gotten some of it through Josh's sobs on the phone. The rest of it came in bits and pieces when I got to Burnsley, told by him and Mom and Audrey, sometimes in a hollow, quiet voice and sometimes between tears. I heard it all, but it wasn't until I was lying in bed that I put all the bits in order.

Mom and Josh and Audrey had sat at the hotel, waiting, first annoyed and then confused, then confused and worried, then worried and afraid.

They tried to call Dad, but it went straight to voicemail. Not unusual, at first—there were definitely spots with no reception on the highway—but they weren't usually that extensive.

They tried to check the traffic reports, but all they could find was what they assumed was the accident he'd been stuck in the last time they spoke.

But it wasn't.

The first accident had been cleared up for a while. The one they saw was his.

It was the end of the last long weekend of summer. There were trailers and toy haulers and motorhomes all over the highway, heading home from a weekend of campfires and cookouts and booze. And yeah, it might have been Monday afternoon, but more than a few people probably had a beer or three or six while they were packing up their sites before hopping behind the wheel and moping about yet another summer being gone.

More than a few people, and at least one.

Part of me wanted to know what happened to the people in the motorhome that hit him head on after drifting over the yellow line. Part of me didn't want to know. It didn't matter; the part that wanted to know won by default because Mom had asked, of course, once the police had finally got a hold of her.

Because of course, Dad had been in the car alone. And for some reason, his phone was drained. And yeah, he had his license and car registration and they'd figured out who he was before even loading him into the ambulance, but when they used that information to track down a phone number, they ended up with two: Dad's number and the home phone, the landline my mother refused to get rid of.

No one answered the landline, obviously. So they unlocked Dad's phone and used that to notify someone.

And that someone wasn't Mom.

"They went to his favourites and picked whoever he'd called last," she said softly. "Which was Mike. They must have hung up just a few minutes before it happened. He and Gary had been talking more regularly after seeing each other at the anniversary party." Her eyes had started watering again. "He's on his way. It takes a bit of time since he's on the island but he—" Her voice broke "—he's coming."

It was after Mike called that Mom talked to the police and they told her the driver of the other vehicle was taken away in an ambulance. There had been two others in the motorhome and both had ended up with minor injuries, but they weren't sure if the driver was going to make it out of the hospital.

I didn't know how I felt about that.

I wasn't sure I wanted to know how I felt about that.

Because I'd always been a vindictive person, but I didn't want to know how deep that cruel streak ran.

I WAS MAKING A pot of coffee when Brad arrived around nine the next morning.

It wasn't the first pot of coffee. I'd made that one around seven when I finally figured that if I hadn't fallen asleep in the two hours I'd been lying there awake, I probably wasn't going to fall asleep at all. I'd tried to be quiet since there were people sleeping in various rooms and on various couches, but the smell of coffee had brought Josh into the kitchen not too long after it was ready.

He'd softly suggested we go sit outside on the deck so Audrey and Dylan and Zain could keep sleeping. I nodded, then carried the coffee pot and two mugs outside while he grabbed cream and sugar.

It was a beautiful morning. Chilly, but a sweater was enough to stay warm as the sun caught beads of dew on the grass that definitely needed a trim. The neighbourhood was quiet, the silence broken only occasionally by the sound of a door closing or a vehicle starting as someone got ready to go to work, since I guess not everyone's world had turned upside down the day before.

Josh and I didn't talk much as we drank our coffee. That in itself wasn't unusual, since we didn't tend to talk much at all. But that Josh wasn't talking much was a bit strange, since he was usually in the running for the loudest person in the room.

After he finished his first cup of coffee, he set his mug on the table and let out a sigh.

"This fucking sucks," he said.

"Yep," I agreed.

And then we were quiet until Audrey came out on the deck a while later. She kissed Josh on the top of the head, then lifted the coffee pot to see how much was left before pouring herself a cup.

Dylan joined us not too long after Audrey brewed a fresh pot a while later, followed by Zain, who looked like he'd taken a shower and shaved before coming outside. Josh said good morning, but it wasn't until Zain sat down and took a sip of coffee that Josh frowned and looked at him.

"Wait," he said. "You're... Dude, it's supposed to be your first day at your job."

"It is," Zain said, his voice even. "I called them this morning."

"What did they say?" Audrey asked, looking worried.

Zain smiled. It was small and it was tight, but it was a smile. "They were great about it. Told me to take as much time as I needed and my manager already approved the time off as bereavement leave even though I haven't worked there for a single minute yet."

"That's awesome," Josh said, looking relieved. "My boss said about the same. I mean, Dad worked there too, so..."

He trailed off, looking down at his coffee mug. Audrey put a hand on his thigh.

Even though there was no real reason for us to stay out on the deck now that everyone who wasn't sleeping in a bedroom was awake, we stayed. Something about the crispness of the air and the feel of the sun was what we needed that morning, so much so that I was almost hesitant to go back inside to make a third pot of coffee when we finished the second.

Unfortunately, I also needed to pee, so I couldn't pawn the task off on one of the others.

Also unfortunately, that was when Brad finally got there.

There was a soft knock on the door, just loud enough that I heard it from the kitchen. Not that it mattered; I heard the front door swing open just a few moments after that.

"Hello?" he called.

I didn't want to respond, but I was too tired to be petty. "In here."

He walked into the kitchen looking as neatly put together as he always did, because apparently Brad couldn't exist like a normal human even after spending the night in an airport and driving two hours from Kelowna first thing in the morning. A look of gentle sympathy crossed his face when he saw me. "Hey, beautiful."

"Don't," I said.

Normally, he would have sighed in resignation so that it was very clear that he was choosing to respect what I'd said, as if it would earn him brownie points or something.

That time, though, he just nodded, as if he was actually respecting me instead of just putting on a show.

And somehow that was even worse.

WHEN SOMEONE DIES, THERE'S a lot to do.

Wills to find. Papers to sign. Appointments to attend. Decisions to make. And all of those things happen far faster than I had ever realized.

Dad had died less than twenty-four hours earlier and somehow Mom already had an appointment at the funeral home.

Josh, as the oldest, ended up as her coordinator. Even as he processed the loss of the man he'd looked up to more than anyone, he was the one helping make appointments, gathering pictures, coming up with the plan. Although, maybe it wasn't because he was the oldest. Maybe it was just because Josh was better suited to doing those kinds of things than me or Dylan were.

I didn't care what the reasoning was. I was just glad I didn't have to deal with it.

Instead, I stayed home with Audrey, Dylan, Zain, and Brad while Mom and Josh went to the funeral home. I think the intent was for us to start looking through photos or something, but no one realized it was going to take all five of us to deal with the veritable parade of people coming by with lasagnas and shepherd pies and flowers.

The neighbours came first. Then coworkers, people from the various committees Mom sat on, retired teachers who had taught Josh and then me and then Dylan twenty years earlier.

And friends, of course. Mom's friends and Dad's friends and Josh's friends and even a few of Dylan's old friends. Zain's parents showed up early in the day and Mrs. Hameed immediately busied herself in the kitchen, tidying up the dishes from coffee and breakfast and helping Audrey rearrange the freezer so more of the massive trays of food could fit in. Dr. Hameed looked out the back window, then waved Zain over.

"Do you know where Gary kept his lawnmower and edger?" he asked. Zain nodded.

"Good. It won't take long if we both work on it."

"Oh, you don't have to do that," Audrey said, but Mrs. Hameed shook her head.

"You have enough to deal with," she said as she picked up a dishcloth and began wiping down the counters. "Your family is our family. Let us help."

I TOOK A NAP that afternoon.

The fatigue hit sometime around when the fourth or fifth shepherd's pie arrived and I was restacking the lasagna in the downstairs freezer so it would fit. Mrs. Hameed was still there and Audrey had things under control, so I slipped into the guest room and crawled into bed.

Luck was with me that afternoon. I fell asleep quickly and deeply and dreamlessly, one of those naps that you wake up from unsure of what day it is and feeling like you're in a different dimension. At least, that's what happens if you aren't woken up by a gentle knock on the door some unknown time into your nap and are still blinking sleepy confusion out of your eyes when the door opens and Zain slips in.

"What are you doing here?" I croaked.

He closed the door behind him. "Sorry to wake you."

"You shouldn't be here," I said.

"Please," he said. "Please just hear me out."

"I don't want to. You need to go. Before Brad comes and finds you in here."

"He won't," he said. "He just left to drive Audrey back to her and Josh's apartment so she can grab clean clothes in case they end up staying the night again."

"Zain—"

"Please," he said. "Just listen. Just for a sec, Teacup."

"You really think this is the best time to do this?"

He sat down on the edge of the bed, facing me. "No. It's not. Which is why all I'm asking is that you don't make a decision about any of this until this is over."

I stared at him. "Until what's over? My dad being dead? Because spoiler alert, that doesn't end, Zain."

"That's not what I meant. You're not thinking clearly right now and—"

"I am thinking perfectly fine," I said. "I decided before any of this happened what I was doing."

"Yeah, but things are—" He cut himself off before finishing.

"Things are what?" I asked.

"Nothing," he said. "I'm just asking you to not decide about Brad right this second. You need time to get back to yourself."

"You don't know what I need."

"I know you need me. You need Finn. You need us, and you know that as well as I do. What you don't need is to give in to that bastard who's taking advantage of you when you're vulnerable."

And that pissed me off.

"Why would I need you?" I snapped, sitting up. "Your selling point to me was literally that you're not as much of an asshole as the other assholes I've been with. Like, congratulations, Zain. You're slightly preferable to Brad and Nathan, but you're still an asshole who apparently thinks I can't make my own fucking choices."

"Tess—"

"And Finn? The guy who—" I stopped, my mouth opening and closing as I thought.

Zain looked at me, unimpressed. "Who you can't even find anything bad to say about?"

I glared at him. "He ghosted me."

"His ex ghosted you."

"Yeah, and he's so stupid he didn't even know she did it."

It was his turn to glare at me. "Don't you dare call him stupid."

I rolled my eyes, even as guilt rushed through me because he was right. I couldn't say anything bad about Finn and those words tasted like poison in my mouth. But that didn't matter.

"So what, you think I can't get by without a guy who can't... can't text more than one sentence at a time and a moody asshole who took a short break from treating me like garbage to fuck me?"

"I didn't—" He started, but cut himself off and drew in a breath. "I've apologized for that. And yes, I do think you need us. Because you're better with us."

"I'm perfect on my own," I said. "I was perfect before you and I am still perfect. I will continue being perfect without you. I don't need you or anyone else to validate who I am, Zain."

"So then why are you going back to him?" he asked. "If you're so fucking perfect on your own, what do you need him for?"

"Because I don't want him to hurt you."

"Why do you care if you don't need me for anything? I know you're not just taking the high road here, Teacup."

"Just because I also don't want the guilt of that on my conscience doesn't mean it's not taking the high road."

"That's bullshit and you know it. You know I don't think it's worth going back to him just so people don't find out I'm bi."

"Yeah, well, he also knows shit about me, Zain," I said. "Did you forget that? The part where he probably has photos of us fucking? Where I've been lying about this for years?"

"And who, exactly, are you keeping that secret from now, Tess?" he asked.

To Zain's credit, the regret was instant.

Like, instant-instant.

And honestly, had I not been hurting the way I was just then, I might not have held it against him. He'd lost someone, too. I knew how close he felt to my dad and my family. I knew he was processing this trauma like I was. And like me, he probably wasn't thinking straight. He was probably exhausted. Overwhelmed. Reacting in strange ways to an incomprehensible situation.

But saying it... saying it just then, the way he did...

"Teacup, I—" he said, horror in his voice as he realized what he'd said.

"Get out," I said.

"Tessa, I'm sor—"

"Get out. Get the fuck out."

"No, wait—"

"It's over. I don't need you. So get the fuck out, get the fuck over it, and just leave me the fuck alone."

I don't know if it was my words or the fact that I stopped being able to control the volume of my voice and he was worried someone might hear me. Whatever it was, Zain held both hands up in surrender and stood, walking out of the room and closing the door behind him. Once I heard the door click shut, I let out the breath I'd been holding as anger began to pulse through my body, so intense and so all-encompassing that I could almost see it in my eyes.

And yeah, I should have let myself calm down.

Yes, I should have taken a few deep breaths and thought before I acted.

But when your heart is so raw, when your brain is so muddled, when everything feels wrong and upside down and hopeless and broken...

I didn't.

Hands trembling, I picked up my phone.

Me

I wanted to do this in person, but I can't and you deserve to know right away, so I'm sorry it has to be like this. But whatever was happening between you and me and Zain is over, okay? We can't do it anymore. You and him have each

> other and that's perfect. But I can't be involved.
> I'm sorry.

I kept my eyes on the little checkmarks beneath the message. The moment I saw that Finn had read it, I tapped on his name and blocked his number.

Like a fucking coward.

Then I went to our group chat and removed myself. I clicked on my message thread with Z Biggest Asshole and blocked him.

I blocked Claire.

I blocked Chuck.

Charles.

Kira.

Julie.

All of them.

All they were going to do was talk me out of it.

All they were going to do was tell me I was wrong.

But none of them would understand. Not then and not ever.

The problem had never been other people. It had always been me. I was a third in a world made for couples. It was Finn and Zain. Claire and Julie. Nathan and Mel. Chuck and Charles. Kira and Jackson.

And me.

And yeah, I thought I'd wanted more. I thought I'd needed something different. But look where that had gotten me.

So maybe Brad was meant to be mine. Maybe this was always the way it had to be. Because there was no place in this world for a woman who wanted more.

And I was done.

I was fucking *done*.

I N WHAT ALREADY FELT like a rare moment, there was no one in the house that hadn't been staying there. Brad was standing at the stove, stirring something. Mom and Josh were back from the funeral home, sitting at the table with Audrey, Dylan, and Zain as they looked through one of the small photo albums Mom had. Mom was sniffling as she flipped the pages.

"Maybe Mike will have some old photos of him," Josh was saying. "And I can check at work. There might be some of his old professional photos around."

"I know," she said, her voice watery. "It's just... the fucking *fire...*"

And that hit me hard.

Most of the photos Mom had were from the past five years.

There were none of my dad with us when we were kids.

No photos of him when he was a teenager or a child himself.

Mom had scrounged up copies of some of their wedding photos from people after the fire, but there weren't many of them.

All of that was gone.

And somehow, it hurt more than it did when we'd first found out how much had been lost in the fire.

Still, I pushed that pain down, taking a breath as I walked into the kitchen, where Brad was cooking... something. It looked like it might be Kraft Dinner.

"Hey, beautiful," he said as I joined him at the stove. "Want some lunch?"

"Sure," I said, staring into the pot. "Want me to make something edible?"

He tried to smile, but it was more of a grimace. "I'd love some help. I've never quite gotten the hang of this."

"Of what?" I asked, picking up the empty box of Kraft Dinner. "Reading the directions and putting cheese mix, milk, and butter into a pot?"

"Well..." he said.

I shook my head and nudged him out of the way, grabbing a wooden spoon and stirring to see if the noodles were salvageable. They were not, so I made him grab two more of KD from the pantry so I could start over.

We cooked together in relative silence except for the moments where I asked him to get something. At the table, everyone distracted as they picked out photos to use at the funeral.

"Can you get the milk from the fridge?" I asked Brad, keeping my voice soft.

He brought it over and set it down. "Anything else?"

"Yeah," I said, not looking at him. "You can have another chance."

He hesitated, apparently surprised. "What?"

"With what we talked about."

"Tess, we don't need to talk about that right now," he said, murmuring so no one else could hear him. "Call it amnesty for a while, okay?"

"You don't get to decide when you're the good guy and when you're not. You put it out there, so there's your answer."

"Are you sure?" he asked, almost suspicious. "Because all I want is a chance, Tess. Just a chance to prove that I deserve you. That I still need you."

"You better start fucking proving it, then," I said.

"I will," he said immediately, and put his hand over mine to stop me from stirring. I looked at him and he lifted his other hand, notching it under my chin and tilting my head up.

"I swear to you, Tessa," he whispered. "I love you. And you won't regret this."

Which was funny. Hilarious, even. Because I already did, especially as he leaned in and pressed his mouth to mine. Part of me was screaming, and part of me was silent, and from the corner of my eye, I saw Zain rise from the table and excuse himself.

Thirty-Four

Mike hugged like an uncle.

They were those tight, rib crushing kinds of hugs that steal your breath not just from the strength of his arms but from the intensity of his emotions. Whether it was ecstatic to see someone, like he had been at my parents' anniversary party, or joining us to mourn like he was that day, Mike hugged with all his heart.

Even if you'd only ever met him once in the part of your life where you had a developed memory. Or once in general.

It was surprising that he had the strength to hug the rest of us like that after he hugged my mom when he arrived the next day. She was the first one he greeted, of course, and that hug was so tight and so long that I wasn't sure either of them would ever let go. Mom had been crying on and off over the past day, but it wasn't until Mike got there that she really *broke*.

"I wasn't ready," she kept saying. "I wasn't ready for this. It's too soon."

"I know, Lola, I know." He shoved a hand across his face. "Fuck. I keep wanting to wake up like this is a bad dream. I was talking to him. Just before, I was..."

"This isn't what was supposed to happen," she choked. "We were supposed to retire. Get old together. Travel the world. We were going to come see you on the island this winter. I don't know what to do."

"It's okay," he said. "It's okay. You don't need to know right now. We'll take care of you. Everyone in this room. I'll take care of you. Gar would haunt my ass from beyond if I didn't."

She laughed, the sound watery and crazy and genuine. "He would. He so would."

"He loved you so much, Lola," Mike said.

"He loved you too," Mom said. "He loved everyone here with all his heart."

I wasn't entirely sure that was true, but maybe Dad just had a smaller heart when it came to me.

When Mike finally let go of Mom, he turned to me.

"Tessa," he said.

"Hi, Mike," I replied.

He opened his arms and hugged me hard, as if he could transfer his sympathy to me through physical contact.

"Good to see you, my dear," he said. "Not under the circumstances, of course. But remind me to grab a package from the car. I brought some paintings for you from Gar's mom."

I'd almost forgotten about the paintings he said he was going to look for, which I'd only found out about at Mom and Dad's anniversary party because no one had thought to tell me that my grandmother was also an artist. Not until Mike, who was also the first person to tell me I looked like her.

Because no one else in my family knew what it was like to feel like you didn't fit in. It would have never mattered to Josh if he didn't look like Dad because he belonged in so many other ways. But all I had was a tenuous connection to a woman who had died before I was born.

MIKE'S ARRIVAL WAS ALMOST the end of me not having to share a room with my ex-husband.

"I can get a hotel, Lola," he insisted when he found out she'd been sleeping in the guest room with me, but she shook her head.

"I have to be able to go in there," she said, gesturing in the general direction of her bedroom. "If you don't want to take it, I'm sure Brad would appreciate not having to sleep on the couch again."

"You're more than welcome to the guest room, Mike," Brad said. "Tessa and I will get a hotel room."

"Don't worry about it," Mike said. "You kids take the guest room. I already booked a room and since I'll be here most of the time, it'll give Lorelei a nice break from me."

Mom slapped his arm. "I don't need a break from you."

Mike laughed, a loud boisterous sound as he put an arm around Mom's shoulders. "You say the sweetest things, Lola."

We spent the rest of the day getting ready for the funeral. I'd known people who had died before, of course, but I'd never realized just how fast everything moved in those few days after death. Dad had died Monday and Mike arrived on Wednesday, and the funeral had already been scheduled for Thursday.

"He wouldn't want it delayed," Mom explained to Mike as we all ate dinner together that night. "He would've been aghast about how much time everyone is taking off work because of him."

Josh laughed, nodding along. "I guarantee you he would expect me to go back to work on Thursday after the funeral. Friday at the latest."

"I'm sure he wouldn't," Brad said.

"I dunno, man," Josh said. "I can almost hear his voice, you know? 'Josh, Fiore can't afford to have both of us gone for a week, and I have unfortunately called dibs on this week. I left the paperwork for the Henderson account on my desk. Can you stop by the office and put it through the nearest Ouija Board so I can close off the sale?'"

Josh wasn't wrong about almost being able to hear his voice. His impression of Dad was so accurate that it was almost haunting, but in the most hilarious of ways. Mom burst out laughing, her fork clattering as she dropped it, and Mike's roaring guffaw was enough to make even me smile.

"Well," Mom said once the laughter had faded. "I thought we couldn't do anything until I found the original copy of his will, but they said as long as I was confident I knew what he wanted for his funeral, we didn't need the original." She sighed and pushed lasagna around her plate with her fork. "We scanned copies of the wills, like we did with everything that made it through the fire, but I don't know what he did with the originals. They're probably in his desk in our room or maybe he put them in the safety deposit box or—"

"There's plenty of time to deal with that later," Mike said, patting Mom's leg beneath the table. "Let's focus on getting through the next day or two."

Mom smiled at Mike, a gentle look on her face. I noticed Brad watching, but didn't think anything of it until later that night when we'd gone down to the guest room and were alone together for the first time that day.

"That Mike is pretty friendly with your mom," Brad said after I'd come out of the ensuite because I'd refused to change into my pyjamas in front of him.

"I believe it's because they're friends," I said.

"That's not what I meant," he said. "I think he's making a move on her."

I gave him an unimpressed look. "He is not. That's just how he is."

"I thought you'd only met him once."

"Yeah, and he was like that then, too. Just because you look at every woman like a conquest doesn't mean everyone else does."

"I don't look at women like they're a conquest, Tessa. I'm just saying, the way he acts around her, the way he's touching her—"

"The way my dad just died and everyone's emotional and unsettled right now and you coming up with this conspiratorial bullshit is about the furthest thing from helpful I can imagine?"

He lifted his hands in surrender. "I was trying to look out for your mom. That's all."

I didn't bother responding that time, instead crawling into bed and lying on my side as close to the edge as I could manage. Brad took off his shirt and followed silently a few moments later.

"Night, beautiful," he said as he flicked off the lamp on his side of the bed.

I didn't respond to that either, just stared blankly at the wall across from me as any thought of sleep evaporated from my mind.

At least, until there was a knock at the door a few minutes later.

"Want me to—" Brad started to say, but I'd already turned my lamp on and nearly fallen off the mattress in my eagerness for an excuse to get out of bed. A moment later, I opened the door to see Mom standing there, her cheeks wet with fresh tears and her green bathrobe tugged tight around her.

"I'm s-so sorry," she hiccupped. "B-But I can't do it. I c-can't sleep in our r-room and the funeral's tomorrow and I need to s-sleep at least a b-bit—"

"It's okay," I said, pulling her in for a hug as she sobbed again. "Brad, do you mind...?"

"I'm sorry," Mom repeated. "Sorry, sweetie."

"Lorelei, it's more than fine," Brad said. From behind me, I heard him get out of bed and grab the t-shirt he'd stripped off a few moments earlier.

I may not have always gotten along with my mom, but that didn't mean I *wanted* her to be so upset and scarred that she couldn't even go into her own bedroom. I wasn't that much of an asshole.

But I was enough of an asshole to feel thankful that she was so I didn't have to sleep in the same room as Brad.

FUNERALS ARE WEIRD.

They're a strange sort of pageantry between the final wishes of whoever is being buried and the funeral that those left behind want.

A lot of a funeral is about what the one person who was attending only in the most technical of ways would have wanted. Or needed. Or found funny. Like Josh refusing to allow anyone to play *My Way* or *Somewhere Over The Rainbow* during the service because "Dad would've never listened to those. He wouldn't have wanted that."

"What do you think he would've wanted, then?" Mom snapped, since she'd been heavily in favour of *My Way* and was getting frustrated that we couldn't agree on a song.

"*If Tomorrow Never Comes*," Josh said. "Garth Brooks."

Mom's expression morphed from one of annoyance to one of pain. "I d-don't know if I'll be able to sit there through that."

Mike enveloped one of her hands in his and squeezed. "You can do it, Lola. Because he's right. Gar would've wanted that."

It was also why Josh asked Zain to pick up a case of Kokanee for us to toast Dad with once the funeral was done. And why Mom insisted that

Mike wear one of his Hawaiian shirts because "Gary would've thought that was hilarious."

I don't know if Dad would have found my funeral outfit hilarious or not.

I mean, I found it funny. But we hadn't exactly shared a sense of humour.

It was perfectly respectful. No one else would've suspected the semi-hysterical laughter I'd stifled with a towel in the guest room ensuite that morning. But I knew.

I considered changing. Having not even had time to go back to my house between the bachelorette trip and returning for the funeral, I didn't have many options, but I was sure Audrey would have had something appropriate that I could borrow.

But I had my trademark outfit with me. And, according to my dad, it was funeral appropriate. Because the last time he'd seen me wear it was at his and Mom's anniversary party, and he'd asked me who died when I walked in with my black leather jacket and black pants and black satin top and black pumps.

"You look like you're on the way to a funeral," he'd said, and I'd thought if my outfit looked like a funeral outfit, then it was the sluttiest funeral I'd ever been to, and then Zain had said he thought I looked great in a way that made me want to shiver and that was enough of reliving that memory.

Regardless, I didn't know if Dad would have found it as funny as I did. I liked to think he would because we always like to project what we think the dead would do or say about something, even if they wouldn't have done or said anything like that in life. If he'd actually been there, Dad would've probably made some comment about me being snarky by wearing that specific outfit, even though it wasn't like I'd planned it.

But maybe, just maybe, it would have been one of those handful of times that our senses of humour aligned.

Dad had picked his pallbearers out and listed them in the will, which was unfortunate. If he hadn't, I would've done anything I could to insist that maybe we only needed four pallbearers instead of the traditional six. Or that maybe all Dad's children could be pallbearers instead of just the boys. Because even though I still couldn't make myself cry at the funeral, it hurt to see Brad up there with my brothers and Zain, Mike, and Dr. Hameed.

Josh was crying when he walked in. Dylan wasn't, but he finally broke down during Josh's eulogy, even though it was an arguably funny story.

"Dad was never too sure about 'those damn computer games,' as he called them, even though we had a PlayStation and an Xbox and a—well, PC was about the only system we didn't have," Josh said. "He would watch Dylan play for a bit and shake his head, not understanding what the big appeal was. And as Dylan will tell you, they butted heads. There was argument after argument about 'those damn computer games' until Dylan finally convinced Dad to try them one day in the middle of winter."

Dylan started chuckling at that point.

"And my brother, you know, he's a smart guy. He mostly liked playing Halo and Grand Theft Auto and stuff. So did he start him on Skyrim or Call of Duty or Portal? Of course not. Did he get him hooked on MarioKart or Zelda or Pokemon? No, no." Josh paused, smiling down at his piece of paper. "No, Dylan knew he had to play to what Dad liked in order to get him to see what the big appeal was. So Dylan dusted off the Wii he barely ever used and got it all set up so Dad could experience WiiSports Golf."

He paused for everyone to laugh because if there was anything everyone knew about Dad, it was how much he loved golf.

"And let me tell you, that was the stupidest smart thing Dylan had ever done," Josh said. "Because Dad saw the appeal of 'those damn computer games,' but Dylan could hardly play anything else for the entire rest of the winter because Dad kept kicking him off the TV so he could 'play his computer golf.'"

There was more laughter, including from Dylan, although after a while his shoulders were shaking for a different reason and Audrey subtly passed him a Kleenex.

Nearly everyone cried at the funeral. Mom's tears were constant, of course, and Mike was wiping tears off his face even as he comforted her. Audrey teared up when Josh talked about how much he'd miss Dad at their wedding in a couple of weeks. Even Zain's eyes were watery and red, though the only reason I knew that was because his niece and nephew were sitting along with the rest of the Hameeds in the row behind us and one of them kept kicking my chair. I'd turned around to ask them quietly to stop, but my eyes went to Zain like they were magnets and I forgot what I was going to say.

And yet, I couldn't cry.

I couldn't during the viewing before the funeral started, even though my dad was lying in that fabric-lined box looking more like plastic than a person and smaller in stature than he'd ever appeared in life.

I couldn't when the casket was walked in.

Not during the eulogy.

Not during the slideshow, even though someone had tracked down an old elementary school yearbook that had a photo of me and Dad from when I was seven or eight. Or when the photo of us dancing at my and Brad's wedding popped up.

Not after the service, when people I hadn't seen for years were giving their condolences.

Not when we moved into the reception room and I saw Kira standing there with her parents, Mrs. Katz holding Velma, who was dressed in the teensiest navy blue lace dress and had a matching bow on her mostly bald head.

"What are you doing here?" I asked as I walked up to her.

"I wanted to be here for you," she said in her wavering voice. "But I think your phone might be broken, Tess. I've been trying to text you."

"Oh," I said. "Um. Yeah. I think it is."

A slight wrinkle of suspicion creased her brow, but only for a moment before she hugged me tight.

"I'm so sorry," she said. "I wanted to get here sooner but Jackson is at a conference in Arizona and couldn't get back in time to come, so I had to drive down myself and we had to stop in Kamloops for the night. But I didn't want to fly with Vel when she's still so little."

And see, that should have made me cry.

The fact that she'd driven from Vancouver to Burnsley all alone with her very young baby just to be here after I had tried to push everyone away should have made me sob.

But still, nothing would come.

Thirty-Five

JOSH WAS STANDING ON the driveway when we all got back to my mom's place after the funeral, directing people to park on the street.

"Everything okay?" Brad asked Josh when we got out.

Josh, surprisingly, smiled brightly. "Yeah, man. Just, you know what my dad would've wanted?"

I half-laughed as I looked past him to see Zain and Audrey in the garage, pulling out the various lawn chairs Dad had stored in there. "Drinks on the driveway."

"His second-favourite summer pastime," Josh said. "After golf, of course."

Audrey and Zain seemed to have the chair situation handled—well, they probably could have used the help, but that would've put me in a situation where I might have to talk to Zain and I'd been avoiding that as much as possible—so I went inside to get some drinks. Sure, Dad had a fridge full of beer in the garage, but I figured people might want something like water, too.

So I was in the kitchen when Mom and Mike got back.

"I just want to change!" I heard Mom call just before the door swung shut. I thought she was alone until she continued talking. "I'll be way too hot if I sit out there in this dress."

"You're way too hot either way, Lola," came Mike's voice.

"Ha, ha," Mom said. I think it was supposed to be sarcastic, but she was actually laughing at the same time she said it. "But, um... would you mind? If it's not too much trouble?"

"Lorelei," Mike said softly. "You're always trouble, but this? Not any trouble at all."

She chuckled, though it was a shaky sound. "It is. It's so stupid."

"It's not stupid."

"I just... I walk in there and it's like I can smell his cologne and all his stuff is there just like he left it and it—"

"I know, love," he said. "You don't have to justify it, okay? I told you I'd take care of you. I'll help you however you need. And if that means getting a little show while you change..."

Mom laughed again. "You're awful."

"You knew what I was like before—"

And he said more, I'm sure, but he was cut off by the closing of my parents' bedroom door. I pressed my lips together, then took a steadying breath and collected the bottles of water I'd pulled from the fridge.

It was none of my business, I told myself. None of my fucking business, and in no way did I want it to be my business.

I SPENT MOST OF the afternoon sitting on a blanket in the shaded grass of the front yard.

I supposed I could've used one of the lawn chairs, but when I initially went over there, it was just me and Kira and Velma. But slowly but surely we were joined by others: first Audrey, who was almost shy as she asked Kira if she could hold Velma, and to whom Kira enthusiastically agreed. While Audrey was basking in her baby cuddles, Mrs. Hameed came over along with one of my mom's friends from the Women of Burnsley club she was part of. They were eventually followed by Mom, then by another woman I didn't know, and suddenly there were two circles of lawn chairs on the driveway: the one occupied mainly by the men, set in the sunshine with a cooler of beer conveniently located in the middle of the circle, and the women, which was more of a half circle with the blanket Kira and I were sitting on at the front of it.

"She's just so precious," Mrs. Hameed was saying as she took her turn holding Velma, who had been surprisingly chill with the whole situation. She'd barely made so much as a peep or—as was more likely for Velma—let out a gurgling rumble from a belly full of gas. "Those beautiful big eyes."

"Definitely her mama's eyes," said one of the other women who must not have known Kira's mom or something since Velma had blue eyes and Kira had brown eyes and hadn't physically given birth to her. But Kira just smiled proudly.

"She definitely has the same eyes as her birth mother," she said with a casual gracefulness. "And we think she'll have the same curly hair, too."

"Oh, I'd nearly forgotten you adopted," Mrs. Hameed said. "The two of you are so natural together."

Kira didn't quite seem to know how to respond to that but smiled all the same.

The conversation turned to the adoption process and I took the opportunity to leave. Not that it wasn't interesting, but it was a story I'd heard countless times already and given the events of the past few days, it wasn't unreasonable that my mind needed a break. As stealthily as I could, I excused myself to the bathroom, hoping no one would notice when I slipped into the house.

Of course, that didn't take into account that Zain was both a nosy and a pushy bastard, so when I came out of the guest room after deciding to use the ensuite instead of the main bathroom, he was standing there with his arms folded.

"What do you want?" I asked tiredly.

"Does she know?" he replied.

I frowned. "Who?"

"Kira."

"About what?"

"About all of this. Does she know you got fired? Does anyone? Because Finn was really fucking confused when he texted me about why you'd blocked him and—"

"Fuck off, Zain."

"Tess—"

"No," I said. "I told you to leave me alone. This—" I gestured wildly between the two of us. "—is not leaving me alone. You understand that I've said it's *over*, right?"

"Fine, it's over," he said, though his voice shook when he said it. "But that's not going to change the fact that I care about you, especially hearing that *no one* can get a hold of you and—"

"It is literally the day of my dad's funeral," I said. "And you're harassing me about this again."

"It is literally the day of your dad's funeral and you didn't know your best friend was going to be here because you pushed everyone away when they wanted to help you," he said. "I'm worrying about you."

"Well, stop," I said.

"I won't."

"You need to. I'm not your problem anymore."

"You never were my *problem*—"

"Exactly. I'm not your problem. I'm no one's problem, now."

He looked pained. "Tess, this isn't you. You're not thinking clearly."

"Fuck off, Zain," I said again, and when I stepped forward to push past him, he silently moved out of my way, even though his eyes were broken.

I couldn't stop my heart from racing as I went upstairs.
My intent was to pause in the kitchen, to let the surge of
anger and embarrassment and self loathing fade before putting
on my happy-but-not-actually-happy-because-it-was-a-funeral face and
returning to the circle, but when I got there, Josh was standing near the
fridge.

"Teacup," he said. "You okay?"

"Fine," I said. "I just had to pee."

He raised his eyebrows. Which was fair. I probably looked very
distressed for someone who was claiming she just had to pee.

"And I needed a minute alone," I lied. "It's been an overwhelming
day."

Suspicion was replaced with sympathy in his eyes. "Yeah. It's been a
hard one. I'm sorry."

"For what?" I asked.

He half-laughed. "In general."

And then, for some reason, my brother hugged me.

DESPITE SHARING A BED for the past few nights, Mom and I hadn't
talked much. Aside from her crying and me trying to comfort her, we
mostly slept.

But even though we spent most of the day drinking on the driveway
sharing stories with every person who was part of my dad's life, when I
crawled into bed that night and turned off the lamp, Mom wanted to
talk.

"Did I ever tell you how I knew I was going to marry your father?" she
asked in the darkness.

"Dad used to say it was when you saw him hit his first hole in one," I said.

She snickered. "He did, but he was wrong. I knew a long, long time before that."

"You did?"

"Mm-hmm." I could hear the smile in her voice. "It was when we broke up."

"When you *what*?"

"In high school." I felt her shift and in the almost-darkness of the room, saw her pull the blankets up to her chin. "We dated for a couple of weeks, but I was one of those vapid, ridiculous teen girls who was obsessed with being popular. Gary wasn't exactly one of the popular boys, but I liked him and I figured he was high enough in the pointless teenager social standing ranks that we could date."

"A meet-cute for the ages," I said, and though it probably sounded sarcastic, my intent wasn't to be mean. Thankfully, Mom laughed at it.

"I know, right? And I figured because it was almost the end of the school year, I could spend the summer getting him integrated into the popular groups and come September, he'd be one of the popular guys. And you know, it was a great couple of weeks. He was a total romantic. Such a gentleman. He always made sure he had his jacket with him, even though it was June, just in case I got cold. He would bring me a flower to school every Monday morning. He was just... sweet."

I couldn't picture my dad acting like that, but I supposed it was possible. "But you broke up?"

"Mm-hmm. Because I found out his deep, dark secret."

I felt my shoulders tense. "Oh?"

"Yep. He—get this—was a curler."

I blinked. "A... Like, curling the sport?"

"Yep." She laughed again. "We weren't in any classes together at the start of the year, so I'd had no idea he was on the curling team. And like I said, I was a ridiculous, vapid little teenager, and curling was not one of the cool sports. Maybe if he'd also played rugby or football or, hell, even did track or something, it would have been fine, but I simply couldn't date a boy who was on the curling team."

"Oh," I said.

"I know," she said. "I know how ridiculously shallow it was. I wasn't the brightest sixteen-year-old. Blame all the bleach blonde dye we soaked our hair in back then. I went and sat down with Gary after school one day and I told him we couldn't date anymore because I couldn't be seen with a curler. And you know what he did?"

"Quit the curling team?"

"Nope. They went to the provincial championships the next year, actually."

"What did he do, then?"

"He frowned at first, then looked kind of confused. Then he says to me, 'Is that the only reason you're breaking up with me?' And it was, so I told him I liked everything else about him, but I didn't want people to make fun of me for dating someone who curled. I thought maybe he was going to cry or beg me not to break up with him or something."

"But he didn't?" I asked.

"Nope. He started smiling and perked up a bit, squaring his shoulders and slapped his hands onto his thighs. Then he says, 'Well, if that's the only thing you think is wrong with me, then I'm a hell of a catch!' And before I could even react, he stood up and walked away, looking like the cockiest bastard you've ever seen."

I may not have been able to picture Dad bringing Mom flowers as a teenager, but I could definitely picture that. I smiled into the pillow. "So what did you do?"

"Sat there in shock as he walked away," she said. "Then he stopped right near this group of girls I was sort of friends with, looked at them, and sauntered right up."

"Right in front of you?"

"Oh, I deserved it," Mom said, laughing again. "And I knew that, even then, but you know, I was livid and I got up and stormed after him. Right when I walked up, he was introducing himself to Stephanie Willow and I grabbed him, kissed him, and told him he passed the test."

I laughed in spite of myself. "And did he believe that?"

"Not at all. He goes, 'Tell you what, Lorelei. If you promise not to give up on this good thing again, I'll pretend that I believe that and we can go back to how things were.'" There was still a smile in her voice, though it started to sound watery. "And I knew right then and there I was going to marry that man. That I was never going to give up that good thing again." She stopped, then sighed. "God, I miss him."

And as bad as it was to think, I didn't know if I agreed. But I did very much regret that I never knew my dad as the person my mom seemed to remember.

I WASN'T A BIG believer in fate.

I believed in luck, or my lack thereof. And I believed in karma, to an extent. But believing that everything happened for a reason, that there was some great cosmic force that decided coincidence was the most efficient method of making things happen?

It was a stretch to me. Although, maybe if I thought of it as a great cosmic force that decided coincidence was an absolutely hilarious way of making things happen, I'd believe in it more.

Regardless, even with my inability to fully believe that fate was real, I couldn't argue that there wasn't something strange going on the following day.

Because there was.

I should have never ended up in the house alone. Not when there were so many of us still using my mom's house as home base.

But Audrey couldn't take another day off work, even though it seemed pointless to go back for a single day before the weekend. Josh had decided to go to the office so he could clear out Dad's desk and had brought Zain with him. Mike took Mom to order copies of the death certificate and to an appointment with the lawyer and to the bank to check for any important papers in the safety deposit box because everything would be closed over the weekend, so she wanted to do as much as she could that day. Dylan decided to spend the day with some of his friends who were still in town. Kira had started the drive back to Vancouver. And Brad?

Brad had to drive back to Kelowna because he had to return the car he'd rented when he'd flown in because apparently, they couldn't extend the rental on that exact vehicle. So while he could rent a different car once he was there, he had to bring back the one he currently had.

And that was strange, right? I'd never heard of that happening before. And it was strange that Brad didn't even bother asking if I wanted to join him for the trip, instead kissing me on the top of the head while we sat at the table and saying that I should stay here and relax for a while.

But that was what happened, and suddenly, the door swung closed behind Dylan and for the first time in what felt like forever, I was blissfully alone.

And no one else had returned when the landline rang.

I almost didn't answer it. It was usually just telemarketers. But there had been had a lot of calls the past few days that weren't, and... well.

I mean, the cops had called the landline first after my dad's accident. So ignoring it felt wrong, even if it was just a telemarketer.

But that day, it wasn't.

"Oh, good, someone's there," Mom said when I answered. "Are you busy right now, hon?"

"Not really," I said.

"Would you do me a favour? The will isn't in the safety deposit box. Dylan said he checked Gary's desk in our bedroom on Wednesday but he couldn't find it and I just..."

"Don't think he looked properly?" I asked.

"Well, maybe," she said. "But if it's not in the safety deposit box and it's not in the desk, I don't know where else it might be. I'm hoping you could take a second look."

"Yeah," I said. "Of course."

It didn't take me very long to go through Dad's desk. Despite it having multiple drawers and cupboards, most of them were fairly easy to glance in and see there were no important papers. Dad's space was fastidiously organized.

Just like Dylan, I found nothing. Which was weird because again, Dad was organized. But, I thought as I sat in his desk chair with my mouth twisted to the side, there were no *really* important papers in his desk. No land titles or bills of sale. No passport. No birth certificates or tax returns or anything like that.

Which meant he had to be storing it somewhere else.

That wasn't helpful on its own. I mean, common sense would dictate that if those things weren't in his desk, then they had to be somewhere else. But maybe I was looking for the wrong thing. Maybe there was a note or something about where he'd kept those things.

So that was how I ended up finding a small key in a tiny coin envelope in my dad's stationery drawer. And it didn't take me long to figure out that the key was to a safe, on account of the fact that Dad had labelled the envelope with the word "SAFE" in his tidy handwriting. And then it was just a matter of finding the safe, which again, didn't take long since under the word "SAFE" was the word "CLOSET" in parentheses, written in the same tidy handwriting.

"I feel like that kind of defeats the purpose of a hidden safe, Dad," I whispered for some reason as I opened the door to the walk-in closet.

But it made more sense when I tracked down the safe in question. It was sitting in a drawer underneath the one where Dad kept all his socks. Mom obviously didn't know about it, since if she knew there was a spare drawer in the closet, she would have probably annexed it for more of her clothes.

If she could have gotten it out, that is. Because that bitch was *heavy*.

It took way more effort than I wanted to give to pull the safe out of the drawer, but there was no other way to get at it. The lock was on the front, not the top, and there wasn't a big enough gap to get the key into it. So I heaved and hoed and finally had the brilliant idea to pull the entire drawer off the sliders and, instead of using my fingertips to lift it out, harness the power of gravity to dump it out of the drawer.

Which worked perfectly, if a bit loudly, since the heavy box landed with a loud thunk on the carpeted closet floor. Panting a bit more than I'd like to admit, I flipped the safe back over, then sat cross-legged in front of it.

GuardBox Fire Safe was written above the lock. So it wasn't a safe so much as it was fire protection, which made sense for a man whose house had burned down five years earlier. But that didn't explain why Mom didn't know about it. I bit my lip, wondering if I should maybe wait for her before opening it, then decided against it.

I mean, chances were good the will was inside. So I opened it.

And the will was there.

But I didn't see it right away.

I didn't see it until Mom and Mike got back from the bank and discovered me sitting on the floor of the master bedroom closet, sobbing.

Thirty-Six

Everyone returned to my mom's house after dinner that night.

Well, except for Zain, who Josh said was spending the night at his parents' place since he hadn't spent a ton of time with them that week, and his mom was getting disgruntled about it.

But after the various errands and things everyone had going on that Friday, everyone returned to my mom's house, mainly because Josh had sent a text out saying there were a few things he needed to talk to all of us about. Once he and Audrey got there, we crowded around the kitchen table, the overhead light casting a bright golden light over everyone's faces and dissolving any shadows we could have hidden in.

"Alright," Josh said once we were settled. He glanced at Audrey, who nodded encouragingly as she put her hand over his. "Auds and I have been talking and there's no easy way to say this, but we're cancelling the wedding."

"What?" Mom said, instinctively reaching for Mike and gripping his hand for support. "Are you—"

"We're not breaking up," Audrey said quickly. "We're still going to get married. But timing-wise, the wedding is supposed to be in a week, and after everything, it doesn't feel like the right time to do this."

"No," Mom said, her voice almost a low groan. "No, hon, don't postpone it."

"The decision's already been made," Josh said.

"But that's not what your dad would have wanted."

"And for once, I'm going to do something the way I want to, Mom."

He said it as gently as he could, but even from across the table and without him looking at me, I could see the flicker of pain in his eyes. Mom blinked, her lips parted, then sniffled and nodded.

"Of course," she said. "I understand."

"We need time," Audrey said. "Josh needs time to recover from this, and I need to focus my energy on helping him with that instead of stressing about who's going to pick up the flowers next Friday. We need to do what's right for *us*. And we've decided that means postponing the wedding."

Josh looked at Dylan. "We're hoping the wedding party will all stay the same and everyone's still willing to be there once we reschedule."

"Of course," Dylan said. "I'll be there."

"Me too," I said. "Unless you want Leslie to take over, which I totally get. I'll support you either way."

Audrey's lips twitched, her smile almost sad. "I haven't quite thought about it yet, but I appreciate you being understanding about it, Tess. That means a lot to me."

"But," Josh continued, "since we'll be losing some deposits and such on this, we're going to be scaling back other aspects of the wedding. Things like changing the catering and shrinking the guest list a bit. But almost everyone in this room is safe."

"'Almost' everyone?" Mike said, a hint of a laugh in his voice.

Josh didn't laugh. Instead, he looked at Brad. His eyes were cold. Angry. Darker than I'd ever seen my brother's eyes look.

And I knew.

I knew the biggest fucking asshole had told him.

"Josh—" I said.

"When we first sat down to plan the wedding, one of the things we did was talk about the couples who inspire us," Josh said, still looking at Brad. "The people who we would look at and think, that's how we want to be when we're married." He glanced at Mom. "Like my parents. And Audrey's grandparents. And for a long time, Tess and Brad."

He finally looked at me. His eyes weren't so cold, but there was still plenty of emotion boiling in them. "You know, I was so jealous of you, Tessa."

Brad forced a chuckle. "Didn't know you felt that way about me, man."

Josh ignored him. "You'd found that person, you know? You had this dream wedding and wonderful marriage. This beautiful, perfect life that seemed so... wrong. It wasn't anything like you."

It was my turn to force a laugh. "Are you trying to say I'm ugly and flawed or—"

"Of course not," Josh said. "But that kind of life had never seemed like your thing, Tess. You stopped seeming like you. For a while, anyway."

"What's that even supposed to mean?"

"I mean that about five years ago or so, you stopped acting like the weird sort of Stepford wife you were whenever Brad was around and more like the stubborn, outspoken, dramatic little sister I knew. And I didn't make the connection, you know? I thought maybe I'd been imagining things or that the fire had changed something for you. But it took being with Audrey and hanging out with her family for me to realize how fucked up my relationship is with my siblings." He shook his head, the corner of his mouth twitching. "How much I failed at developing that relationship."

"You didn't fail," Dylan said.

"I did," Josh said. "I'm the oldest. I set the tone. I could've been a better brother. Because if I was—" He looked at Brad with that same darkness he'd had before. "—I would've figured out what a piece of shit he is a lot sooner."

"Excuse me?" Brad said.

"Nah," Josh said. "You're not excused. There's no fucking excuse for what you did to her."

Fuck.

Fuck.

"Josh, wait—" I said.

"I know, Tess," he said, looking at me. "Okay? I know what he did and I know what you've been doing and I know you think it's because that's the only way you would fit into this family and you're wrong, okay? You are *wrong*. We all failed you and didn't even know it because you were so damn good at making it seem like you were okay." His voice creaked a bit, not quite a crack, but more than a shaky nervousness. "I always thought you were in on the joke with us, you know? But you weren't and I never checked to make sure you were. None of us did."

And like, yes, that was a lot. That sent a lot of emotions rushing through my heart and my veins and through each of my nerves, the kind that made my eyes sting and my throat feel tight. But beside me, Brad was fuming, and my palms were sweating so much that I was itching to wipe them on my pants.

"Just stop," I said, my voice high. "Okay? There's a lot more to this than—"

"What more? You and Zain?" Josh asked. "Because I know about that too, Tess."

The room went silent and my face went red. Because yeah, I'd figured Zain was the one who spilled all of this to him.

But I did *not* think Zain had told him... well.

Everything.

"Josh," Brad said, his voice sympathetic and warm. "I know you think you know what you're talking about right now, but you very much don't. It's been a shocking and emotional week for everyone, but Tessa and I are together."

"No, you're not," Josh said. "She doesn't have to keep faking it. We all know now."

"She's not faking it," Brad said. "We're back together."

"You cheated on her!" Josh said. "The whole fucking time you were together! She fucking divorced you."

Dylan's mouth dropped open.

The warmth in Brad's tone faded as he clenched his jaw, but his voice was still patient. "We're giving things another shot."

"You can't be serious." Josh looked at me. "You cannot be serious right now, Tess. You're not actually taking him back."

"Oh, absolutely not," I said.

"What?" Brad said, twisting towards me.

"I mean, it's kind of pointless now," I said.

"Are you forgetting that I still know?"

And yes, I knew what he knew. I knew he was the kind of asshole who would do exactly what I thought he would with that information, even though he'd resisted outright saying that he'd out Zain. I knew he hated Zain, hated that I'd fucked Zain, hated that I liked Zain better than him, and that he would *jump* at the chance to fuck Zain over.

I knew all of that.

But Zain also would have known what would happen if he told Josh *everything*, just like he would have known there would be no way for me to stop that information from getting out.

All I could do was hope beyond hope Zain was ready for it.

"Know what?" Josh asked. "That Zain is bisexual?"

I caught Brad's face turning red before he looked at my brother, stunned. "I never said—"

"—because he told me you're the type of fuckweasel that was going to out him to everyone as a way of blackmailing Tessa into taking you back."

"You did what?" Mike said, his voice dangerously low.

"That's not—" Brad said.

"Or is it the throuple thing?" Josh continued, and it was my turn to gape at him. "Because Zain thinks that Finn and I will have a lot in common, so I'm looking forward to meeting him. Or is it Tessa's girl-friend-not-girlfriend? Because Claire sounds like a fucking blast, honestly."

Brad's eyes went even wider. "Her *what*? Who the fuck is Claire?"

Josh grimaced, the tendons on his neck sticking out a bit as he looked at me apologetically. "Oh. Shit. Sorry, Tess. I... fuck."

Brad snorted. "For someone who's accusing me of threatening to out someone as blackmail, you sure just outed my wife to everyone in this room, including your mother."

"She's not your wife," Audrey said vehemently.

Josh's face turned red, panic flaring in his eyes. "Tess, I'm sorry."

And here's the thing.

Yes, I could have been mad at him.

Yes, he did technically "out" me.

But only technically.

And only because he was trying.

He was fucking *trying*.

Which was a hell of a lot different than what Brad was going to do.

So I looked at Brad, a resigned sheepishness on my face. "I know you think you're being all clever right now, but it's not actually news to my mom."

Josh's shoulders sagged as relief crossed his face, though it was quickly replaced by confusion. "Wait, Mom knows?"

Mom nodded firmly, her eyes matching the same iciness that Josh had in his as she set them on Brad.

"Yeah," I said. "I kind of might have told her all of this earlier after I found Dad's will."

"You found Dad's will?" Dylan said.

"What does his will have to do with this?" Brad asked.

"Nothing," I said. "It's not so much as the stuff he had with the will."

"What did he have with the will?" Audrey asked, her eyes wide.

I glanced at Mom, then at her. "It's really not my place to say."

Brad rolled his eyes. "Of course it's not."

"Your attitude is not welcome here, Bradley," Mom snapped.

And that was what finally made Brad look scared. "Lorelei, I—"

"Get out," she said.

"What?"

"Get out," she said. "Out of my house. Out of my daughter's life."

Brad looked at me, disbelief on his face. "You can't be serious."

"You heard what she said," I said.

"Tessa—"

"Dude, you cheated on my sister and you threatened my best friend," Josh said loudly. "Get the fuck out now or you'll be leaving in an ambulance."

Brad half-laughed. "You couldn't—"

"I have no qualms in going two-against-one," Mike said.

"Make it three," Dylan added, glaring at Brad.

"And if you think I'm gonna sit around while the guys kick your sorry ass because of some kind of patriarchal bullshit, you're as stupid as you look," Audrey said.

Brad looked at her, then back at me.

"So you're just going to go back on what you said?" he asked. "What happened to taking the high road, Tessa?"

Half the table jumped as I burst out laughing.

Seriously.

I couldn't stop. It had to be about the funniest thing I'd ever heard in my life, Brad telling me to take the high road after all the shit he'd pulled.

"Please, beautiful," he said, even as I shook my head and tried to stop giggling long enough to respond. "All I wanted was a second chance. After all of this, after everything, you know I still love you. You know—"

"No," I said. "It's over."

"Tess—"

"Shut *up*, Brad."

There couldn't be a single shred of doubt that I was related to the people sitting at that table. Not when I blurted those three wonderful words at the same time as my brothers and my mom, all at the same speed and in the same inflection, all of us wearing matching glares. And maybe, after all the times I'd told him to, that was what convinced Brad to finally, *finally*, shut the fuck up.

That I'd finally figured out I didn't need him to keep my family happy.

That I belonged perfectly well without him.

I mean, the chances of him staying shut up were low. Brad had spent five years trying to get me back and a little setback like everyone discovering the one thing he had to hold over my head wasn't going to stop him forever.

But for now... for now, he was giving in.

Josh stood up after Brad had left the table, making sure he did nothing more than grab his suitcase before leaving the house. The rest of us sat in silence, not quite looking at each other until he returned. Once he had, Mom looked at me and took a nervous breath as her hand moved beneath the table. I couldn't see it, but I knew Mike had just taken it and squeezed. She looked at Josh, then at Dylan.

"I have a lot to tell you," she said.

Thirty-Seven

THE FIRE SAFE HAD been full of paperwork.

All the things I'd suspected were there. The deed to the house. Dad's social security card. A piece of paper with a list of what seemed to be banking passwords on it. I lifted things out piece by piece, looking for the will and setting anything Mom might need to one side, which was most of it.

Partway through the stack of papers was a letter-sized brown envelope. I opened it because of course I did. Because it looked like the kind of envelope you might keep a will or something in. But when I pulled out the stack of papers inside, it was just a bunch of letters in handwriting I didn't recognize.

And I mean, I wasn't going to read them. They were clearly important to my dad, but I didn't feel like I had the right to read through something so personal, no matter how intriguing a handwritten letter in a safe might be to someone with a propensity to snoop.

But then I saw my name near the top of the page of the first letter.

Dear Gary,

I know what the three of us agreed on. I know you're her father no matter what. I know Lola doesn't want to know.

But she doesn't know why it's so important. You do. Please, Gar. For Tessa's sake, get a paternity test.

And come on.

Who wasn't going to keep reading after seeing that?

You don't have to tell me the results. You don't have to tell anyone you did it. But you know what I could've passed on. You know what my mom went through, and her dad. I don't know if I have whatever causes it and I don't know if there's a way to find out, but you CAN find out if Tessa's at risk by finding out for sure if she's yours.☐

Please, man. Just consider it.☐

Mike

I read it two or three times, slowly processing the words one by one.

Paternity test.

Mike.

Mike and my *mom*.

Finding out for sure if my dad was my dad.

And something... something I might have.

The letter was at odds with the story Mom had told me last night. The woman who had been deep in that memory of two high school kids falling in love didn't seem like the kind of woman who would cheat on her husband. Regardless of any problems I'd had with my parents in the past, I'd never thought they were anything but faithful to each other.

I'd never thought they were anything but deeply in love.

My hands shook as I lifted the letter and set it next to me on the floor. Dad's response to that letter wasn't there, of course, but there was another letter beneath it in the same handwriting.

Dear Gary,□

I trust you, man. I just couldn't live with myself without at least asking you to consider it. You know I'm fucking terrified of it happening to me, but that's nothing compared to how scared I am of passing it on to some innocent kid. I've never wanted kids of my own because of it.□

And I'm sorry. For this mess and for everything else.

I feel like I fucked everything up at the same time I feel like it was inevitable. We knew, didn't we? That it'd come to this eventually. And I guess this was the wakeup call, but fuck if it doesn't hurt more than I thought anything ever could. It's not fair to you or her or me, at all. □

But me staying there wouldn't have been fair to your kids, and yeah, they're not mine, but I want the best for them like you and Lola do.□

And imagine them growing up trying to explain us. WE can't even explain us. You'd lose your job if the wrong person found out. Burnsley's not exactly a free-spirited place, you know? Josh will be old enough to start wondering soon. He and Tessa deserve the best life you can give them. And I would prevent that from happening. □

Miss you both something fierce. The development on Paradise Island is coming along nicely. I've spent a good amount of time in Nassau but to be honest, my heart lies with that little island I told you about. It's got no potential as a resort, far too small a place for that, but for a place to escape...□

Well, not to be cheesy, but it could be our own Paradise Island one day.□

I hope that made you groan. I'd hate to think I'm losing my touch.

Give Lola my love and a kiss from me.

Mike

Oh.

That...

That was not what I expected.

I mean, it wasn't like it came right out and said—but the implication was there, wasn't it? That they... that I...

But they couldn't have. My parents wouldn't—*my* parents would *not* have ever...

I was reading it wrong.

I had to be.

That's what I told myself until I read the next letter.

Of course it breaks my heart. It already has. I miss you. I miss her. And I know Lola said that if you want to come here for a while or whatever, then we can. And I'd love that, Gar. But it can't be forever.

Still not proof, I told myself. Friends miss each other all the time. That didn't mean—

Maybe in another life, it would've worked. But you and her... you've got kids, Gary. I'm the outlier here. But that doesn't mean I don't dream about waking up between you two, one of you on each arm like we used to. That doesn't mean I don't think about the way you like to—

"Oh, God," I said, hurriedly putting that one down as my face turned red.

There was just one letter left in the stack after that. One letter, and then a long white envelope torn open. A shiver ran through me as I picked up the letter first.

Just promise me that if—

And then there were a bunch of scratched out half thoughts, scribbles so dark I couldn't make out what they'd meant to say.

—genetically speaking, you find out there's any relation to me, you tell her. Wait till she's old enough or whatever, I don't know. You're her dad. You know best. But tell her it might happen.

That left the envelope.

I was sure it was the test results. Partly because it made sense and mostly because the return address on the envelope said it was from a lab of some sort and I was pretty sure that's where DNA test results would come from. My hands were clammy, shaking so badly as I slipped my fingers past the torn-open top to work the papers inside out I was almost afraid I'd tear them.

I never stopped to think of if I wanted to know or not. I wasn't the person who would sit there declaring it didn't matter what a piece of paper said, that Gary Lane always had been and always would be my father.

Because it did matter.

That way of thinking was an impractical romanticization at best and dangerous at worst, apparently, since Mike had... something.

Something he didn't want me to inherit.

No, I wasn't that person. I was the person sitting in my parents' closet, discovering puzzle piece by puzzle piece, that she'd been conceived in what seemed to be some kind of throuple situation.

That, almost disturbingly, the kind of relationship I preferred was something my parents had wanted for themselves.

That my birth had led to the shattering of that relationship.

That I'd been a wakeup call.

That Mike had moved far, far away because he didn't feel like he could safely be with the people he loved.

Because even now, even years after the fact, even being as outspoken and unashamed as I claimed to be, there was fear in telling people that I didn't want a traditional relationship. That I didn't want to choose between people I cared about. That I was attracted to people regardless of what was in their pants, regardless of the norm, regardless of anything but my own desires.

Decades after the fact, that fear still guided so much.

And it had been so much worse thirty years ago.

Tears had already started blurring my vision before I even unfolded the results. I blinked them away, though one fell and splattered on the paper as I opened it. I tensed, staring at the page, at the numbers in front of me until they made sense.

Two columns. One labelled Tessa Lane and one labelled Gary Lane, with meaningless markers and genomes and whatever other random science shit they scienced for. Dr. Jackson Clark would have been able to tell me, I guess. But thankfully, for un-sciencey people like me, there was a summary at the bottom:

Probability of paternity: 99.999%

So he was.

After all that, he was my dad.

After all that, I was his daughter.

And after everything, after all the secrets I'd kept, after all the things I'd thought would make me the outlier in my family, I was wrong.

Because of everyone in my life, my parents would have understood more than anyone.

And after years, after a *lifetime* of feeling like I had nothing in common with him, my dad and I had... this. This odd, strange, weird similarity that connected us.

And because of me, because of what I'd done, it was too late.

I was too late.

That was when the tears broke free. The ones that had been stuck since Monday night, the ones I'd craved every day since, flooded down my cheeks as I clutched the DNA test results in my hands. I sobbed, regret making my heart splinter, anger making it bleed, grief making it curl into itself like the smaller and tighter it could be, the less things could hurt. I sobbed for the version of my dad that I never knew, for the version that I did know, for the guilt of my existence being what had separated my parents from the person they loved.

And that was when Mom and Mike walked in and found me.

"Oh, Teacup," Mom said, her face crumpling as she moved in to hug me. "What's—"

"Where did you find those?" Mike asked, disquieted panic in his voice.

"S-Safe," I choked through my tears.

"I didn't even know we had a safe," Mom said. "What are you—"

"Lola, no," Mike said. "Don't look at—"

But she'd already taken the results from my hand and was looking down at them.

"I can explain," she said, her voice high-pitched. "Sweetie, I can explain, this isn't what it seems. There's m-more to it and I can prove it, I can p-prove—"

"Mom," I choked, then heaved another sob. She put a comforting arm around my shoulders and it took a minute, but once I caught my breath and used the back of my hand to wipe away the hot tears on my cheeks, I let out a shaky breath and looked at her.

"Mom, I have some things I need to tell you."

Thirty-Eight

SPILLING ALL THE SECRETS didn't fix everything.

In a fairytale world, it would have. Mom would have explained the story of two star-crossed best friends and the woman they both loved. I would have explained the snowball of circumstances and pain and fear that led to the avalanche of lies I'd been caught in. There would be a lot of hugging and tears before we declared ourselves one big happy family.

And some of that happened. Mom did explain how she and Dad and Mike had come together. How they'd had an undeniable connection for years. How Dad and Mike had been inseparable before my mom came along, and she refused to be the thing that separated them, so she became part of that inseparable relationship, too.

How Dad had been so intense, so focused, so dedicated to working his ass off and building the life he wanted my mom to have. How she had been so dramatic, so over the top, with feelings bigger than she knew what to do with. And how Mike had balanced them, steadied them, brought laughter when things were complicated and joy when things were hard.

How it wasn't until Josh had been born that they realized the depth of that connection. How Dad had felt so guilty, how he'd struggled, how Mom had seen the way they looked at each other and never quite known what it meant until she did.

How they'd finally given in.

How it had felt so right.

How there had been two years of ignorant blissfulness as they pretended what they had could work.

But then there had been that one fateful day when Mom realized she was pregnant again. And that as she sat there, staring at the test, she didn't know which of them was the father.

"It wouldn't have mattered," Mom said. "But they said… well." She looked at Mike. "I guess I didn't know all of it until today."

Mike had been mostly silent until then, but looked up, pain on his face.

"My mother had Huntington's disease," he said. "And her father had it, too. We're fairly sure my mom's grandpa also had it. Which meant there was a damn good chance I'd end up with it, too. Back then, it wasn't as easy to test for and let me tell you, it was…" His voice broke and he shook his head. "Mom got it young. It eats away at a person's brain. Changes them completely. Watching her go through that… I knew I didn't want to have kids when I was in my teens. Not that I didn't *want* them, but I didn't want to pass that on. So Lola getting pregnant was a wakeup call."

"We wanted you to stay," Mom said softly.

"I couldn't," Mike said, and his voice shook again. "I wanted to, Lola, but it was too hard to see you all when—"

"I know." She sniffled, then laughed. "I know. We've been over it a thousand times and you know I always wanted you to do what was best for you. Even if I thought it was very stupid."

Mike chuckled. "Well, either way. We all agreed that no matter what, Gary was Tessa's dad."

"I said I didn't want to get a DNA test or anything," Mom said. "I thought it didn't matter. In another world, we would've continued on, the three of us being together and raising babies together and just… living our lives."

"But with my fear of passing on Huntington's..." Mike sighed. "I begged Gary to get a test done. I told him he didn't have to tell anyone the results. Just find out if she'd be at risk for it. And he never told me he'd even done it. But he did."

"Wait," Audrey said. "So was Gary...?"

"He is Tessa's father," Mom said. "We, um, found those results. Earlier today. In the safe."

"There's a safe?" Josh said.

"I didn't know about that either," Mom said. "He must have had one even before the fire because otherwise I don't know how the hell those letters and results survived. But they did."

"Did you ever get genetic testing or anything done?" Josh asked Mike.

He nodded. "By some miracle, I don't have the gene. Let me tell you, I cried with relief when I found out because it means I couldn't have passed it on. But it wasn't until the anniversary party in March that I knew Tess was Gary's kid." He looked at me, chuckling as he shook his head. "You look just like his mom. Just like her."

Dylan and Josh were surprisingly relaxed by Mom revealing her story. I thought Josh might be a bit more accepting considering Zain had told him literally everything about me, so it wouldn't seem as shocking, but there was still a difference when it was your parents versus your sibling. But he listened, laughing here and there as they told the story for the second time that day—since I'd gotten a version while we were all sitting in the closet earlier—and looking morose as we all saw the heartbreak on Mike's face.

Dylan reacted in much the same way he reacted to anything: barely. It wasn't until Mom finished talking that he spoke up.

"Okay, so Dad was like... bisexual?" he asked.

"Something like that," Mom said.

"And you were all, like, in a relationship sort of thing?"

"Yes," Mike said. "Your dad and I were friends for a long time before he and Lorelei got married, but there were a lot of, uh... feelings. Between all three of us."

He turned to Mom. "So does this mean you and Mike are going to be together now?"

"Dill," Josh said. "Not the time, man."

"Right now, we're still coming to terms with Gar being gone," Mike said. "But if it gets to that point, I promise we'll be open with you all about what's going on."

That seemed to satisfy everyone, though I wondered if I was the only one who caught him already referring to himself and Mom as "we." If anyone else did, they seemed as unbothered by it as I was.

Because it didn't bother me. Of course it felt far too early for Mom to be with anyone else. Dad had been gone for less than a week. But if Dad was anything like me—and I was starting to see that we were more alike than I'd ever wanted to consider—he would've wanted them to be with each other.

He would have wanted to know they were happy. Or at least, as happy as they could be as two rather than three.

Because I got it. I got how incomplete it would seem for any of them. I barely knew Mike, but I could see how he balanced my parents. They had needed Mike's heart, its empathy and its exuberance and its optimism. But Mom had also needed Dad's dedication. His drive. His practicality. And they'd needed her drama. Her loyalty. Her humour.

Just like how I needed Finn and Zain to balance me.

I needed the easy, unbothered way Finn approached life. I needed Zain to challenge me. I needed the way Finn doted on me, cared for me, gave me the space to be vulnerable without worry of judgement. But I also needed Zain's passion. I needed the intensity. The fierceness. The way he knew I could handle myself but was there when I wanted someone to lean on.

Dad would've wanted Mom and Mike to love each other when he couldn't be there, like I wanted Zain and Finn to be together when I couldn't.

Because it wasn't about them moving on. It wasn't about them replacing someone.

It was about wanting the people you... the people you *loved* to have as much happiness as they could.

Once Mom and Mike had told their story and cleared the air, it was my turn to come clean about everything.

There were a lot of tears as I talked. From me and from Mom, but also from Josh. Dylan didn't cry, at least not that I knew of, but Dylan wasn't a big crier to begin with. The pained look on his face was more than enough to understand.

And like I said, spilling all those secrets didn't fix everything. It wasn't all better just because we had everything out in the open. The course of one conversation, no matter how life changing, couldn't fix years of dysfunction.

But it was a step.

And honestly, I felt peace. I felt calm, despite the heaviness of the conversation. And it was *heavy*; hashing out a lifetime of not knowing how to interact with each other, of secrets and separation and resentment over things the others didn't even know about—those weren't easy things to talk about. But it was necessary. Of course it was necessary. It was the motivation for so much of what I'd done.

"I can't believe you hated being called Teacup," Josh said when I'd finished.

"I told you that," I said. "Multiple times."

"Well, yeah," Dylan said. "But Dad always said it too, and it seemed like it was an inside joke or something."

"It wasn't funny," I said. "And I don't know why Dad couldn't see that."

Josh sighed. "Look, Dad was my hero. I can't say he wasn't. I spent my whole life wanting to be just like him because that was what he wanted me to be."

"That's not—" Mom started, but Josh held up a hand.

"Dad wanted me to have the same kind of job he did. Do the same things he did. Live the same life he did. And I went along with it because I looked up to him like no one else in the world. But that means I think I also need to admit... well..." He looked at me, then at Dylan, but couldn't quite meet Mom's eye. "I love Dad, and I'm gonna miss him like you wouldn't believe but he wasn't always a... a great person."

It was shocking to hear that come from Josh's mouth. Accurate, but shocking, simply because in my mind, Josh had always been a second version of Dad.

"He didn't know how to show he cared in a way that other people understood," Josh continued. "He was mean. I don't think it was on purpose, but he didn't know how to show things properly. He didn't know how to tell you he was proud of you."

"That's because he wasn't proud of me," I said. "He knew perfectly well how to tell people he was proud of *you*."

"But he was proud of you, too," Josh said.

"Don't bullshit me."

"He was, though," Dylan said.

I looked at Dylan, who was frowning down at his hands folded on the table.

"Dad did this thing where he'd complain about the things he liked most, you know? Like, he always said that streaming was a stupid career choice and playing video games all day was a waste of time and I'd never make anything of myself. But then when I did, he... he'd say the same things, but kinda different. Like he'd tell people 'Oh, Dylan just sits around and games all day. Do you believe people give him money for that?' Like, it was still mean, but it was more like he was saying other people were stupid, not me."

"He never thought being an artist was anything but stupid," I said. "Even when I was doing well at it. Nothing I've ever done made Dad proud except bringing Brad here."

Josh shook his head. "Do you remember that day, though? When we were all sitting here and Brad said you were stubborn and Dad made that comment about you talking him into paying for art school?"

I nodded. My face turned red as I remembered how embarrassed I'd been.

"It was like that."

I frowned. "Like what?"

"It sounded mean but he meant, like, he was proud of how stubborn you were. That you stood up for yourself, even to him."

I couldn't say I believed Josh and Dylan. Part of me wanted to. It was the same part of me that wanted to forget all the problems between me and my dad and make him more myth than memory. To remember him as nothing more than a good man and forget all the things that made him real.

Death does that. It warps memories, taking away the bad and replacing it with only the good. And that's not necessarily a good thing. Humans aren't perfect. You weren't supposed to speak ill of the dead, but it felt like it dishonoured them more to pretend they were something they weren't. To pretend that I had no bad memories of my dad would have only taken away the significance of the good memories I had of him.

It would have made it feel like those good memories didn't matter, and they did.

My dad and I didn't have a good relationship. Regardless of the similarities I could see in us now, that wasn't how I knew him.

He never told me he was proud of me. The meaning my brothers were assigning to his actions was their interpretation and nothing more. They couldn't have known what was in his heart. They couldn't know if they were guessing right or if they were just trying to comfort me, to justify the unjustifiable, to give me closure.

But the only thing closing was the casket, and the only person who truly knew if my dad had been proud of me was inside it.

And I could have pointed that out. I could've told Dylan and Josh that they looked up to a man who had hurt all of us, though deep in my heart, part of me did believe that hurt hadn't been intentional.

I could've said that.

I could've told them to stop.

That I didn't need their comfort.

But all that would've done was hurt them and the fragile relationships we'd just started building.

And we were all hurt enough.

So that time, I chose the high road. And sure, maybe Brad had been right when he said taking the high road just meant you had farther to fall.

But maybe it also meant there would be more arms to catch you on the way down.

Part 7

Confession: Home is where
your bra comes off.

Thirty-Nine

"So," Josh said, setting a beer each on the table in front of me and Dylan.

"So?" I asked, cracking the beer as he settled in his seat next to Audrey.

"Now that Mom and Mike are gone, I have some additional questions for you," Josh said.

I glanced at Dylan, who shrugged, then back at Josh. We'd been talking for ages at that point; Mom and Mike had stuck around for a bit but decided to take a walk together a while ago, even though it was getting late.

"What questions?" I asked, trying to hide my nervousness by sipping my beer.

"You and Zain," Josh said with a knowing sort of teasingness. "And, uh, Finn?"

Fuck.

"What about it?" I asked.

"How's that going?"

"I haven't talked to them." I motioned at the table. "I've been here the whole time."

"Yeah, but you're going to, right?"

"I mean..."

"Tess. Come on."

"What?" I twisted the beer bottle between my hands, not looking at him. "Just because it all worked out doesn't mean I'm not kind of annoyed he did the exact thing he promised he wouldn't do and ran to tell you everything the second he wasn't getting his way."

"I mean, he didn't, though," Audrey said.

"Oh, Josh just magically found out all the details through his telekinetic powers."

"That would be telepathic," Dylan said.

"Not the point."

"No, Zain told me," Josh said. "But he didn't want to."

I looked up at him, frowning. "What do you mean?"

Josh glanced at Audrey, then back at me. "I mean I asked him, Tess."

"Asked him what?"

"What he had going on with my sister."

I gaped at him, lips parted in shock, until Josh chuckled and snapped me out of it.

"But how...?"

"Uh, let's see," he said. "There was the random texts and phone calls he was getting while we were camping that he refused to tell anyone about, even though it was clearly someone he was into because he was taking selfies around the fucking fire. Not that I thought it was you at the time. But then there was the random disappearing act during the bachelor party that was a little weird. And then the whole thing with him being downstairs in the guest room after you 'had to pee' yesterday when we were all here."

My face burned. "We did *not* do anything yesterday."

"Well, yeah, I know that now," Josh said. "But it was enough that I was trying to figure out why the hell my best friend was sneaking around with my 'married' sister. So when we went to get Dad's stuff from work this morning, I asked him what he was doing. In fairness, I thought it was going to be a very different conversation from what it was. I mean, he wasn't going to say anything until I said I was going to give you shit for cheating on your husband. And honestly, I thought he was making it all up at first because he was trying to protect you or something."

I looked down at the beer again, unable to bring myself to say anything. Josh's voice softened.

"Tess, he only said something because he didn't have much of a choice," he said. "I thought... well. It was one thing to think he was being a homewrecker. It was another to hear how much he cares about you."

My eyes were still fixed firmly on the beer. "You're not mad at him for that?"

"For wanting to be with you? Fuck no. If there's anyone out there that I can guarantee is going to treat my sister right, it's him, and I know you'd treat my best friend right, too. But I was pissed he never told me he was... you know."

That got me to look up, mostly because I couldn't stop myself from glaring at him. "You're pissed at him for not telling you he's bi?"

"I'm pissed at *myself*." Josh's voice was quiet but emotional. "He told me a lot of things today. Things about you, yeah, but things about him, too. Stuff I should've known because he's my best friend and that he never told me because he didn't know how I'd react. And I'm mad that I came across as the kind of person who wouldn't support him." He looked at me, almost pleading. "I'm gonna fix that about me because that's not who I want to be. Just like I'm gonna be a better brother to you and Dill."

I nodded slowly. "Well, I... I appreciate that. And I'm sure Zain will be glad he can talk to you about things. Maybe it'll make it easier when he has to finally tell his parents."

"What do you mean, finally?" Josh asked.

"Like... because he isn't out to them?" I said.

"Wasn't."

"What?"

Josh gave me a look that wasn't quite pity and wasn't quite disbelief. "What do you think he was doing tonight?"

"But he must've known once you told Brad you knew, he wouldn't..." I looked from Josh to Dylan to Audrey, as if one of them would know what to say. "I mean, Brad barely even knows Zain's parents. He doesn't have to tell them."

"He wants to, Tess," Josh said gently.

"No, he doesn't!" I stood from the table so abruptly that the other three jolted upright. "He literally said on Sunday that they wouldn't support him. That he'd end up—fuck. Is he there? Right now?"

"I mean, probably, but—"

I grabbed my phone and tapped at it frantically, unblocking Z Biggest Asshole. I could feel three sets of eyes on me as I hesitated, trying to figure out if I should call him or text him before figuring a text would be better in case he couldn't respond.

You don't have to do—

And then my phone died, because of fucking course it did.

"Fuck!" I swore, then bit my lip, looking down at my phone as my heart started to slam in my chest.

Because this...

This was it, wasn't it?

I was the one who told Zain it was over. And yeah, Zain had broken his promise to me, but... well. I mean, the truth was going to come out one way or another because we'd been sloppy and Josh had noticed.

Which meant if there was any chance, any hope, any minute possibility that we could be together again, it was up to me.

So this was it. This was the moment. This was when there needed to be one of those grand romantic gestures, and I was the one who needed to make it.

Because I needed him.

I looked up at Dylan. "Lend me your car."

"What?" he said.

"Lend me your car. I need to go to the Hameeds'."

"Tess—" Josh said.

"I will give you forty bucks."

Dylan laughed. "Forty bucks? That's it?"

"I'm unemployed. That's like twenty percent of my weekly income right now."

"Oh," he said. "Right. Well..."

"Forty... five," I said. "And the rest of this beer I've taken one sip of."

Dylan shook his head as he leaned back in his chair and dug into his pocket. "Don't worry about it. Just don't, uh, crash."

"Promise." I pushed my beer across the table at him, then plucked the keys from his hand.

"Tessa, wait," Josh said. "Maybe you should—"

"I don't want him to do this because of me," I said. "He's given up enough for me already."

Josh inhaled as if he was going to say something, then hesitated before letting his breath out.

"Okay," he said. "Good luck, Teacup." The nickname left his mouth and he looked instantly mortified. "I mean—"

"It's fine," I said. "I don't mind it so much now."

"But you said—"

"Zain changed my mind about it." I turned to leave the kitchen, grabbing my purse off the counter where I'd been storing it. "He's changed my mind about a lot of things."

I PLUGGED MY PHONE in to charge while I was driving, but it wasn't like Burnsley was a big town. The Hameeds didn't quite live within walking distance of our house—though that had never stopped Josh and Zain from trudging to each other's houses if their parents refused to drive them over—but it wasn't a long drive. Certainly not long enough to charge my phone more than a few percent and nowhere near enough for me to actually call anyone.

So, with a sigh, I turned Dylan's car off and got out, walking up the driveway with the intent of steeling myself once I reached the front door and rang the bell.

Except I didn't reach it.

Mrs. Hameed was sitting on the wooden steps that led to the front door, wearing a light blue hijab and clutching a tissue in her hand. She looked up as I rounded the corner of the garage, illuminated by the golden glow of light filtering through the windows next to the front door.

"Tessa?" she said, her voice hoarse.

"Hi, Mrs. Hameed," I said. "Are you alright?"

"Mm-hmm," she said. The sound came out high-pitched and another step forward made it clear that she was crying.

Fuck.

"What are you doing here, dear?" she asked.

"I was looking for Zain," I said.

Her chin trembled. "He left a while ago. After he..." She trailed off, then let out a tiny sob. "How did I mess up so badly?"

It was not my place, I told myself. It was not my place to confront Zain's mom about her reaction to him coming out and I needed to focus on finding Zain and being there for him and—

"What do you mean, messed up?" I asked bluntly.

She sniffled again, dabbing the tissue in her hand against her eyes. "I always wanted my sons to know it was *their* life. That they could do anything they wanted. Be who they wanted to be. Love who they wanted to love." She sniffled again, then brought the tissue to her nose and let out an echoing honk of a blast as she blew it. "How badly have I done that my boy doesn't seem to know that?"

Oh.

That wasn't what I'd expected.

"What happened?" I asked, trying to soften my tone.

She looked up at me, pressing her lips together into an uncomfortably familiar smirk. "If you're here, I believe you know, dear."

"Well, yeah," I said. "But I don't know, like, what actually happened."

Much like when my mom told a story, Mrs. Hameed responded with several details that didn't matter and a semi-rambling train of thought that eventually summed up the situation. Zain had gone over for dinner, like he'd said, and when they finished eating, said he needed to tell his parents something important.

"I thought perhaps he had a girlfriend," Mrs. Hameed said. "Or that he'd gotten some girl pregnant."

But, of course, he told them that he was bisexual.

And maybe if it had just been him coming out as bi, it would have been okay. His mom felt bad she'd never realized it. His dad had frozen a bit, but he'd steeled himself and nodded. So maybe if he'd left it at that and told them he'd moved to Vancouver because he needed space from them, and that he knew that they didn't think he was as accomplished as his brother, but that this was who he was and that was what he needed to be happy... maybe it that would have been okay.

But his dad did *not* like the fact that Zain was polyamorous.

"He kept telling him it was wrong," Mrs. Hameed said, still crying. "That we were not the kind of people who believe in polygamy, even though Zain kept trying to explain that wasn't... I don't fully know. I know it only in the context of where I grew up and where Ahmed grew up. I know Ahmed never agreed with having multiple wives, though I had no idea how... how passionately he disagreed. But if Zain says it's different, I have no reason not to believe him. I know my son. He's always been a good boy. He wouldn't choose to do something if it was wrong. So I don't need to understand why he wants this to keep loving him." She buried her face against her hands. "But I didn't know how to say that. I didn't say it in time."

Zain had left, saying he'd give them some space to process and would get in touch before he left for Vancouver on Sunday. And then his parents had argued, his mom insisting they could support him even if it was unusual and his dad insisting that was enabling immoral behaviour that went against what he believed in. And then he'd stormed off to his study and Mrs. Hameed had come out here, alone and upset and wishing she'd known what to say before Zain had left thinking they didn't love him.

"If you find him, dear, please... please just tell him I love him," she said, wiping her eyes again. "No matter what, I love him. If you don't mind."

And of course I said I would.

Forty

He had to be at the Mountainview.

There were a couple of hotels in Burnsley, but the Mountainview was the only nice one. And knowing Zain the way I did now, he wasn't about to stay at Beddy B's—the motel near the highway whose name was supposed to invoke feelings of a bed and breakfast but actually just became slang for the type of bugs that infested the personal items of one in three reviewers on Yelp—just to throw me off.

There was no lineup at the check-in desk when I walked into the lobby, but that was only because I was the one who started it. Two clerks were working: one was helping an elderly couple who couldn't seem to understand why they needed a credit card on file for their reservation and the other was helping an exasperated-looking man in a crisp suit.

"I understand that," the man was saying. "But I promise you, that is my actual name."

"Sir, you expect me to believe your name is Michael Torris?" the clerk said flatly.

I couldn't help it. I snorted back a laugh, then clapped my hand to my mouth. The man didn't seem to hear me, thankfully.

"I have my ID right here," Michael Torris said. "And if you don't mind, I go by Mick."

I didn't hear the clerk's response, mostly because someone behind me started talking in a loud voice. And, more significantly, I recognized the voice.

"...bastard's not answering his phone. So not only did she block all of us, now we can't even—"

She stopped speaking suddenly. Probably because I turned around, my eyes wide, and immediately caught hers across the lobby.

Time whirled around me. I was trapped in that moment, staring straight at her—well, not just her, but them—but before I could even register that my jaw had dropped, she was storming across the lobby, so fast and so intently that her long brown hair was fanning back from her face.

"Mick!" she shouted, and suddenly the man dealing with the clerk bolted past me.

"What's wro—*oof.*" He had just enough time to grab the phone she thrust towards him, her burning eyes still locked on mine.

"Claire?" I finally said, and then she was in front of me.

"Never do that to me again," she demanded, then cupped my face in her hands and kissed me so hard, I thought I was going to see stars.

It was fierce, the way she kissed me. Fierce and intense and angry and relieved and comforting, so fucking comforting somehow, even though I could almost taste wrath on her lips.

"You're so stupid," she muttered between kisses.

"I know," I said, inhaling sharply as she bit down on my bottom lip. "I'm so stupid."

"So fucking stupid," she said, then she pulled away. Her eyes were watering as she tenderly brushed my hair off my face. "I love your stupid ass, but you're so fucking stupid."

"I'm sorry." The words got caught in my throat. "I just—"

"—went nuclear on your own life because of your asshole ex-husband?" she finished.

"It... made sense at the time," I said.

"How, in any way, did that make sense?" Chuck said, coming up behind Claire and folding his arms. "Also, I hope you're not expecting the same greeting from me. Because I will gladly tell you how stupid you are, but we're not kissing."

"Not even a little?" I asked.

"Maybe a peck on the cheek," Charles said from beside him.

"I could go for a peck on the cheek," Julie said. "But I'll leave the tongue kissing to Claire."

"That seems fair," Charles said. "No tongue kissing Tessa, Chuck, but everything else is fair game, okay?"

Chuck rolled his eyes, then looked back at me. "Why?"

"What?"

"Why did you block me? Why did you block all of us?"

"Because I knew you were going to talk me out of what I was doing," I said.

"So you knew we'd all tell you how stupid it was, and yet you still tried to do the thing," he said.

"Well, as the record can show, I'm really stupid," I said.

"I don't think you're stupid at all."

Those words almost broke my heart, as did the voice that spoke them. I knew he was there, obviously. He didn't have the stature of a person you could easily miss. But I'd been doing everything I could not to look at him.

Until then.

"Thanks, Finn," I said, my voice quiet.

He smiled. It was a little sad. A little uncertain. Not quite its usual brightness. But it was a smile all the same.

And it made my heart ache so much I had to look away again.

"Sorry, Tessa Bernice Lane, but that is not good enough," Chuck said. "Not this time. You are my friend and I love you endlessly, and I am so, *so* sorry you've been going through all of this. But the fact that you'd shut everyone out instead of asking for help is... it hurts, okay? And I want to know why."

That hurt, too, but I couldn't deny that it was fair. "I didn't want to bother anyone."

"You know it's not a bother," Claire said.

"Isn't it, though?" I said before I could stop myself. "I constantly have shit going on in my life. I'm constantly making the wrong choice about things. I'm constantly acting like an asshole to all of you. Now that everyone's paired off, it's like I'm... I'm just the extra."

"Well, that's stupid too," Julie said, which was a surprise because Julie never called people stupid. "I mean, for one, you're not the 'extra.' You're the glue."

Confused, I looked up at her.

"You're the whole reason all of us are together," she continued. "If you want to talk about us as couples or whatever, you brought me and Claire together." She looked at Chuck and Charles. "They wouldn't have met without you. Same with Finn and Zain. Bringing this group of us together—that was you, too. You're not some afterthought, Tess. You're the connection."

I didn't know what to say to that. Julie waited, in case I had something to say, but then smiled.

"Two, you're not an asshole. I'd be willing to claim you're the kindest person in this room."

That made me laugh. I mean, I was standing in a room with Julie. And Finn.

"I mean, not to be that person, but that is a stretch," Chuck said, stifling a laugh of his own.

Julie folded her arms and gave him an unimpressed look. "Is it? Because you know what Tessa did after I was a total asshole who ghosted her? She didn't just accept my apology, Chuck. She got me in touch with Claire so I could go to Paris. She triggered a huge life change for me after I was awful to her."

"But that was after you showed up to do me a favour at Kira's," I said.

She raised her eyebrows at me. "So you're saying you called in a favour with someone who hurt you in the past for the benefit of your friend? You didn't even call in a favour for *yourself*, Tess."

"And you also left halfway through a sex date to help her in the first place," Claire added. "Not to brag, but I'm pretty sure I could have made you come a few more times that night. You gave that up to help Kira."

"Yeah, but—"

"You worked your ass off to make the date auction work after I snapped at you multiple times," Chuck said, looking slightly disgruntled as he admitted it. "You covered for me a ton of times at CARE, even though you were the first person to claim you were useless. You could've thrown me under the bus because you know as well as I do I was at that lunch with you and Claire, but you didn't. And even though you have your own stuff going on, you always set things aside to help me when I was panicking or worried or freaking out about meeting Charles's parents."

"I get paranoid and jump to conclusions," Claire said. "I've made assumptions about your motives that were completely unfounded. Even if we argue about it, you never make me feel like I'm a bad person. And you safe worded me one time because you were worried about me, then sat there and listened as I trauma-dumped on you before telling me you still enjoyed being around me."

"You always tipped really good when you came to Bar One," Charles said. "And you were always super nice to whoever your server was." He glanced around at everyone, almost nervously. "I mean, it might not sound like much, but it really does matter."

"You let me live with you," Finn said. "When I had nowhere else to go, you helped me, even though we hadn't talked in a long time and you were kinda mad at me."

"Sorry to inform you about this, but the jury has apparently decided that you, Tessa Marie Lane, are not an asshole," Chuck said. "We're still out on whether you're stupid or not, but you've lost your asshole designation with all the nice things you've been doing and all the forgiveness you've been laying down on people."

"And it wasn't really that stupid," Finn said. There was a beat of silence where everyone glanced at him, confused, and he shrugged. "I mean, when you're going through a hard time, sometimes you do things that don't make sense. Like not telling your family you're living in your car."

"Or your ex-girlfriend," Julie said, and Finn gave her an embarrassed smile.

"Exactly. But like, you had a lot happen in the last week, Tess. Probably when you did all of this, it did make sense to you, even if it didn't to anyone else. Or even to you now. Right?"

I bit my lip, trying to force my chin to stop trembling as I nodded. "Yes. Exactly."

"Cool." He smiled, looking relieved for half a second before something nervous flitted across his face. "But then, are we still broken up?"

I let out a shaky laugh. "I don't want to be. If you'll let me apologize and un-break-up with you."

"Oh, God yes," he said, the words coming out as a relieved sigh. "Because I really wanted to greet you the way Claire did—well, like, the kissing part, not the calling you stupid part—but if we were broken up I thought that might be awkward and—*mmmph*."

His arms went around me as I kissed him, familiar and strong and so, so right. I felt his smile against my lips, felt the muffled little chuckle that was the precursor to a soft but appreciative sigh that only I could hear because my friends were laughing at us. He held me close and held me tight, cradling me as we kissed like no one else was around.

But there were, of course. There were plenty of people around, including two very concerned looking desk clerks and a scandalized old lady, so eventually I had to stop kissing him.

But that was okay, because Finn was grinning, and the sight of that smile was making my whole body feel warm.

"So, you all came here to tell me I'm stupid?" I asked as Finn put an arm around my shoulders.

"Well, most of us were worried as fuck about you," Chuck said.

"I think we can safely say it was all of us," Julie said.

"And we're your friends," Charles said. "We wanted to be here for you."

It took a while for the full story to come out, mainly because half of them were trying to talk at the same time and the other half were interrupting with details or corrections or reminders as they spoke, but eventually they got the whole thing out.

And what it boiled down to, yet again, was Zain.

Zain telling them how worried he was about me.

Zain updating them with the details of what was going on, first because I was in such a state of shock after my dad's death that he just took that job on without saying anything because I wasn't capable of it, then because I went and blocked everyone I knew.

Zain begging them for help because I was about to go back to Brad and I was angry at him and he couldn't do anything. I didn't want to see him. And so he got ahold of Claire and pleaded with her to try reaching me because he'd rather have me happy and supported, even if he couldn't be the one to do it.

"Zain told me what was going on," Finn said. "Especially after you... you texted me."

My face went red and I had to look away from him again.

"And then when Zain realized just how much you were spiralling, he got Finn to tell Charles," Chuck said. "Since the only person Charles texts as much as me is Finn, apparently."

"You said I needed more friends," Charles said.

"You do. They're just not supposed to be hotter than me."

"You're the hottest man I know," Charles said. "And besides, pretty sure he's taken, babe. More importantly, he's not you."

"Nope," Finn said. "I'm Finn."

"Glad we settled that," Julie said. "Finn also texted me so I could tell Claire."

"It was like a very panicky, very effective, very gay phone tree," Claire said. "Especially when we realized that none of us had heard from you and couldn't get a hold of you. And since you were refusing to listen to Zain, I figured a visit to small town interior BC was in order so we could talk you out of the very, very, very stupid thing you were about to do."

"So she just flew us out here on her private jet," Chuck said casually. "By the way, the mile high club? Fabulous."

"You joined the mile high club before me, too?" I asked, offended. "On your flight to talk me out of doing something stupid?"

"What else were we going to do?" Chuck said. "Although, we almost didn't have enough time. It's not a long flight."

"I told him he had to bring his own sheets," Claire said.

"They were easy to find since the bed is *not* round," Chuck said.

"Wait, you had sex on the plane?" Finn asked. "Like, on the way here?"

"Uh... yeah," Chuck said. "Where did you think we were for most of the flight?"

Finn shrugged, then grinned at Charles and held his hand up. "Nice, man."

Charles's face turned red, but he was smiling as he high-fived Finn.

"Anyway, then Zain texted Finn about everything with Josh today," Claire said. "But we figured even though we didn't have to talk you out of what was, again, the stupidest thing I've ever heard, you'd probably need some support."

"Even if that support was just us telling you how stupid you are," Chuck said.

"Except *now* we can't get a hold of Zain," Claire finished. "So we had no idea where you were, have no idea where he is, and had no way to get through to either of you that we hadn't already tried."

"He's—" I started, then looked at Finn.

"He's what?" Finn asked.

"He came out," I said. "To his parents. I don't think it went particularly well. With his dad, at least. And now I don't know where he is. I thought he'd be here."

"You can't think of anywhere else he might be?" Charles asked.

I pressed my lips together, trying to rack my brain. "Honestly, if he's not here, not at my mom's, and not at his parents'... no."

"He doesn't have any friends he might be staying with?" Julie said.

"I mean, I'm sure he's got other friends around here, but I can't imagine he'd go to any of them after coming out," I said. "He hasn't come out to anyone else in Burnsley except—"

And then it hit me.

"Except?" Chuck urged when I stopped speaking.

"Oh, that asshole," I breathed.

"Who?" Claire asked. "Zain?"

I shook my head, almost laughing. "I know where he is."

Forty-One

"Tess? What are you—"

"Go get Zain," I said. "I know he's here."

If Josh thought I didn't notice his eyes dart to the side, he was as stupid as I was. "I know you're looking for him, but he's not—"

"Josh, I've been on a fucking wild goose chase trying to track that man down. I have seen his mother, I have scarred an old lady in a hotel lobby, and I have definitely used way more of Dylan's gas than I was hoping to and I really, really don't want to fill up the tank for him. So I swear to God, if you don't go get Zain right now, I will shout what I need to say through your entire apartment and I promise you don't want to hear even half of the details that I definitely do not need to include but will just so you get to hear them."

He hesitated again and I thought he was going to just do it, but then he shook his head. "I don't know where he—"

"Zain, get your ass to the door right now or I'm going to tell him all about that special nickname you like and the reason you like it so much, even though you're damn insistent that it's not a 'massive' kink and—"

There was a soft banging noise from somewhere to Josh's left, followed by a curse.

"For fuck's sake, Tessa," Zain said. "Fine. Give me a second."

Folding my arms across my chest, I raised my eyebrows at Josh. He shrugged.

"Sorry, Tess," he said. "But bros before... uh... girls."

"Imply I'm a hoe again and I will give you all the filthy details you don't want to hear about my hoeing ways with your *bro*," I said.

He rolled his eyes. "Look, if you two end up together, I'm not playing the pick-a-side game whenever you inevitably get on each other's nerves because you're both in the running for biggest drama queen I know. And I know we just had that whole long conversation about how we should be better siblings and shit, but just so you know, I'm not sorry for this. Not in this situation."

"Good," I said. "I'm glad he has a friend like you and had somewhere safe to go after this. But I need to talk to him now."

He glanced to the side again, then looked at me and lowered his voice, his lips barely moving as he spoke through his teeth. "Don't yell at him. He knows he's fucked up, but he's had a fucking hard night, okay? And he's been trying to do the right thing, but—"

"Josh," I said. "I know."

He studied me for a moment, then nodded. "Fine. One sec."

He didn't invite me in, which was fair, but left the door open while Zain took his sweet ass time coming to it. I folded my arms, shivering in the cool air.

Josh and Audrey called it an apartment, as did most people in Burnsley, but their building was more like what would happen if an apartment building had a baby with a motel. The structure itself wasn't enclosed; each of the apartments had a door that led outside, so there were no buzzers or anything to let people in since they could walk right up and knock like on a normal door. Which was great, because it meant Josh didn't have a way to warn Zain as soon as I'd arrived, and less great because it was September and it was nighttime and I was cold.

But any complaints I had about being cold faded when a shadow approached the door and a moment later, Zain was standing there.

He didn't look good.

Like, he looked good because Zain always looked good. No amount of bags under his eyes could change the fact that they were gorgeous. No drawn and haggard look on his face could take away the slope of his jaw or the height of his cheekbones. No amount of downturn to the corners of his lips could stop them from looking inviting.

But he didn't look like he felt good.

I felt a little bad. I mean, I probably should have felt really bad, considering how much of this was my fault. Zain's day had to be about as crazy as mine had. It had started with his best friend confronting him about what was going on with his sister and ended with Zain coming out to his parents as both bi and poly, and that was after the hellish week he'd had. My dad might have been the one who died, but Zain looked up to him too. I'd broken up with him, I'd yelled at him, I'd refused to listen to any logic or sense. Even still, he'd been there for me. He'd quietly made sure I had what I needed. He'd gotten me from Vancouver back to my mom's house when I could barely remember my name. And he'd arranged for my friends to be here, because even when I pushed him as far away as I could, he wanted me to be happy. And that didn't even get into the fact that he was supposed to have started a new job four days earlier.

Okay.

I did feel really bad.

"What do you need to talk about, Tessa?" he asked.

"I'm sorry I've never been fair to you," I said.

His reaction wasn't big enough that most people would have noticed it, but it was there. I saw the twitch of his eyebrow, the blink of his eyes that wiped away the hint of resigned suspicion and replaced it with cautious hope.

It might not have seemed like a huge reaction, but for me, it was like a neon sign.

"I'm sorry," I said again. "The entire time this... thing has been going on, I haven't been fair to you. I've been downright horrible, actually, and you've responded by taking care of me. You've sacrificed a lot for me and never asked for anything in return that I didn't make you ask for. You've let me lean on you when you needed someone to lean on yourself. And I won't sit here and say that you've never done things that hurt me because we both know that's bullshit, but I think if we put everything on scales, the things I've done to hurt you would be much heavier."

"Tess—"

I held up a hand. "This whole situation started because I was too afraid to tell the truth and admit I'd failed. And it took me too long to realize that the things I was afraid of weren't real. You were the first person who found out about all the lies I was telling and your response wasn't to use it against me but to stand up for me. Every single time, your response was to protect me. And then even when it came time for me to return that favour, I was selfish. I didn't want the guilt of knowing you came out to your parents because of my fuck ups. And rather than listening to you be all logical and shit, I just felt like I was the one who needed to be punished and refused to see any option that wasn't the worst-case scenario. So I'm sorry. Regardless of what... whatever happens, if this is... like, if this is it or not or you want to forgive me or don't or whatever, I want you to know I'm sorry for how I've treated you. How I always assumed the worst of you. How I didn't trust you. And how I hurt you. I'm really, really sorry for that especially."

He nodded slowly, his eyes focused down and his throat flexing before he looked up at me. "You think this is it?"

"I don't know," I said. "I'd love for it to not be, but you're the only one who can decide whether to forgive me."

"What about all the things I have to apologize for?" he said. "Because there's a lot I'm sorry for too."

"Nowhere near as much as I have to apologize for," I said. "And regardless, it's forgiven. But I understand if… if that's asking too much. For you to forgive me, I mean."

He studied me for another moment, then folded his arms across his chest. "You know, besides you and Finn, there was only ever one other person I thought to myself, like, 'This could be it.' That this person could be my endgame."

I wasn't sure where he was going with this, but I nodded all the same.

"Their name was Parker," he continued. "We met on this baseball team we both played for and just hit it off. They were amazing. Really smart, successful, funny as hell. And it was getting to the point that I almost, like… I was starting to plan how to tell people.

"The thing was, though, Parker was in a shitty relationship before me. So sometimes Parker was a little suspicious or overreacted to things, but it had started getting a lot better as time went on.

"So this one day at work, I'd gotten overlooked for a promotion I thought I was for sure going to get and I was pissed. Parker wasn't off work yet, so I was messaging Josh about it and ranting about how it was such bullshit and the guy who got it just got it because of nepotism. Then when Parker came over, I told them all about it, of course. And they were all sympathetic and said all the right things… until they mentioned how frustrating it was that nepotism was such a big thing at my company.

"And see, I hadn't told them that. I'd told Josh, and *only* Josh, about that. And there was no fucking way Josh and Parker knew each other, but when I asked Parker about it, they tried to convince me I'd mentioned it earlier in the conversation. Which I know I didn't. But anyway, I checked my phone later, logged into the account I was using to talk to Josh, and checked to see which devices I was logged into. And wouldn't you know it, there was a device I didn't recognize. An iPhone, last logged in just after I'd talked to Josh."

"They were spying on all your accounts?"

Zain shook his head. "Just the one. I'd borrowed their phone months earlier and must've forgotten to log out, and they'd never bothered telling me. They'd just check it a few times a day for their own peace of mind. And of course they were sorry about it when I confronted them. Of course they apologized and tried to explain it was because of their ex and how they'd been treated and all that. But I just couldn't, Tess. I couldn't trust them. I couldn't forgive them for that.

"So I broke it off. And yeah, maybe it was the right choice, but let me tell you, I wondered for a long time if I should've just given them a second chance. Because yeah, sometimes people hurt you, and sometimes you can't forgive them, but life gets pretty fucking lonely if you never try. And I never even tried. I just ended it."

I bit the inside of my lip, hoping he couldn't tell that I was shivering. Or trembling. Or both. "So... would you consider forgiving me, maybe?"

"No," he said.

It felt like a cannonball had launched itself into my stomach. My heart cracked and my breath disappeared, leaving my lungs hungry for air that I couldn't breathe.

I hadn't been lying. I didn't know if Zain was going to forgive me or not. But to tell me that whole story, to make me think—

"I already have," he said. "Without question. And if you can forgive me for *that*—"

"You *asshole*," I gasped.

He knew what he'd done. He was laughing about it as I launched myself forward, throwing my arms around his shoulders and kissing him hard. His hands slid around my sides, pulling me in, holding me against him as he kissed me back.

"I had to," he murmured. "I had to get a little even."

"You're the worst." I kissed him again. "I hate you. You're terrible."

"I hate you back, kitten." He sighed against my lips. "Fuck, I missed you."

"Are you staying here tonight?" I asked.

"That was the intention."

"Right. Well, I'd like to fuck you tonight but I'm not sure Josh would appreciate that occurring on his couch."

"I'm sure your mom would appreciate it happening in her guest room even less."

"Good thing Finn has a hotel room."

He pulled away, eyes wide. "Finn's here?"

"Yeah, I've been over here the whole time," Finn said from just down the hall. "I thought you might want some privacy but Mick already left so I wasn't sure where else to wait."

"Wait, who's Mick?"

"Claire's personal assistant."

"Claire's... wait, so Claire brought Finn and—"

"And everyone," I said. "Chuck and Charles and Julie, too. And Mick obviously. I thought you knew that. You're the one who got in touch with everyone."

"Well, yeah, but I didn't know she was coming," he said. "I just wanted you to feel supported. And since I couldn't do that for you, I thought... well. That explains why she's been calling me all night."

"Oh. Well, surprise. "

He let out a short laugh. "Right, so then... Mick drove you here?"

"Well, no. I drove us here. But Claire lent Mick to us so he could bring Dylan's car back to my mom's."

"You sent him with Dylan's..."

"Well, yeah. I figured you could drive us back to the Mountainview in the rental."

He raised his eyebrows. "So you were betting on me for sure forgiving you, eh?"

"It was more that I was for sure betting on you being here and was willing to do what it took to get Josh to let me talk to you."

"With Finn."

"Well, I figured if you were dead set against talking to me, then at least I could send Finn in to be there for you."

"...in front of Josh."

I shrugged. "You're the one who told him that he and Finn would get along."

Zain opened his mouth, then closed it and chuckled. "I did say that."

"Wait, who's Josh again?" Finn asked from down the hall.

"My brother," I said.

"My best friend," Zain said at the same time. "And... wait, what are you still doing over there?"

"I dunno," Finn said. "I wasn't sure if you were done or if I should wait here or—"

"Finn," Zain said, sighing as he stepped out into the cold. "Come here, bud. I haven't seen you for over a week."

"Oh, thank *God*," I heard Finn sigh, and Zain had barely taken two steps out of Josh and Audrey's apartment when Finn reached him, a beaming smile on his face. Zain's hand went up, sliding along Finn's jawline and to the back of his head, and then Finn was stooping down so their lips could meet in a relieved kiss.

"Fuck, I missed you too," Zain murmured when they parted. "What are the two of you doing to me?"

"Ruining your life, obviously," I said.

He smiled. "Couldn't be happier about that, Teacup."

Forty-Two

IT TOOK A WHILE for us to leave Josh and Audrey's place.

That was because Zain had been unbearably right: Finn and Josh clicked so hard it was almost audible. Not that it was hard to make friends with Finn, but it was almost shocking to see how easily the two of them connected.

Almost as shocking as the fact that Josh—my brother, who had started the day not knowing his best friend was bisexual and the sister he thought was married was in a polyamorous relationship with said best friend—was meeting Finn.

Like...

Like it finally could be real.

"He's nice," Audrey whispered to me as Zain collected his bags while Josh and Finn debated which historical figure they'd want to physically fight and why, with both of them eventually agreeing they'd at least try to punch Hitler.

"Too nice," I said, though I was being at least three-fifths sarcastic.

She smiled, watching Josh lean against the wall as he and Finn chatted. "I'm happy for you."

"You are?"

"Of course. Why wouldn't I be?"

"I mean, I lied to everyone for years. I'm kind of surprised no one's been harping on that."

"Well, I can't speak for anyone else, but I know when Josh told me, my first thought was about how alienated you must have felt from your family that pretending to be with a man who did what he did to you was the better option. And how painfully unfair that was." She shrugged. "You lied because you wanted to feel like you fit in with your family. Sure, that's not a common way of handling that situation, but it's like that whole idea of three fingers pointing back at you whenever you point a finger at someone."

I didn't know what to say to that. It was... I could barely explain it. How relieving it was. How vindicated I felt.

How stupid I was to have spent all this time keeping it to myself.

"I've known you for years now, Tess," Audrey said when I said nothing. "But there was always something about you I couldn't quite put my finger on. I'm not upset about this because now it's like I can finally see you. You only told us about this just a couple of hours ago but you're the you-est *you* I've ever seen. If that makes sense."

It did, to me at least. "And that's a good thing?"

"It's the best thing." She reached out and put a hand on my shoulder. "I've always been a fan of yours, Tess. You're cool and unapologetic and have a big heart that you try to hide beneath a no-bullshit exterior. But I know I speak for both myself and Josh when I say I'm so excited to get to know this version of you, if you'll let us."

And I already knew I would.

More importantly, I wanted to.

Because either way, I was going to have to. Zain was my... something. I didn't know what to call him yet. I didn't know if we were official or if I was going to call both of them my boyfriends or if there was some other term I should use. Regardless, Zain was important to me, and I knew Josh was important to him. So being with Zain meant I was going to get to know Josh better whether I liked it or not.

But given everything he'd said and done that day, given the way I'd been so certain I'd known the kind of person he was only to see how wrong I'd been, I was pretty sure I was going to like it.

After saying goodbye to Josh, Zain drove us back to the Mountainview.

And here's the thing.

We should have probably talked more.

I mean, we did talk. Finn filled us in on how his dad was doing—good—and I updated Finn with a brief rundown of how my family found out about Brad and the discovery I'd made in the safe earlier that day.

And then Zain told us what had happened when he came out to his parents.

"My mom was just silent as my dad lost his shit," he said, tapping his hand on the steering wheel as we waited at a traffic light. "More about me being poly than about being bi, which... honestly, I don't know if I expected that or not."

"I'm sorry, Zain," Finn said.

"It's okay." He sighed. "So I let my dad say what he had to say then told them I was going to give them some space and I'd call on Sunday before I left if they wanted to talk then."

"Your mom asked me to tell you she loves you no matter what," I said.

Zain looked up, his eyes meeting mine in the rear-view mirror. "You saw my mom?"

"It was the first place I thought you'd be," I said. "She was crying on the front steps when I got there. She said she'd been fighting with your dad."

"But they never fight."

"Yeah, well, your mom doesn't understand why you would want something like this, but she knows that you've always been—and these are her words, not mine—a 'good boy who wouldn't choose to do something if it was wrong' so she doesn't need to understand it to keep loving you." I twisted my mouth to the side. "Although she also seemed upset that she didn't say it to you in time because she didn't know how to say it, so I guess it wasn't just the fight. But that's what she told your dad."

Zain didn't reply. His head bobbed as he nodded, his face blank but completely readable, at least to me. In the front seat, Finn reached over, taking Zain's hand in his.

"Thanks for telling me," Zain finally said. "I'm gonna, uh, not think about this anymore tonight. I need a break."

"You know we're here if and when you wanna talk about it," Finn said. "But if you need a break, would you rather take a nap inside a giant burrito or between two giant slices of French toast?"

And when Zain laughed, I knew he was going to be okay.

So we spent the rest of the drive back to the Mountainview talking about that instead of taking a step back and made sure we were doing the right thing after a week of hell and a whirlwind of emotions.

Because I needed a break, too. But honestly, it didn't matter. Not anymore. Over the course of a day, the biggest barriers we faced had been shattered. And yes, we would eventually need to talk about these things, but I was confident that no matter what the details were, that discussion would lead to one place: me and Zain and Finn, together in whatever capacity we decided.

And that was enough for now.

Besides, it had been over a week since I'd seen the—

My.

It had been over a week since I'd seen my boys together. A very long, very hard—and not in the fun way—week where I'd done my damndest to ruin my own life and happily failed because of all the other stubborn assholes in my life who wouldn't let me self-destruct.

So I needed them.

And they needed me.

Claire, being Claire, had booked everyone their own rooms. And Claire, being a billionaire, had picked the most expensive rooms the Mountainview had to offer, which were all on the top floor. There was a harrowing moment after we got off the elevator that I thought Finn was going to lead us to the same room Zain had stormed into all those months ago and discovered my secret, where Brad had cowered behind me as though I could protect him from Zain drowning him in my lavender-scented jacuzzi water.

But luck, or karma, or coincidence, or whatever was on my side and Finn led us the other direction.

I barely got the door closed behind me before Zain had me pressed against the wall with his lips on mine. And I'd barely caught my breath from that when Finn leaned in to take his turn, his mouth warm and inviting and dizzyingly delicious.

And I expected things to get intense.

I expected Zain to pin me down, to murmur in my ear not to leave him again, to command my body with his tongue and fingers and cock as he directed Finn to help punish-but-not-really-punish me for all of my stupid actions over the past week.

But that wasn't what we needed.

After an emotional day and week, after heartbreaks and reconciliations and a snowball of events that were about to change our lives forever, it wasn't even what we were capable of.

So instead, Zain kissed my neck, his lips treating me as if I was as delicate and sweet, while Finn caressed my cheek, both of them showering attention onto me like I was... well.

Like I was worth it.

"I thought you'd be mad," I whispered as Zain used his tongue to trace a pattern on my collarbone.

"At what?"

"Me. I thought you were going to be all growly or something."

I felt him smile before he pressed a kiss against my neck.

"Kitten, when we get home, I'm going to use everything I've learned about your beautiful body over the past few months against you," he said. "I'm going to fuck you harder than you've ever been fucked before. I'm going to fuck your throat so deep you'll be tasting my cock for days. Then I'm going to edge you until you're crying and begging to come while Finn fucks your pussy. And I'm not going to let you. Instead, when he's ready to finish, I'm going to make you use your mouth to clean up the wet mess you leave all over his cock until he's coming down your throat, too. I'm going to show you exactly why you're never, *ever* going to think of pulling the shit you did this week again."

He nipped at my neck, making me gasp, then soothed the spot with another gentle kiss.

"But tonight, kitten... tonight I need you softly," he continued. "Tonight, you're finally ours."

Forty-Three

MY BOYS STRIPPED ME slowly, kissing me all the while. Zain methodically removed my top and Finn my jeans. Zain took off my bra and once he was done, Finn let me tug off his shirt and pants. He stopped me once he was down to his boxers so he could stoop down to kiss me before letting his lips trail down my chin to my neck.

Then to the tops of my breasts.

Then my nipples.

Then in a meandering trail across my ribs and down my belly, inch by inch until he was kneeling in front of me. When he reached the waistband of my panties, he hooked his fingers in them so he could tug them down. And once my panties were around my ankles, Finn looked up at me, those gorgeous blue eyes wide with something wondrous and full of blatant desire, then held my gaze as he pressed his lips against my mound.

"That's it," Zain said. "Get our girl nice and ready for us, baby."

"Yes, sir," Finn said, his words vibrating against my skin.

I barely had time to react before he lifted his hands to my thighs, pushing them apart just enough to spread my folds and run his tongue along my clit. A soft whine snuck past my lips and I felt Zain laugh, the bulge in his jeans pressing against my ass as he kissed my neck again.

"Are you ready for us already, kitten?" he asked.

"Of course I am. I've been ready since before we got here."

"Mmm. God, I can't wait to fuck you."

"Then why aren't you?"

"Because." He sank his teeth into my neck again. "Because I like seeing him play with you. I like the noises you make when you're so needy. But mostly because I don't want to let go of you and if I'm gonna take my pants off, I'll have to."

"I—oh." I gasped, losing my train of thought as Finn slipped a finger inside of me. My head tilted back and my eyes fluttered closed and Zain made a soft noise before slipping his arms around me so he could cup a hand around each of my breasts.

"You have no idea, Teacup," he said. "No fucking clue how much I love seeing him touch you. How much I love knowing exactly what both of you feel like when I watch him lapping at your sensitive little clit with his tongue. I love knowing that same tongue has licked every inch of my cock, spoiled my balls, and had my cum on it." He thrust his hips forward and I whimpered. "You have no goddamn idea how happy I am right now."

"Not true," I whispered. "It's nowhere near as happy as I am."

I felt him smile, then the tenderness of his kiss as I looked down at Finn, who was doing his best not to grin so he could keep licking my pussy.

We stayed like that for a while, Zain playing with my nipples while Finn teased my pussy. I leaned back, resting against Zain with my eyes closed as I submitted to sensation, to the feel of hands on my breasts and my thighs, to lips on my neck and my pussy, to the filthy words whispered in my ear and gentle groans of appreciation coming from between my legs. Desire rushed through me, warming my skin and making every touch feel heightened, from the soft breath brushing my neck to the finger curling inside me to press my G-spot.

"Oh, do that again," Zain whispered when Finn pushed another finger inside me and my whole body trembled.

"Dunno if she can take another finger yet," Finn said.

"She can," Zain said. "Can't you, kitten? You can take three of Finn's thick fingers in that wet little pussy, can't you?"

"Yes," I whispered, and proved it a second later when I let out a loud cry as Finn added a third finger to my pussy, making me shake in Zain's arms and sending me back into that blissful place where I existed only between the two of them and nothing, fucking *nothing*, else mattered.

I don't know when we moved to the bed or who suggested it. It was like I was half-dreaming in the best way, like the world wasn't even real because it was so fucking good. But that was where we ended up. Zain's clothes disappeared somewhere and then he was the one in front of me while Finn had his cock nestled against my ass. I had one hand up, fingers running through Finn's thick blonde hair as he kissed my neck and took his turn playing with my breasts, and the other on Zain's hip, holding his body against mine as he teased my clit with his cock.

"So fucking wet already," he murmured. "I wanna fuck you, Teacup."

"Do it, then," I said.

It wasn't like most of the times the three of us fucked. Usually when we were together, everything was relatively equal. If I was being fucked by one, I had the other in my mouth. Or if someone was going down on me, the other had his cock in his ass.

But that night, they made it about me.

That night, Zain guided my body away from Finn's and, save for a moment where he pressed a heated kiss against Finn's lips, focused all his attention on getting me onto my back and parting my legs so he could sink inside me, both of us hissing in pleasure as his cock stretched my dripping hole open.

"Fuck," Finn said, and then I felt him lie beside me, his long body pressed up against mine and his hand slipping between my and Zain's bodies so he could play with my clit again. I reached down, intending to wrap my hand around him, but he pushed it away.

"Just relax and take him, Tess," he said, as if he had no fucking idea that he'd started picking up the same mouthiness Zain used to make me melt.

Instead, he kissed me, capturing my gasps and sighs and moans as Zain fucked me slowly and steadily and deeply, his thick cock pressing against my hip. He stroked my clit, dragging me closer and closer to that moment of overwhelming intensity, groaning as my breathing grew faster and I had to clutch his arm as my body tensed.

"Come for us, kitten," Zain murmured. "Show us how good we make you feel."

And I did.

My back arched as my orgasm ripped through me, shattering beneath Zain and beside Finn, a hand clutching each of them as if I'd be torn away if I didn't hold on. Finn held me, lips pressed to my shoulder, and Zain kept moving, groaning as I clenched around his cock before finally relaxing with a deep sigh.

When I opened my eyes again, he was leaning slightly to the side, kissing Finn heatedly.

"Your turn, bud," Zain whispered, and before I'd even finished catching my breath, he'd pulled out and Finn was kneeling between my legs, pulling me up into his lap.

He guided my hips down so I was riding him in a strange but satisfying half-squat sort of way, where he was still kneeling and I was bouncing on top of his thighs. My breasts bounced against him, even as he wrapped both arms around me and buried his head against my shoulder.

"You feel so good, Tess," he groaned.

"She does, doesn't she," Zain said, kneeling beside us as he lazily stroked his cock and watched us fuck. "It's gotta be a fucking scientific marvel, kitten. The way you can take his cock so deep and take mine so hard. You and your perfect fucking body that feels like it was custom made for both of us."

"Maybe it's just practice," I gasped, and both of them laughed as Finn thrust up into me.

"Well, practice definitely made you perfect," Finn said, and I felt heat rise up my neck. He kissed one of the flushed spots, his breath hot against my skin. "You're so perfect, Tess."

And fuck.

Fuck.

I was going to come again.

I mean, I knew I was perfect. I'd said it a million times. But hearing it, hearing those men say those things to me... my heart had been so burned so raw that week that it was like their words were fabric drenched with cool water, soothing and healing and comforting me. And the way Finn was fucking me, the spots his cock was hitting as I bounced on top of him, the sight of Zain stroking himself to the sight of us...

I was going to come.

Which they, of course, realized immediately. Because both of them were versed in what I looked like when I was about to come.

"That's it," Zain said. "Squeeze that fat cock of his with your sweet little pussy. You've got no idea how amazing it feels when you come on us. How tight you get and the noises you make and the way you throw your head back."

"Yes," Finn groaned. "He's right, Tess. You coming is one of my favourite things in the world."

And who was I to deny Finn, amazing man that he was, one of his favourite things?

So I did, again, and again I felt like I had to hold on with the way Finn was fucking up into me and the intensity of the trembles rushing through my body. He groaned in my ear, arms tight around my waist and holding me to his chest as my vision flashed light and dark, my muscles tense with ecstasy until I swore I was floating and had no choice but to come back down.

It was only when Finn guided me off his lap so Zain could come up behind me and slip his cock in my pussy that I realized what they were doing. I doubt it was planned; there had been no time for them to discuss it before we started, so it had to be a simple matter of them instinctively understanding what they wanted to do.

While the two of them always shared me nicely, they seemed to have an unspoken agreement that whoever was fucking me got to fuck me until he came. Then, if the other wasn't finished, he'd take over, taking his turn until he came, too. They didn't tend to switch back and forth, which seemed fair to me. Like it was some kind of common courtesy for threesomes with two men unless there was some reason for them not to.

And that night, the reason was to drive me crazy.

As Zain sank into me, I reached for Finn's cock, intent on guiding it into my mouth, but he had dipped down and captured my lips instead. That was when I realized they were switching off so they wouldn't come; that for some reason, they wanted to drag things out and prolong their pleasure while simultaneously bringing me to peak after peak.

"What are you doing to me?" I whispered against Finn's mouth

He smiled and reached up, brushing my hair back off my face. "Making sure you know how fucking much we need you."

And just...

Fuck.

I could have cried.

"I need you too," I said. "Both of you. More than anything."

Zain hunched over, pressing his lips to the back of my neck as he buried himself inside me. "We know, kitten. And you've got us."

His turn didn't last as long that time, maybe because he'd already been holding back for a while and maybe because Finn finally let me put his cock in my mouth so he could reach over and kiss Zain while he fucked me. Whatever the reason, he pulled back with a sudden curse, putting a hand on my ass and squeezing as he inhaled deeply.

"I'm not gonna make it another round," he said. "Her pussy is too fucking good."

"Don't I know it," Finn said brightly as he carefully guided his cock from between my lips. "Want me to come in her first or do you want to?"

"You know if you come first I'm barely going to last because I love fucking your cum deeper inside her," he said. "So you better make her come hard."

"Yes, sir," Finn said, then a wicked little grin spread across his face. "Come here, Tess. I want you to ride my cock."

Which was incredibly smart of him. Finn knew as well as I did that I'd come as I rode him because I almost always did. Something about the angle, the way I could control my pace, being able to plunge his cock as deep in me as I could before rocking back and forth, grinding my clit against him... there was no way I wasn't going to come hard.

And I, of course, didn't mind one bit.

Finn lay back on the bed, his head propped up on one pillow as I straddled his hips. Just behind me, I felt Zain crawl forward, then reach between my legs so he could guide Finn's cock inside me. Once his cock was buried as deep as I could get it, I moaned, closing my eyes and relishing the feel of him, of Zain's hand on my hip and Finn's sigh of relief.

And then I started fucking him properly.

Despite having come twice already, it didn't take long for the third one to bubble up inside me. I could barely think, barely process the overwhelming sense of ecstasy as I stilled on top of Finn. When I finished, I pitched forward, barely catching myself as I collapsed against him. Finn reached up and wrapped his arms around me, holding me in place as I gasped for breath. A strong hand rubbed my lower back, my pussy twitching uncontrollably as little shocks of pleasure still shot through my nerves.

And behind me, Zain was still touching my ass, his fingertips tracing a light pattern along it.

"Finn," he said distractedly. "Would you be game for trying something a little, uh... different?"

"Different how?" Finn asked.

"I want us both inside her."

"You can't fuck my ass tonight," I mumbled. "I'm nowhere near ready."

"I know, Teacup." His fingers moved down my ass towards the back of my thigh. "I'm not talking about your ass."

It took me a minute to figure out what he meant. I mean, of course it did. Because we'd never talked about that. I'd never considered it. I'd never imagined that both of them could fit in me at once.

Though, I wasn't really sure why. I mean, I'd sucked both their cocks at once. I could barely get the tips of them in my mouth, but I'd done it. And I'd rubbed their cocks together, using both hands to jack them off at the same time. So had they; grinding and stroking and, on one hilariously ridiculous occasion, literally trying to sword fight with them.

So fucking my pussy at the same time... it wasn't unreasonable to think about trying it.

"You can say no, kitten," Zain said. "It was just a thought. I don't even know if—"

"Do it," I said. "Try, at least."

"Oh, fuck yes," he said.

"There's lube in my bag," Finn said. "I brought it just in case."

Finn kept his grip on me, holding me against his chest as Zain grabbed the lube, then positioned himself behind me and between Finn's legs. I was excited, certainly, but also nervous, my heart racing as Zain opened the lube cap and then reached down to trace the spot where my pussy was already stretched around Finn. I bit my lip as the cool sensation of the lube spread around my pussy, then shivered as Zain slipped a finger in, like he was testing to make sure I could open even more for them.

Then he pulled his finger out and I felt his cock nudge against me; a moment later, the tip was pressed to my opening.

"Be careful," I breathed. "Please."

"Always, Teacup," he said. "You tell me if it's too much."

"I will."

"Good girl," he murmured, and then he pushed his cock in.

All three of us made a noise as he entered me. Zain gasped, Finn groaned, and I don't even know what the fuck to call the sound I made. It wasn't a noise of pain; there was the slightest pinch, barely enough to be called anything more than discomfort, and it faded the second Zain stopped moving and I relaxed from the instinctive way I'd tensed as he penetrated me. It wasn't a noise of pleasure either, though; not solely, anyway. There was surprise there, since somehow Zain's cock had slid in smoothly and easily even though I was already stuffed full of Finn, and something else. Something intense.

I knew exactly what it was.

And for once, it wasn't terrifying.

"Tess?" Zain asked, his voice strained. "You okay?"

"More," I whimpered.

He groaned. "You sure? I—"

"*More*, Zain," I repeated. "Just fucking *do* it."

He did not just fucking do it. He did do it, but slowly, carefully, inch by inch, making me freeze in pleasure as Finn tried not to squirm beneath me.

"You okay, bud?" Zain asked as Finn panted.

"Uh-huh," Finn grunted.

"You sure? I can—"

"Can you not feel the same thing I do?" Finn blurted. "Because oh my God, this is fucking amazing."

Zain laughed, the sound dry and shaky. "Oh, I can feel it, baby. I just want to make sure everyone else is okay because once I start going, I don't know if I'm going to be able to stop."

"Go," I said.

He laughed again. "Patience, Teacup. I don't want to hurt—"

"*Go*," I demanded, trying to push back and failing because of the whole Finn being inside me thing. "Fucking *fuck* us, Daddy!"

And even though I wasn't usually the one telling Zain what to do, he listened without hesitation.

I was barely conscious through the whole thing. I mean, I was awake, obviously. It wasn't like I passed out on their cocks as they fucked me together, even though the sensation of it all was so intense that I probably could have. But it was that intensity that took that amazing experience and turned it into a clouded pile of memories, as tangled as the pile that was our legs and arms and bodies.

Moments melded together. One moment Finn was kissing me; another I could feel him pushing up, meeting Zain's cock inside me. Zain spoke his usual stream of filthy words that made me tremble, but there was no way I could remember what he said since I could barely process those words in the first place. Someone's hand was on my breast, but there were fingertips digging into both of my hips and my thigh. It was all I could do to hold on as they took me, used me, completed me in a way I could have never dreamed of being completed.

Although, I took full credit for making them both come, mostly because me coming was what set both of them over the edge.

"I-I-I," I stuttered, my breath coming in short gasps. "Gonna c-c-come."

"*Yes*, kitten," Zain growled. "Come on our cocks together like you were always fucking meant to. Because this is what you were fucking made for. You were made for me and him just like we were made for you."

"Yes," Finn groaned. "Yes, you were. Come for your boys."

I'd had a lot of orgasms.

A lot of them.

Neither Zain nor Finn had ever asked what my body count was and that was a good thing. I wasn't ashamed of the number, but it was mostly because, truthfully, I didn't know it. It adds up when you're fucking people two at a time with a policy of only seeing them once. And then on top of that, as much as I fucking despised my ex-husband, I couldn't deny that Brad and I had a lot of sex when we were together.

So for that orgasm to hit and nearly break me the way it did was saying something.

I couldn't have said what it was. There was the sensation of being so full that I couldn't move, of being propped up on their cocks and completely at their mercy because getting off of them would have required me to use my legs and I couldn't feel those anymore. There was the way my body was trying to tighten, tense, clench around them as a way of enduring those waves of delirious euphoria, but couldn't because it was like there wasn't room, so I had no choice but to submit to that ecstasy unprotected and unprepared.

Then there was their finish; the tiniest shred of my mind noting the sound and sensation of one, then the other, coming inside me. The sound of one of them cursing, the other groaning that he could feel it, he could feel the way both their cocks were twitching as they unloaded. As could I, of course. I could feel the way they came and the way I was sure it was already leaking out because how could there possibly be enough room left for both of their loads?

And then there was the way my heart and my soul felt like they had shaken and cracked and erupted. The way words spilled out of me, words I didn't even know I was saying until I realized I was lying in between them on the bed, half-gasping and half-sobbing.

Words I didn't need to know I was saying to know that I meant them.

Words that were mumbled and far less coherent than I initially thought they were, given the confusion in Zain's voice and the concern with which Finn was holding me.

"...Teacup, just breathe," Zain was saying.

"You're okay, we've got you," Finn added, his lips pressed to the side of my head.

"Take a couple of breaths, Tess," Zain said. "We can't understand you, okay? You need to—"

"I'm in love with you," I said, my voice quiet and shaky.

Both of them stilled and silenced.

"I'm in love with you both," I said again. "You already fucking know that, I'm sure, but I just need to... I... F-Finn, I love you."

His arms tightened around me and I could feel him grinning.

"I love you too, Tess," he said.

I opened my eyes to see Zain staring at me, blank shock in his dark eyes.

"I love you, Zain," I whispered.

"Teacup—" he said.

"Don't say it if you don't," I said. "I j-just needed you to know I—"

"Of course I fucking love you," he said. "Tessa Lane, I've loved you for so fucking long it's actually kind of concerning, and I'm gonna keep loving you forever."

"Good," I said, and he laughed as he leaned in to kiss me.

When we parted, he looked past me, a vulnerable look on his face. "Finn—"

"Oh, if you don't think I love you, too, you're crazy," Finn said.

Zain chuckled again, the sound relieved. "Good. Because I love you too, bud."

Behind me, Finn shifted, propping himself up so he could lean in and kiss Zain.

And God, did I feel like the luckiest person alive just then.

Forty-Four

LIFE DIDN'T GO BACK to normal.

I mean, obviously.

It couldn't. Going back to normal would have meant denying that night at the Mountainview, whispering to my boys how much I loved them and listening to them whisper it to me.

There was no coming back from that. There was no way I could return to the person I'd been just two weeks earlier, denying what I wanted for the comfort of people who wouldn't have been uncomfortable if I'd just told the truth.

There was no way I could disrespect my boys, my family, and my friends like that. Not anymore, and never again.

Plus there was the whole thing where my life had been completely uprooted, even before Brad had discovered me and Zain together, my dad had died, and three decades of secrets were revealed over the course of a day and the discovery of a hidden safe that wasn't all that hidden.

I didn't have a job.

I was back to living alone.

Zain was starting his new job. He had to set up his new apartment that he hadn't even seen yet. Finn was still checking on his dad, making sure his mom and sisters weren't overwhelmed with anything even though his dad seemed to be healing incredibly well.

There was no more normal.

"

And God, didn't *that* make me the luckiest fucking person alive, since my previous normal kind of sucked.

There was still a lot I needed to do. Apologies to make and accept. Conversations to have. Some easier, some harder. But none of them so hard as they could have been without those people behind me.

Some of those conversations happened that weekend. When I woke up in the hotel room the next morning, it was to a loud knock on the door. I'd been sleeping so deeply that it took me a moment to remember... well. *Everything.* So there was a second loud knock that made Zain stir and groan blearily.

"Who the fuck needs us at—" He glanced over at the nightstand. "Oh, shit. It's almost eleven."

"Yeah, you guys were really tired," Finn, morning person that he was, said as he stood up from the couch, where he'd been sitting on his phone.

"Probably from all the sex," I mumbled.

"Probably," Zain agreed. "Are you sore or anything?"

I laughed, shaking my head. "Thanks for checking, though."

"Well, you had a lot in there last night. Had to make sure we didn't break you."

"It's okay. I have a large capacity vagina."

"You have a what?" he asked, bewildered.

But before I could explain, the door opened.

"Oh, hey Cl—" Finn started.

"Morning, Finn," I heard Claire say, then a surprised noise from Finn as she apparently let herself in the room. "Good to see you. I hope you all had fun last night, but as it turns out, it's my turn to talk to Tessa."

"Uh... okay. But also—"

"I know it's your room," she continued. "And I hate to swing my dick around because I don't have one, but if I have to remind you that I paid for the room, I will, because I need—oh, fuck!"

"I was just gonna say they're still naked in bed so maybe give them a sec," Finn said, coming up behind Claire, who had nearly punched herself in the face in her hurry to cover her eyes.

"Sorry," she said loudly as I burst out laughing. "Sorry, Zain, specifically. Nice tats, though. Also nice to finally meet you in person."

"Thanks," Zain said dryly. "You too. Mind passing me my pants, Finn?"

They went down for breakfast while Claire and I talked. And by talked, I mean we called each other stupid a few more times, agreed that we were both right, apologized and promised each other we were still best friends, then ate each other out until we both came.

That evening after promising Chuck I would actually be back in Vancouver on Monday and we would actually go for the drinks we were supposed to have last week and I *actually* was not going to do any more stupid things like block him, he and Charles caught a ride back to Kelowna with Claire, Julie, and Mick. Claire had to fly to Buffalo for work, which was fair, and Chuck said Burnsley was the most boring shithole town he'd ever visited, which was also fair. Zain, Finn, and I spent the night together again, though it was far less intense than the previous night. We still fucked, of course, and it was still tender and gentle compared to our usual encounters, but it was just as passionate.

Just as amazing.

Just what I needed.

And what I wanted, forever or as long as they'd have me, because I was so fucking in love with them.

So in love.

The next day, the three of us were booked to fly back to Vancouver on the usual flight Zain and I used whenever we were in Burnsley for the weekend. The problem with that was the flight was later in the day, which left us with a somewhat strange gap between checking out of our room and needing to leave for the airport.

"We could go see your mom and say goodbye," Zain, asshole that he was, suggested as we packed up our suitcases.

"That sounds fun!" Finn said.

"Does it?" I asked, my voice pitching high. "Isn't that maybe a little too much for right now?"

"Teacup, you're going to have to introduce them eventually," Zain said. "Pretty sure we're beyond the not-casual-but-not-serious territory and into the 'we all admitted we're in love multiple times this weekend' territory."

I gave him a dirty look. "It's not that I don't want to. He met my brother the other night. But like, with everything this week and the safe and Mike's still there..."

"Those sound like convenient excuses to me," Zain said.

"They are," I replied. "They just so happen to also be correct excuses."

He looked at me for a moment, then a wicked little smirk flashed across his lips and he leaned back, digging his phone out of his pocket.

"I've got an idea," he said.

"What?" I asked.

"Just a sec." He typed quickly on his phone, then locked the screen and looked up. "Wanna make a bet?"

"What are we betting on?" Finn asked interestedly.

Zain nodded towards me. "Her phone's going to go off in five minutes. Is it going to be a call or a text?"

"What did you do?" I asked, but he shook his head, even as I lunged across the bed and tried to steal his phone so I could find out. It was pointless, of course, partly because he was stronger than me and Finn ended up coming over to help hold me down as Zain absorbed my laughter and cursing with his lips. And mostly because he was wrong.

My phone didn't go off in five minutes.

It was two.

And it was a phone call.

"What is this I hear about *Josh and Audrey* getting to meet your other boyfriend before I did?" Mom demanded as soon as I picked up the phone.

I looked up at Zain, who was still hovering over me, but had allowed me to get my phone out to answer it. "You texted my mom, you asshole?"

"Of course not," he said. "I texted Josh and he texted your mom."

"And I also haven't seen Zain since he *became* your boyfriend!" Mom added, her voice loud enough that Zain could hear her through the phone. "Just because I've known him almost his whole life does *not* mean he's exempt from having to make a good impression on me."

Zain's lips parted in shock and I burst out laughing.

"You brought that on yourself," I said.

"Zain? What's the hold up?" my mom said.

"We only, um, figured this out last night?" Zain said.

"You know where I live," Mom shot back.

He pressed his lips together, trying to hide a smile. "You're right. Sorry, Lorelei."

So we had no choice but to go to my mom's for a bit. I mean, I guess we did. I guess I could have said no.

But I just...

For once, I wanted to go there.

I wanted her to meet Finn.

To see me there with Zain.

To know that the three of us were together, and happy, and that I finally felt like I could share that.

Contrary to her dramatics, Mom didn't give Zain a firm talking-to or interrogate him when we got there. She greeted the three of us in the front hall, first wrapping her arms around me to give me a tight hug that almost made me cry—in a good way, not because she was squeezing too hard—then turned to Finn.

"And who's this you've brought over?" she asked.

I played along, even though she could obviously figure out who he was. But I'd spend almost the entire drive over nervously practicing in my head how I was going to do this.

What I was going to say.

What I was going to call him.

"Mom," I said, thankful my voice didn't waver. "This is my boyfriend, Finn."

I wasn't looking directly at Zain, but from the corner of my eye, I saw the smile flicker across his face.

"Hi, Finn," Mom said, extending her hand. "I'm Lorelei."

"It's so nice to meet you," Finn said earnestly, shaking her hand. "Thanks for inviting me over."

"Anytime, sweetie," she said, then looked at Zain. "And who's this, then?"

The corners of Zain's eyes crinkled. I rolled my eyes.

"I'd like you to meet, for the first time ever, apparently, my—"

And then I stopped.

Because yeah, I'd figured out what I was going to call Finn when I introduced him. But I hadn't thought of what to call Zain, since I didn't think my mom was going to pretend not to know him.

It should have been easy. He was my boyfriend, too. But no matter how hard I thought, I couldn't figure out how to phrase it in a way that felt *right*. Calling him "my other boyfriend" or saying "he's also my boyfriend" made it sound like he had a lesser role in my life. Like he was second to my first.

And neither of them were second. Both of them were my firsts. They were equals, not others or alsos. But it also wasn't like I could use the only other term I could think of for Zain at the moment, which would be *especially* inappropriate to use when introducing him to my *mother*.

Before I could keep overthinking it, Zain, somehow blessed with the ability to read my fucking mind, put a comforting hand on my lower back.

"You can use whatever term you want, Teacup," he said. "As long as it starts with the word 'my.'"

"My bitch it is, then," I said, because I wasn't quite in the place yet where I could let everyone see me swoon when Zain said something sweet and romantic and touching.

Luckily, Zain just chuckled. "Whatever. As long as I'm yours." He extended his hand to Mom. "Hi, I'm Tessa's bitch, Zain."

Mom burst out laughing as she shook his hand. "Finn and Zain. How will I possibly be able to keep the two of you straight?"

"Oh, you won't be able to," Finn said. "We're already not straight."

And I couldn't help it; I laughed. Finn looked at me, a pleased smile on his face, and Zain shook his head with a soft chuckle a moment later.

It wasn't until we'd taken off our shoes and started towards the kitchen that Mom dropped the façade of not knowing Zain.

"Come here," she said, then hugged him. "I'm so sorry you had to deal with that asshole—" She didn't say his name, but she obviously meant Brad. "—but thank you."

"For what?" Zain asked.

"Taking care of my girl." She kissed him on the cheek before letting go. "How are you, sweetie?"

"I'm, uh, good," Zain said.

"And your parents?"

She didn't need to say more than that for us to know what she meant about that, too. Zain's expression didn't change much, but I caught the twitch of his jaw and the quick glance he made to the side before responding.

"It'll be okay eventually," he said.

Something like pain crossed my mom's face and she put an arm around him again as we all went to the kitchen, where Mike was waiting. Mom grabbed coffee for everyone as Finn and Mike immediately got into an in-depth discussion about how many French fries it was okay for someone to take before you told them to order their own French fries and, more importantly, whether that number stayed the same if you ordered yam fries or poutine.

Which was good, because it gave Zain a chance to duck outside for some privacy to make the call he'd said he'd make before leaving Burnsley.

It wasn't a long phone call. When he came back inside, his face was carefully neutral. I tried to read it, tried to telepathically ask him how the call went because I doubted he wanted to talk about it in front of my mom, but it wasn't until we left so we could make the drive back to Kelowna that I finally got an answer.

"My mom and I talked for a bit," he said. "She said pretty much what you told me she said, which was nice to hear. I mean, better than the absolute worst case scenario, right?" He cleared his throat. "My dad is... I dunno. Not quite ready to accept any of it."

"I'm sorry," I said, because of course I was. Because of course I had guilt about all of this. But Zain just looked in the rearview mirror and smiled.

"I'm not," he said. "This was more than worth it, kitten."

Forty-Five

When we got back to Vancouver that night, I went home.

Alone.

It wasn't like they didn't offer for me to go to their place. And it wasn't like they didn't argue that they could come to mine instead. They did, almost excessively, until I told them that I needed a night to myself.

That I needed time to process everything.

That I loved them, so much, but my body was craving at least some sense of the normality it used to have, even if nothing was normal anymore.

Which was mostly the truth, and enough of the truth that they accepted it and finally let me get into an Uber back to my place.

Because of course part of it was because I wasn't sure that I wanted to see their apartment.

I knew when the moment came to see it, I would be fine. I would be happy for them. I would smile and tease Zain for being extra because there would for sure be some accent or touch that showed off how high-maintenance he was.

But I needed some time to build the strength for that up.

I spent the week attempting to give my life some semblance of routine. I went back to my place. Made fun of Dottie. Walked Millie. Hunted for a job. Started picking up the bits of my life left after everything had fallen apart. Then began adding them to the new life I'd built from the other pieces while trying to figure out how I'd be able support said new life on a shoestring budget until said job hunt worked in my favour.

Although that mattered less once Friday morning hit.

"Did you get the letter?" Chuck asked without even saying hello as he picked up the phone.

"Why do you think I'm calling?" I replied. "What the *fuck*—"

"Thank Claire," he interrupted. "And me, of course, but I would've only been able to get you a fifth of that as severance. Claire was the one who had her lawyers point out to Loni the many things you could use against her should your wrongful termination case be brought to court, such as the discriminatory behaviour, lack of notice, and on-the-record disdainful actions of your boss over the past number of years."

"This is more than I made in a year, Chuck," I said.

"Hmm, that's so funny," he said. "I distinctly remember Loni saying a year's salary should be fine because it was barely a dent in her funds but—oh, would you look at that, you were overdue for a raise. You'll likely see the back pay for the raises Dinah was supposed to give you in a different payment."

I opened my mouth to protest, then closed it and took a breath. "Just don't get yourself fired for this."

"They can't fire me," he said. "And if they do, I know this billionaire who would one hundred percent lend me her scary lawyers because I made a point of asking her about it before sharing confidential records with her to allow said lawyers to build a more thorough case."

"I love you," I said.

"Gross," he replied. "I love you too."

So that was a weight off my chest. More than a year's salary could buy me a lot of time in my little garden suite while I tried to find a job. I spent the rest of Friday morning making a mental list of things I absolutely needed to spend some of the money on, like paying off my line of credit.

Then I went to the place I'd been spending most my time that week.

It had started because I wondered if I really needed it. If maybe, just maybe, that part of my life was done. Because if it was, if I could give that piece of me up, I could have something else.

In hindsight, it was stupid. I could give up wanting to paint the same way I could give up pasta. Like, I'd survive, but at what cost? At what level of happiness?

But, I'd reasoned with myself, I barely painted anymore. It had been years of dull, lifeless pieces that were intended to fill wall space. The meaning of them didn't matter. The look of them barely did, either. They were pretty, non-offensive, boring pieces meant to drum up the same amount of emotion as a generic print on a hotel room wall.

If I barely painted, there was no reason for me to have a studio.

And if I didn't need a studio... well.

So I'd gone into the room on Monday intending to imagine what it would be like not to have that space. And maybe if it was in the same state it had been for the past five years, I would've felt nothing. Maybe I would've taken a breath in, then let it out, then began packing up my supplies as I tried to figure out how to bring this up with my boys.

But their faces were staring at me when I walked in.

The painting I'd been working on when I couldn't sleep the night before I'd left for Burnsley was still sitting on the easel. I froze when I saw it, my breath catching as I looked at the blueness of Finn's eyes and the intensity of Zain's brown ones and the woman standing between them.

I'd captured my boys pretty well, but her...

She was wrong.

She'd been right at the time. I couldn't deny that. When I'd painted her, the pain in her eyes had seemed like a permanent piece of her. The slight downturn of her lips was something that seemed to come naturally.

Now, though.

Now I needed to fix her.

Now I needed to start again.

I was out of clean canvases, but that was okay. The one I'd ruined with thick, bold streaks of green paint spelling out *THIS IS BULLSHIT* was still there, and it was salvageable. I brought it to the easel and set it down.

Then, instead of doing something smart like sanding the paint off or painting over it and letting it dry, I just started working.

I didn't finish it that day. I didn't finish it any day. Truth be told, I wasn't sure I'd ever finished a painting in my life; there was always one more thing to fix, one more spot that could use a touch up, one burst of colour that would bring everything together even more. But it took me until Friday to get it to a point I would have considered it presentable enough to show to other people.

Which was good, because that was the first day someone saw it.

"Teacup?"

I jumped, nearly sending the canvas crashing off my easel and onto the floor. Catching it, I steadied it on the easel before whirling around to see Zain, still dressed in one of his sharp-looking suits, standing there.

"Where did you come from?!" I gasped, my heart somewhere in my throat.

"I knocked on your door and tried calling you and didn't get an answer, so I was a little worried you were hurt or something."

"I... I was painting," I said, my cheeks flushing warm.

"I gathered that." He looked past me at the easel. "You're painting... us?"

"I just... I needed something to do," I said. "And it's not done yet. I don't know if I'll finish it. It was just something to pass the time."

A soft smile spread across his face and he stepped further into the studio. "Are you sure, Teacup? Because it's..."

I tried not to wince. "It's what?"

"Amazing," he said, and another step brought him up beside me as he studied the portrait. "God, you're good at this."

I felt my face burn even more. I mean, I knew I was good at this. I'd spent almost my whole life honing these skills. There was nothing wrong with being proud of that.

But the way he was looking at the painting and, more specifically, at a painting that meant as much to me as that one did... well.

It made me feel something.

The background was dark green, a shade that almost matched the *THIS IS BULLSHIT* smears that had been there originally. Now, though, I didn't know that anyone other than me would be able to tell they'd ever been there. I knew, of course, that the S in *BULLSHIT* made up some of the waves in my hair and that a hint of the two Ls was hidden in the tattoos on Zain's arm. I knew that Finn's hair colour had taken forever to get right because a good chunk of *IS* was hidden behind it.

But even if someone else had looked, I don't know that they could have seen any of those hints. Not with the way I'd captured us looking at each other: Zain in profile, his eyes soft as he looked at Finn. Finn not quite straight on, blue eyes smiling down at me. And me facing backwards, my head turned just enough that the viewer knew I was looking at Zain. I had a hand on Finn's chest and just past my silhouette, had painted the two boys with their fingers pressed together. Zain's hand was on my waist and I had mine resting on his bicep.

That painting was everything I felt about them.

"You give paintings titles, right?" he asked.

I nodded.

"What's this one called?"

I hadn't considered it yet, but the answer came out without a second thought. "Death of a Unicorn."

Zain laughed. "Dark. But perfect."

"You like it?" I asked.

"It's fucking beautiful, Tess," Zain said. "I love it."

"Good." I set my brush down on the table beside my easel. "Then do me a favour and pretend to be surprised when I give it to you and Finn."

He looked at me, eyes wide. "What?"

I shrugged. "A housewarming gift. For your new place."

"Why don't you bring it over tonight so I don't have to pretend anything?" he asked.

I frowned. "What do you mean, tonight?"

"You're coming over to have dinner with us."

"You think so?"

"Yep."

"Maybe I already had dinner plans."

"Finn's making four-cheese fettuccine Alfredo."

That was fine, I told myself. Like yeah, I'd had his fettuccine Alfredo before and it was delicious and probably half the reason Zain fell in love with him because that was the first meal we'd all had together, but I didn't need that, not when I knew damn well this was just a trick to get me over there and—

"Let me put a bra on and grab my purse," I grumbled.

"Neither of those things are necessary," Zain said. "The bra especially."

I ignored him and grabbed one off the hook by the door anyway.

He drove us to a building close to Denman Street that looked exactly like the kind of place I would expect Zain to live. It wasn't brand new or ultra-modern, but it had sleek lines and that glossy shine of stacked windows reflecting in the evening sun. When we got to their apartment, Zain unlocked the door and held it for me. I walked in to that familiar smell of something cheesy and creamy, and as soon as the door closed, Finn turned around with a grin on his face.

"Tessa!" he said. "Hope you're hungry."

"Always," I said, distracted as I glanced around. "Wow. This is..."

"What?" Zain asked, and if I didn't know better, I would've thought there was something worried in his voice.

"...nice," I said.

Which was an understatement. The apartment was gorgeous. It was tidy and organized, but didn't have that just-moved-in feel even though they'd just moved in. The door opened into the kitchen and dining area, which had crisp white cabinets and granite countertops. Just beyond that was the living room, which had floor-to-incredibly-high-ceiling windows that opened out onto a balcony and a strange but cute little alcove beneath a slanted ceiling that Zain had turned into a kind of home-office area.

"Should we give her the grand tour?" Finn asked. "The sauce'll be fine on the stove for a bit; it's on low."

I humoured them, despite the fact that I thought I could see most of the apartment from where I stood. But I said nothing as I followed Zain down the hall to the left, nodding as he showed me the large main bathroom and the in-suite laundry beside it and a smaller bedroom which I guessed was Finn's. It was a generic space, probably because Finn hadn't had much in the way of furniture to bring, but the bed was neatly made and there were extra throw pillows on it.

And then there was the master bedroom.

"Jesus Christ," I said as Zain opened the door. "You *are* the most extra person I've ever met."

He burst out laughing. "What? You don't like it?"

I gaped at the bed, which was fucking gigantic.

Seriously.

It wasn't a king size. It was way bigger than that. Like way, way bigger than that. I hadn't expected the master bedroom to be so large, but I guess it made sense—the other side of the hall had three rooms to its one. There was room for the gigantic fucking bed, plus a dresser and some nightstands, with a closet on the far wall and a door that I thought must be the ensuite.

"I didn't even know they made beds this big," I finally said.

"It's an Alaskan king," Zain replied. "And it was worth every fucking penny. Trust me."

"It is a nice upgrade from the queen size," Finn said as he came up behind us. "Not that I'm complaining, but it is kinda awesome that my feet don't hang off the end."

"I bet," I said. "Wow. Weekend sleepovers will sure be a lot more fun here than at my place."

Neither of them responded as I looked around. Once I was done, Zain stepped out of the way so I could get to the door.

"You should check out the view from the balcony," he said.

But I never got that far.

"There's an upstairs?!" I gasped after I realized the slanted ceiling above Zain's office area was actually a fucking staircase.

Zain smirked. "Yeah, Teacup. It's got a loft."

"Remind me to be a business risk person or whatever it is you do in my next life," I said. "What did you put up there?"

"Go see," he said.

"Is it a sex dungeon?"

"I think a sex dungeon would be downstairs, not up," he said.

I rolled my eyes as I went to the staircase and started climbing. Finn and Zain followed, though not closely enough that they ran into me when I stopped at the top of the stairs.

"What?" I said as I froze in place.

"What do you mean, what?" Zain asked.

It was a beautiful space. The far wall was windows, like the living room had been, and the floor was light coloured laminate that didn't quite pass for hardwood, but came pretty damn close. Two of the walls were an off-white colour that gave the room a clean but relaxing feel, and the other wall was exposed brick, making it hipstery in the best way.

But that was all there was.

"It's... empty," I said. Neither of the boys spoke. I glanced around, then looked back at them, a confused frown on my face. "Why is it empty?"

Zain shrugged. "Didn't know what we were putting here yet."

"Seriously? This is like, the nicest room in the entire apartment and you're not using it?"

His eyebrows flicked up. "What would you put in here?"

I twisted my mouth to the side. I knew exactly what I'd fucking put in it, but I didn't want to say that.

"Well, if you don't want to use it as an office, you should set it up like a second living room area." I moved into the room, gesturing to the areas I'd put everything. "Big TV, couch, a bar area. Like a man cave but not a cave."

"Teacup," Zain said. "That wasn't the question."

"What?"

"I asked what *you* would put in here. Not what you think we should put in here."

I stared at him.

He stared back.

Finn also stared back.

"I... I would use it as a studio," I whispered.

"Funny," Zain said. "That's exactly what I thought would be perfect here."

I looked from him to Finn and back again. "Wait. Just... what?"

Zain's face softened and he climbed the rest of the stairs, joining me in the empty loft.

"I just wanted to be ready," he said. "Just in case there was ever a day when this thing could be real."

"Little presumptuous of you," I said, a shaky laugh coming out with the words.

"A guy's gotta have hope, Teacup. And I figured that way, when you inevitably freak out because I'm asking you to live with us, I can address as many of the terrible excuses you'll come up with right away."

"Terrible?" I said. "Like what?"

"I dunno. Give me one reason you can't move in with us."

I snorted. "Easy. I can't afford this place."

"I can," he said immediately.

"That's not fair—"

"If I cared about that, I would've found a place we could split equally," he said. "But as you said, I'm extra. I wanted something a little... more."

"It's not just you, though." I looked at Finn. "It's not fair to you, either."

"Neither was you refusing to take rent money from me while I was living with you," Finn said promptly.

"I..." I stared at him, then looked back to Zain. "Did you coach him on what to say?"

"Yes," Zain said.

"So you're already teaming up on me."

"We were teaming up on you before," Finn said. "I believe you usually like it."

Zain pressed his lips together hard and I knew. I fucking *knew* he'd told Finn to say that, too.

He'd known exactly how I would respond.

He'd guessed at the things I'd be worried about. Scared of. The insecurities that had been swirling in the back of my mind. He'd known so well that he and Finn had a script of retorts.

If I said we'd been "official" for a week, he'd say something about us doing this for a lot longer.

If I said we'd only been doing this for a couple of months at best, he'd remind me he'd known me my whole life, we were all in love, and I knew as well as they did those timelines didn't matter.

None of us had experience doing something like this. There was a big difference between one-night-only threesomes and living together in a three-way relationship. But Zain would say we would figure it out together. That we'd never know if we didn't try.

I was broke, jobless, and had no idea what to do with my life, but he'd already addressed part of that. And then he'd say that was okay, he knew I would find something, and he wanted me to be happy.

And if I said I couldn't leave Dottie in that big house by herself, because what about Millie, what about her knee, who would take out her recycling and if she died in her sleep, make sure to take off her bonnet and put a little blush on her because she would mortified if a cute paramedic showed up and she didn't look her best, even if she was dead?

Well, he'd either promise we'd go see Dottie every time she needed us, or more than likely, he'd offer to move Dottie into the fucking building if he could manage it.

Both of them knew I wanted to be there. That I wanted to share a home with them. It would've been stupid of me to assume otherwise, and I was trying my hardest not to be so stupid anymore.

So I responded with the only thing I could think of that Zain *might* not have thought of.

"What are you *doing*?!" Zain exclaimed, half-laughing and half-startled as I shoved my hand up the back of my shirt and unhooked my bra. Shimmying out of it, I sighed in relief as I let my tits bounce free.

"You're gonna have to put a hook near the door," I said. "Because I take my bra off as soon as I get home and I'm not changing that just because I'm living with a couple of boys."

And somehow, they had no complaints about that.

What's Next for Tessa?

Catch up with your favourite chaotic trio six months later in the bonus epilogue.

Get your copy here: **bit.ly/doau_epilogue**

Acknowledgments

Holy shitsnacks, I can't believe we're finally here.

The Unicorn Confessions series has controlled my life for what feels like forever right now. I don't quite know what to do with myself now that it's done.

That's a lie. I'm working on another series with a chaotic bisexual mess of a main character. But that sounds way less dramatic than what I just said.

I have to give thanks to my hype-up squad, supporters, sounding boards, and reassurance technicians. Jason Caldwell, Nora Fares, thank you for being my author buddies. I couldn't do any of this without you.

To the folks who beta read, proof read, and offered up feedback along the way: Charlie, Peyton, Lisa, Dragan, Sipho, and Kristi – you rock. Thanks for helping this story get to the place it needed to be.

To Paul M, Kevin Matheny, centralsquareguy, KW, PM, ED, KJ, MidNyt, RP, Alex, GW, my ARC readers, friends in my Cheryl's Terrors Facebook group, and wonderful supporters on Patreon: every single one of you is an awesome person who deserves the absolute best.

My family and friends who are still cool despite me being decidedly uncool, thank you for everything you do to support me in this.

And to my husband, who I love more than anything: you rock, don't ever change, and would you please hurry up and light that candle so I can get my present out of it?

Xoxo, Cheryl

Join The Chaos

Every hot mess deserves a happy ending.

Get exclusive bonus scenes, short stories, novellas, and more by joining my newsletter: **cherylterra.com/newsletter**

Find even more bonus content, early access to new work, and weekly updates that I sometimes actually do post every week on my Patreon (free tier available!): **patreon.com/cherylterra**

Also By Cheryl Terra

Also By Cheryl Terra

Find all of Cheryl's books at cherylterra.com/stories

Aurora Flats Series

Fate and Fried Chicken

If You Can Series

The Boy Next Door
Kiss Me If You Can
Hold Me If You Can
Keep Me If You Can
Sleigh Me If You Can

Unicorn Confessions Series

The Unicorn Confessions
Unicorn For Sale
Death of a Unicorn

Love Across Canada Series

Get Over It
The Devil Made Me
Runaway
Finding Home

Standalones

When It Rains
Hearts at Play: Special Edition
One Little Question
What Happens In Vegas
Selfish Love
Another Last Call